Dragon Waking

THE DRAGON CIRCLE: BOOK TWO

Obar nodded curtly. 'We are all of us here to play out some little drama of the dragon's devising. What his true purpose is I cannot hope to guess. We can only hope to survive.'

Jason looked at the others in the silence that followed. Nick looked very uncomfortable. He had risen to his knees and now stared at his parents, his lips pressed together tight, as if he would never say another word. His knuckles were white where he gripped the hilt of his sword.

'So, how do we survive?' Mrs Smith asked.

'There is only one way,' Obar replied. 'By finding the other dragon's eyes.'

Craig Shaw Gardner is the bestselling author of *Batman* and *Batman Returns*. His popular humorous fantasy series include *The Ebenezum Trilogy* and *The Cineverse Cycle*. He lives in Cambridge, Massachusetts.

Also by Craig Shaw Gardner

The Ebenezum Trilogy
The Ballad of Wuntvor
The Cineverse Cycle
The Sinbad Series
Raven Walking*

NOVELISATIONS

The Lost Boys
Wishbringer
Batman
The Batman Murders
Batman Returns
Back to the Future II
Back to the Future III

* available in Mandarin

Dragon Waking

THE DRAGON CIRCLE:
BOOK TWO

Craig Shaw Gardner

Mandarin

A Mandarin Paperback
DRAGON WAKING

First published in Great Britain 1995
by William Heinemann Ltd
This edition published 1996
by Mandarin Paperbacks
an imprint of Reed International Books Ltd
Michelin House, 81 Fulham Road, London SW3 6RB
and Auckland, Melbourne, Singapore and Toronto

A CIP catalogue record for this title
is available from the British Library
ISBN 0 7493 2050 8

Printed and bound in Great Britain by
Cox & Wyman Ltd, Reading, Berkshire

MAJOR PLAYERS IN THE DRAGON CIRCLE

The Neighbours

Nick Blake

Joan Blake, *his mother*

George Blake, *his father*

Todd Jackson

Carl Jackson, *his father*

Rebecca Jackson, *his mother*

Mary Lou Dafoe

Jason Dafoe, *her brother*

Rose Dafoe, *her mother*

Harold Dafoe, *her father*

Bobby Furlong

Margaret Furlong, *his mother*

Leo Furlong, *his father*

Evan Mills

Constance Smith

Old Man Sayre, *currently deceased (but reviving)*

Charlie, *a dog*

The Islanders

Nunn
Obar   *three wizards*
Rox

Oomgosh
Raven
Zachs, *a creature created by Nunn*

The Captain, *formerly Nunn's second-in-command*
The Newton Free Volunteers, *comprised of*
    Thomas
    Wilbert
    Stanley
    Maggie

Nunn's soldiers
The Anno
The Wolves, *now without a leader*

The Dragon

Prologue

It wasn't a dream after all.

Nick had given up trying to figure out what was real. But seeing his father again, in his old house on Chestnut Circle, was just too, well, normal.

Normal was something that didn't happen any more.

No, he and his whole streetful of neighbours had ended up *somewhere else*, no longer in a small suburb in 1967 America. Not even in America, or the world that held America. No, they had come to a whole new world, where a Raven and a wolf talked, where wizards had jewels embedded in their flesh and a dragon rumbled underground, where the girl from across the street was almost boiled alive by a bunch of little men, and where he had been given a sword that made him a great fighter; but it was a sword with a curse, for every time he used it, the weapon forced him to draw blood.

'Nick?' his father asked. 'Oh, god.' He looked like he wanted to run across the room and hug his son.

Something held him back.

'It really is you, isn't it?' he asked instead.

Something always held them both back. His father glanced down at the dinner tray he had spilled on the floor.

'Dad,' was all Nick could say in reply.

Maybe it was just the harsh light from the floor lamp, but there seemed to be more wrinkles in his father's face than the last time Nick had seen him. The rest of the place looked pretty much the same; the battered couch, the bookcase full of book club editions that his parents never got around to reading, that watercolour of the cabin over the fireplace. It was maybe a little bit cleaner than usual; his father had always been the really neat one in the family.

But it looked like home.

This was the one place Nick really knew. Maybe it was the other place, that whole other world, that was the dream.

His hand brushed the sword hanging at his side.

'I've been so worried about you,' his father said. He took a couple of steps forward, as if his feet might finally overrule his head. 'Where have you been?' He frowned down at Nick's sword. 'What have you got there?'

Nick answered with a question of his own. 'What are you doing here?'

'Here?' His father frowned, a bit of anger creeping into his voice. 'What do you mean? This is my house, isn't it?' He stopped himself and looked back at his son. He smiled a bit, as close as Nick would ever get to an apology. 'Well, it used to be, didn't it? Before all that other stuff got in the way.' He shrugged. 'When the police found out that you were missing, not only you, too, but all the neighbours, well –'

His father finally walked towards him across the room.

'I should never have walked out on you and your mother. I was having problems at work, and maybe problems with getting older –' He stopped, still at arm's length, and shook his head at his son. 'Well, I wouldn't expect you to understand.'

The older man turned away, looking out at the darkness beyond the living-room window. The night was covered with fog and all Nick could see was the dull glow from a distant street light. His father turned to him again, his frown going deeper still, then jerked his head away, as if it would be easier to look someplace else. He began to walk across the room again, his heavy shoes crushing the worn wall-to-wall beneath.

All this movement was making Nick uncomfortable. He became aware he was gripping the hilt of his sword.

'I didn't have a purpose,' his father said suddenly, still not looking at his son. 'But, with your disappearance, I did.' He made a noise that could have been a laugh if it had had more energy. 'It was time to come back and wait.'

2

His father turned and really looked straight into his son's eyes.

'After both you and your mother disappeared I moved back in.' He laughed as if that was silly. 'Maybe it was only then that I realised how much I missed you. Somehow, I knew that if I came back, I'd see you again. You and your mother. And that's half come true, hasn't it?'

Nick didn't answer. He didn't know what the answer was.

His father kept talking anyway. 'So I waited.' He shook his head, his mouth stretching towards a smile. 'Sometimes, whole weeks would go by when I thought I was crazy.'

Whole weeks? Despite all that had happened in the new world, Nick had only been gone for two days.

'So where have you been?' His father opened his hands before him as if he might reach out and grab the answer. 'I was so worried. It's almost been a year.'

A *year*? Nick would swear his father was crazy, if he didn't think the whole world was crazy instead.

But his father wanted an answer.

'I don't know,' Nick began. 'I don't think you'd understand.'

His father shook his head in irritation. 'Oh, come on, Nick, give me some credit. A lot of strange things have happened here. Maybe I'm a little more open than I was before.'

Nick didn't think anyone could be open enough to accept what had happened to him and all his neighbours in the last forty-eight hours.

'No, Dad,' he answered slowly. 'I don't think you could understand, unless you'd been there.'

'What?' His father's hands leapt forward, as if they wanted to tear apart Nick's stubbornness. 'Here I am, trying my best to figure out what's going on, and this is what I get from you?'

Nick felt the room shift beneath his feet. His father grabbed on to the couch for balance. 'What was that?' the older man demanded.

Nick looked around the room. He had the feeling there was more here than just the two of them. 'Oh, shit!' he blurted.

'What did I tell you about talk –'

3

His father's voice disappeared when he also saw what was on the other side of the picture window.

The fog was gone, replaced by one giant, unblinking eye; a large yellow orb with a wide slit across its middle, like the eye of a lizard.

Nick knew it was the eye of the dragon. And, somehow, he knew he'd seen it before – more than once – many, many times.

So much for normal.

'What the hell is that?' his father asked, his voice no longer so sure.

'I think it's something from where I've been,' Nick replied, trying to choose words that wouldn't upset his father any more than he had to. He remembered talking to Todd about this. What had Todd said?

'It has something to do with anger,' Nick explained. 'Maybe our fighting brought it – or maybe it was here all along. Maybe', he added, his voice even softer, 'it brought us to it.'

His explanation just seemed to make his father mad all over again. 'What are you talking about? I don't want to hear your flights of fancy. God damn it, Nick, make sense!'

It was Nick's turn to shake his head. 'Dad, I can't make sense if the world doesn't.'

His father jumped back as smoke began to seep through the window's edge.

'No!' His father's voice was so loud and frantic it was almost a scream. 'I won't accept this!'

'Dad!' Nick grabbed his father by the shoulders and pulled him back towards the centre of the room. 'Get away from there!'

The picture window shattered as the surrounding wall was engulfed by flame.

BOOK 1

THE ISLAND AND BEYOND

One

The wall crumbled into dust. Shards of stone flew out into the trees, cracking trunks and shredding leaves. A great wind rose, tossing the few splintered remains of furniture into the air.

The wizard Nunn would destroy them all, as easily as he demolished the remains of his castle wall.

So the dead man Sayre would escape without his permission? He had blasted a hole in the wall, had he, with the power Nunn had given him?

Well, Nunn would demolish every wall in the castle, and tear apart the forest beyond. And then he would make sure that Sayre stayed dead for ever.

The wind increased again, so loud now that it screamed with fury. The jewels embedded in Nunn's hands pulsed with his power, and his anger. They were two of the dragon's eyes and they would bring him dragon's fire. Flames shot forth from his fingertips, sculpted by his power into the shape of little men, Nunn's own children of destruction. For there were other things that angered him far more than that worthless Sayre:

Mary Lou had escaped him!

Anger leapt from his fingers. One of Nunn's new children embraced a tree, encasing the wood in flames.

All thanks to his meddling brother Obar and that impudent newcomer, Constance Smith!

Nunn waved his hand. A second of his offspring ran through the branches of another great tree, leaving a trail of flaming leaves.

The great wolf that Nunn had enlisted into his service had died before he could kill more than one of his opponents!

The wizard pointed to the sky. A third child ran to the top of another tree, turning its crown into a giant torch.

Even Nunn's creature Zachs was becoming unreliable. And the wizard had lost his third jewel, ripped from his forehead by a being held captive in his own skull!

Nunn sat heavily. As much fury as there was inside him, there was even more exhaustion. He looked up and saw the fires dying out in the moist wood without his wizard's power fuelling them.

His foes were more bothersome than he had expected. Nunn had taken them for granted as unschooled newcomers, placed here as Nunn's playthings. But they were slightly more worthy than that. After all, the dragon had picked them for their talents.

Of course, Nunn had an advantage over all of them. He had survived the dragon. He had lived and prospered as the great flying beast cleansed the world around it with its terrible fire.

Nunn and his brother Obar had easily defeated all their foes in that last encounter with the dragon. That was, of course, before Nunn decided that Obar would get in his way as well.

But the dragon was near again. And Nunn could feel a difference this time, a difference not only in his foes, but in the energy that surrounded all of them, an energy that came from a beast that still slept, but would wake very soon.

This time, they would really see the dragon. And this time, one of them would control the beast, or they all would die.

Nunn had spent years preparing for this moment; he had energies of his own. There were alliances he could call on. There were certain creatures, little more than whispers floating in the night, that would join him for a price. And things that dwelled on the deepest part of the desert floor, with lizard teeth and human brains, that liked the soft salty taste of flesh; and great leviathans upon the bottom of the seas that lived to feed off human souls. He could use all of these, and more.

All these bargains would cost him, but the price would be nothing compared to what he would gain.

He had lost one of the dragon's eyes, but there were three more out there to be taken. His brother and the Smith woman had two of the jewels as well. He would not confront them quite

8

yet. Two against two was all too fair. He much preferred two against five.

He knew from the jewels within his palms, and the few short hours when the third eye had melted into his forehead, that each gem increased his power by an order of magnitude. Once he had adjusted to the great power of the new stones he could defeat the others and gain their eyes to control both them and the dragon itself.

The world was changing around him. Already, he could vaguely sense the existence, and something of the location, of the remaining jewels, the first time he had the awareness since the last visit of the dragon. But he would have to call upon all his remaining strengths to gain these jewels before his foes.

He had need of one of those strengths now, no matter how unreliable.

'Zachs!' he called.

But Zachs didn't answer. Nunn frowned, thrusting his consciousness into those inner recesses where he had banished his creature of light until Zachs was needed again.

The tell-tale spark was gone. Zachs had left him.

Mills must have done something.

Mills! The insufferable upstart who had invaded Nunn's mystical form and then had somehow escaped Nunn with his life!

Some might escape Nunn for a short time. But no one took something from Nunn and lived.

The others Nunn would kill. But he would not allow Mills to die until he had truly suffered. Once the wizard had recaptured Zachs, he would have his creature eat the upstart from the inside out. Not that Nunn would allow Mills to die – until the wizard was quite ready.

No one did this to Nunn! No one!

Nunn's scream brought his fire children back to life, higher and higher, until he was surrounded by a wall of flame.

Nick heard a dog barking. It was Charlie; his dog. He opened his eyes and saw green. This wasn't his house at all. Instead he saw those huge trees with their strange green leaves, half-way between an oak and a willow, the trees that filled this other

9

place. And when Charlie bounded into the view he no longer looked like the dog from Chestnut Circle. The whole shape of his head had changed so that he already seemed more like a great beast from this new place, all muscles and teeth and red glowing eyes.

Nick groaned. He had been with his father and the dragon. And he had been with them more than once, over and over again, like some dream that he couldn't wake from. And every time the dream returned, his father had grown angrier than the time before. Until the final confrontation, when they had been surrounded by fire.

'Nick?' cracked a young teenager's voice. 'You're back!'

Nick was flat on his back, staring up at the trees. He turned his head and saw Bobby Furlong running towards him. He was back in the clearing with all the neighbours, away from Chestnut Circle on this strange new world. He had trouble focusing on anything. His eyes wanted to close. It must have something to do with the dreams.

'And you brought somebody with you!' Bobby added.

Nick turned the other way and saw his father on the ground by his side.

So that part of it wasn't a dream. Nick breathed in sharply. He wasn't sure if he wanted his father here or not.

The other man opened his eyes. 'What happened?' he asked after a groan of his own. 'How did we get out of the house?' He looked over at his son. 'I thought we were going to be burned alive. What did you do?'

Nick thought about trying to explain that he had nothing to do with it. But he didn't know how to put the words, and he wasn't sure his father was ready to listen.

'George?' Nick looked up and saw his mother standing above both of them.

'Joan!' his father called. 'I'm so glad to see you again!' He tried to sit up, but fell back to the ground, groaning with the effort. 'I knew, if Nick was around, you wouldn't be very far away.'

'George, you don't know the half of it.' Nick's mother shook her head. 'Although you'll figure it out if you want to stay alive.'

'What are you talking about?' George grimaced as he pushed himself up on to his elbows. 'I'm afraid I don't understand any of this.' He shook his head and laughed. 'You're beginning to sound like Nick.'

'That's because Nick knows what's going on,' Nick muttered, half to himself.

'What's that?' George frowned at his son. 'Please, Nick. Can't you speak up if you have something to say?'

'George,' Nick's mother said sharply, 'don't get mad at your son until you understand what's going on. Maybe Constance Smith can explain a little bit of what this is all about.'

Nick's mother turned to the elderly woman seated at her side. 'Frankly, Constance, I think I need a thing or two explained myself.' She waved in George's direction. 'Why is he here in the first place?'

'Oh, dear,' Old Mrs Smith called from the other side of the clearing. 'I'm sure it has something to do with the dragon. I don't know how much I understand, even now.' She smiled as she began to rise. 'Perhaps Obar can help me.'

Nick turned his head the other way, and saw the chubby wizard in the wrinkled white suit conferring with a couple of the other women from the neighbourhood. He looked up across the clearing at Mrs Smith. 'Well,' he said with a tug at his moustache, 'it is most unusual. And it is most likely the dragon.'

Nick's father made an embarrassed sound, half cough, half laugh, as if he had only now noticed the wizard. 'I'm sorry. I probably should introduce myself.'

'No need,' Obar replied as his mouth curled to a smile, 'I know who you are.'

'Yes, dear Obar,' Mrs Smith chided as she moved across the clearing. 'But perhaps dear Mr Blake needs to be introduced to you.'

Nick's father yelped, a high, strangled sound.

'But –' he half whispered, half choked as he pointed a trembling finger towards Mrs Smith.

Perhaps, Nick considered, his father had finally noticed that, in her trip across the clearing, Mrs Smith had chosen not to walk. Instead, she floated straight towards them.

'No,' Nick's father continued, his voice shifting down to a moan. 'This is all crazy. Who are you people? I don't want to be a part of any of this.'

'Unfortunately, George,' Nick's mother replied gently, 'I don't think any of us has any choice.'

AROUND THE CIRCLE:
Meeting the Dragon

The dragon is not the same as others.

It has waited, since perhaps the beginning of time, for a moment that may never come. But it is for that moment that the dragon exists, for it is only then that it will be fulfilled.

So the dragon rises, looking for that moment. But that moment is never there. So the dragon destroys. Its great wings send buildings crashing to the ground. Its claws cut living things in two and its huge mouth always hungers for more flesh. And what it doesn't eat, it burns, its fire scouring everything so there is nothing left behind but barren earth.

Perhaps, from the ruins, the moment will arise at last.

The dragon does not hope. The dragon only waits.

It waits until the time comes again. And it sends for those who might make this time different from those before.

The dragon stirs. It calls for a sacrifice and one is given. But once the dragon has claimed a soul it longs for blood.

A single eye opens, a great orb the size of a city, an eye the colour of night. The eye sees everything, all those newly brought and all those from before. It watches them move, and act, and struggle towards a goal that only the dragon understands.

Over and over again it has been the same, perhaps since the beginning of time.

The mortals will try. The mortals will fail. The mortals will die.

It begins again.

Two

Jason looked down at the tree-man on the ground in front of him. The eight-foot giant, his hide so rough it was more bark than skin, groaned once, the first real cry of pain Jason had ever heard from the Oomgosh.

Jason didn't know what to say. What if the great, green man didn't recover? What if this time the poison did more than shrivel his arm and instead attacked the tree-man's heart?

Before yesterday, Jason had never seen anybody die. Then the soldiers had stabbed his neighbour, Old Man Sayre, in the stomach. So much had happened after that it seemed impossible that all of it could have taken place in two short days, one thing building on top of another until even Jason ended up fighting for his life.

But those creatures they had fought earlier, those things brought by Nunn, seemed more like animals than men. And even their murdered neighbour had been a sour old man whom nobody liked to talk to.

This was somebody Jason really cared about. This was the Oomgosh.

Jason pushed his thick glasses back up on his nose. For a change, he was glad he had to wear these things. They gave him something to hide his feelings behind.

He wished he could tell somebody how scared he was. But he really didn't know how to talk about it. His parents never wanted to hear about that sort of thing, and the other guys only wanted to talk about cars and monster movies and maybe girls. Guys weren't supposed to have any feelings.

But the Oomgosh wasn't his parents, or the guys in his

neighbourhood. And the rules back home weren't the rules around here.

'Hey,' he said, trying to get the large man's attention.

The Oomgosh didn't answer. The tree-man was very still.

Jason felt as if he couldn't breathe. The Oomgosh had to get better! Jason started talking again, saying anything, not caring any more what it sounded like. 'Hey, trees have to rest, too. You've told me about that, the seasons and all.' He stared down at his silent friend. 'Hey, are you going to be OK?'

The Oomgosh opened his bright green eyes. 'I am not gone yet.'

Raven cawed from his perch above Jason's head. He flapped his great black wings. 'The Oomgosh is always with us!'

'Yeah,' Jason insisted. 'Didn't you say that the Oomgosh never dies?'

'Yes,' the tree-man agreed, his voice more hoarse than Jason had ever heard it. 'There will always be fertile soil for trees to take root. There will always be warm sunlight and cool rain to let them grow. And there will always be an Oomgosh.'

Jason smiled at that. 'Really? Then you're not going to die?'

The Oomgosh sighed then, the sound of an autumn breeze ruffling fallen leaves. 'I did not say that, friend Jason.' The green man smiled, but the humour did not reach up to his eyes. 'Trees die by degrees. So it is with me. In the end, I am no less dead.'

Jason felt he would never understand anything that happened here. He tried to think what else he could say, how he could keep the good things here with him.

'About time!' Todd shouted almost in Jason's ear. Jason looked up, startled out of his thoughts. Sometimes, when he was with the Oomgosh, he forgot about everything else.

'Some things can't be rushed, hey?' Stanley shot back. The Newton Free Volunteers had returned. The four of them, three men and one woman, strode silently back into the clearing, their green clothing making them almost invisible at first as they walked out from under the trees.

Stocky Wilbert was in the lead, the usual smile curling the edges of his beard. Stanley was next, the thinnest of the four, and a man who seemed to take pleasure out of being sullen.

Maggie followed. With her short hair and quick reactions, it seemed to Jason that she was always trying to be a more complete soldier than any of the men. Last was Thomas, their leader, a man who acted much more quickly than he talked.

It looked to Jason like they hadn't met with any trouble. Their bows were on their backs, their knives in their sheaths. Somehow, with the taut way they held themselves, and the look they'd give to the smallest noise, they still seemed ready to leap into action at the slightest notice.

Jason looked around at the other neighbours in the clearing. It startled him that they were still all here; Todd and Bobby stood above Jason's sister, Mary Lou, who lay sleeping on the ground towards the clearing's centre. Hovering nearby was Mrs Smith, floating a few inches off the ground the way she did these days. His mother stood behind her, along with Mrs Blake and Mrs Jackson, all clustered together like they were talking over each other's fences back in the neighbourhood. Bobby's mother, Mrs Furlong, squatted between the other women. She was moving her fingers along the ground at her feet, like she was drawing pictures in the dirt. Jason wondered if her pictures would make any more sense than her words. Ever since that other wizard, Nunn, had eaten her husband, she'd been pretty far gone.

Their resident wizard, Obar (the good one, or so Jason hoped), popped up in the middle of the group in that way he did. Jason realised that there were two more men lying on the ground just beyond the wizard. One looked like Nick. The other one looked like –

Nick's father? He hadn't seen Nick's father in over a year. What was Nick's father doing here?

Jason really did need to pay more attention to the other things going on around here.

Thomas, the leader of the Volunteers, stopped just short of the assembled neighbours. 'There's nothin' out there. No sign of Nunn or any of his creatures.'

'They disappeared much too fast,' agreed Maggie. She scratched fretfully at her short, ill-cut hair. 'Nunn is planning something else.'

'And the sun will rise tomorrow morning,' Wilbert shot back with a laugh. 'There are certain things you can depend on.'

Stanley frowned at Nick's father as if the newcomer was surely part of Nunn's evil plan. 'And who is this?' he demanded.

'My ex-husband,' Joan Blake spoke up first.

'A divorce, then?' Maggie said more to herself than to Nick's mother. 'No love lost between the two of you, is there?'

Stanley looked at his fellow Volunteer with a wicked smile. 'Maggie wouldn't know anything about that, hey?'

His question was rewarded with an angry look from Maggie. And Mrs Blake looked about as upset as Jason felt. She glared at Nick's father as if the two of them were in the middle of a fight that had been going on for a long, long time.

'Is this another neighbour, then?' Thomas asked with a nod at Blake.

'Well, he was once,' Mrs Smith agreed. 'But we haven't seen him in over a year.'

Obar stepped forward at that, staring at the newcomer as if he were some sort of creature the magician had never seen before. 'Even more interesting. Then he was nowhere near the neighbourhood?'

'I moved back in', Mr Blake said defensively, 'after everyone else moved out. Or you all – vanished. I thought maybe –' his lips twisted toward a feeble smile, 'I might be able to find everybody again.'

'Most assuredly.' Obar rubbed distractedly at one arm of his soiled white suit. 'It truly appears that the dragon is not done with us yet. This is still beginning.'

Mrs Blake shook her head sharply. 'What, you mean the dragon went back to get George, specially? Why would he do something like that?'

'Oh?' Obar replied, as if he was once again surprised anyone was asking questions. 'Well, George here was needed, no doubt.'

'Needed?' Mrs Blake snapped.

Her former husband shrugged apologetically. 'I'm as much in the dark about this as any of you. Nick showed up, and then –'

He paused, then laughed sharply, as if he didn't believe what he had been about to say.

'You saw the dragon,' Obar announced for him.

'Well, we saw something,' Mr Blake admitted. 'How did you know?'

Obar nodded curtly. 'We are all of us here to play out some little drama of the dragon's devising. What his true purpose is I cannot hope to guess. We can only hope to survive.'

Jason looked at the others in the silence that followed. Nick looked very uncomfortable. He had risen to his knees and now stared at his parents, his lips pressed together tight, as if he would never say another word. His knuckles were white where he gripped the hilt of his sword.

'So, how do we survive?' Mrs Smith asked.

'There is only one way,' Obar replied. 'By finding the other dragon's eyes.'

Mrs Smith looked at the wizard with some exasperation. 'But haven't they been hidden for years?'

'Yes,' Obar replied with one of his all too knowing smiles, 'but I don't think they'll be hidden much longer.'

There was a moan from the back of the crowd. It was Jason's sister, Mary Lou, still asleep after her ordeal with those small creatures who tried to sacrifice her. She jerked about, her eyes still closed, as if she was locked in a dream.

Obar was suddenly at her side. 'Yes, I was sensing this from somewhere within our little group.' He placed the back of his hand gently against the sleeping girl's forehead. 'In fact, I believe we will have our answer – now.'

Mary Lou opened her eyes and screamed.

Three

It was like learning to walk all over again.

He was suddenly aware of muscles that he had taken for granted his entire life, could feel the pull of tendon against bone when he moved a leg, a hand, even took a breath. The sensations came and went. Colours would be much too bright, then noises much too loud. His balance would be fine one minute, then completely desert him the next.

He lowered himself carefully to sit against the bole of one of the great trees that surrounded him.

Or should he say – *them*.

Strange did not begin to describe this feeling. He was still Evan Mills, high school vice principal, all too close to forty, with his hair starting to thin out on top, generally in good health and, somehow, after all these years, still single. But he was also so much more.

He was a creature created by Nunn, a wild thing that seemed all made of light, a child that might be full of joy one minute, full of malice the next. And he was a wizard, a being so long without a physical body that he had forgotten how to resume his once-human form and now appeared only as a great puffy cloud in the most serene of skies.

All three of these beings were inside this shell that looked like Evan Mills. All three had escaped from within the thing that was Nunn. In one way or another, Nunn had collected them all, feeding on the life energies of such as Mills, and then giving that energy to Zachs, his creature of light, to do Nunn's bidding. Nunn had collected others, too, hundreds at the least, some human, some not, including Leo Furlong, another of the neighbours.

Evan wished they could have brought Leo out with them. But Leo had never been very brave. He couldn't risk leaving the darkness, so whatever was left of him still resided somewhere within the wizard.

'Free!' cried the part of him that was Zachs, but the creature used Evan Mills's lungs, and Evan Mills's lips. 'Nunn won't get us now! Zachs can do what he wants, when he wants! Free, free, free!'

'Maybe we will be free, some day,' another voice issued from Evan's throat, the voice of the wizard Rox. 'But we will have to learn what we have become before we can do anything else.'

'Zachs is powerful!' Mills felt a tingling in the palms of his hands. Sparks flew from his fingertips. 'No one will hold him back!'

'Wait a moment,' Evan Mills managed, his own voice sounding strained. 'This is new to all of us. I think – we should work together – at least for now.' Part of him wanted both of these other creatures simply to go away. But a part of him was afraid that Evan Mills really didn't exist any more; that he was dead already, but would only realise it when his three parts tried to go their separate ways.

Somehow, in their escape from Nunn, the panic had taken over and let the three of them work together to come this far. But now, with his muscles acting strangely, or under the command of minds other than his own, Evan felt like some sort of spastic, untrained child. Maybe he should hold on to that image. A child was far more symbolic of a new beginning than his life coming to an end, a sign of innocence rather than decay.

We are still too weak, too disorganised, the wizard inside him counselled, silently this time, without the use of Evan's voice. We will need allies.

'We need more than allies!' Mills said with a disbelieving laugh. 'I have to learn – we have to learn – to use my muscles.'

Zachs needs no muscles! Somehow, the light creature's voice was still very loud inside his head. Zachs will eat muscles, eat flesh, then fly away!

Maybe once, the wizard answered. But it is different now. We are all different.

'So different that we don't seem able to move any more,' Mills said. 'What's happened to us?'

You were the strongest at first, the wizard replied, when we were escaping Nunn's domain. We were still integrating with this new form. You have a history here – your experience and instinct saw us through.

Mills raised his right hand through sheer force of will. 'If we're going to get anywhere, you'll have to let my experience take over again.'

For now, most certainly.

For now? Mills thought. What did that mean?

Later there will be other modes of travel. As he has been so eager to tell us, Zachs can fly. And I know ways to get places with even greater speed.

Somehow, Mills did not find this reassuring.

'When you can control my physical form,' he asked bluntly, 'what happens to my mind?'

I don't know, Evan Mills. We can only see what happens. I am telling you all I know.

'Telling you all I know.' Evan Mills remembered the exhortations of others on trusting wizards. Or rather, not trusting them. And now he had one inside him.

Actually, the wizard continued, I know one more thing. The only way any of us will survive is to find the dragon's eyes. To do that we must find the others.

'The others?'

Your neighbours. If there is anyone else of importance, I imagine they will find your neighbours as well. The dragon will see to that.

Constance Smith stepped out of the way as Mary Lou's mother rushed to her side.

'Mary Lou!' Mrs Dafoe called. 'Dearest! What's wrong?'

Mary Lou shook her head. 'It was almost too much, but it's all right now.' She smiled. 'I can see it!'

With that, Mrs Smith felt as if she could see something too; shifting scenes, two or three of them, seemed to brush against the very edges of her consciousness.

'The first one waits in a busy place –' Mary Lou began. 'Hidden from all the thousands of people who walk there.'

Mrs Smith saw the place as soon as the words had left the teenaged girl's mouth. It was a bright, sunny spot, filled with open-air stalls and small, crowded shops, a riot of people and goods and bright banners.

'A market-place,' Mrs Smith said.

'Yes,' Mary Lou agreed. 'That sounds right.'

The vision of the market vanished from Constance Smith's mind.

'The next is much brighter,' Mary Lou continued softly.

Mrs Smith almost lost her balance as her mind was filled with light, as if someone had opened a long-shuttered window and found the sun.

'But there is a dark spot, deep within the glare.'

The brightness faded for Mrs Smith, as one might turn down the contrast on a TV screen. She could see a bright white expanse beneath a blue-green sky. The vision took place on this world, then. And in the midst of all this whiteness was a great black smudge.

This time, Mary Lou had the answers. 'White sands. And a great slab of obsidian.'

Mrs Smith could see it now, a huge, jagged stone rising from the flat desert floor, almost like a mountain that defied the sun and wind that turned everything around it to sand.

'The second one is there,' Mary Lou concluded.

'And the third?' Obar was suddenly at the young woman's side.

'The third? It waits for us here, somewhere nearby. It calls out, doesn't it? Can't you hear it?'

Obar's brow furrowed in a frown. 'There is something. I don't – quite – sense its exact –' He shook his head in frustration.

Mrs Smith had the same sensation, a slight buzzing at the very back of her head. 'Perhaps', Mrs Smith said, 'it only wants Mary Lou to find it.'

'B-but she would never know how to handle it!' Obar sputtered. 'We fight great forces here, not just against my brother Nunn, but against the dragon as well. There will be no time for training. Only I have the experience to control this kind of power –'

'Excuse me, but can someone tell me what you're talking about?'

Mrs Smith glanced over at Nick's father. The question had to come from the newcomer. Everyone else here could easily guess what they were discussing.

'This.' Mrs Smith held up her own green gem, her dragon's eye. 'Obar has a great fondness for these.'

'You will too, as you use them more,' Obar shot back, the slightest hint of bitterness in his voice. 'The power grows on you. But we will need that power, if we're going to survive.'

'Then we will get it,' Thomas said from where he stood in the shade of a tree. 'There are enough of us. If we plan well, there is no reason why we cannot succeed, no matter who is ranked against us.'

'No matter who?' Joan Blake asked from the centre of the clearing. 'Then we will be fighting more than Nunn?'

Thomas nodded at Joan's ex-husband. 'There are still new players being added to the game. Who knows what we will fight?'

'Raven is ready!' the great black bird called down from his perch overhead. 'That is enough!'

Why, Mrs Smith wondered as she felt the heat of the dragon's eye in her palm, did she have the deep conviction that Raven was wrong?

Mary Lou stood up, waving away her mother's offers of help. She muttered something about needing some air as she pushed her way through the group that surrounded her. She took a few steps beyond the group, leaning at last against one of the great trees at the clearing's edge.

'There is no more time to talk!' The wizard waved a hand in Constance Smith's face. 'We have to go,' Obar insisted. 'And we have to go now!'

Constance frowned at the wizard. The usually evasive Obar seemed suddenly very emotional; his voice was full of passion, but his eyes looked afraid. She wondered how dire the situation had to be for him to be so direct.

'Perhaps we do,' she replied carefully. From everything she had learned, their lives could very well be in danger. Or more danger than usual. Sometimes she marvelled that they were all still alive.

But Joan wasn't quite ready to follow Obar's lead. She looked at both of those who already held the jewels.

'Having more of the eyes would make us safer, then?'

'Even more important –' Obar agreed, his moustache quivering, '– is to prevent Nunn from obtaining them.'

Joan's frown deepened. 'Then Nunn will kill us if he gets the jewels?'

Obar mopped at his brow. 'I wish it was as simple as that. I think, if Nunn triumphs in this, we will be worse than dead.'

Nunn stood among the ruins of everything that he had built; his castle, his fortress, his life. But the anger had left him. There was no reason for it any more.

Suddenly he could see.

The three remaining eyes were within his reach.

Two were on other islands, quite accessible, if demanding a little effort. He got a clear vision of the location of both.

The last one, however, was tantalisingly close, on this very island. Oddly enough, he could not picture the surroundings for this final prize. Perhaps it was too close, the very power of its proximity clouding his sight. But he could sense it through the other eyes, one embedded in each of his hands, and in the aching crater where a third jewel had rested in his forehead.

But that new jewel was almost within his grasp. He shivered, nearly overcome with the ecstasy of it. He took a deep, lingering breath. He could feel already the new jewel's power mixing with his blood.

Yes. He would have them all, all three of the eyes yet to be taken, and then the other jewels that Obar and Mrs Smith kept from him. But he would have to be clever. He had the greatest power, the greatest experience. But his enemies, untried as they were, were far superior in number. And the dragon had plans all of its own, which none of them could fathom.

Nunn.

The wizard felt the word rather than heard it, like a chill along the back of his neck. The first of those he called had arrived. He turned away quickly as he saw the first deep flickers out of the corner of his eye.

He closed his eyes in acknowledgement. It was best, even for a wizard, not to look at these things too directly.

He had called all his creatures for this, the beginning of the dragon. Nunn would need his spies to watch the others, and his most subtle spells to lead them astray. But if his enemies could not be fooled, he would have to stop them with the likes of what hovered in the air about him now.

NUNN.

The feeling was more insistent this time. The wizard had made promises. The dark creatures expected their due.

He held up a hand to let them enter. He would have to give them a bit of his power; it was in the bargain.

They touched him then. He felt as though his fingertips were encased in ice. The cold shot through his veins, the ice scraping at his flesh from within. A part of Nunn wanted to cry out, to scream from the pain, but he kept his silence. No one would ever find any weakness in Nunn.

The odd voice that was also a feeling grew ever happier as the cold spread. It seemed to purr as it drained vitality from the wizard's form. Nunn's hand, his arm, his shoulder, all seemed lost to him, as if they had turned to stone.

'Enough!' the wizard declared.

Reluctantly, the dark things withdrew. When he made the bargain, Nunn had also showed them what would happen if they did not obey.

The creatures gone, Nunn's arm fell to his side, all feeling fled. He knew it would be of no use to him for quite some time. If he had let the dark things stay for another moment, the same would have happened to his heart.

Of course, this inconvenience was nothing compared to the agony the dark things would bring to others. He had a wizard's strength, and the resilience of magic. The dark things could kill lesser beings with the slightest touch.

Nunn?

A question this time, from a voice filled with power.

'Soon,' Nunn replied. There were others to wait for and a few final plans to make.

He laughed as the castle walls reassembled themselves around him. No one would deny him ever again.

He had planned for all of his real existence, since the dragon brought him here so long ago, for what was to come. The dragon had let him survive that last onslaught of wind and fire, and Nunn knew that was no accident.

Now he would prove himself truly worthy of the dragon's legacy. And that legacy said that all his enemies should perish, in fire at the very least.

Although Nunn had better ideas for some of them.

Four

Evan Mills had never known such pain.

A moment before he had had a vision. And in that vision he saw two jewels and sensed the presence of the third.

We will see no one! We must go now!

Mills stiffened with the message. It sounded like a scream in his brain.

Zachs will no longer have to fear Nunn. Zachs will have a dragon's eye!

Mills realised he was holding his skull. If he didn't hold it, it would surely explode. Every word of the creatures inside him pushed out behind his eyes and ears, as if only flying eyeballs and eardrums could set the pressure free.

We will have a dragon's eye! And the one with experience shall control it!

You want it all for yourself? Perhaps our host has something to say about that. Mills's pain lessened for an instant. Zachs's inner voice had lowered, as if the creature was, for once, giving the matter some thought.

No one has any say in this! the wizard roared back. *We will have these dragon's eyes, now!*

Zachs will —

Zachs will die if he doesn't keep quiet!

'Stop,' Mills managed. He had fallen to his knees.

'Yes,' the wizard's voice came from between Mills's lips. 'We are putting undue pressure on our gracious host.' This spoken voice seemed as serene as the one inside his head was strident. 'But you know, with a stone, we might be three beings rather than one.'

Three? Evan Mills took his hands away from his throbbing skull. Then there was some hope that he might survive this?

Zachs must have a stone! the creature shouted in his skull.

Evan grunted as new pain shot through his forehead.

Then, Rox replied within, this time most reasonably, *we'll have to gain all three, won't we?*

One for each? Zachs shouted. *Oh, how lovely!*

'Wait,' Mills said. His head seemed to be adjusting slowly to the commotion inside. 'Whatever we do, we have to do it together.'

'So our condition suggests,' the wizard's voice again said through his mouth. 'But I think it is time for the one with knowledge of the jewels to lead the way.'

He found one of the visions suddenly before him again; a market-place, filthy and full of life, a hundred voices calling his attention, a thousand scarves and carvings, bracelets of gold and hunks of meat, all waiting to be taken. Somehow, though he knew he was still in the forest, he could see and smell and hear the market as if it were all around him.

There are too many here, Rox announced abruptly, and the vision faded just as quickly, the sharp smell of spices replaced by the too-sweet odour of great trees and dead leaves. *Too much chance for opposition. We will try the desert. It will be the easiest place to begin.*

Zachs will shine in the desert!

So shall we all, Rox agreed, *with any amount of fortune.*

And Zachs will have a stone.

Not the first one.

The voices were growing stronger in Mills's head again.

Zachs issued a cold mental chuckle. *We will see who is faster, wizard. And brighter. Won't we?*

The wizard's reply was far more sombre. *I'm afraid that we will.*

Zachs is beginning not to like you. What Zachs doesn't like, he devours!

Well, that will have to wait for the proper time.

Mills grimaced. How could they go to the desert if he couldn't even walk them across the clearing? How could they

27

do anything until he managed some sort of basic motor control?

Allow me, the wizard said.

The forest faded around them, becoming blurry, like a camera that was out of focus. The blur shifted again, and the trees still surrounded them. Mills shivered, taken by a sudden chill.

I am a bit out of practice. This time, Rox's voice sounded more tired than agitated. *Besides, where we are going, we will need some water first.*

The forest blurred again, the colours running together until they all mixed into white. Mills heard the faint sound of running water. It grew louder as new colours emerged from the white, colours that solidified into trees, rocks and a rushing stream.

'Much better,' Rox announced aloud.

Evan Mills did not reply. With every passing minute, he was realising how little control he had, over his body, or anything.

For a while, Harold Dafoe had never expected to see the sun again; any sun, even the one in this crazy blue-green sky.

But then a door had opened before him and Carl Jackson; not in the wall, that would be too simple for someone like Nunn. No, this doorway had appeared in the middle of a corridor, the bottom of the door maybe a foot above the castle floor.

The door had appeared without warning, from Nunn or anyone else. Not that Harold doubted for an instant that Nunn caused it to open. In this castle, Nunn was everywhere. But that didn't matter just now, for on the other side of the door was sunlight. That was an invitation that even Harold couldn't refuse.

He stepped through the doorway and into the clearing where Nunn's men had brought them – how long ago? Perhaps a few hours, perhaps as much as a day. Time didn't seem to work in quite the same way around here as it had back home.

At least he was free of Nunn's castle. Now he wished he could get free of Nunn.

Not that Harold had any illusions. It was his fault that he was in this. That was the sort of thing his wife, Rose, said all the time. He didn't think quickly enough, he was afraid to act, he always let opportunity slip away.

Harold admitted that he was a cautious man. Before, in the world he had come from, where the worst problems were how you were going to pay the mortgage and whether or not you should yell at your kid, that caution worked. Here, however, it had led him to stay with the smooth-talking wizard rather than dare the unknown world outside with the other neighbours.

In the hours that had passed since, Harold realised he might have made a mistake. Not just because of the way Nunn had treated the two neighbours who remained, more like property than as allies, but because of other things in the wizard's castle. Things like those horrible screams in the night, screams that never seemed to end, that began as cries of pain and ended up as cries of the damned; voices without hope, voices beyond reason. If it truly was night in this castle. Who could tell without any windows; the only light some weird wizard-trick hanging over their heads? And there was something else, too, worse than the screams, which Harold felt rather than heard, a coldness that seemed to leak from the walls of this place, a coldness that didn't so much want to brush against his skin as it wanted to burrow into his heart.

Harold shivered, even though he had stepped into sunlight.

'Wait a second, Harry,' Carl said at his side. 'I don't think we're alone here.'

There, half in the shadows that circled the clearing, were Nunn's soldiers in their strange battle garb, their almost-conquistador helmets, their breastplates that looked like they were made of shell rather than metal.

The soldiers began to walk towards Carl and Harold, as if they had only been waiting for one of the newcomers to announce his presence.

'Hey!' Carl called out to the silently advancing men. 'We're on the same side now!'

Nunn's guard didn't make any reply, as if they hadn't heard what Carl had said. Or maybe, Harold thought, they hadn't understood it. He remembered how most of them had spoken some other, guttural language. The most eloquent among them, their captain, was gone. And after he had been taken away, only one of the other guards seemed to speak any English at all.

'Maybe we should put up our hands or something,' Harold suggested.

'Hell, I'm not about to surrender to these guys,' Carl muttered back. He clenched his fists and pulled in his beefy stomach, as if he was getting ready for a fight.

As they advanced, the soldiers drew their swords.

'Unless I have to,' Carl added. Both he and Harold were unarmed.

'Ah,' an all too cheerful voice called from behind them. 'Glad to see that you're getting acquainted!'

Harold looked back. The doorway was gone. Nunn stood in its place. There seemed to be a patch of shadow behind him for an instant, but it vanished as if it flew away faster than the eye could see. Nunn paused for an instant, a shiver passing through his form. The wizard opened his eyes; two pools of fathomless black. The green jewels embedded in each of his palms seemed to glow in the sunlight. His skin looked even more deathlike than usual. When he smiled, it made his too-pale face look like a skull.

The wizard shouted to the guard in that other, guttural tongue. The soldiers stopped and sheathed their swords.

'So, Carl,' Nunn called as he strode forward to stand between the two neighbours, 'you've decided to review your troops? Or should I call you – Captain Jackson?'

Carl frowned. He half looked like he wanted to strike the wizard. That seemed to be Jackson's way of dealing with anything that he disagreed with. Nunn looked so frail that a single push might knock him over, except, of course, for those gems glowing in his hands, and his bottomless eyes, two jet-black orbs that appeared to be filled with the stars. Jackson unclenched his fists. Somehow even he thought better of attacking a wizard.

'That's right,' Harold hurriedly said to his neighbour. 'I

remember Nunn talking about that in the castle – your promotion.' He found, at this moment, that he very much didn't want Nunn doing anything to Carl. Jackson might be a loose cannon, but at least he was human.

'Yes, you both have a very important part in my plans,' Nunn continued. 'I believe, Captain Jackson, that you will be quite good at maintaining discipline.'

Carl glanced from the wizard to the nearest of the soldiers. He still didn't talk, but he allowed himself the slightest of smiles.

'And you, Harold Dafoe, will be the Captain's lieutenant. It will be up to you to see that his orders are carried out.'

Harold disliked that suggestion so much that he actually found the courage to speak. 'Pardon me, but how can we order these men to do anything if they don't understand us?'

'Oh, they will understand you.' Nunn's hand was suddenly at Harold's throat. The tips of the wizard's fingers brushed against Harold's Adam's apple. Harold gasped as if his throat had been stabbed by a frozen dagger.

'Now,' Nunn said, 'tell the men to stand at attention.'

Harold struggled for breath. He pushed his own warm but shaking hand against his windpipe. He didn't know if he could say anything.

'Please,' Nunn insisted, 'humour me.'

Harold decided he'd better speak before something very bad happened.

'Stand at attention!' he called. But his words came out different, guttural.

The soldiers snapped to attention.

'What was that?' Harold whispered, his words again in English.

'Just my little gift to you,' Nunn murmured. 'When you speak to others, your voice will be normal, but when you speak to the troops, it will be in their tongue. Our new Captain will give the orders, but you will be the one to relay them. That way, everybody is useful.'

Nunn turned to the soldiers and called out to them in their language. Now, Harold understood it too.

31

'These are your new officers!' Nunn barked at the troops. 'If they are not obeyed, you know what will happen. But quickly! Your new superiors need to be outfitted! They need their choice of weapons!'

Two of the soldiers ran back into the forest as if their lives depended upon it.

Nunn turned back to his new officers. 'I am so glad that you have decided to join me.' He paused for a moment, as if listening to something that no one else could hear. 'I believe that I may be able to recruit someone else shortly to help you along.'

He looked directly at Jackson and Dafoe with his bottomless gaze. 'Now I have a little project in mind to test your worth.' His skeleton smile grew even broader. 'Or your loyalty.'

Mary Lou had to get away from all this noise. She needed some air. There were still too many images swimming about in her head. Obar was beginning to shout at all those around him and everybody else's voice was rising in turn. Everyone was upset, because of what she'd told them. Somehow, Mary Lou was to blame all over again. Obar, Mrs Smith, Volunteers, neighbours, even her own mother and brother; she wanted to get away from all of them.

She knew she shouldn't go far after all that had happened. She'd just walk a short distance into the woods and find someplace that was quiet. She had to do it; like an insistent voice at the back of her brain said she had to move.

She turned and walked towards the forest, putting distance between herself and the half dozen conversations that came from her revelations. Everybody was talking about what she had said, but no one was speaking to her.

'Mary Lou!' a harsh voice called from above. It made her remember how she had grown to hate the sound of her name when the small, cannibalistic Anno had chanted it over and over again, as they captured her and prepared her – for what? She still wasn't quite sure if the Anno wanted to sacrifice her or honour her. Maybe they had wanted to do both.

She looked up and saw Raven on a perch above, preening his feathers.

'Too many people?' the great black bird called.

Mary Lou was surprised. 'How did you know?'

'Raven often feels that way. Too many people, too much talk. Raven needs to stretch his wings!' The bird fluttered his wings to demonstrate. 'You need some quiet?'

Mary Lou nodded, reluctant to slow her pace. 'Maybe I need to walk around a bit too.' She was having trouble even stopping to talk, as if, now that she had started walking, her legs had urgent business somewhere else.

Raven tilted his head as he regarded her. 'You're clever for a human. Perhaps that foolish dragon has made a wise choice for once.'

The bird spread his wings. 'Raven should fly as well. Remember –' he called as he took flight, 'Raven is always nearby!'

Mary Lou smiled as the bird disappeared above the trees and she started walking once more. The great, self-important Raven had paid her a compliment. She felt special again for a minute.

Maybe that's what was really bothering her.

Ever since she had come to this place, she had been singled out, first by Nunn, then by the Anno, or 'the People' as they called themselves, and by Garo, the People's sometime servant, a handsome ghost that Mary Lou had called her prince.

She had felt special before, with the People and with her prince, until she found out that all they wanted to do was use her to get to the dragon. And then the dragon had used her too, to pass along its visions to the others.

It felt like everybody wanted her for something, but nobody wanted her for herself.

Mary Lou looked up. Her urge to wander was suddenly gone. Maybe she should head back. The huge trees surrounded her now, their leaf cover plunging the forest floor into gloom. She couldn't even see the sunlight of the clearing behind her. How far had she walked while she was thinking? Maybe she should be getting back.

She turned back the way she had come.

Something hit the ground behind her.

She jumped and spun around.

An Anno smiled up at her; one of the People who had worshipped her and tried to kill her.

Mary Lou, the Anno called. Except this time the creature had not used its high, grating voice to call her.

This time, she had heard it with her mind.

AROUND THE CIRCLE:
How Raven Brought Forth Humans

Once was a time when the world was new, and the sun had only recently begun to shine over the face of the River Nass, which was the home of all the animals. And over this river flew Raven, who had stolen the sun, the moon and the stars to give this river light. But today, Raven was bored.

So it was that he flew down to observe two of the many who crowded the shores of that great river, for those two, the Stone and the Elderberry Bush, were engaged in a loud and lengthy argument.

After a moment's listening, Raven realised that the two argued over who would be the one to give birth to humans. Stone insisted, in that slow way common to all of its kind, that it would be the better one to bring humans to the world. 'For', as Stone said in its slow, deep voice, 'if I am the first to give birth, then people will live for a very long time. Should they come from the Elderberry Bush, they should wither and die in the same way as the bush from which they come.'

At that, the Elderberry Bush ruffled its leaves. 'But if I were to give birth to humans they would grow towards the sky, and they would shake their limbs in the wind.'

Raven had heard enough, for he knew whom he preferred. Further did he see that Stone, in its own slow way, was already on the way to giving birth. So it was that the black bird flew quickly to the bush, which, with its deep-green leaves and bright-red berries, was far more lively and colourful than any stone would ever be.

'Give birth to humans,' Raven urged and the Elderberry Bush did just that.

So was the nature of things set. If Stone had been the first to bring forth its children, humans would live a great long time. But the Elderberry Bush was first, so that humans are bright and quick enough to please Raven, but they also die far too soon, so that elderberry bushes may grow on their graves.

And then, the birthing done, Raven spread his great black wings and took to the sky, knowing these humans would see great joy, and great grief.

But Raven would never be bored again.

Five

'Mary Lou!' her mother called out suddenly. 'What's happened to Mary Lou?'

Nick turned round from where he'd been watching the trees. After a brief talk with his mother he'd let the others carry the conversation and removed himself from the middle of the action. He'd seen Mary Lou walk away, first from the group surrounding her, then from a tree she'd used for support. She only seemed to be stretching her legs, walking in no particular direction.

Nick had just thought she was as fed up with this meeting as he was. He'd nodded and smiled at her as she walked past, but she hadn't been looking at much of anything. And Nick had had other things on his mind, including a sword handle that felt very warm in his grip, and a father who was suddenly back in his life.

'She walked into the woods – that way!' Jason called, pointing to his right. Mary Lou's brother had also kept out of the crowd, hovering around the sleeping tree-man who had befriended him.

The rest of the older neighbours, Mrs Smith, Mrs Jackson, Mrs Dafoe, Nick's mother and father, all clustered around the wizard Obar. Even Mrs Furlong, who seemed lost in her own little world since she'd lost her husband, sat by Obar's feet. And the four Volunteers were right behind them, with Todd and Bobby close by.

'How could this have happened?' Mrs Smith demanded.

'We're the ones who should keep guard,' a grim-faced Thomas announced. 'It's our fault that she's missin'. We'll find her.'

'No.' Mrs Smith shook her head sharply. 'I don't think it was anybody's fault. I don't think we were meant to see her go.'

'Someone hid this from us?' Mary Lou's mother hugged her arms as if suddenly cold. 'Was it Nunn?'

Obar answered this time. 'No, Nunn would be more obvious than that. He likes brightly coloured assassins and lightning storms, dramatic things that enhance his power. I think this comes from the dragon.'

'So the dragon can make us – *forget* about Mary Lou?' her mother demanded.

'How can we win against something that can play with our minds?' Nick's mother added.

'I don't know,' was Obar's frank reply. 'But I think we'll win if the dragon wants us to.'

'Plus the dragon – if it is the dragon – doesn't make us forget,' Mrs Smith reasoned. 'It only misdirects us. Now that we know Mary Lou is missing, we can go and find her.'

'Some of us can,' Obar insisted. 'The rest of us must go after the stones.'

'The stones can wait!' Rose Dafoe insisted. 'My daughter can't!'

'Besides, I think –' Mrs Smith said slowly, '– this will only take – a minute.' She vanished from sight with the slightest of popping sounds.

'That woman!' It was Obar's turn to shake his head. 'Very well, while she is gone, we'll prepare. We need to split into three groups to find three stones.'

'Is that safe?' Nick's mother asked.

'Our largest advantage is in our numbers,' the wizard answered. 'We have two here who have magical abilities.' He paused to look at the crowd around him. 'At least two.'

He nodded to the Volunteers. 'And we have others with experience of this place, who can think on their feet. Nunn may have made alliances with all sorts of creatures, but he holds an iron control over all of them.' Obar paused to chuckle. 'At least, he attempts to control them. And because all decisions must come from Nunn, these things are not as flexible as we are. This might be another advantage.'

Obar paused to scratch beneath his oversized moustache. 'But we have three jewels to rescue. Two are on other islands. I believe that Mrs Smith can claim the eye that waits in the market-place quite efficiently. I will go and find the one that waits in the desert.'

Todd stepped forward, as if he felt left out of the action. 'Why the desert?' he asked.

'Because, from what I know of my brother, that is the one Nunn will seek first. I know the way my brother thinks. I will have the best chance of outmanoeuvring him. But I will need a couple of assistants to protect me from Nunn's less sorcerous accomplices. Nick will be one.'

Nick looked over at the wizard. Didn't he have any say in this?

It was Nick's mother's turn to push herself forward in the crowd, a determined expression on her face that somehow made her seem a foot taller than her five feet two inches. 'My son? I don't think he knows how to fight anybody.'

'Perhaps he didn't,' Obar admitted. 'But his sword knows how to fight and Nick is learning fast.'

Nick frowned. This time, maybe the wizard really did know best. From the warmth of the sword handle in Nick's hand, his weapon wanted use soon.

Obar turned from Mrs Blake and looked to the other side of the crowd. 'I'd also like to be joined by one of the Volunteers.'

Stanley burst out laughing. 'You want us to go with a wizard? There's a great chance of that, hey?'

Maggie stepped forward. 'I'll go. I think it's time for a change of scene.'

Stanley stopped laughing abruptly.

'I'm thinkin' this is bigger than anything we're used to,' Thomas interjected. 'No time for old quarrels.'

Obar nodded. 'It's the biggest thing any of us will ever face, and maybe the last. But Mrs Smith will need some help as well.'

'Well, we can't let dear Maggie show us up, can we?' Wilbert boomed.

'I always wanted to see that market-place,' Stanley agreed.

'I'm also thinkin' one of us should stay behind,' Thomas added. ' 'Case Nunn has any plans locally.'

'I'll go,' Todd announced. He waved at the weapons in the hands of the Volunteers. 'I may not be too good with any of these, but I know how to fight.'

'I do believe you,' Obar agreed. 'And I think your talents can be of use.'

Todd frowned, not sure if Obar's comment praised or poked at him.

'What about me?' Bobby piped up.

'You can use a bow,' Thomas replied. 'I'll be needin' help here.'

Bobby smiled at that.

'We'll do what we can too,' Nick's mother offered.

'After we find Mary Lou,' her mother added with a quick nod and a frown.

A cawing sound came from the trees behind them. 'What about Raven?' The cawing was the sound of Raven's laughter. When nobody answered, the great black bird replied for himself: 'Raven will be everywhere!'

There was a groan behind Nick, followed by a great deep voice. 'We would expect no less, oh my Raven.'

Nick turned. The Oomgosh was awake and was trying to sit up. Jason frowned down at his friend, the boy shifting from foot to foot, as if he would help the tree-man if he only knew how.

The tree-man nodded as others in the clearing turned to look at him. 'Perhaps', he added as he managed to lift his torso at last, 'if the worst occurs, the Oomgosh could stir himself to help as well.'

'But, but, but –' Jason sputtered, his hands waving to help his explanation, 'you need to rest, to heal –'

'Then I will need your help,' the large fellow agreed. 'The Oomgosh and Jason will help together.'

'Raven feels better already!' the black bird called.

'We have other problems here, too,' Mrs Jackson spoke for the first time, a slight smile on her face, as if even she didn't believe she was speaking up. 'I'm afraid Margaret

39

Furlong isn't much good to anybody in her current condition. And poor George here looks a little shell-shocked by everything going on.'

Nick's father shook his head slightly, surprised to be part of the conversation. 'I guess I am,' he admitted. 'I'll do what I can.'

'I'll find you something to defend yourself with,' Stanley announced, pulling off his pack.

'But what about Mary Lou?' her mother insisted again. 'What will happen to her if Mrs Smith can't find her?'

Obar shook his head. 'Mary Lou doesn't need to take care of herself. The dragon will do it for her. And the beast may find her the third jewel as well. Of course, what the dragon will do with Mary Lou is another matter entirely.'

Mrs Dafoe made a sobbing sound at the back of her throat, as if that was the last thing she wanted to hear.

They would have warmth.

Nunn had kept them away from the living for far too long. Oh, he would give them a small creature here and there to keep them from withering away completely. And they would devour the small, pitiful, mewling things in an instant, barely waking from that slumber Nunn imposed upon them.

They had slept, then, for a very long time.

But now Nunn had woken them, and given them the slightest bit of his warmth. And that first taste had shown them how hungry they were.

It was only right, then, that Nunn had found them a place to feed.

There were so many in that clearing, pulsing with life, and so blissfully unaware of those who watched them. It was so long since they had tasted a full-grown human. Oh, Nunn would give them an infant now and then, but it would be gone in an instant, nothing more than a tantalising taste when they needed a full meal.

There was enough flesh and blood and energy waiting beyond the trees to satisfy them all.

They whispered to each other. So close, and yet they had to

wait. How could they control themselves with such a feast before them?

Nunn said that they could take, but they could not kill. There had to be a spark of life remaining for the wizard's perusal. How could they hold themselves back, when they wanted to gorge on the vigour of those who waited so unwarily?

Something else stopped them. There was a wizard here, a wizard who could hurt them. They didn't want to feel a wizard's fury again.

But they listened and whispered softly among themselves. This wizard would not be there for ever.

And, when he was gone, they would satisfy their hunger at last.

Six

'Hello?'

Where was she?

Mrs Smith had been quite sure she could find Mary Lou. Ever since she had held the dragon's eye, all she had had to do was get something firmly pictured in her mind. Then, she only had to believe herself to be a part of that picture and she was there.

Until now, that is.

'I don't know how to –'

Now she was nowhere at all. And everywhere.

There was no light. She was surrounded by a total darkness, an absence so complete that, for an instant, she felt she might be lost in nothingness.

'It's so close!'

But in the place of light there was sound.

'Won't anybody listen?'

Voices swirled around her.

'No. No one understands. No one ever –'

Conversations poured, one over another, as if people swirled around her in the void. Some shouted in her ear, while others were farther away, as hazy as those voices you'd hear behind a bad telephone connection.

'But how do we get out?'

'Out? I think we need to get in.'

There seemed to be an awful lot of people here, if people matched those voices; hundreds at least, perhaps thousands. She was suddenly struck with the thought that these might be the voices of everyone who had ever found their way to this world; everyone, perhaps, both living and dead. What an odd thought. Of course, in this place, the odder the thought, the more likely it might be true.

'You don't understand. We finally have time.'

'I can't remember what happened yesterday!'

Time? She didn't think time was the same around here. Another odd thought? She still knew so little about this place that they had come to.

'Maybe she knows.'

'If anyone can know anything!'

She? Until that moment, Constance thought that she was only eavesdropping on a hundred conversations. Could some of the voices be talking to her?

This seemed like another lesson.

That's what she had begun to think of many of the things that happened around her now; that they were here to teach her something. She could learn from everything in this place. She supposed that was true everywhere. But it was something she had forgotten, back when she lived on the Circle.

'Maybe I know what?' she said aloud.

The voices stopped, but only for a second. When they started again they redoubled, words flowing faster, higher, louder, as if all the hundred or thousand voices were trying to answer her at once. The sound rushed around her, the noise like water, buoying her one minute, threatening to drown her the next.

Constance Smith would not let this happen. She had discovered she had power in this place, and she could use that power to survive and learn. She willed herself to calm and the noise to lessen. The voices retreated. They still clamoured, but at a distance. And it was still too much. Before, she had been able to distinguish phrases and sentences. Now she was lucky to discern a word here and there.

'Help . . .'

' . . . here . . .'

' . . . at last . . .'

' . . . don't . . .'

' . . . away . . .'

' . . . interfere . . .'

Now it seemed as though *all* the voices were talking to her. And all of them were saying something different.

'Would you please –' Constance could barely hear herself over the cacophony around her. She decided to finish her sentence with a shout:

'BE QUIET!'

The voices stopped; again, the silence was as total as the darkness.

'Now,' she said in the sudden stillness, 'if only one of you will talk at a time, I'm sure we can all get our turn.'

And all the voices started up again.

'*You must . . .*'

'*No, listen . . .*'

'*. . . distractions . . .*'

'*. . . most important . . .*'

'*. . . life or death . . .*'

'I give up!' she shouted back at them.

She didn't have time for this. She had to find Mary Lou. She formed a picture of the young woman in her mind again.

'*No!*'

'*. . . must . . .*'

'*. . . imperative . . .*'

'*. . . destruction . . .*'

The voices grew even more urgent as they faded away. They knew she was leaving.

Maybe Mrs Smith was making a mistake by not trying really to understand what the voices had to say. What if they were attempting to tell her something she should know, about Mary Lou or the jewels or even the dragon? But they could just as easily be some creation of Nunn's, put here to stall and confuse her.

Well, she had found this place once. No doubt she could find it again, when she didn't have a young woman's life to save.

The voices stopped as the forest rematerialised around her. But Constance was alone. There was still no sign of Mary Lou.

George Blake found himself staring at his hands.

People were talking all around him. They were planning

some sort of expedition; an adventure that he would no doubt have to join. He had trouble understanding any of it; it seemed better if he just stayed quiet.

He wondered how he had got here in the first place. Oh, not all that mumbo-jumbo about magic and some dragon. It had all begun with his returning to that empty house, back on Chestnut Circle. His wife and he had separated, but – no matter what Joan had said to their son – they had never gone through the official motions of a divorce. The house was still half his, legally at least, and once his wife and son had vanished he felt he had to see it again.

He had wanted something real, something familiar, something down-to-earth. The house, with its reminders of simpler times, was that in a way. But it held more than memories. It was filled with empty space and silence, all the places where Joan and Nick used to stand and move and talk. When George had moved back there, he had accepted both the memories and the emptiness. And, somehow, both of those things seemed to be a part of what happened next, some kind of wild set-up for his trip here.

George almost laughed. He was beginning to sound like his son Nick, with all his wild ideas.

But George didn't want those ideas; talking birds and trees, people who could appear and disappear right in front of you, and your own neighbours making plans to steal something from a dragon. Who believed in dragons? Who even wanted to think about them?

So his mind kept wandering, wanting to go somewhere else. It was easier to stare at the ground or study his hands. But even his hands, with all their familiar scars and ridges, didn't look right in this place. They were the wrong colour, too orange maybe, and the shadows they cast looked a little green.

He should be happier than this. He'd found his wife and son; the two people who he thought would make his life complete. Well, they were the people who used to be his wife and son. Now Joan, after her first few words to him, hadn't bothered to pay much attention to him at all. And every time he looked at Nick, the boy looked afraid of something. Nick was jumpy, distant, uncommunicative. Neither one of them seemed to want to talk to George. Nobody appreciated the fact that he'd come back to the house, that he wanted to change, to have another chance. How could he get through to the two of them? They were both so distant. Was it even worth a try?

George closed his eyes. There was just too much going on here. And he'd have to figure out at least some of it if he ever wanted to talk to his wife and son again. But every time he looked at something new, half his mind still wanted to shut down.

His eyes snapped back open as he heard a loud cry. It was that talking bird, he thought. But this time the cry was full of alarm.

Another shadow flowed across his knuckles, somehow deeper than all the rest, somehow darker than black.

He looked up and saw other shadows where shadows couldn't be. They hung in the air above the clearing, great spaces of black blotting out the sunlight. They moved silently downward as he watched, half floating, half flying towards the ground and the people below.

Others were shouting out in the clearing, ducking and running as the moving shadows flowed ever nearer. The neighbours seemed to be forming a ragged circle; or maybe the shadows were herding them in that direction.

Only Mrs Furlong didn't look up at the darkness swooping closer overhead. But then, she didn't seem aware of anything. For an instant, George wondered if he was like that too, hiding in his house of memories.

But now was not the time to get lost in thought. Whatever was happening with the shadows and the neighbours, there was suddenly a distance between him and the others. George pushed himself away from the tree he had leaned against. He had to get to the neighbours. Alone, he was much too vulnerable.

He thought about shouting out, calling to the others. But he was the outsider here; why would they want to save him? Better if he got himself over there with the others before the shadows got too close.

He pushed himself on to hands and knees, wondering if he could dare to stand. Or would it be better to stay close to the ground, as far from those dark things as possible? He glanced overhead. There, directly above him, was one of the patches of dark, its ragged edges growing wider as he watched. He realised the shadow was falling directly towards him. It would cover him in an instant.

George Blake cried out at last, as he was engulfed by total darkness and total cold. He could no longer see. He could no longer feel.

And he could no longer hear himself scream.

Mary Lou wondered if it had been like this for her prince; the flood of thoughts that now came from the Anno, not in words but in images.

The first image was of the forest, warm and green, a huge nest made of the great trees, and the singing vines that connected them, a nest whose centre was the Anno's village, high up in the trees. This nest was the Anno's home, Mary Lou realised, their safe haven.

The image shrank, as if she were flying high above it, until the green became a ragged oval surrounded by darkness. Were they showing Mary Lou that she was on an island? But then the darkness erupted into flame and the whole island was circled by fire.

Fire had to mean the dragon. So this had something to do with the dragon bringing them here, or maybe the dragon creating them? There had been a sense of peace that had come with the images of green. The fire was accompanied by a growing excitement, as if the Anno were looking forward to serving the dragon.

The island disappeared from the middle of the ring of fire. In its place, still surrounded by flame, there stood a woman. Mary Lou realised it was a picture of herself.

What did this mean? Was she here to serve the dragon too?

She remembered that Garo, her prince, had complained about this sort of thing when he was the emissary of the Anno;

47

the way the People, as they called themselves, would only tell him bits and pieces of what he wanted to know.

That was the second time she had thought of Garo. Not that he had really been a prince; no, he was another one of those wizards who seemed to trick people as readily as they spoke. Garo had deceived her into being trapped by the People, being drawn into what seemed like a sacrifice.

But in the end, Garo had sacrificed himself instead.

And what about her? Did the Anno want her to take Garo's place, as an interpreter between the People and the humans? Somehow, she felt there was more to it than that.

And then the Mary Lou in her mind walked into the fire.

Seven

It took Jason a moment to figure out what was happening.

Raven had called, then the Oomgosh.

A minute before, Obar had muttered something about Mrs Smith. He had excused himself and disappeared. The wizards were always doing that sort of thing.

And as soon as the wizard was gone, the other things had come. Great dark blobs had appeared in the blue-green sky above the clearing. They scared Jason the moment he saw them floating soundlessly down towards them, as though they were blotting out the world around them rather than travelling through it.

'In the sky!' Raven called at the same time Jason saw them. 'Danger in the sky!'

'Around me, oh people!' Jason looked behind him and saw that the tree-man had got to his feet. 'It takes a lot of energy to overcome someone who is ten feet tall.'

Both neighbours and Volunteers drew nearer, using the Oomgosh as their focus as the dark things drifted silently down from above. There were so many of them that Jason thought they might blot out the sky.

Wilbert whistled. 'Lord, look at those things. Will our arrows do any good?'

The Oomgosh considered that. 'I think they will disturb them at the very least. We must use every means of defending ourselves!'

'Raven will pluck them from the sky!' the bird called from high above.

'And we will fight them from below, my Raven!' the

49

Oomgosh boomed as he raised his one good arm towards the attackers. 'We will not go easily.'

The tree-man glanced below. 'Jason, I will need your assistance. I can tell from your sympathies that you can feel the earth.'

'What?' Jason didn't understand. But he would do anything to help the Oomgosh. He pushed his glasses back up his nose to get a better look at the tree-man's face above him. 'What do you need me to do?'

'Take strength from the earth!' The Oomgosh's smile widened, as if each word he spoke increased his joy. 'Feel the dirt, feel the leaves, feel the life of the trees pass through their roots. The warmth of the earth, the energy of the plants will pass into your skin and blood and bones, pass into your eyes and mind and fingers. Fight for the pebbles that support your feet, and the rich loam that gives us wild flowers in the spring. Fight against those things that would destroy it.'

Jason would do it if he could. 'But how?' he asked.

'Do as I do, and it will come to you.' The Oomgosh looked back up to their silently falling foes. He planted his thick legs a yard apart and lifted his good arm again to the sky.

Jason spread his legs wide and lifted both his arms.

'Now, Jason,' the Oomgosh called to him. 'Feel the air. See how it moves.'

The Volunteers were shooting arrows at the things above. The shafts disappeared into the darkness, but the great blobs twitched and paused in their descent, as if the sharp points of the arrows caused them pain. Raven flew among them, always just beyond their reach, the air from his wings making the dark things flutter from his path.

'The air, Jason!' the Oomgosh insisted.

Jason realised he had to shut out everything around him but the air. The Oomgosh had closed his eyes. Jason closed his as well.

He felt a breeze against his cheek.

The air, the Oomgosh had said. Jason could feel it brush his skin. The breeze ruffled his hair. The gentle wind brought the green smells from the surrounding trees.

'Catch the air, Jason!' the tree-man urged. 'Follow its patterns!'

Suddenly, all of Jason's feeling was concentrated at the tips of his fingers. He could feel the dance of the wind, the push and pull and spiral of air, warm breeze over cold. Even though he stood completely still, his fingers seemed to join the dance, cascading around and about in great sweeps and circles above Jason's head.

'Now, Jason,' the Oomgosh instructed, 'take the wind and push it at our enemy!'

Jason could feel the air speed up as the Oomgosh began a push of his own. Jason's feet felt warm against the earth. And his hands could push the breezes, making them whistle, then howl.

'Push!' the Oomgosh cried.

'They can't get down here!' someone else cheered.

The wind thrust against Jason now, almost pulling him from his feet. Somehow, though, he held his ground and used the force of the gale to push even more.

'I surrender!' Raven called out. 'The Oomgosh has given us the king of storms!'

'The Oomgosh, and Jason!' the tree-man called back. 'This storm is too strong for any single being to bring it!'

'Those things!' This time, Jason recognised the voice of Nick's mother. 'They can't take the wind. They're blowing away!'

'They are gone!' Raven agreed. 'Raven and the Oomgosh have won again!'

'Is that all, my Raven?' the Oomgosh screamed above the gale.

'Raven and the Oomgosh and Jason!' the bird corrected himself.

'As it was meant to be!' the Oomgosh cheered. 'Jason, that is enough!'

Jason released his grip on the wind and the storm reduced itself to a gentle breeze. He opened his eyes. He felt as if he'd just run five miles.

'We have all worked together,' the Oomgosh announced, 'and the danger is gone.'

Everybody looked so relieved. And he had helped. This was wild.

His mother was staring at him with a frown. Why did his mother look so worried?

'George?' Nick's mother called out. 'What's happened to George?'

'Could he be hiding somewhere?' Mrs Jackson suggested.

Stanley laughed at that. 'Those things were enough to scare me into hiding, hey?'

But Thomas shook his head and hurried over to where Nick's father had been resting by a tree. Jason wondered what he was looking for. Tracks, maybe, or signs of a fight?

The Oomgosh closed his eyes for a moment, as if he was silently communing with the trees all around. 'No, he is gone. They have taken him.'

Thomas nodded at that. 'Yep. Looks like they snatched 'im where he sat.' He looked up sharply at the other Volunteers. 'This is all our fault. We're the ones with experience hereabouts. Should've been watching the perimeter.'

The Oomgosh raised his good hand in protest. 'It was I who wasn't careful enough. I should have acted sooner, and more forcefully.'

The tree-man swayed and fell to his knees.

'Oomgosh!' Jason called. His sneakers pulled free of the ground with a sucking sound, as if he had sunk into the earth during his dance with the wind.

'I am not as recovered as I might like.' The Oomgosh tried to smile, but there was too much pain in his great face.

'George?' Nick's mother called at the edge of the woods. 'Come on out, George!'

Nick followed her to the spot behind the tree where they had last seen him. 'Dad?' His knuckles were white where he held the hilt of his sword. The weapon was still in its scabbard, but his arm was poised to pull it free in an instant.

Jason wondered why they didn't believe the Oomgosh? Or Thomas, for that matter?

Nick's mother had acted like she had been so angry at George Blake that she couldn't talk to him. And, until Nick's father was gone, Jason hadn't thought Nick cared at all about him one way or another.

'Oh, dear, something has gone wrong.'

Jason turned round at the sound of the new voice.

Obar had returned. 'We've lost somebody?' he asked with a frown, but continued to talk before anyone else could answer. 'Nunn again. I would have thought he would be too busy planning for the dragon's eyes.' He stroked at one side of his drooping moustache. 'Ah, but this would be part of his plan, wouldn't it?'

Nick rushed across the clearing to confront the newcomer. 'Wizard, why did you leave us defenceless?'

Obar placed a protective hand on the rumpled white fabric stretched across his chest. 'I didn't leave you defenceless.' He nodded at all those gathered around. 'Apparently, almost all of you survived. Even the one who is gone – George Blake? – has only been captured. Nunn means to demoralise us. He'd like nothing better than to see us milling aimlessly about, grieving over our losses, so that he could pick us off one by one.'

'Nunn!' The great black bird spat out the word as if it was a curse. 'Raven will steal the other jewels Nunn still holds!'

'No doubt you will, when the time is right,' Obar agreed with an approving nod. 'And none of us has any time to waste. We will lose more than one of our number before this is done.'

Nick's mother walked up behind her son. From the look on her face, she seemed about to launch into an angry speech of her own.

'We must calm down.' Mrs Smith suddenly stood beside Obar. 'We can do no good fighting among ourselves.'

'Where's Mary Lou?' Jason's mother insisted.

'Someplace that I cannot reach.' Mrs Smith tried to smile. She looked nowhere near as sure of herself as she had before she left. 'But I feel that place makes her far safer than any of us here.'

Jason's mum still looked like she was about to break down, as if there was just too much happening to both her son and daughter.

'Again, we must act,' Obar stated loudly, 'with or without Mary Lou –'

But Jason had lost interest in the conversation, at least for the moment. The exhaustion had finally overcome him and he had sat heavily, his sneakers once again sticking to the soil. He glanced at the bottom of his shoes and was startled to see half a dozen small holes in each, as if roots had burrowed up from the ground to touch his feet.

Or maybe roots had grown from his feet to seek their place in the earth.

AROUND THE CIRCLE:
BEFORE THE STORM – 1:
When Harold Dafoe
Was the King of
Everything

His eldest daughter, Susan, was gone. And Harold Dafoe still didn't quite know how it happened.

For some reason, he thought of the day Rose, dear, pretty Rose, said 'Yes'. That had been close to twenty years ago. The world had been a different place. Harold had been different too.

What a day that had been. 'Quite a catch,' Harold's parents had told him. Even the guys at Tech had shown a grudging admiration. Not that a lot of them would admit to wanting a wife. College was the time to 'play the field', after all. But hey, if you had to be tied down, you could do a lot worse than Rose.

To be honest, Rose's answer had startled him. Harold had never considered himself particularly good looking. And heaven knew he wasn't particularly adventurous. But Rose hadn't been searching for looks or adventure. She was looking for somebody solid, dependable. She didn't want the flashy guys. And Harold was an engineer (well, almost). He was dependable. He'd hold down a job for his whole life while they raised a family.

And so he did hold down a job. And so they did raise a family. That was the way it was supposed to be, wasn't it? They had moved from an apartment to a small 'starter' home and from there to their current home on Chestnut Circle.

Still, Harold remembered that one day when Rose had said yes. For one shining instant, he was the king of everything.

But how had the king of everything come down to this?

He knew where it started. His daughter, Susan, had made a mistake. She had let one of the local boys go too far and now she was with child.

Rose thought it was the end of the world. At first, Harold had wanted to take the boy's head off.

But then he started thinking about Susan. Why had she done it? Maybe they hadn't given their daughter enough love. He wished there was a way to make up for it now.

Rose wouldn't listen to any of his suggestions. She insisted that they send Susan away, to one of those places for girls with 'her sort of problem'. If she stayed around, what would the neighbours think? How could she go to school? How could the family attend church on Sunday?

And Harold didn't press the issue very hard. Since the day they were married, he'd always done what he thought was best for Rose, always followed her lead in family matters. Rose always knew what was best for the family.

Whatever he said now would be wrong. So he didn't say anything at all. His family was everything to him. He couldn't stand to lose any more of them.

At least, he thought, Mary Lou and Jason would always be there.

So he'd helped his oldest daughter pack up her room and arranged for the transportation to take her away.

Everything was going just the way he and Rose had planned until the moment he'd met their second daughter, Mary Lou, on the stairs.

Mary Lou stared at the suitcases in her father's hands with the sort of wide-eyed confusion you would only see in a twelve-year-old.

'Daddy, are you going away?'

Oh, dear. Rose had been going to talk to their daughter, just as he was going to talk to their son, Jason. They just hadn't seemed to find the time just yet. He hated to see Mary Lou so upset. Maybe, if he told her a little bit about it, his wife could fill in the rest.

He nodded down at the suitcases in his hands. 'I'm not going anywhere, honey. These are – for Susan. She has to go –'

'Harold,' Rose spoke up sharply. 'I'll tell her later.'

Harold nodded at that and shrugged towards his little girl. If anything, Mary Lou looked more upset than before. Still, they had agreed that Rose would be the one to talk to her. And things were bad enough around here without getting Rose angry too.

Why, then, as he carried the bags down the stairs, did he feel like he'd let his younger daughter down?

Rose stood at the bottom of the stairs, arms folded, looking both at her husband and her daughter beyond. Harold risked a final glance back at Mary Lou.

His daughter had started to cry. She turned and rushed up the stairs.

Harold took the bags out to the front steps, feeling as if his whole world had fallen apart.

What had ever happened to the King of Everything?

Eight

Carl Jackson stood on the platform Nunn had given him and looked out over the troops. His troops.

'How many?' he barked to Harold Dafoe, his second-in-command. Carl had no idea what the hell he was supposed to do. But if he shouted long enough and loud enough, no one would have the balls to question him.

He glared at the nearest of his soldiers, a man shorter than Carl, but with muscles showing where he had torn off the sleeves of his uniform. If uniform was the right word for what these soldiers wore. They all had chest plates and helmets made out of something hard and greyish-brown, something that looked more like shell than metal. But the clothes beneath the armour were anything but regulation. Some might have been uniforms once, but more of them looked like rags even the Salvation Army wouldn't touch.

And the soldiers matched their clothes. As they silently stepped into the clearing, man after man, to present themselves to their new Captain, Jackson was struck by how little each new recruit resembled the last; short, tall, thin, bulky, white, yellow, black and brown, like they came from every godforsaken corner of the earth.

What did Nunn want Jackson to do with this mob? Carl wanted to be anywhere else than where he was right now. He had no idea what had brought him to this crazy place. And he didn't trust Nunn, who seemed even crazier than all the shit around him.

Not that he'd talk about this, even with Harold. Jackson almost smiled. Especially with Harold. It would make him look weak. He hadn't been under anybody's thumb since his bastard father died, thirty years ago, and he'd sworn he'd never let anybody lord it over him again.

But Nunn had given Jackson a job to do.

Harold turned back to him, the counting done. 'Ninety-seven, Carl.'

Ninety-seven? That was a goddamn army, and all under his command. Jackson took a deep breath. He'd better come up with something. He *had* been in the army back in the States, even made corporal for a couple of weeks before he was busted back down to private for fighting. Got out of the army six weeks later on a medical disability, a knee problem that cleared up as soon as he was a civilian. But it boiled down to this – the army didn't want him, and he didn't want them – and he got an honourable discharge besides.

So how hard could this be?

'Harry, tell them to stand at attention.'

Harold barked out an order in that weirdo language.

About two thirds of those in front of them went rigid; real professional soldiers. Some of them glanced at Harold and Carl as they came to attention; Carl thought he saw a little fear.

There were a few, though, that didn't snap to quite so fast. Maybe they were confused. Or maybe they didn't respect their new Captain as much as they should.

The muscular guy in the front was one of the slow ones. And Jackson swore the guy had the slightest trace of a smile.

'Harry, follow me!' Jackson shouted as he leapt from the platform. He didn't look back to see if Dafoe was with him. It was time for a little discipline.

He stopped directly in front of the smirking soldier.

'You got a problem, asshole?' Jackson demanded. Any trace of emotion left the other man's face. His eyes snapped straight ahead, looking to some point behind Jackson's head. Maybe the soldier didn't know the words, but he understood his Captain.

Good for a start, Jackson thought. But he needed to set an example.

'Harold!' he yelled.

'Yeah, Carl.' Dafoe rushed up to him, out of breath. What took him so long? The wimp must have taken the stairs down. Maybe someday Harold would need to be an example too.

Jackson found a big smile stretching across his face. 'I think these soldiers need a little lesson. Tell them that, Harold.'

Harold barked out a short and ugly sentence.

What now? Carl felt a strange sort of excitement. He remembered what the other Captain had done to Hyram Sayre, their crazy neighbour, taking a sword and gutting him to get the others to obey. And he remembered Hyram falling to his knees, trying to hold his stomach together with his hands as his guts oozed between his fingers. Well, if that's the sort of thing it took, Carl was ready.

He reached down and pulled the soldier's sword from its scabbard.

The soldier didn't move. Any trace of a smile was gone from his face. Well, it was a little bit too late now, wasn't it?

'You will obey me.' Jackson got no reaction from the soldier. He glanced sharply to his side. 'Harry?'

Harold barked out the sentence.

Jackson lifted the sword, holding it only a few inches in front of the soldier's face. The soldier continued to look straight ahead, as if the sword wasn't even there.

Jackson pushed the sword forward until the point pressed into the other man's cheekbone. Still nothing. The point drew a thin line down the soldier's cheek. Blood welled from the wound. The soldier didn't flinch.

It wasn't enough. Jackson felt like he needed something more.

He pulled his sword back and studied the man that had to be humbled. The soldier's whole chest and stomach was covered by that hard shell. So no guts spewing between his fingers just now. Very well. Jackson put the point of the sword at the soldier's throat.

'If you do not obey me –' Jackson turned his head quickly to his lieutenant. 'Harold, repeat it!' Dafoe was sweating. He looked like he was going to throw up. He managed to mutter a few guttural words.

Jackson turned back to the soldier. 'You're dead,' he said in the calm sort of voice you'd use to discuss the weather, or last night's game, or the death of scum.

Harry's voice echoed his own.

Jackson smiled. He had total control here. He could do whatever he wanted. And he would.

As soon as he realised that, his anger went away. Knowing he could kill the soldier any time, in any way he wished, made Carl not want to kill him at all, at least for now. The threat was probably enough this time. He could give the soldiers the real lesson the next time they acted up.

Jackson threw the sword in the dirt at the soldier's feet. He turned smartly and marched back to the steps of his reviewing platform.

'Uh, Carl,' Harold said close by his ear as he passed, 'are you sure you should have –'

'Shut up, Harry!' Jackson cut him off. He stopped and looked at the quivering idiot that was his second-in-command. 'And don't call me Carl any more. From now on, I'm the Captain.'

With that, he climbed the steps, two at a time. When he reached the top again, he snapped his mind back to the soldiers lined up before him in the clearing. All of them were very much at attention. He doubted that any of them would even twitch until he gave the order.

Jackson nodded curtly at his troops, showing his approval.

He was beginning to like this.

Nunn was pleased. He watched it all in that way he had, walking invisibly among his troops. His new Captain was everything the wizard had hoped he would be. Cruelty was such a wonderful tool.

But Nunn had already spent more time than he could afford. He could pursue his more important tasks knowing the island was in capable hands.

Of course, when he returned, he would have to remind this

Jackson of his real place beneath the wizard. Perhaps Nunn would even use a little cruelty of his own. It would be interesting to see how the new Captain reacted to that.

Nunn chuckled. He had already forgotten about those small setbacks he'd had earlier, except of course for how much he would punish those who turned against him.

He could already feel the dragon's power flowing into him. With three of the eyes, he would be unstoppable. With four, he would turn all his enemies to dust and collect the jewels they once held as their remains danced away in the wind. And once he had all seven, he wouldn't even fear the dragon.

He withdrew from the common mortals. One more small piece of business; yes, he could hear the whispers now.

The darkness flocked around him, eager to please. They had brought a gift; one of the so-called neighbours.

The gift huddled on the floor by Nunn's feet, gasping in great breaths. Yes, it was another little quirk of Nunn's dark assistants that they froze the very air through which they moved, making it quite unbreathable.

'What were those things?' the newcomer managed, obviously deluded into thinking he was still among friends.

'They were my servants.' It took Nunn a moment more to search out the name. 'George Blake.' Ah, yes, the new one. He had wanted a final disruption to his foes before he left; something to increase their doubt and distract them from their search. George Blake, the new one, snatched almost as quickly as he had arrived, that was a particularly good distraction. He would have to reward his servants.

George Blake turned his face up towards the wizard. 'Have I met you?'

The only light here were the two dragon's eyes, glowing where they were embedded in Nunn's palms. Blake squinted into the glare.

His next question was a bit more hesitant. '*What* – are you?'

Nunn was in such a good mood, he decided to allow the impertinence.

'I am your master. I am your god. I am everything you will ever need.'

'Oh, god,' Blake replied, apparently referring to someone besides Nunn, 'how have I got myself into –'

Nunn stroked one of his jewels gently with his index finger. Blake screamed as he folded into a foetal position.

'Yes, the pain is quite dramatic, isn't it?' Nunn asked softly. 'There will be more, if you don't obey me.'

Blake remembered to breathe again. He nodded his head, shocked into silence. Yes, this one was quite malleable. He would make a fine addition to Nunn's collection.

'I can waste no more time with you now. I will give you over to a couple of friends –' Nunn smiled at the fear on Blake's face, '– friends of yours. When I return, we will talk some more.'

Yes, Nunn was quite pleased. Everything was in place at last.

The Captain couldn't believe it.

Nunn no longer seemed to have time to repair the little tears and holes in his world. And he appeared to have forgotten all about his former Captain of the Guard.

He guessed he shouldn't call himself that any more. It had been so long since he'd used his real name. He'd been the Captain for so long, he'd stopped thinking of himself as anything else.

But now he'd have to learn to think for himself again. He climbed carefully through the ruin of Nunn's castle wall, still glowing faintly where Hyram Sayre had blasted his way to safety. For a time, Nunn had forced Sayre and the Captain to think with one mind; Sayre had been dead, after all, and, with what Nunn had done to him, the Captain had not been all that lively. But Nunn had given Sayre a bit more power than he had anticipated. The not-quite-dead man was suddenly more than alive and he had left Nunn behind. Not to mention the gaping hole he'd left in the wizard's defences.

So after regaining a bit of strength, the Captain decided he'd better leave as well. He'd found a twisted piece of metal in the wreckage. Whether it had once been a sword or some part of one of Nunn's arcane devices, it now made a perfect club. It wasn't much of a weapon, but it would serve until he found something better.

He climbed down the far side of the wall and found himself too weak to walk any further. He crawled instead, desperate to get some distance from Nunn's domain. It was only after he was past the first line of trees that he allowed himself a moment's rest, out in the sun he'd thought he'd never see again.

He woke suddenly. It was dark. Hardly any light penetrated through the forest cover above. He could vaguely make out the pale shape of his hand at his side and the irregular metal of the club just beyond that. All else was lost in total black.

He hadn't meant to sleep like that.

He knew that something had woken him. He could smell it on the wind. Wolves.

He pushed himself up to a sitting position.

'I'm armed!' he called out with all the force left in him. He grabbed the club. The metal felt very cold in his hand. 'I'll use it!'

He was answered by a growl in the darkness.

'Fresssh meat!' one of the wolf voices howled.

'Humansss are too trricky,' another answered.

The Captain waved the club above his head with whatever strength he still had. It whistled in the night air. With luck, he could knock one or two of them senseless before they took him.

'Humansss kill us!' a wolf barked.

'Hungrry!' another insisted. 'Mussst feed!'

There was a series of angry barks and growls, as if the wolves were fighting among themselves.

The Captain pushed himself so that his back was to a tree. Maybe, with the wolves so disorganised, there was a way he could survive.

'Your leader is dead!' he called. Actually, he only knew that their leader had changed, turned by Nunn into a great wolf-monster. But Nunn had returned to his castle without the monster, and Nunn had been in a rage. If the Wolf King wasn't dead yet it soon would be.

The fighting stopped.

'Man hasss killed ourr king!'

A throaty growl. 'We will kill man!'

'I did not kill him!' The Captain waved his club in the air

63

again, to let the wolves know he could kill another of them. 'The man who killed your leader is my enemy!'

A wolf howled at that.

'Ssshow him to ussss!'

'We will rrip the meat from hisss throat!'

'He is not here!' the Captain called back. 'He is far away. You cannot kill him. Neither can I, by myself. Together, though, together we will tear him apart.'

'Togetherrr?'

'Humansss can't be trusssted!'

Nor could wolves, the Captain thought. Still, he had kept the wolves from attacking. Maybe he really could save himself.

'I am a good hunter,' he called out into the darkness.

He had had to survive in this wilderness before. The tough vines made an adequate sling and there were plenty of small rocks around for ammunition. In the morning, once he'd rested, he could pull down a few of the local rodents to give to these creatures.

'Together', he added, 'we will catch much food.'

The barking and growling started up again, not quite as loud as before, as if the wolves were arguing more than fighting.

'Be careful of humansss –'

'You'll find usss food?' another voice howled.

'Keep ourr dissstancce! Keep ourr dissstancce!'

'We mussst avenge ourr king!'

'Come back tomorrow,' the Captain called back. 'We will hunt together in the daylight. Then, once I have brought you food, we will find the killer of your king.'

'Verry well, human. We will give you until tomorrow.'

'But if you trick usss –' The sentence ended in a growl.

The wolves' voices faded with distance and their odour soon followed.

The Captain sat with his back to the tree and listened to the silence. Apparently the wolves were gone for the moment.

But he had to sleep. If they came back and attacked him during the night it couldn't be helped.

Wolves were not to be trusted.

The Captain smiled despite his exhaustion. After all, he wasn't to be trusted either.

Once upon a time Hyram Sayre only had a lawn. Not a particularly big lawn, but not too small either. It was a third of an acre, and a corner lot. It was what Hyram lived for.

It had not always been this way. Once, when he had first bought the house in the centre of the lawn, he had had a wife and a daughter, Cheryl. But having a house was far more of a responsibility than the rental that Hyram and his family had shared before. The house and the property had to be properly kept up to retain their value. And nothing was more important to the appearance of a house than a well-maintained lawn.

Not that it had been easy. At first, the lawn had been quite difficult, full of dry patches and crab grass, and one shaded corner where nothing would grow at all. How, Hyram argued, could you hold up your head when your lawn looked like that? What would the neighbours think?

So it was that Hyram accepted the challenge. Nothing would be as important as a perfect lawn. He experimented with seeds and fertilisers and weed killers and sod and extra water, worked night and day, in and out of growing season. It had taken years, but at last he and his lawn understood each other and his yard was all that it could be.

Of course, there were always difficulties. His wife and daughter had left him years before, unable to see his vision. And he knew that many of the neighbours laughed at him and let their teenagers run over his perfect grass with their damned hot rods. But he was beyond that, for he had found his higher calling. Constant maintenance had its own rewards.

So Hyram's life fell into a pattern until the day that the storm came, the world changed and he was killed quite painfully.

Not that he was entirely dead. No, a local wizard kept Hyram moving. So he went to the wizard and the mage gave him a certain power for some reasons that the wizard never fully explained. Or maybe Hyram hadn't been listening, for he saw the world around him in a whole new way.

You see, once Hyram had got over his first discomfort, being dead and all, he could see some advantages to this situation. This new world was not ruined like the one he had come from. Green was not restricted to tiny lawns and public parks. Green was everywhere.

He could feel the green all around him. Whatever the wizard had given him was only the beginning of his power. Hyram Sayre would be truly whole once he had merged with the green.

So it was that he visited the forest. And should he find a tree or shrub that was small or sickly, he had but to give it a touch and that plant would grow. His touch was surely green and – far beyond a single lawn – all the world would benefit.

He had left the wizard behind. He had a purpose here now, no longer tied to the petty concerns of mortals.

Forest grow! Flowers multiply! Trees bear fruit!

He would live quite happily ever after.

BOOK 2

VISITING DAYS

Nine

The ocean had been quite a surprise, even for Constance Smith. The survivors of Chestnut Circle had spent two days on this island and besides a small stream, she had seen no sign of water. But then Obar had simply announced 'This way', and Mrs Smith and those coming with her had followed him through the forest.

They had walked for what Mrs Smith would judge to be half an hour. Actually, she had floated for a good part of that trip. Her broken hip, while healing remarkably well, was still a bit on the weak side.

But it had only taken a few minutes before she first felt the breeze and smelled the salt on the air. The trees were getting smaller around them, and more scraggly, as if their roots could not sink as deeply into the soil.

'Ah,' Obar remarked as he climbed a small rise. Constance floated close behind him.

The world opened up before her. Instead of the claustrophobic forest she saw the ocean everywhere, the sky a bluish green, the sea that same green with an added shade of grey. It looked like every ocean she had ever seen and still completely different.

The sand was the wrong colour; more of a greyish brown than a yellow. And she realised there were no seagulls here. Instead, she saw sleek black birds with sharp, blood-red beaks flying above the waves. One swooped low, skimming the water with its claws, and was rewarded with a small silver fish. The other birds called to their lucky brother, their voices somehow sounding much too low and hoarse.

As much as her trips to the other realities, this vista gave

Constance the feeling of being somewhere totally new, with a different ocean and a different sky.

The wizard looked at her for a moment, then glanced out to the ocean. 'You will need a suitable craft.'

With that, Obar frowned and muttered and waved his arms. The sea grew perfectly still for a moment, the water sparkling in the sun. The black birds flew quickly away, their cries higher than before, as if they wanted no part of this. The world around them was totally silent. Even the breeze was gone.

Perhaps a hundred feet from shore the ocean began to move, white water crashing everywhere, as if something was rising from the bottom, frantic to get out.

A pole rose above the churning waters, then a cross-piece to show that the pole was truly a mast. Water flew around the dark wood, a fountain in the sea, as two lesser masts appeared.

'It's a ship!' Wilbert called for all of them.

And indeed it was, for, as the water fell away, a great wooden craft had risen to the ocean's surface.

Todd whistled in admiration. 'Did you just – like – create this?'

'Well, um, yes.' Obar coughed. 'Well, that is, I believe I have got rid of any trace of the former occupants. No need for unnecessary unpleasantness.'

So in other words, Constance thought, he had scavenged this thing rather than creating it. Obar was nothing if not indirect. The craft reminded Mrs Smith of some pirate ship from an old Errol Flynn film. It seemed a little large for a crew of four. Still, she hoped that Obar knew best.

'And we really need to use this?' she asked again.

Obar nodded emphatically. 'As I've said before, water is tricky. Your magic is new to you. It is best not to overtax yourself.'

Constance thought again of her fruitless search for Mary Lou and her stop in the midst of the voices. Perhaps there was a certain wisdom in what the wizard had to say.

'It is only half a day's sail to the closest of the islands.' The magician pointed somewhere out at the middle of the ocean. 'You can almost see it from here.'

Todd squinted out across the water. 'Only half a day? So how do we get there?'

Obar shrugged agreeably. 'Oh, the boat will pretty much steer itself. Should there be a problem, you can certainly ask the rigging to bend one way or another and it will be most happy to oblige.'

Stanley scowled as if he wasn't buying any of this. 'Why should we need to do that, hey, when the boat can steer itself?'

'Mrs Smith will easily get the feel of it.' Obar frowned and shook his head. 'Just obtain the jewel and bring it back here. Our lives do depend on it.'

The boat rocked on the grey-green water. It looked whole and dry; not at all as if it had spent considerable time rotting at the bottom of the ocean.

Obar waved a hand and a row-boat appeared on the shore before them.

'This boat is not quite as real,' Obar admitted, 'but it should be able to transport you for short distances with no difficulty.'

'I guess, then,' Mrs Smith said with very little conviction, 'we should be on our way.'

She looked out again at that galleon riding the waves, her straight and true transport to the dragon's eye. According to Obar, it was all very simple. Why did she feel she was missing something?

Obar never told the whole truth when he could help it. Not that he didn't want her to succeed. It just seemed as though that secretiveness had been trained into him from his years of magic, so that he was now incapable of thinking any other way. The only way to get the magician to tell the whole truth was to pin him down with questions; grill him until you had covered every possibility.

But the possibilities before her were almost entirely unknown. And until she knew more about what lay in front of her, she didn't know what questions she should ask.

Her three companions had walked down the beach to the boat. She floated after them.

71

Wilbert and Stanley pushed the small craft out so that it was entirely buoyed by water. The heavy-set, bearded Volunteer was first into the boat.

'Well, here's a place we can lend a hand.' Wilbert retrieved an oar from the bottom of the boat. Stanley climbed in after him and grabbed a second oar.

'What about me?' Todd asked as he, too, jumped aboard. The row-boat rocked precariously.

'Go up to the bow,' Wilbert replied. 'You're our look-out.'

Constance waited for the three men to be settled, then glided into the centre of the rearmost seat on the dinghy. She settled in so gently that the boat didn't rock at all.

She wondered if she could propel this boat through water in the same way she nudged herself through the air. 'I might be able to give us a little push as well.'

'Careful!' Obar called from where he still stood on the beach. 'As I said, water is tricky. I look forward to seeing you back on the island.'

She looked at her three companions. 'Let me give it a bit of a try.'

Wilbert smiled and said, 'Have at it!' Stanley said it sounded easier than rowing. Even Todd nodded silently from the front of the boat. It was a little frightening, really, how much all the others trusted her.

She would just have to do her best to earn that trust. She thought of water, thrusting her consciousness into the shallows at the rear of the boat. Once down there, all she had to do was give the boat a little nudge.

Water felt different. She was surrounded by swirls and eddies. There was a weight here that covered her. Currents fought with cross-currents as the waves encircled her. The water was pulling her under, dragging her towards the bottom.

She felt the slightest moment of panic as she broke free, but calmed herself with a single breath. The dynamics were different here than they were on land. It was rather like when, in flying, she had learned the magical equivalent of walking. To deal with water, she would have to learn how to swim.

'Perhaps rowing is better,' she admitted, glancing back towards Obar on the shore. But Obar was gone, no doubt pursuing another of the new-found eyes.

'You know best,' Wilbert agreed as he fitted the oar into its lock. They were supportive even when she failed.

She smiled at the others, not letting her uncertainty show through. Soon, both Stanley and Wilbert were rowing side by side, their strokes setting up a rhythmic counterpoint to the waves. Mrs Smith closed her eyes and listened to the sound of the wind, the sea, the rowing, the returning birds. Obar was right; she was a creature of air, not of water.

'There's a rope ladder up ahead!' Todd called. She opened her eyes and saw the young man was pointing at the ship.

'So there is!' Stanley said with a glance over his shoulder.

With no further words between them, Wilbert and Stanley adjusted their stroke so that the dinghy angled slightly to the right. Stanley glanced over his shoulder again. 'That should do it!'

The large bulk of the ship appeared to screen out the worst of the waves now and they seemed to fly across the surface of the water. Half a dozen strokes and they were covered by the boat's great shadow.

'Whoa, there!' Wilbert cried. 'Don't want a crash.' Both Volunteers dragged their oars in the water, slowing the dinghy's forward motion.

The thinner of the two glanced sceptically at the boat beneath their feet. 'I don't feel that this trip was entirely natural, hey?'

Wilbert shipped his oar and scratched at his beard. 'There he goes. Stanley, the master of understatement.' He twisted round in his seat. 'Todd, boy! Grab hold of that rope!'

Todd scrambled to the very tip of the boat and got his hands around one strand of the rope ladder.

Stanley had jumped to another seat and somehow got himself turned around facing the bow. 'Tie the boat to that loose end there, hey?'

Todd frowned down at the rope in his hand.

Wilbert shook his head as he straddled his own seat. 'Uh-oh.

I don't think our young friend has spent much time at sea.' He stood carefully and moved forward in the boat. 'Let me show you how to make a couple of knots, Todd boy.'

Stanley peered up the rope ladder to the deck above. 'So who gets the honour of going first?'

Without another word, Mrs Smith lifted herself from her seat and flew up the side of the ship. She wanted to inspect what was ahead of them before any of the others risked themselves. Obar had mentioned certain unpleasant things that he had supposedly removed from this craft. She wanted to make sure they truly were gone.

It wasn't, she reflected, that she didn't trust Obar. It was more like she didn't trust the world.

She set herself down on one corner of the deck. The whole ship looked brand new, full of dark wood and polished brass fittings, thick sturdy ropes and billowing white sails that appeared to be newly hung.

She sent her consciousness below decks and found four fully furnished cabins and a large store of food, and what appeared to be large bolts of cloth. The rest of the below-deck area was completely empty, as if it had been scoured clean. Which she supposed it had. This time, Obar seemed to have done all that he had promised.

She leaned over the side of the boat and called to the others. 'All clear up here! Come aboard!'

Wilbert had just finished tying the boat up below. Todd swung on to the ladder first and came up so fast Mrs Smith was sure he would slip and fall. Wilbert and Stanley followed at a slightly more careful pace.

'Mrs Smith,' Todd said breathlessly when he reached the deck. 'Shouldn't you have – I mean, we could have – What if it hadn't been –'

'I appreciate your concern, Todd,' Mrs Smith replied with a smile. 'But I've found ways to take care of myself around here that I didn't know I had. They've kept me alive – at least so far.'

She was sure Todd still thought of her as that quiet, older, slightly frail lady who lived across the street back on Chestnut

Circle. And, deep down, she still was that person. It wouldn't do to get too full of herself; these new powers were far too unpredictable.

'Ah,' Wilbert added as he gained the deck, 'Mrs Smith, you can protect us any time you want.'

Stanley was right behind him. He looked around as he planted both his feet firmly on deck. 'I never did much like boats.'

Todd looked above them at the sails, slack for lack of wind. He turned to Mrs Smith. 'So how does it go?' he asked.

'I was hoping Obar would have taken care of that,' Constance replied. 'I imagine we just have to let the ship know we're ready and we'll be on our way.'

She heard the sound of flapping canvas overhead. The mainsail was filling with the wind and the ship began to inch forward. It had been waiting, then, and she had let it know it was time.

'Sail, ho!' Wilbert cheered.

'I'm going to find someplace to sit,' Stanley answered as the boat began to roll with the waves.

'There's food below,' Mrs Smith said.

Stanley's hand went to the knife at his belt. 'Anything else?'

She shook her head. 'I could find nothing. We are the only ones on board.'

Wilbert laughed and patted his belly. 'Well, since we're not needed to sail this thing, let's eat!'

Constance waved for the others to go ahead. 'I think I will remain above. It feels good to be in the sea air.'

Stanley followed his fellow Volunteer, a worried look still on his face. 'Call if you need us, hey?'

Constance assured him that she would and watched Stanley follow the other two through the door that led below. She was glad, for the moment, to be alone.

She could not shake the feeling that something would go wrong. And she wanted some quiet. Ever since she had come to this place, she had either been surrounded by others or busy using her magic. She hadn't had a moment to take stock, to reflect on everything that happened around her. It was another

75

way her life had become so much different; after years of spending days by herself, just her and her house, waiting for her husband to come home from the city.

Her husband? She hadn't thought of Ralph since a few minutes after she'd come here. She doubted she would ever see him again. What would he think of what she'd become? Constance wasn't at all sure that he would like it.

She took a deep breath of the sea air. It was nice to slow down for a moment, to have a chance to collect her thoughts. It felt cool here compared with the muggy heat of the island they had left behind. The boat creaked as it laboured beneath the wind. The groan of masts and boards sounded like some sad, distant song for all the sailors who had trod the deck before.

She gently rose above the boards of the deck and floated forward, lifting herself to the foredeck and the bow of the boat. What bothered her the most, she guessed, was not knowing what faced them. She could see no land ahead with her normal eyes. She wondered, if she looked with her dragon's eye, might she be able to see their goal.

She took the green jewel from the pocket above her breast and held it in both hands. She could feel the familiar power shoot through her fingers, her hands, her arms and shoulders, spreading to every corner of her body.

She closed her eyes and willed her mind to rush forward above the waves, seeking land. She had a sense of speed, of water below, clouds above.

But the speed was gone. Her senses had stopped. She tried to feel around her, to find the island that was their destination. But there was nothing but the waves beneath her. Was this another trick of the water?

Then she knew that there was something else here, something far beneath the waves, but something that was coming closer. Now that she had found it, she was aware that this thing beneath her was huge, rising from a vast patch of the ocean floor. And she realised with a start that the thing was aware of her too, in fact might be rising to find her, to overwhelm her and those she protected, enveloping them and dragging them down to the ocean floor.

76

It was coming faster. She had to get away.

Mrs Smith opened her eyes. Her consciousness had snapped back from the ocean ahead. She noticed that she had dropped the jewel. It lay quietly beneath her feet.

She bent down, scooping it back up and into her pocket.

That huge thing before them was real. And while she could escape it through a trick of the dragon's eye, she doubted that the ship, as it rushed forward to its meeting with this leviathan, would be spared so easily.

She looked up at the wind-filled sails. She had no way to change this ship's course and wouldn't know where to sail it if she did. Somehow she felt that great thing beneath the sea would find them wherever they sailed.

She would have to find a way to face and defeat it, or she and her dragon's eye would be lost beneath the ocean for ever.

AROUND THE CIRCLE:
BEFORE THE STORM – 2:
The Day Carl Jackson Found Truth

Carl Jackson only knew one place to find truth, and that was at the bottom of the glass.

He took another swig of the good stuff. And why not? He deserved it, especially after the way his family treated him. His lazy wife, his snivelling son, he'd give them what they deserved.

He looked back at the tumbler in his hand. The light was funny down here in the rec room. He could swear he saw his reflection in the brown Scotch at the bottom of the glass. Except it wasn't him exactly.

It looked more like his father.

Carl almost threw his glass across the room, but stopped himself just in time. It would have been a waste of good Scotch, all because of some stupid thought he had. After all, his father had been dead a long time.

Carl closed his eyes.

'If I wasn't tied down to you two, I could've made something of my life. How do I even know he is my son, the way you're always whoring around? You're both a drain on me! Why do I beat him so bad? Because I feel like it!'

Carl's eyes snapped open. That sounded like his father's voice, right here in the room with him. But he was all alone in the basement, the house around him perfectly still.

Carl hadn't seen his father since he was fourteen. The old man had finally made good his threats and left. Carl had always sworn, if he ever saw his father again, he'd beat him the way he'd been beaten himself.

He was getting angry all over again. But no, it was something in the booze. How could that be? He was drinking the good stuff.

Yeah. The good stuff. He'd never desert his family the way his father deserted them.

That's why he'd got his family this great home in a nice neighbourhood. What would his father say if he knew that Carl Jackson, the boy who would never amount to shit, was living on Chestnut Circle?

Carl chuckled. That called for another drink.

Not, of course, that his own wife and son appreciated everything he'd given them. Why did they have to cross him at every turn?

His eyes were drawn back to the glass. The reflection there had changed.

Now it looked like his mother.

'Why do you stay out all night that way? I'm not going to be around that much longer. Your father crippled me and you don't care. You'll end up in jail and they'll throw me in the streets! What have I done to deserve this?'

His mother had become impossible after his father had gone. She clutched at Carl, demanding he give up his whole life for her, sometimes keeping him home from school so she wouldn't have to be alone.

A couple of months after his father left his mother stopped going out of the house altogether. Soon, Carl was doing his best not to come home. But every time he did the house looked worse, and his mother looked older and frailer. He could still feel his mother's crooked fingers, more bone than flesh, plucking at his clothes, trying somehow to hold on to him so he could never leave again.

Carl looked at the glass in his hand and shuddered. Why wouldn't his mother listen to him? Didn't she know he had to get out of there, to do something for himself, to prove he wasn't the good-for-nothing fuck-up his father always branded him? He couldn't have her clawing at him all the time. He couldn't live his life for her!

She had died a week after he joined the army. Too many pills, the doctors said. She was getting feeble-minded. She must have got confused.

Carl drained his glass. Why couldn't she leave him alone? Why couldn't they all just leave him alone?

Why didn't any of them ask what Carl wanted?

Yeah. Why not? That was the problem, really. He was surprised he'd never seen it so clearly before. Maybe he should go upstairs, find Rebecca and Todd, and just flat tell them that.

Yeah. Maybe this time he could really talk some sense into them. Maybe he could get them to stop their whining long enough to see his side of things. Maybe he could stop all the screaming and hitting for a little while.

Not, of course, that the two of them didn't deserve a good smack now and again.

Carl chuckled. This Scotch was good. He'd have to do this more often.

Yeah. Maybe this time they'd really listen to what he had to say.

Hell, he'd make them listen. He'd sit them down and slap them silly until they knew everything he needed. He'd show his father who ran the house now. He'd show his mother he could do whatever he wanted.

Yeah. He'd finally figured it all out.

If only he could get out of his chair.

He couldn't feel the empty glass in his hand. His fingers were numb. The glass fell from the arm rest of the chair, very slowly,

79

and bounced on the shag carpet.

He giggled. That glass was ready for a refill! If only he could focus on it better. When you finally figure things out, that calls for a celebration! Why was it getting dark in here? Was Todd screwing with the lights?

He'd show Todd what it meant to screw with somebody.

But not just now. His eyes were closed. His whole body felt heavy and smooth, as smooth as the Scotch going down his throat. He was free. Nothing could stick to him now.

Yeah.

Carl Jackson felt it all just slipping away.

Ten

Things were moving too fast for Harold Dafoe and there seemed to be no way to slow them down.

Somehow, he had got himself thrown into this mess with the wizard and his neighbour Jackson. Somehow? It was his own fault. He could never figure out what to do. He always let other people make decisions for him. It had got him through his life so far; his boss told him what to do at work, Rose told him when it was time to get married and time to have kids. Real life, though, the life back on Chestnut Circle, the life before now, that hadn't been quite so dangerous. Harold could let other people make decisions back then. But now he was stuck with both Nunn and Jackson. Harold thought they were both crazy. No. This new world was crazy. Nunn and Carl were psychotic.

But there seemed nothing Harold could do, except to go along. And then things got more complicated with every passing moment.

Now George Blake was here. Nunn had brought him, along with something else that really had Harold worried.

'Welcome your neighbour!' the wizard had announced in his usual sardonic tone. 'And I have another small aid for Carl's use alone.' He held up a globe that appeared to be filled with some dark liquid, except within the deep blue fluid Harold could see flashes of crimson light. 'Come, my Captain. The explanation of its use is for your ears only.'

Jackson walked forward at that and Nunn raised one of his hands, the green stone shining where it was embedded in his palm. Nunn spoke to Jackson, then; Harold could see the wizard's mouth move, but no sound reached Harold's ears. Jackson laughed when the wizard was done, a long and hearty laugh, as if he had just heard one of the best jokes ever. Or maybe Nunn was giving him a joke to play on the world. Harold didn't trust Jackson already. How much more of a threat would the new Captain become if he started to use magic?

The wizard handed Jackson the globe; Carl grinned like he had just won a million dollars. Nunn closed his raised hand.

'– and I expect good things from both of your assistants as well.' Nunn's voice abruptly reached Harold again. 'I do not appreciate being disappointed.'

Nunn smiled at the soldiers around him, soldiers who were doing their best not to look at the wizard. 'I leave all you men in the most capable hands. Obey my new Captain and his two lieutenants, and you will be well rewarded when the new world begins.'

The magician waved once and popped right out of existence.

The new world? Harold wondered what the hell that meant. Not, of course, that he could ask anybody about it.

'Harry?' Jackson said in his ear. Harold snapped to attention. 'You nervous about something?'

Harold turned to his neighbour. Carl bounced the softball-sized globe in his hand, a shit-eating grin on his face. 'It couldn't have anything to do with the little surprise I have here.' He looked around at the soldiers still in rank behind him. 'I could drop it, here and now, but – there goes the surprise. I think it would be far better if everybody just obeyed me totally. Don't you?' He turned back to Harold. 'Harry, go take care of George. Nunn has given us things to do.'

'Take care of –' Harold replied hesitantly.

Carl almost frowned. 'Don't be an idiot, Harry. Get him up, get him with the programme.' The globe in his hand made him smile again. 'In this outfit, you either move it or lose it.'

Harry nodded and ran back to the platform, where Nunn had deposited their latest recruit.

George lay there on the boards, curled into a foetal position.

'George!' Harry called as he approached.

His neighbour didn't reply. He didn't even move.

Harry walked up to him and pushed George's shoulder with his toe. George managed a grunt.

'Come on, man,' Harold insisted, his tone verging on desperation. 'Stand up!'

It took him a moment, but George turned his head and opened the eye closer to Harold. 'Why?' he croaked.

Harold risked a look back at Carl and the soldiers. 'Stand up', he whispered hoarsely, 'or you'll be dead!'

'Is he up and around yet?' Carl called merrily. Harold thought Jackson was just looking for an excuse to kill someone.

'Now!' Harold said between clenched teeth.

'Oh, god, I suppose I have to.' George rolled on to his back with a sigh and raised his arms to Harold. 'Give me a hand and I'll see what I can do.'

Harold pulled him up into a sitting position. From there, George managed to scramble to his feet. He started to sway. 'Mind if I lean against you?'

'Be my guest,' Harry said, greatly relieved. 'You just saved your rear.'

George nodded as he answered softly, 'I never did much like Carl Jackson. I wouldn't give him the satisfaction.'

'Ah, sleeping beauty joins us!' Jackson cheered. 'Come on, gentlemen, we have work to do! We have to visit our neighbours and hold them for Nunn!'

Harold couldn't help himself. 'We have to capture our own families?'

'Hey,' Jackson shot back, 'that shouldn't be too hard. As long as we can get them to see the justice of Nunn's cause, we shouldn't have any problems!'

'I still don't understand any of this –' George said softly.

'Come on, George,' Carl called up to him. 'Join our little army. Show that you're good for something!'

'– but I still don't think I like him,' George added even more quietly. As soft as his voice was, he was beginning to sound angry.

Harold liked that.

He hoped George Blake could be angry enough for both of them.

★　　★　　★

It was the heat and then the blazing sun that hit him, one-two, as surely as someone had slapped him, one cheek after the other. Evan Mills shook his head to clear it as he shielded his eyes from the glare.

He giggled and said with another voice, 'Enough heat even for Zachs!'

The wizard's deeper voice replied, 'I told you we would need water.'

Somehow, Evan thought, Rox's smug attitude was a little suspect. The wizard hadn't mentioned how much water they'd already seen when they had accidentally materialised twice, once some six feet or so above the ocean, the next time six feet or so below the water's surface. Still, Evan's clothes would dry quickly in this heat. The salt was already making the cloth feel stiff and scratchy.

'I can't see a thing,' Mills complained.

'We can make certain adjustments,' the still-smug wizard's voice replied. 'It's not as though we are only human.'

With that, the world darkened around him, as if he were surrounded by tinted glass. Even though it improved his vision immensely, Evan still couldn't see anything but sand.

The wizard sighed. 'I should have suspected this. We are not alone.'

'What are you doing here?' another voice demanded behind them.

Evan turned round. It was Obar.

'What are you even doing alive?' the white-clad wizard demanded. He didn't seem at all pleased to see them.

Answer him, Evan, Rox said, silently this time.

What should I say? he thought. Evan supposed he could start with the truth, or at least part of it. 'I survived my encounter with Nunn. He got a little careless.'

Obar waved his explanation aside. 'You must be here for the jewel. Why would you be doing something like that?'

He showed Evan his own jewel. It glittered in the sun. 'You must be working for someone else. I'm afraid I can't allow –'

There was a laugh as a cloud of sand exploded at Obar's

right. 'Rather,' a dry voice announced from deep within the maelstrom, 'we can't allow –'

Evan was already far too familiar with that voice. They had been joined by Nunn.

The dark wizard grinned as the sand settled around him. 'Like old times, hey, brother?'

Obar nodded slowly, holding his jewel with both hands as if it were a shield. 'Like old times, until you tried to murder me.'

'Murder?' Nunn's smile only seemed to broaden with the word. 'And was I the first to try? I seem to remember that somewhat differently.'

Evan found himself talking again. 'What's the difference?' his most authoritative voice interrupted. 'You were both murderers already.'

Both the wizards stared at him.

'Rox?' Obar asked softly.

Even Nunn's smile faltered. 'Apparently we weren't as final at this as we imagined.'

Obar shifted his jewel slightly so that it was pointing more at Evan than at Nunn. 'This is rather – unexpected.'

'We can finish it now,' Nunn encouraged. 'He has no eye of his own.'

'You are both so good at murder,' Rox agreed in a surprisingly cheerful tone. 'And will one of you kill the other while that one is killing me?'

Obar glanced down at the jewel in his hands. 'No doubt.'

'We haven't built up a tradition of trust, now, have we?' Nunn asked his brother. 'But perhaps we can still work together when we have a common goal. I believe you were the one who said that before.'

'Why should either of you ever trust the other?' Rox said through Evan's voice. 'I think it would be far more amusing if one of you trusted me.'

Nunn raised his arms. 'I have had enough amusement.' He opened his fists to reveal the dragon's eyes glowing in his palms. 'I have two stones. I will kill you both.'

'Not if I gain the new stone first!' Zachs cried as the world

85

faded around Evan. They were using Rox's magic, then, to jump again.

There was a moment of blackness that always came when Rox magically shifted them from one place to another; another moment for Evan Mills to realise how much control he had lost.

Both of those who shared his form were coming forward, trying to wrest command of Evan's body for their own ends. With every passing moment, he felt more like a puppet with three completely different sets of strings. Evan wished there was some way he could fight them, to push them into a secondary role until the three of them could be free of each other. But to try something like that now would leave him vulnerable to the other magicians; vulnerable and no doubt dead.

The world came back into focus; more sand, with a great black stone rising from the dunes in the distance. There was a flash before the stone, an explosion of rock and sand that threw Evan off his feet. Sand rushed above them on a sorcerous wind.

They missed us, Evan thought. He closed his eyes to protect them from the whipping sand.

They wouldn't have if I had jumped where I wanted, Rox admitted.

You were going for the jewel. Quick in and quick out. Zachs would have done it that way!

There appears to be a certain advantage to our awkwardness, Rox assured them.

You mean that we're still alive? Evan thought sceptically.

Rox chuckled in Evan's head. You lose patience with us. Everything will change when we have the stone.

But how do we do it? Zachs shrilled.

'He isn't there!' Obar screamed above the storm. 'How could you miss him?'

'Brother,' replied Nunn, his cool voice somehow cutting through the gale, 'I have lost patience with you.'

'And I have none for you, either!' Obar's shriek was being lost to the howling wind.

'Why, Rox,' Nunn called out in a much more pleasant tone, 'you are becoming unpredictable. Could it be the school-teacher's influence?'

Mills giggled. 'There are more here than schoolteachers, my dear Nunn.'

'So even my Zachs has turned traitor?' Nunn laughed. 'It's getting a little crowded in there, schoolteacher! I will enjoy punishing all three of you in turn.'

<u>Run!</u> Rox screamed inside Evan's skull. <u>Now!</u>

Evan Mills pushed his shoes against the sand, hardly making any headway at all. He had never heard the wizard in a panic before.

A bolt of green fire sliced through the swirling sand, hitting a spot only a few feet behind where they struggled through the sand. Mills found himself thrown forward through the air. Things seemed to slow around him, although whether that was due to his own adrenalin or the wizard's intervention, Evan couldn't tell.

<u>Do not talk</u>, Rox insisted. <u>It makes it easier for them to find us.</u>

Mills didn't understand. Shouldn't the dragon's eyes do that anyway?

<u>They are distracted by each other, and the eyes they hold</u>, Rox explained. <u>It is a momentary distraction, at best.</u>

Somehow, Evan landed on his feet.

Distractions? Zachs can make some distractions of his own.

Evan felt a sudden warmth in his hands. He opened his eyes the slightest bit. Even through the shifting sands, his hands looked like they were on fire!

Zachs threw the fire ball behind them. The great orange ball was met with another bolt of green. The force of the explosion lifted Mills off his feet again.

This time he fell to his knees.

The great obsidian rock loomed out of the blowing sand.

Zachs will get us to our goal!

Evan found himself throwing another ball of fire behind him. This one was met by two bolts of green. Mills turned away as what felt like a giant hand pushed him somersaulting towards the rock.

Some part of him, somehow distanced from all this, marvelled at the cleverness of the light creature's plan. Considering

87

the trouble they had when either the wizard, or Evan himself, tried to move them, this was probably the only way they could actually reach their goal.

Mills felt another explosion at his back, throwing him face first into the sand. Of course, that removed part of himself realised, by the time they did reach that obsidian rock, he would no doubt be maimed or dead.

The sorcerous wind picked up his whole body like a leaf and threw it towards the jagged black stone.

Eleven

At least, Todd thought, he knew how to eat.

He'd felt like a fool when they'd asked him to tie up the boat. He'd had no idea what to do with the rope in his hands. He thought again about how it had been back in high school, him and his gang ruling his corner of the playground. If he couldn't get something done, he'd have one of his guys do it for him.

He wished he had his gang with him now. He wished he had something, anything going for him here.

He supposed he had some sense when he'd followed the two Volunteers below. They were looking for food and there, in a large, central room at the bottom of a short flight of stairs, they had found barrels full of fresh water, boxes with some kind of dried biscuits and a cabinet that held what looked like a whole carcass of some smoked and salted meat. Ship rations, Wilbert had called them. The meat and biscuits certainly tasted better than the bitter sand lizard Todd had eaten earlier.

Still, none of this, the ship or the food, fitted in with what he knew about this place. How was he ever going to handle anything around him if the world kept handing him surprises?

He stared at the half-eaten biscuit he held between his fingers. 'And where do these come from? Magic?'

Wilbert washed down a mouthful of meat with water from one of the silver tankards they'd also found. 'You give the magicians too much credit.' He waved his hands to take in everything they'd spread out on the table. 'Oh, Obar might have used his magic to steal all these things from someplace. But no, this food, this table, these utensils were all made on one of the other islands.'

'The other islands?' Todd looked at his biscuit with new respect. 'You mean there's other people here?'

It was Stanley's turn to nod. 'Oh, people and all sorts of things. Or so we're told. Not that we've had a chance to see this first hand.'

Todd looked back and forth between the two Volunteers, half annoyed, but also a little excited, about finally learning this. He dropped the remains of the biscuit on the table, all appetite gone.

'Why didn't you tell us about this stuff before?' he demanded.

Stanley shrugged. 'Well, you have to ask, hey?' He took another bite out of what looked like a leg of the carcass they'd dismembered on the table, closing his eyes as if this was the finest pleasure in the world.

He had to ask? How could he – Todd stopped himself before he could get worked up all over again. Wow. It was one thing if this world was nothing more than a primitive island or two. It was quite another if there were sailing ships and people making food and who knew what else.

Stanley opened his eyes to take a drink. He grinned at Todd. 'Feels a little overwhelming, hey?'

'We're overwhelmed all the time.' Wilbert laughed. 'Here, it's always an adventure.'

'Yeah, an adventure,' Stanley said, the sour edge back in his voice. 'And you're ahead of the game as long as you're alive.'

An adventure? Todd thought. He was only beginning to realise the Volunteers didn't know everything either. Perhaps everybody felt the same way he did.

'But', he asked the others, 'if there are other places full of people, why didn't you go there?'

'The wizards control the boat traffic,' Wilbert explained. 'We probably could have talked Obar into getting us across, as long as we could trade him something in return.'

'Some of our party did just that,' Stanley agreed.

'You mean there were more Volunteers?'

'Besides the ones who got killed?' Wilbert answered. 'Yep. Might be living in luxury this minute.'

'They could just as likely be dead,' Stanley objected. 'That's one thing we do know – about wizards. Your chances of survival are a lot better if you stay out of their way.' He looked over at his fellow Volunteer. 'So why are we doing this, hey?'

The ship lurched suddenly, throwing half the food on the floor.

Wilbert looked up from where he had steadied himself against the table. 'Think it's time for us to go topside.'

Stanley had already started up the stairs as the boat shifted again. 'One of us should have stayed up there with the lady,' he muttered, half to himself.

Todd was thinking just the same thing.

He rushed up the stairs right after them, bursting through the doorway a second later.

'Mrs Smith!' he called as he reached the deck. 'What's happening?'

'I believe we're going to have visitors,' the old woman replied. 'Or perhaps only one very large visitor –' She paused, as if she didn't know what to say. At last, she added, '– and there doesn't seem to be anything I can do about it.'

Todd turned to the rail where the two Volunteers were already watching something come out of the sea.

There was a great churning in the water ahead of them. The ship was being tossed about by the sort of waves you'd see in a storm, even though the sky was clear overhead.

Something was emerging from the roiling waves; a point thrust itself upwards, water sloughing from its sides. From this distance, it looked jagged, rough-hewn like a piece of stone. But the stone kept rising, higher and higher, until Todd was sure it must be a submerged island, or even a small mountain rising from the sea.

The mountain twitched.

'Lord,' Wilbert called to the others, 'that thing is alive!'

'I knew there was a reason that I didn't like boats!' Stanley agreed.

It was a living thing, then, its rough-hewn edges really loose pieces of skin. The top of the thing started to wave back and forth, a tentacle of some sort. Somehow, Todd still had the sense it was only a small part of something much larger, something huge; as if the tentacle rose all the way from the bottom of the sea.

Stanley had pulled out his bow, but not even notched an arrow. Todd knew how he felt. Something that big wouldn't even feel an arrow. What could you do against a creature like that?

Wilbert turned away from the railing, as if he couldn't stand to watch it any more.

Todd glanced back to Mrs Smith. Even she seemed over-whelmed, staring open-mouthed at the looming tentacle.

'Mrs Smith!' he called out to his neighbour. 'You've got to do something!'

'Oh, yes.' She blinked and shook her head, as if trying to wake herself up. 'Yes, yes, yes.'

The way she kept repeating the word made Todd wonder if she was trying to convince herself.

She reached into her pocket and retrieved her green dragon's eye. 'I most certainly do.'

She frowned in concentration as she held the jewel at arm's length.

A beam of green light shone from the eye, starting as a small point of light but widening as it travelled upward and outward, until it shone on the whole upper half of the tentacle above them.

The great appendage jerked back as the light struck it, as though the huge limb were trying to escape. But the green light held on to it, making the whole great tentacle glow with an amber radiance.

The tentacle froze in place as the waves quieted around them.

'There.' Mrs Smith took a deep breath. 'I seem to have it under control, at least for the moment.' She shook her head. 'There was something about it that was so – over-whelming.'

It seemed to Todd that Mrs Smith had been having trouble ever since she had come out on the ocean. She had stilled the tentacle, but he could see the strain on her face. And her arms shook ever so slightly as she held the jewel.

'Well, you've got the critter now!' Stanley exclaimed.

'It's not quite time to celebrate,' Wilbert added from where he stood on the deck. 'Look on the far side of the ship.'

Todd turned round. There, at the ship's stern, the water was beginning to bubble and roll on the ship's other side.

Wilbert nodded his head. 'Things like that always have more than one tentacle.'

Todd felt the hopelessness grow inside him as he waited for the white water to part, allowing another tentacle to rise from the sea. And, somewhere in between the two tentacles, Todd could picture a giant, gaping mouth.

But there was something else inside him, fighting with the fear. Somewhere, deep within, Todd could feel his anger. And his anger would not let this happen.

For all of his doubts and complaints, this was someplace new, someplace away from his father, someplace where he could prove himself.

Damn his father anyway! Damn his drunken rages. Damn his quick fists knocking over a smaller Todd. Damn all the bruises Todd's father would lay on his mother, so many that she had to hide in the house for days.

Todd's hands balled into fists.

Damn the wizards! Damn them for throwing Todd out on the sea. And damn the dragon for bringing Todd here in the first place.

He wanted to hit something.

Damn this thing in front of them!

It wouldn't end like this.

Todd remembered his cleansing anger. He remembered that moment when he had been lost inside the dragon, when he had been beyond fright, even beyond anger, when he had found an odd sort of peace.

He stared up at the second great tentacle, risen from the sea, snaking down towards the ship.

'No!' Todd screamed. 'You won't do this!'

But his scream did not end there. It rose from his throat, beyond words, his voice a siren of rage.

Mrs Smith gave a small cry of surprise as the jewel in her hands leapt from her fingers to dance in the air above them.

The second tentacle erupted in flame.

Todd turned his head to stare at the first tentacle, no longer frozen by Mrs Smith's spell. It thrashed above the ship, the loose pieces of skin somehow causing the air to moan with their passing. Then those loose pieces were devoured by flame, red and yellow, blue and white flaring out as the tentacle was consumed. The great thing retreated, the flames hissing as they were swallowed by the ocean.

Todd shook his head, stunned at what had happened. The great anger inside him left in an instant, like air from a burst balloon.

Somehow, he had spoken with the dragon for a second time. And the dragon had let him use his anger.

Mrs Smith snatched the dragon's eye from the air. She looked back at Todd with a frown. Was she jealous that he had used the jewel?

He looked around quickly, for someplace to sit, or something to lean against. Once the anger left, his strength seemed to follow.

Wilbert was suddenly at his side. 'Here, Todd, lad. Let me find you a place to rest. I tell you, you newcomers are loaded with surprises.' His cheerful voice seemed full of admiration.

'I don't know,' Stanley called from his place by the rail. 'Too much mumbo-jumbo for me. Any time you use magic, it's going to come to a bad end.'

Todd nodded as Wilbert lowered him gently on to the steps that led up to the foredeck. It was nice to get Wilbert's respect. But Todd was all too sure that Stanley was the one he should listen to.

Twelve

Harold Dafoe had a job to do.

He always did. But now, instead of trying to keep his wife happy or his kids fed, this job was whether or not he was going to stay alive.

'We are going to hunt down our families,' Carl Jackson had told Harold and George. 'Once they see us marching in on them, they'll realise how wrong they were. You'll be surprised how happy they'll be to see us.' He glanced back and forth between the two other men. The superior grin seemed to have taken up permanent residence on Jackson's face. 'So why are you standing here?'

'What do you want us to do, Carl?' Harold asked, trying to keep the desperation out of his voice.

'Captain,' Carl snapped.

'Captain!' Harold replied.

'Much better,' Carl agreed generously. 'You have to be careful not to make mistakes.' He turned away from the two neighbours to look at the troops still in rank behind him. 'I think I want the men in two columns, ready for a quick march. I will lead the way. Harry, you and George will take up the rear.'

'So you really can find our families?' George asked. He hastily added 'Captain?' as Carl glanced round.

'Child's play,' Carl replied. 'Thanks to Nunn's little gift here.' He held up the globe for both the neighbours to see. Something moved inside the ball, something half total darkness, half blinding light. 'The gift will show me the way. And that is the least of the things that it will do. But I believe the two of you have received my orders?'

'Yes, Captain!' Harold replied, waving for George to follow them as he left the platform. The sooner he was away from Carl Jackson, the better. And he didn't even want to think about what was in that globe. George and he were in a bad place right now. He felt like Nunn and Jackson already had use of the two men's bodies; but he feared that Nunn's gift wanted both of their souls.

Harold barked out orders as he approached the troops. Form two lines. Prepare to march. He turned back to Jackson, overseeing it all. 'Which way, Captain?'

Jackson regarded the globe. 'Left, I think.'

Harold called that to the troops too.

'What language are you talking?' George called to him as they walked.

'Damned if I know,' Harold replied. Maybe he could explain more to his old neighbour once they had started marching.

'Very good, Harry.' Jackson balanced the globe on his upraised palm as he took the steps, two at a time, down from the platform. The globe was only a bit bigger than a softball and, from the way Jackson played with it, appeared to weigh hardly anything at all.

Harold wondered how long it would be before Carl used it. He also wondered, for only a second, if there was some way he could get the globe away from Jackson.

Where had that come from? Harold's own desperation, no doubt. But the thought scared him almost as much as Carl and his globe.

Jackson marched to the front of the line.

'Repeat my orders, Harry!' Carl called. 'Forward march!'

Harold did as he was told.

'Fall in with me at the back, George.' Harold waited for the last of the soldiers to pass them by, then swung in behind him. George hurried forward to match his pace.

It was only a moment's march before the trees closed in above them.

'This forest is everywhere, isn't it?' George spoke softly after a few minutes' march. He looked overhead at the tree limbs, their thick foliage blocking out the sun. 'It's all a little spooky. Claustrophobic, I guess.'

'Yeah,' Harold agreed, 'and I don't think I'll ever get used to it.' It was also starting to get dark. Why would Jackson begin the march this close to evening? But Harold already knew the answer to that. Their new Captain didn't care. He would probably march his new troops all night and into the following morning if he had to.

Somehow, he didn't want to share this insight with George quite yet.

'Actually, this isn't as bad as it could be,' he said instead. 'We're moving pretty fast. Sometimes, the vines grow so thick in front of you, it's hard to make any progress at all.' He thought of the first time he had been a prisoner of this army, and how the Captain and his men cut through the strange vines that cried out in pain.

Now that he looked at it, the path before them was remarkably broad and even for this forest, almost as if it wasn't natural.

'I don't think I'll get used to any of this,' George replied after another moment's march. 'I think I made a mess of things when I first came here, especially with my wife and son. It's all so different.' He took a deep breath, then let it out slowly. 'I don't do so well when things are different.'

Harold almost laughed at that. 'And I do? I think, to do well around here, you need an ego like Carl's.'

They had begun to climb a hill. Harold could finally see all the troops strung out before him, all the way to Jackson at the front of the line. There were bursts of bright light before their leader, coming from something Jackson held high above his head. It was the globe. This path really wasn't natural, then, but was scoured from the forest through Nunn's magic. The globe must destroy the trees before it. Harold was sure the globe could destroy people with equal ease.

'Harry?' George asked softly.

Harold turned to his old neighbour and saw that he pointed above them, to a point close to the front of the line. There, some twenty feet in the air, was another light, green and bright against the gloom of the forest floor.

'Get ready to find some cover,' Harold counselled George.

'Where?' a voice called out of the light. It was a woman's voice, somehow familiar.

Some of the soldiers looked up at the sound overhead. A couple of them shouted. Others stopped dead, the marching rhythm gone from their steps.

'Don't know how –' The light was trying to resolve itself into a shape. And the voice wasn't that of a woman but a teenage girl. It was his daughter, Mary Lou.

Now all the soldiers had stopped in front of Harold. All eyes were turned to the sparkling light above them. Many of the soldiers were talking, muttering something over and over again. One word; Kennake. Harold said the word to himself and suddenly knew its meaning. The dragon. But what did the dragon have to do with his daughter?

'Can you hear me?' his daughter called tentatively. The light above swirled about so that it might have looked like a face framed by dark hair.

'Mary Lou?' Harold answered.

'Daddy?' There was a new strength in Mary Lou's voice. The face shape suddenly showed two eyes and a smiling mouth. 'I'm so glad I found you!'

Harold was suddenly afraid. Would Mary Lou abruptly arrive here from whatever place, or maybe spell, she now spoke from? He didn't want that to happen. It was bad enough that he was forced to obey Carl Jackson's whims. He had to save his daughter from being pushed into this madness.

'What is happening back there?' Carl Jackson called from the front of the line. 'Why do you disobey me?' He held the globe high above his head. 'Harry, ask them if they want to die!'

'Where are you?' Harold called to his daughter instead.

'I'm not too sure,' she replied. She laughed. 'I'm certainly learning my way around.'

Jackson started to move back through the crowd of soldiers. 'Unless you want to die first, Harry!'

'What's that, uh – Captain?' Harold turned his attention back to the man with the globe. It seemed that Carl couldn't see her. Maybe his daughter would be safe after all.

98

'They said I'd be able to talk to people!' Mary Lou's bright voice said overhead. 'You're my first try!'

Jackson looked up at last. 'What the hell is that?' Apparently he could hear, and see, the apparition now.

'Oh!' Mary Lou cried in alarm. 'This wasn't supposed to happen. Daddy, I've got to go!'

'No, you don't!' The new Captain raised the globe towards the lighted face. 'Nothing stops Carl Jackson any more!'

'No!' Harold shouted as a dark tendril swirled out from the globe and headed for the light. The thing swirled through the air like a snake seeking its prey.

The tendril branched once, then again, as three of the snake-like things sought to encircle the light above. A great, roaring rush filled the air as the face exploded in flame. Fire consumed the tendrils and raced towards the sphere in Jackson's hands. Jackson screamed as he dropped the globe.

'Kennake!' Someone shouted this time. And the shout was taken up by the troops all around them, the same word, over and over again.

All around them, soldiers started to run.

There was nothing like a solid meal of tree squirrel and hopping bush-rodent to let folks get along.

The Captain looked down at his new troops as they tore into their food, ripping off bloody gobbets, then swallowing them whole. The Captain, of course, preferred his squirrel cooked. The wolves had no such problems.

He sat on a fallen log, the wolves in a semicircle around him, and tended a fire that kept his troops at a respectful distance. The squirrel that he had skinned and impaled on the spit was roasting nicely.

One of the wolves growled as it worried the remains of a particularly fat bush-rodent. A couple of others in the pack barked back at their fellow. It was odd, the Captain thought, how the wolves sometimes spoke as animals and sometimes as men; odd, but no more surprising than anything else in this place. Unless, of course, the wolves were talking in such a way that they kept secrets from their new leader.

He wouldn't worry about that now. This alliance would never be any more solid than when his troops' bellies were full. In that, he supposed, wolves were not all that different from men.

The Captain stared back at the fire. His own squirrel looked cooked at last. He removed the spit from above the flame and waved the meat about for a moment to let it cool. This was his first free meal, the first meal beyond Nunn's control. He took a bite from the leg. The tough squirrel meat, seared on the outside and close to raw inside, tasted as sweet as anything the Captain had ever known.

The wolves were already done with their dinners. Four of the five beasts seemed content to doze on their full bellies. The fifth animal watched the Captain eat, its pale eyes shining in the firelight.

The Captain nodded to his audience as he took another bite.

'Yesss,' the wolf replied in its growling voice. 'We will work togetherrr.' It paused, looking at the bones between its paws, the only remains of its own meal. 'At leasst for now.'

The Captain wondered what reply he should make, if any. He decided on something neutral. 'Things look better with a full stomach.'

The wolf rolled the small bones in the dirt before it with a casual paw. 'It fills ourr bellies. It is not the besst, but it will do.'

So, the wolves would let the Captain know it would be difficult to buy their loyalty. But that also meant their allegiance could be bought, and he would have it, even if he had to promise them finer things. 'There will be other meals,' he replied.

'We could alwayss use morre,' the wolf agreed.

The Captain took a drink of water from a short, hollow tree branch he'd made into a makeshift canteen. He wiped his mouth and looked back at the wolf that had spoken. 'Is there something you prefer?'

The wolf licked its chops before replying, its tongue very red in the firelight. 'Fressh human. Morre to ourr liking.'

'Human?' The Captain was careful to keep his voice calm. 'That can be arranged.'

There were a few humans he would quite enjoy seeing torn apart. He wondered if the wolves would eat wizard too.

Another of the wolves opened its eyes and barked softly. 'Human. They come thiss way.'

The animal who had spoken first pricked up its ears. 'Many humanss,' it added a moment later. 'Too many for uss.'

The Captain stamped out the fire. No need to advertise their presence. 'Should we hide?'

The first speaker among the wolves considered that for a moment. 'We may wait herre. They will pass uss by.' It made a sound deep in its throat, almost a gruff laugh. 'We are silent and as swift as evening turrrned to night. Humanss cannot smell. They make enough noise to wake the wood.'

Both wolves and Captain waited in total silence for a long moment, until the Captain heard the shouts.

'Something is wrrong,' one of the wolves muttered.

'Humanss arre running,' another agreed.

'Maybe some of them will come to uss,' the first speaker said. 'We will have human meat afterr all.'

'Let me talk to them first,' the Captain demanded. 'Humans have other uses.' He wanted to know what had gone wrong, especially because he had heard what the men were shouting about; the dragon.

A couple of the wolves growled softly at his words. The first speaker turned sharply towards its fellows.

'This human is not like the otherss. He hass fed us once, and promised us morre. Let him keep a human orr two. Therre will be many more for usss.'

Then this first wolf could be the Captain's ally. He would have to reward that kind of thinking as soon as possible.

'They come this way!' one of the wolves announced in a low growl.

'Two of them, rrunning swiftly,' the first speaker agreed. 'So swiftly, they do not guess we arre herre.'

The Captain quickly extinguished the remains of the fire.

Even he could hear the people now, crashing across the fallen leaves and branches of the forest floor.

They burst into the clearing, one man quickly following the other. All five wolves rose, growling. The two men both reached for their bows. The wolves looked ready to spring.

'Not so fast,' the Captain called from the far side of the clearing. 'Before we all kill each other, why don't we talk a bit?'

He turned to the newcomers. 'Pator. Chen. I had not anticipated meeting you again so soon.'

The two soldiers froze. This was obviously far beyond what they had anticipated.

'Captain?' Pator managed at last, speaking in that guttural polyglot that passed for a language among the troops. 'We thought you were dead.'

'So did I, a number of times,' the Captain agreed. 'But I am not. I've got free from Nunn –' He paused to nod at the wolves around him, '– and made other arrangements.' He nodded back at the two soldiers. 'Now, you two have the chance to join us.'

Pator glanced back at the other soldier, then looked to the Captain. 'You mean, go against Nunn?'

The Captain nodded. There was something different about Pator. He had a new, deep scratch on his cheek.

The Captain touched his own scars, one for each cheek, part of a ritual he would rather not remember, back at a time he thought a ritual might change things. 'So, Pator. Are you trying to imitate me?'

The soldier touched his own wound self-consciously. 'It is a gift from your successor.' He looked back at the second soldier one more time, as if he might say something to him, but turned back to the Captain instead. 'I would be dead soon if I stayed under that pig. Better I die in the open forest. I will join you.'

'Fight the wizard?' Chen demanded, his voice a mix of fear and surprise. 'Are you mad? He can kill us at any time.'

'Perhaps he could, once,' the Captain interjected, 'but now he has a great many more things on his mind.'

'You will go against both Nunn and his army? How will you defeat them, with a bunch of animals?' Chen waved dismissively at the wolves. 'I will tell the new Captain I was lost. He needs all the men to follow Nunn's orders.'

'Then I can't convince you to stay?' the Captain asked.

Chen shook his head. 'I would be as good as dead.'

'So you say.' The Captain thought for a moment and sighed. 'Think about it for a minute. Your only chance is to stay here with me.'

'Then I have no chance at all.' Chen looked from the Captain to the wolves and back again. 'Am I free to go?'

The Captain waved him away. 'I have no use for you.'

The soldier turned his back as the Captain nodded to the wolves.

All five of the animals attacked Chen together.

The wolves pulled him off his feet. In an instant, he was lost beneath the pack. His screams ended abruptly.

Pator turned away from the wolf pack. He looked very pale in the fading evening light. 'Chen was right. You are mad.'

'No doubt we all are,' the Captain agreed. 'But we will survive.'

Thirteen

'Land! Straight ahead!'

Todd's eyes snapped open with the voice. He had been sleeping on a folded piece of canvas. They must have carried him here after the fight with the sea creature. He didn't remember anything after the tentacles caught fire. The dragon had given Todd a chance to use his anger, but it had taken all his energy in return.

'There's the harbour!' Wilbert called from the bow of the boat. 'I can see half a dozen ships at anchor. Obar has set us right where he said he would.'

Did he? Todd wondered exactly what the magician wanted from their journey here. Did he know about the sea creature? Maybe he didn't want them to succeed, but wanted to use them as decoys while he collected the jewels.

Stanley had said he would never trust a wizard. And Todd noticed that the thin, sour-faced Volunteer was silent now. Maybe he should talk to Stanley, someplace where Mrs Smith wouldn't overhear.

Todd sat up, then stood. His exhausted sleep seemed to have put him back together. He didn't feel bad at all.

He walked to the ship's rail, and forgot all about wizards.

There was a whole great city before them, built up from the water's edge; large buildings of red and yellow and green, maybe three or four storeys tall and three times as wide. And the city stretched beyond the seaside structures, with smaller homes built all up and down the surrounding hills. There must be hundreds of people, maybe even thousands, living here.

Had all these people been brought by the dragon? That's

what the others had told them; there was no other way to get to this world but by the dragon's choice. Somehow, Todd no longer felt quite so special.

Their ship was sailing straight for the middle of the harbour, moving between the other craft at anchor. Two of the other ships looked much like the one that Obar had rescued. Two more were long and low, with one great mast at each of their centres. Another ship was a squat brown craft with three sails on which were painted fantastic creatures. One of the sails, bright red and white, seemed to show a dragon. Maybe, Todd thought, the creatures weren't all that fantastic around here. The last craft was the strangest, a great square ship, riding low in the water, with a large wheel at its stern. It looked like a Mississippi riverboat, save for the dozen oars resting at its side and the two sails built high above its upper deck.

'We've got a welcoming committee!' Wilbert called.

Todd looked to see that they were approaching a long dock that reached far out into the harbour. At the end of the dock were maybe twenty people. Most of them carried spears or bows and arrows.

Mrs Smith came up next to Todd. She leaned on the rail and looked at what was ahead.

'Oh, dear,' she said softly. 'Obar didn't mention anything about this.'

'Wizards only mention what's convenient,' Stanley said from where he stood in the middle of the deck. 'Begging your pardon, ma'am.' He had quietly unrolled his pack on the deck and seemed to be examining every weapon he still kept inside.

There was a shout from the dock. Todd shook his head. He couldn't understand anything that was being said.

'Oh, dear,' Mrs Smith murmured again. 'Well, maybe I can fix this at least.' She pulled the jewel from her pocket and frowned at it for an instant. Three sparks flew from the top of the eye. One rushed straight towards Todd, speeding so quickly he had no chance to duck away. But when it hit him, he didn't feel a thing.

The voice shouted from the dock again. This time it said, 'Hello the boat!'

Or maybe, Todd realised, he could now understand the words.

Wilbert turned back to the others. 'Mrs Smith? Shall I?'

She nodded. 'Be my guest.'

'Hello the dock!' Wilbert called to the rapidly approaching platform. In fact, they seemed to be approaching it a bit too rapidly. At this speed, they would ram the wooden pilings in another minute. Obar had given them a way to get here, but had he given them a way to stop?

'Stop, boat!' Mrs Smith called as she must have realised the same danger.

The boat slowed suddenly, as if restrained by a giant hand against its bow. Todd stumbled forward a step. Wilbert had to grab the rail before him to avoid being tossed into the sea.

The ship drifted forward slowly now, still approaching the dock.

Three of the people on the dock fell into a quick conversation. Todd wondered if their boat's odd behaviour had them worried.

One of them looked up at last and shouted out, 'What have you to trade?'

Wilbert looked back to Mrs Smith again. 'Trade? What are they talking about.'

'Oh,' Mrs Smith replied. 'Of course. The bolts of cloth. Obar thought of everything.' She looked up at Wilbert. 'Tell them we have cloth to trade. Fine cloth.'

Wilbert nodded and turned back towards the dock. 'What have we got to trade? Why, only the finest cloth in all of the seven islands!'

The three people at the centre of the group fell into another quick conversation. Apparently, they were the dock officials, surrounded by some sort of police force armed with every weapon that would work around here.

The ship had got quite close by now, maybe ten feet away. But its forward motion had almost entirely stopped, so that the only way they would meet the dock would be if someone threw a rope to pull it in.

One of the three officials stepped forward. 'We will be glad to trade you for your cloth. Assuming the cloth is of sufficient quality, we will offer you a basket of fruit for every three bolts.' He glanced at the army around him. 'Of course, as soon as the trading is complete, you must depart.'

'A most pleasing offer,' Wilbert agreed, 'but not quite what we were looking for. For cloth this fine, we should have three baskets for every single bolt. And once your merchants have seen the quality of our merchandise, they will wish us to tour the market-place for days so that we might take orders for our next shipment.'

The three officials stared out at Wilbert for a long moment. Todd wondered which one would instruct the police to start throwing their spears.

Instead, the leader called out that they would offer a basket for every bolt. Wilbert countered with another offer, and the three, after some conversation, accepted two baskets, or their equivalent, per bolt. And a party from the ship might spend one night in the town.

Wilbert turned to his shipmates with a grin. 'We are welcomed with open arms.'

Todd was impressed. 'How did you know they would bargain?'

Wilbert shrugged his broad shoulders. 'I used to own a dry goods store. Some things are universal.'

He turned back to the dock. 'We ask your permission to come ashore!'

The lead official gave it without hesitation. Stanley tossed out a rope which one of the spear carriers caught and tied to a piling.

'We will bring a small party,' Wilbert further announced. 'Only four, with a sample of our goods.'

'Four?' Stanley frowned at that. 'That leaves no one on board.'

'True.' Wilbert's brow wrinkled at the thought. 'Still, does any of us want to miss exploring what lies out there?'

Todd certainly didn't, and since he was the one with the least experience, he'd be the one left behind. Why did it always have to work out this way?

'The boat will have its guard,' Mrs Smith announced. She nodded towards the stern. There stood two men, one a bald-headed Wilbert, the other something like Stanley with a beard. 'I'm afraid I used our current crew as models.'

Stanley snorted. 'I knew there was a reason I never grew a beard.'

'And I'd better work mighty hard at keeping my hair,' Wilbert agreed. 'But what say Todd and us ship out the gang-plank so we can take a tour?'

'I will find a couple of fine examples of our merchandise,' Mrs Smith volunteered as the three men figured out how to untie the long wooden ramp and secure it once it was over the side. Wilbert took charge, telling Stanley to move this rope here and that rope there, and Todd to tug on the planks from his end. They freed it easily and lowered it over the side, perhaps a bit too carefully from the impatient expressions of those who waited for the ramp below. Still, it took only moments to secure their passageway from boat to dock.

'I think these will do,' Mrs Smith announced behind them as they had just finished securing their end of the ramp. Todd turned round to see her float back down to the deck with two airborne bolts of cloth, one by either hand. The one to her left was a rich and royal blue. The cloth to her right was even finer, woven of some thread that seemed almost metallic, so that it gleamed and shifted from pale green to golden yellow in the sunlight.

'Are we ready then?' she asked.

'Whenever you are, ma'am,' Stanley answered.

Mrs Smith nodded. 'There is a bit more preparation. I think it would be inadvisable for me to float down into the crowd. So I'm afraid Todd will have to help me get around until we're away from other people. And if our Volunteers could carry a bolt of cloth each, that would help immensely.'

Wilbert and Stanley moved quickly forward to pick up their wares.

'I think the two of you should go first,' Mrs Smith further instructed, 'so that I don't slow you down.' She held out an arm to Todd. 'If you could give me your assistance?'

Todd moved quickly to Mrs Smith's side, letting her put her arm round his shoulders. He was surprised by how thin and frail she was. Somehow, the dragon's eye had made her seem stronger, almost invincible. The way Mrs Smith had risen above the rest, able to save them from any trouble, made her seem like some sort of great leader, somebody who would always be there to guide them. But the ageing woman next to him, who tried to match his slow steps with her own, seemed so weak in comparison, so fragile, so human.

'Easy,' he whispered, as she almost stumbled moving her bad leg forward. 'We'll get it.' He wondered, just for an instant, on how willing he was to help now. It was so different from being told what to do by his father, or being told what a shit he was no matter what he did. His father was really good at that. But here, he was really needed, even if he didn't always know the best thing to do.

By the time Todd and Mrs Smith had reached the top of the gangplank, the two Volunteers were stepping off the other end and on to the dock. Wilbert made a great show of presenting the bolts of cloth to the town officials. They tried to appear sceptical as they examined the blue fabric, but they couldn't hide their surprise, or their eagerness, when they saw the second, shining cloth.

'Yes, yes,' one of the officials was saying all too quickly, 'I think this will be acceptable. Why don't we unload the rest of the cloth and conclude the deal?'

'The rest of the cloth?' Wilbert said as he caught the mood. 'Well, of course, we will be glad to sell you the remainder of our regular fabrics for the agreed-upon price. But for the special fabrics, and this woven sunlight is only the beginning of the marvels we hold on the ship, we may need to negotiate separately.'

One of the officials began to object. He had not uttered three syllables before Wilbert added smoothly, 'Of course, we will sell you these samples of fabric at the regular price as a gesture of goodwill.'

That seemed to quiet the townsfolk down for the moment. 'Come,' Wilbert continued. 'Take these two bolts. We will collect for them later. But now we need someplace to rest and refresh ourselves, before we return to conclude our business.'

The officials quickly held another conference before one of them pulled a small bag from his pocket. 'Here,' he called, tossing it to Wilbert, 'you will need a way to pay for your meal.'

'And this is –' Wilbert started to say, weighing the tiny bag in his hand.

'Why, payment, of course –' the official began.

'A down payment for the value of our first two pieces?' Wilbert smiled broadly at their generosity. 'Most thoughtful. After we eat, we shall return to collect the balance.'

The official opened his mouth to reply, but no words came out. He glanced at the armed men nearby, then looked back at the cloth in his hands. He coughed and closed his mouth.

'There are many fine places to dine only a few paces –' another of the officials interjected instead.

'Follow me,' Mrs Smith said abruptly. 'I have heard of just the place to go.'

The two Volunteers fell in behind Mrs Smith and Todd. Now that they were on more level ground, they seemed to be able to move at a more normal pace.

'I will get us quite a nice price for the goods,' Wilbert muttered as they left the dock behind.

'If you don't get us killed first,' Stanley agreed.

'Where are we going?' Todd asked.

In answer, Mrs Smith raised her closed fist and opened it just enough to show the faint green glow of the dragon's eye within.

'This thing in my hands will find its mate.' She frowned, then nodded to their left. 'We should walk down the main street.' A wide street ran between two of the large dockside buildings. 'Or should I say up?' As they turned the corner on to the broad boulevard, the street began to climb the central-most hill.

There, on either side, were small stalls filled with all sorts of things, food and clothing and metal utensils and swords and any number of items Todd couldn't find a name for. Slightly up the hill, he could see that the street widened even more and levelled out into a vast collection of even larger stalls; a regular market-place, full of people, livestock and noise.

Todd realised he didn't want them to find the eye right away. The island they had come from was dangerous. This place could be exciting.

'This way.' Mrs Smith directed them to the right of the bigger market. 'Right here.'

She indicated a sign in front of them, showing a large, carved wooden dragon.

'The Dragon Tavern, hey?' Stanley grunted. 'Sounds awfully convenient.'

'It also sounds dark and crowded,' Wilbert added with a frown. 'It may be difficult to protect you in this sort of place.'

Mrs Smith raised the fist that held her jewel. 'This should protect us, unless someone else already has control of the new eye.'

If somebody already had control? Todd had never thought of that possibility. But if a simple trip to this island included a fight with a tentacled monster, it probably made sense that there'd be problems here too. Nothing around here ever seemed easy.

The actual establishment was down a short flight of steps below street level. Stanley led the way and Wilbert took up the rear, keeping Todd and Mrs Smith between them.

It took Todd's eyes a moment to adjust to the dimness within. It was indeed crowded. And very quiet, for every face in the place had turned to watch the newcomers.

They did not look friendly.

'It is here somewhere,' Mrs Smith whispered. 'I should find it quickly.'

'And if someone else has already grabbed it?' Todd whispered back.

Mrs Smith sighed. 'Then I think we are in for quite a battle.'

Fourteen

Nick had no idea why Obar had brought him here. What good would his sword be against another wizard?

Not that he wanted to do anything for Obar now.

He threw an arm in front of his face as there was another explosion out in the sand. Hot crystals scraped against his hands and lower face as the sand-filled wind rushed by again.

Mr Mills laughed, a strange, high cackle, from somewhere beyond the swirling sand, as if this was some sort of wonderful game, and there weren't two wizards trying to kill him.

Two wizards – Obar and Nunn – who hated each other, but were working together. And Obar was working with Nunn, who kidnapped Mary Lou and killed a couple of the other neighbours. Nick wondered how different Obar really was from his brother.

'You'll have to do better than that!' Mr Mills called in a voice that sounded higher than usual. 'You are nothing without your eyes! They have made you old and slow!'

There was a moment of silence as the two wizards waited for the sand to clear enough to show their adversary. As much as Obar and Nunn hated each other, they had to hate Mr Mills more.

Not that Mr Mills was acting that much like himself either, speaking in different voices and appearing and disappearing across the sand. This world was changing all of them from Chestnut Circle.

Nick might feel better if Obar had explained why he was attacking Mr Mills; the same Obar who had brought Maggie and Nick along for protection and then proceeded to ignore them. The wizard never explained anything if he could help it.

Obar could just as suddenly turn around some day and attack Nick.

'Get down!' Maggie grabbed at his sleeve.

An explosion roared over them as he buried his face in the sand.

'Zachs is too fast for the wizards!' Mr Mills called in a high singsong. 'Old, decrepit wizards can't catch Zachs!'

'Stay down!' Maggie called as another explosion thundered above them.

Mr Mills, or whatever he called himself, was trying to make the wizards as angry as possible. And it was working. It was as though Obar and Nunn didn't even care that Maggie and he were there any more. Everything was expendable to the wizards except the jewels.

Maggie pushed herself up slightly as the latest cloud of sand blew away.

'Oh lord, no,' she said quickly, making all three words sound like one.

Nick almost didn't want to know what was happening.

'What are the wizards doing now?' he asked anyway.

Maggie shook her head. 'The wizards are still busy trying to kill each other. I'm more worried about our new visitors.'

Nick raised himself, looking to where Maggie pointed. He could see another distant cloud of dust on the horizon.

They were not the only ones who noticed the newcomers.

'Wizards need help?' Mills called in mock astonishment. 'You're bringing somebody else to fight us? Wizards can't do it by themselves?'

'What?' Obar demanded. 'I never –' He paused and peered at the cloud, growing closer in the distance. 'Who are these newcomers?'

Nunn smiled as his eyes stayed focused on Mr Mills. 'Another of my many alliances. That was one thing my brother never understood. It is important to make the proper connections, for times like these.'

'Nunn will never fight fair!' Mills called out, his voice suddenly much deeper. 'He wants to distract us and kill us all!'

Obar closed his hand over his dragon's eye and glared at his brother. 'It ends this quickly?'

Nunn shrugged slightly, as if he barely could be bothered to answer. 'I thought you would be handy in getting rid of this inconvenient maggot. But apparently you aren't very good at anything.'

'And you are so much better?' Obar waved at Mills, who now seemed content to stand and watch the others. 'This maggot is of your creation.'

Nunn turned angrily to the other wizard. 'What? A momentary oversight –'

'Oversight?' Obar laughed. 'Your whole life was an oversight. You always were sloppy on details, ever since you were a child.'

'Me – sloppy?' Nunn cried out in disbelief. 'This, coming from fuzzy Obar, the man who can't make a decision?'

'Why do I even bother speaking to you?' Obar's jewel reappeared between his fingers, like a coin another kind of magician might snatch from the air.

'I should have killed you long ago,' Nunn replied dismissively, his own gems glowing where they were embedded in his palms.

'You'll never get me now!'

Nick turned to look at Mills as he ran to the black obelisk that rose like some giant sentry over this kingdom of sand. Mills had covered quite a distance while the wizards were arguing.

'Oh, no!' Obar cried.

'He doesn't have it yet!' Nunn turned his palms towards the fleeing Mills.

'Behind us!' Maggie whispered in Nick's ear.

Nick heard a new sound, a strange, high cry that shifted tone up and down, first slowly, then with increasing speed. He turned to see six horsemen galloping towards them. They veered away from the duelling mages, bearing down on Maggie and Nick.

Their long robes and horses were all of grey, much the same tone and colour as the surrounding sand, so that they almost seemed to disappear as they charged down a large dune towards Nick and Maggie.

Another explosion filled the air with grey. The onrushing horsemen vanished in the clouds, the only real sounds the muffled beat of horses' hooves in the sand, and those strange, high cries. Their attackers were there one minute and gone the next, like ghosts that preferred the daylight.

'I think', Maggie said softly as she rose, fitting an arrow in her bow, 'that we finally have something to occupy our time.'

The six riders burst from the cloud, their cries high and quick, one long, ululating scream.

The hilt of Nick's weapon was warm in his hand. It knew blood was coming.

Nick drew his sword with a scream of his own. A phantom warrior and his horse bore down on him. In an instant, Nick saw the horse's spotted coat, the shadows in the folds of the rider's robes, the narrow slit in the grey headdress that allowed an inch of cracked and pale skin to show around the warrior's eyes – strange, yellow eyes that would look better on a lizard than on a man. Things had slowed to a fraction of their normal speed and Nick was a spectator in an endless ballet, as horse and rider gracefully pirouetted towards attack. But the sword guided Nick's hand, thrusting upwards. The lizard rider leaned towards him, his own sword held high, beginning a deadly downward arc.

But Nick's sword had already found the rider's heart. The rider screamed like a human being as the sword was almost jerked from Nick's hand with the warrior's forward momentum. The lizard eyes were wide as horse and rider fell away and Nick's sword glowed red with blood.

He pulled his weapon free as he heard a second cry behind him, ducking low as another sword whistled overhead.

Nick's sword jabbed forward, pulling him behind it. The blade sliced the flank of the second horse before the rider could turn. It reared once and shrieked as the sword drained the blood from its body. The rider pulled hard on the reins, trying to regain control of his mount, but it was too late. The horse stumbled and fell, its rider still half under it. The second lizard warrior struggled to drag himself free as Nick pulled the sword from the steed and impaled the rider.

Nick risked a look around as the sword drank its fill. Maggie had killed two of her own with bow and arrow, but had discarded her bow and now held a knife. The last two warriors, seeing how easily their companions had been dismounted, had got off their own horses and approached warily, each one sporting a great oval shield that seemed to be made from woven reeds.

Maggie grinned over at Nick. 'Lucky for them I broke my bowstring. Now they think they can take us hand to hand. After all, what are we? Only a woman and a boy.'

Nick smiled back at his companion. He was filled with energy, as if the sword passed the vitality of the victim's blood straight up his arm to his heart. His sword swung around from its last meal, pointing like a hunting dog that has found some easy prey. The sword wanted their blood. And Nick wanted their death cries.

His mind raced, feeding on the agony of his enemy. As much energy as he had, he wanted more.

The last two warriors separated, one advancing on Maggie, the other on Nick. The sword in Nick's hand glowed red, as if the metal was hot. The warrior who had chosen Nick held his own sword close behind his shield, so that Nick could only see its curved point peeking out from behind the close-woven reeds. The warrior did not approach Nick in a straight line. Instead, he almost appeared to be dancing, a few paces right, a few paces left, looking for the best angle of attack. Nick did not move. He stood and waited. His sword was ready.

The warrior rushed forward, silently this time, his shield angled towards Nick's sword. Nick's sword arm pulled him left, bringing him round the ghost rider's guard. The warrior tried to change his own angle of attack at the last moment, shifting slightly off balance as Nick's sword caught the edge of the shield and yanked it straight up into the air and out of the soldier's grasp. Quicker than Nick could see, the sword sliced down again, straight through the arm that had held the shield, severing it at the elbow.

The rider stared at his wound for an instant as dark blood spurted on to the sand. His mask fell away to show a face that looked like some cross between human and cobra, with no nose to speak of and a pink tongue that darted from a mouth full of fangs.

The lizard rider screamed at last as he lunged forward with the hand that still held his sword. But the loss of his arm made him stumble. Nick side-stepped him easily, his own sword seeking out the warrior's heart, then plunging deep inside his chest.

The sword made great sucking sounds as it drained the now-dead warrior of all his life fluids. Nick watched the robes before him grow loose as the thing that had once been almost human shrivelled inside. Nick laughed. He had never felt so strong. He could do anything.

The sword yanked free, its feeding done. Whatever was left bounced to the ground within the now voluminous robes, which had no weight left to them and flew away down the dune, blown by the desert wind.

The sword jerked Nick round. Maggie and her warrior were still circling one another. The sword wanted more. It would never be satisfied.

The world was filled with green.

'No!' somebody called behind Nick, more than one voice, the one word stretched on and on, a cry of loss that would never end.

Nick turned his head away from his sword and saw Obar and Nunn, both staring at the obelisk. There, surrounded by a bubble of green, stood Mr Mills.

'The battle grows interesting now!' Mills called to the others. 'And we would like to thank the wizards for all their help!'

The green bubble, with Mr Mills still inside, seemed to pop from existence.

'We could not keep him from it,' Obar said softly. 'Three dragon's eyes, and he still –'

'So I will follow him and kill him, and let this unpleasantness go on a little longer,' Nunn snapped back. 'But I will kill you first.' He opened his arms wide, palms forward, so that one jewel faced Maggie and Nick, the other Obar.

Out of the corner of his eye, Nick saw Maggie moving. The

warrior had turned to look at Nunn and Maggie leapt behind him, pushing at his back with both her feet.

The last lizard rider stumbled forward, straight into Nunn. The man in grey burst into a pillar of green fire.

Nick's sword swung towards Maggie. He tried to pull it back, to place it in its scabbard, but his weapon still pulled towards blood. There seemed to be nothing he could do to stop it.

'We must leave and follow the eye!' Obar called to them. The desert faded around them as the wizard worked his magic, Nick's sword-arm suddenly falling as the sorcery seemed to drain the weapon's energy as well.

Nick quickly threw the blade back into its scabbard.

He began to shake as the desert disappeared.

Fifteen

Mrs Smith could feel the heat pulsing beneath her fingers.

She barely noticed the other occupants of the Dragon Tavern and couldn't care less that most of them watched the newcomers cross the floor. The new dragon's eye was very close. But how close could that be? She had tried to form a picture of the new jewel in her mind, see its hiding place, but without success. There seemed to be certain things her own dragon's eye could not do. Or perhaps she simply didn't know how to ask her jewel for those things.

As casually as she could, she slipped the green gem back into her pocket. Maybe she would do better, once she had the second eye.

'What do we do now?' Todd asked in a quiet voice.

'I think it's time for a drink,' Wilbert announced. 'I wonder if they have something that passes for beer?'

Conversations were slowly starting up in the room around them. Apparently, the crowd had decided they could stay.

'And why don't you sit here?' a girl's voice called from further inside the room. Mrs Smith looked through the crowd to a teenager, maybe sixteen, with long red hair and a bright smile, who waved them forward towards an empty table. It sounded like an invitation to Constance; one that she would gladly accept.

'Let's sit,' she said to those around her as she urged Todd towards the table.

'And what might I do for you fine gentlemen and lady?' the teenager called as the four of them sat on stools around the square wooden table.

Wilbert smiled up at her. 'Talking to us is a wonderful start.'

She nodded as she glanced about the room. 'You are strangers,' she said in a quieter voice. 'New traders. We hardly ever see new traders. Odd for a harbour town, don't you think?' She made a sour face. 'Here, there is nothing but habit.'

'And here I was hoping for a beer,' Wilbert replied.

The girl smiled at that. 'We might be able to find you something to your liking.' She paused, as if debating whether to fetch the order or to keep on talking. Talking won out.

'We do have three dozen traders, always the same three dozen, from three different islands,' she said in a quick, confidential tone. 'We never hear from the other three. Until now, that is.' She smiled knowingly at her customers. 'I imagine you folk come from somewhere else altogether.'

Mrs Smith shot a warning glance at her three male companions. Both Todd and Wilbert seemed quite charmed by their server (she didn't think Stanley was capable of being charmed by anyone), and were capable of talking about all sorts of things that strangers didn't need to know. As good as it was to find someone who would talk to them in this place, Constance wondered how much they could take this young woman into their confidence.

'Sala!' a man called from the other end of the room. 'There are orders to be taken!'

'Sorry,' Sala said as she backed into the crowded room. 'My father expects me to earn my keep. Perhaps we can really talk later.'

Wilbert leaned his elbows against the table and grinned. 'Now that's what I call a friendly welcome. Although it will only be complete once we get some beer!'

Stanley frowned, his whole body rigid, as if he had to be ready for an attack from any quarter. 'And how will we get that?' he demanded. 'I don't remember ordering anything.'

Todd said nothing. His eager smile left his face as Sala faded into the crowd, and now he stared at the table, his expression in neutral. He had the habit Mrs Smith often saw in young people of sort of fading into the background and watching everything around them. But she was not about to take him for granted, especially after the way he used the dragon's eye.

'Todd?' she asked gently. 'Is anything the matter?'

He looked up suddenly, startled perhaps that someone would ask him about his problems. Certainly, for that instant, he looked very young and alone.

His gaze slid down to the table again. 'Nothing any of us can do anything about.'

'You never know. You used the dragon's eye to save us, Todd. Someone who can do that is capable of quite a lot.'

Todd looked up at her then, his gaze very serious, checking no doubt to make sure she was serious too. Again, he didn't seem to know quite how to react. Constance doubted that Todd had got many compliments in his life.

'It's true, Todd lad!' Wilbert boomed. 'We should have thanked you sooner for saving our carcasses. Amazing what you did back there.'

'Maybe Obar had a reason for sending him along, hey?' Stanley added dourly.

A grin tried to break out on Todd's face. Back in the neighbourhood, Constance remembered, the boy had a talent for being brash; a bit of a bully, really, around the other kids. She hoped his victory over the tentacles wouldn't bring that sort of behaviour out in him here.

Todd was saved from any further reaction by the arrival of Sala carrying a tray with four metal tumblers. She placed a cup in front of each of them in turn.

'Foam!' Wilbert cried as he looked at the drink before him. He carefully picked up the cup and raised it to his face, sniffing at it and then taking a sip of the liquid contents.

'You really do have beer!' he announced before taking a heartier drink.

'Well of course we do!' Sala answered behind her ever-present smile. 'What do you think we are, uncivilised?'

'Enough prattle, daughter,' said a man behind her. He was a compact man, not much over five feet high, but unusually broad in the shoulders and chest. Where his daughter smiled, he scowled. The expression sat on his face as though it was frozen there. Constance thought that he and Stanley could have a scowling contest.

'Newcomers!' he called to the table. 'You are as welcome as a brisk west wind. We hope your faces become as familiar as the sun and the sea.' This seemed to be some litany of greeting, probably expected for anyone new to the establishment. With the tavern keeper's fixed expression, however, the words didn't appear to be terribly sincere.

The next sentence might have revealed the true reason for his sourness. 'As new customers in the Dragon Tavern, your first round is on the house.'

'Now that's what I call civilised!' Wilbert agreed. Stanley stared down at his own beer in suspicion.

The tavern keeper nodded at Wilbert's reaction and pulled up a stool.

'So,' he said to Wilbert, 'tell me something about your-selves.'

So he was looking for information too. It appeared that even a free drink had a price.

Wilbert wiped the foam from his beard with the back of his hand. 'What is there to tell?' He glanced at the other three members of his party. 'We are simply traders, new to this port.'

The tavern keeper's frown actually deepened. 'Most certainly. But we so seldom see new faces here, you must forgive a certain curiosity. I understand that you trade in fine cloths?'

'News travels fast,' Stanley observed from above his still untouched drink.

The tavern keeper shrugged his broad shoulders dismissively. 'Our port is really only a small town. Your ship's arrival is the biggest news we've had in weeks. But tell me, if you deal in fine fabrics, why is it that none of you has used them for clothes of your own?' With this question the townsman almost smiled. It did not suit his face at all.

Oh, dear, Constance thought. That was an oversight on her part. Wilbert and Stanley still wore the rough garb that let them blend with the forest, and Todd was dressed as you'd expect from a teenager from Chestnut Circle; black T-shirt, jeans and sneakers. Only Mrs Smith had used her magic to reclothe herself, deciding at last on a simple set of grey robes in place of her forest-tattered dress.

Of course, the people around them seemed to be dressed in all sorts of different fashions as well, from rich robes and jackets to a group of men in one corner who wore no shirts at all, their chests painted with bright patterns of yellow and red. Still, what could she say to put this man at ease?

Wilbert answered for her. 'What do you want us to do, cut into our profit? This cloth is much too fine for the common likes of us. Only Constance here, the guardian of our shipment, will wear some of the more understated fabrics.'

The tavern master nodded. 'The cloth is as wonderful as that? Not having seen it myself, I had thought that the stories were exaggerated.'

'Not in the least!' Wilbert pounded a fist on the table for emphasis. 'Soon, you will see a much finer grade of clothes upon this island.'

'If that is the case, I hope that this is only the beginning of a long and successful trading career for you and your fellows. But we also have many unique and unusual items of our own on this island.' The tavern keeper leaned close to Wilbert, his tone lowered so that it would travel no further than the edges of the table. 'If you would like, I might be able to show you something really special.'

Mrs Smith felt an electric spark over her heart. It came from the pocket where she kept the dragon's eye. Was her own gem telling her that the townsman spoke of its sister stone?

'A trader is always on the look-out for the unusual,' Wilbert replied non-committally. 'We are not here for long. If you might find a way to fit this showing into our busy schedule –'

'I can show you the items this very night!' the tavern keeper replied quickly. He looked about, realising that he had raised his voice in his eagerness. No one around them seemed to take particular notice. He lowered his voice to its earlier confidential tone. 'We will, of course, have to meet after regular business hours. There are certain of these goods that it would be best not to – show in public, shall we say?'

'And who exactly will be at this meeting?' Stanley asked sharply.

The tavern man's eyebrows rose, as if he was truly surprised by such a question. 'Why, only myself and a pair of associates who will bring the merchandise, and, of course, all four of you, if you wish. This is strictly a business proposition. If the cloth is as fine as you say, you will certainly be able to trade it for other items of great value with our port authorities. Of course, the items that come my way are rather more special than those down at the docks. You are most valued customers, and I would like to be able to trade with you for a long time to come.'

'Very well,' Mrs Smith said before anyone else could speak. 'We will take a look at your merchandise. When will we be able to see it?'

'My tavern is open from mid-afternoon until the first light of dawn. Why don't you arrive when the sun shows itself out over the ocean? It is a quiet time around here and we aren't likely to be disturbed.'

The tavern man spread his arms wide, as if to include the whole table before him. 'You, of course, should get yourselves a good night's sleep in the meantime. I know of a particularly fine inn that is but a few paces from here. My daughter would be glad to show it to you. Then, at sun-up, we seal our bargain!'

Mrs Smith nodded once. 'We will see you then.'

The tavern keeper stood at that. 'Until then. Sala!' he called. 'Another round for our honoured guests!'

'He plans to rob us,' Stanley mentioned as soon as their host was beyond hearing range.

'At the very least,' Wilbert agreed. He drained his glass, then belched in contentment.

'But he has the dragon's eye,' Constance said quietly. 'I can feel it.'

'He would, wouldn't he?' Wilbert agreed again.

'Probably plans to kill us, too,' Stanley continued. 'Would save a lot of messy questions afterwards, hey?'

'Well, we will have the money, or whatever it is that they will trade us for our fabric, this afternoon.' Wilbert looked appraisingly at his fellow Volunteer. 'Do you think he'll try it at the inn, or wait for the actual meeting?'

'The meeting, most likely,' Stanley answered after a moment's thought. 'We might have managed to hide some of our money while at the inn. An inn is a public place and our deaths might be noisy. Our fellow guests might get curious. That would give our murderers no time to conduct a proper search.'

'Unless', Wilbert interjected, 'they have made some special arrangement with the inn, like bribing the other guests?'

'Wait a moment,' Todd finally spoke up. 'You're all sure this guy is going to try to kill us. But nobody's talked about not going!'

Constance smiled sadly at the inevitability of all this. 'I'm afraid we have to go, Todd. Otherwise we might never find the eye.'

Todd had figured out a way to make himself useful after all.

Oh, there was that thing he had done with setting the monster's tentacles on fire. But that was the dragon's eye's doing really. He never understood exactly what he did to make the fire happen. Now, though, he had a real way to find out some information and maybe save Mrs Smith and the others a lot of grief.

The idea had come to him after they had left the tavern and Sala was showing them the way to the inn. Not that they had ended up at that particular inn anyway. As soon as they had reached the street, Wilbert started to ask questions of the tavern keeper's daughter about the quality of all the inns in the neighbourhood, and she had admitted that, yes, there were two or three others that were almost as good as the one her father recommended. Wilbert had immediately asked that she point out these establishments. Sala pointed casually to another inn along the way, leading Wilbert to exclaim that this was the very place to stay!

He claimed it was because of the inn's ocean view. Todd knew it was because it might be safer than the one the tavern keeper had chosen.

Sala had become flustered at that. She looked helplessly from one of the newcomers to the next, until her gaze turned to Todd.

She just stood there, for one long moment, looking at him. And he looked back at her. She had a wonderful smile that formed dimples deep in her cheeks. He couldn't help but smile back.

Todd had thought she might have found him interesting, back there in the tavern. With her long, red hair, her graceful body dressed in a billowing white blouse and a strangely uneven skirt that swung about to show glimpses of her long, bare legs as she moved, he had certainly thought she was the best-looking thing he'd seen since he got to this place.

'Come over here,' Todd said. 'Please?'

She looked at the other three for an instant, but then followed him across the street.

'Look,' he whispered to her when she was close, 'my friends can be stubborn and set in their ways. But maybe I can talk to them, get them to see that your father has recommended the best inn in town. I can't guarantee anything, but I can try.'

She sighed at that and looked at him with big, hopeful eyes. Todd decided he'd tell her anything to have her look at him like that. She must be awfully afraid of her father. Todd wondered whether he beat her if she didn't do exactly what he told her to. Somehow thinking that made Todd want to do even more for her.

'Listen,' he added, 'maybe we can get together when my friends and I have finished our business. You know, down at the docks?'

To his amazement, his suggestion made her smile.

'I'd like that,' she said.

Todd didn't know what to say next. He didn't know this place at all. He didn't know where to meet, or when.

Sala, however, had her own ideas. She explained how she was always given some time off for dinner when the night help first arrived. After that, she was banished to the kitchen to wash dishes and help with the food preparation. Her father thought the night-time crowds too rowdy for her to be around.

'Meet me at dusk,' she concluded, 'at the back door of the tavern.'

So they would see each other in a few hours. Maybe, Todd thought, he could find out a little about what her father was really planning.

She waved happily to him before she turned and ran quickly back towards the tavern.

'Todd, lad!' Wilbert called. 'What say we investigate our new accommodations?'

'Sure,' Todd said, hurrying to help Mrs Smith up the three steps that led to the inn's front door. They would have to make plans for how to get the dragon's eye, and how to prevent any obstacles, whether they came from the tavern keeper or anybody else.

But first he had to stop thinking about the way Sala smiled.

Evan Mills had never expected this.

He, and the two others inside him, had manipulated the two wizards into almost throwing him on top of the dragon's eye. Then, in a moment when both wizards were distracted, Mills had grabbed the eye and let Rox spirit them away.

The jewel tingled in his hand. He could feel the sensation in the muscles of his arms and legs, and somewhere in his head behind his eyes. Deep inside him Rox was laughing, and Zachs seemed to be singing a song.

There was no world around them for a long instant, only a great grey blur as Rox transported them to a new destination. Once there, Evan thought, they could use this thing to become three again.

Then the world came back, and with it, the pain.

Evan felt his head would split apart. The agony was unbelievable, far worse than anything he had felt before, as if bone and muscle and flesh and eyes and tongue and brain were all pushing to get out. He had a vision of the top of his skull blowing off, letting the wizard and light creature free, but leaving him dead, his brains spread across the floor.

No, Rox spoke inside his head. This pain would kill us all.

With that, the pain lessened to a dull throb.

Somehow, this discomfort comes from our possession of the stone. I had not foreseen this. I believe I can make adjustments. The pain will go away.

Deep inside, Zachs moaned. So this misery affected all of them.

But the pain was bearable for the moment. Evan chose to ignore the discomfort that remained, hoping he might discover something about this new place Rox had brought them to. It was dark here, and he lay on something soft and dry that rustled when he moved. Grass maybe, or hay. He smelled animals. This could be a barn, then, or a stable. There was an open door some distance away. The square of the doorway was filled with bright light, showing a perfect little picture of buildings across the way and dozens of people strolling up and down a street in between.

'You've brought us to – a city?' Evan managed.

'I thought it best,' Rox whispered through Evan's mouth. 'It will be more difficult for them to find us in this crowd.'

Another, higher voice spoke next. 'How can Zachs run when Zachs hurts?'

'Perhaps the jewel cannot deal with three separate beings in one form,' Rox suggested.

'What should we do?' Evan asked.

'Get rid of the jewel!' Zachs demanded. 'No! Hide it! Come back when we learn to use it!'

'Never,' Rox replied with finality. 'People will kill for the power of the dragon's eye. We will have to learn to harness it in some different way.'

'How can we harness anything', Mills demanded, 'when it does this to us?'

All three voices were silent for a long moment.

'Maybe –' Rox said at last, '– we need a second jewel.'

'A second?' asked Zachs, suddenly eager. 'But how?'

'That is the other reason why we're here,' the wizard informed them. 'The second jewel is quite close. After all, we already have one eye in our possession. The second one should be even easier to obtain.'

The first jewel had not done what the wizard had promised and now Rox wanted them to look for another? Evan didn't like this at all. Not, of course, that he had much to say in the matter.

He groaned as he sat up. 'Find a way for us to stop hurting and we'll look for the other stone.' His arms threatened to buckle when he leaned back against the hay-strewn floor. 'Of course, first I have to remember how to stand up.'

'This will come soon,' Rox said with a strength that Evan Mills wished he could share. 'Soon, we will have everything.'

Sixteen

Nick could barely stand.

The wizard had brought them someplace new. They were in an alley, with tall wooden buildings on either side. The alley was dark, but the bright sunlight where it opened to the street hurt Nick's eyes.

Where were they?

He had trouble concentrating on anything but the battle he had just left behind. His eyes closed and he saw the sword impaling his enemies, opening deep, bloody gashes, pausing for an instant to drink before it pulled itself free and sought another victim. He could hear the screams and feel the power in his hands.

He thought of the sword, swinging towards Maggie.

His eyes opened and he looked at the dried blood spattered across his shirt. Even though his hand no longer gripped his sword, he wanted more.

More of what?

The world swayed around him. He lost his balance, falling backwards.

'Nick!' Maggie called.

His back banged into the wall behind him. It was the only reason he stayed on his feet.

'This is all moving rather quickly,' Obar mused, as if that was Nick's only problem. 'I should be able to help a bit.'

The wizard reached out and brushed his fingers across Nick's forehead.

Nick felt the warmth spread from his head, down through neck and torso and arms and legs. The tiredness fell away like dead leaves scattered by the wind. There was strength to Nick's muscles again, but it came from a different kind of energy than that given by the sword. Nick pushed himself away from the wall. He still felt a little dizzy, but he should be able to walk.

'Here, Nick, I'll help you.' Maggie grabbed one of his arms and slung it over her shoulder.

Obar considered both of them for an instant. 'These encounters can be trying. We will find the two of you a place to stay while I search the town.'

'No,' Nick protested as Maggie leaned his weight against her. He was surprised she helped so quickly after what had almost happened with the sword. After that, he felt uncomfortable with her help. 'I should walk by myself. I should look like a swordsman.'

'So you'll look like a drunken swordsman,' Maggie answered. 'I imagine there's a lot of that around here.' She glanced over at the wizard. 'I guess, from the salt air, that we're in some sort of port town?'

'You can never fool a Volunteer.' Obar took a step towards the street. 'What say we take a look at this place?'

Nick nodded down at his shirt. 'But the blood?'

Obar stopped and turned back toward the others. 'Oh, the blood.' He held the green dragon's eye in his hand. It glowed faintly in the dim light. He waved the jewel an inch away from the fabric of Nick's shirt. The cloth sparkled green for an instant, then faded like the embers from some strange-coloured fire. The blood-stains were gone.

'Sometimes', Obar said with a smile, 'magic can actually be useful. But come. We aren't the only ones looking for this eye.'

Obar led the way, with Nick and Maggie close behind. Nick found he could lean against Maggie without her having any difficulty. While she was shorter than Nick, and fairly thin, her more delicate bones were covered by a thick layer of muscle.

Nick let himself glance over at his benefactor as they reached the end of the alley. Maggie looked at him and grinned, then turned back to where Obar was already stepping into the sunlight. Up close like this, he could see her finely chiselled nose, her warm brown eyes, how pretty she was when she

131

smiled. She didn't really seem that much older than he was. Somewhere in her twenties, probably. Her short brown hair made her appear even younger.

This was the first time he'd really thought of her – well, as a woman. Before this, she was just one of the Volunteers.

They walked together out of the alley into the light. It was afternoon and the sun was low over the hills behind them. They were on a hillside, on a street paved with stones sunk into the ground. The wooden buildings to either side were brightly coloured, painted in strong reds and greens and yellows, the shades even more dramatic framed in afternoon patterns of golden light and shadow.

Obar stopped only a few doors up from where they had entered the street. 'This looks like an acceptable place.'

It must, Nick reasoned, be an inn, although he wasn't quite sure how Obar knew this. Perhaps it had something to do with the wooden sign over the door, a carved rendition of a setting sun.

'Follow me.' Obar quickly climbed the steps. With Maggie's help, Nick followed with hardly any difficulty. Whatever Obar had given to him seemed to be making him even stronger as it settled into his muscles. Nick could probably walk without Maggie's assistance now. Still, why should he move away before he had to?

They walked into a small room crammed with four tables and a counter at the far end. Nick wondered if this was where the guests had their meals.

An elderly man stood behind the counter, polishing the wood in front of him with a dark-brown cloth. Nick was startled to see that the man had only his right eye. There was a hole where his left should be, a shadowed recess full of scar tissue.

The old man smiled as they approached, or half smiled, for only the right side of his mouth seemed to work as well.

'We need a room –' Obar paused to consider, scratching beneath his moustache, '– a pair of rooms, actually – for the night.'

The man looked them over with his one good eye. 'And who be you?'

Obar lifted his hand, waving the clerk's question aside as if they were above such petty concerns. 'We are from that ship that just arrived.'

'Be you?' the clerk replied. He made no further move to get them a room, or even to indicate this was really an inn.

'Payment in advance, of course.' Two coins dropped from Obar's hands on to the counter.

'Ship's gold?' The man's head bobbed up and down once, as if he and Obar had just struck a bargain. 'I be expecting you.' He turned abruptly and disappeared behind a curtain.

'He was expecting us?' Nick whispered.

Obar turned to his two companions. 'That's one good thing about a harbour town. There is *always* a new ship arriving. It saves us from having to answer too many questions.'

The curtain stirred, and the old man re-emerged, carrying a large key.

'I have one room ready now,' he said, offering the key. 'There be another by evening.' He snatched the key back as Obar reached for it. 'Now who do I have the honour of addressing?'

'I am Obar,' the magician said quickly, as if impatient to be done with this. 'My companions are Nick and Maggie.'

'They call me Pit.' The old man pointed at the crater where his eye should be. ' 'Tis a witticism.'

Pit pointed the key towards the top of a set of stairs to his left. 'Room's up there. End of the hall.'

Obar snatched the key from the old man's fingers and handed it to Maggie. 'I will see you as soon as I complete my business.'

'We serve a fine dinner!' Pit called after the retreating wizard. ' 'Tis extra, of course.' He raised his voice to a shout as Obar escaped down the stairs. 'And careful if you wander about after dark. The town has unsavoury elements.' Pit grinned his crooked smile. He turned to Maggie and Nick, his voice lowered to an almost confidential tone. 'He be a temperamental sort, aye?'

'Only when he has business,' Maggie replied. She tugged Nick towards the stairs. 'Now if you'll excuse us?'

'You got a wash basin in your room!' the old man called after them. 'And there's facilities down at the bottom of the back stairs. When you're out there, mind the chickens!'

He waved at the two of them as they started up the stairs. 'Nothing but the finest service at old Pit's!'

They took the stairs slowly. The steps were uneven, with a board missing here and there. The stairway appeared to sway as Maggie helped Nick round a bend. Maybe, he pondered, he wasn't as sure on his feet as he'd thought. The wood railing groaned as he grabbed it for support. So the bannister was none too steady either. Maggie pushed him up, step by single step.

Somehow they managed to reach the top of the stairs. A doorway was open at the end of a short hall.

'Almost there,' Maggie encouraged. She was breathing almost as heavily as Nick. She swung him through the door into the room, then let him go to fall back on the bed.

Nick's groan came from exhaustion. The bed beneath him was full of lumps and bits of something sharp that dug into his back. Besides that, he'd swear he could feel small creatures crawling around underneath him. But it was a bed. All in all, it felt wonderful.

He forced his eyes open to look around the room. It wasn't very large, only big enough to hold a small table and chair to one side of the bed and a grime-encrusted window on the other side.

There was only one bed for the two of them?

Nick struggled to sit up. Maybe he'd better sleep on the floor.

'And what are you doing?' Maggie demanded.

'You should have the bed.' Nick was surprised by how hoarse his voice sounded.

'Should I?' She shook her head. 'You can forget that chivalry stuff around me, Nick. I left it back in my other life.' She smiled then, her head shaking a second time. 'Not that I got so much of it then, either.'

Nick wasn't going to let her win that easily. She really should have the bed. After all, he was so exhausted, he could sleep anywhere.

134

'Come on, Maggie,' he insisted. 'Let me do something for you for a change. You probably haven't slept in a bed since you ended up in that forest.'

The wistful smile was still on her face. 'It *has* been for ever.'

'Well, come on, then.' He managed to sit up.

'Get yourself back down, Nick.' She walked to the side of the bed, only a single step from the door and gently nudged his shoulder to urge him to lie down.

Nick pushed against the pressure of her hand, lifting his own to swat her away. 'No, get away. I think it's time someone was chivalrous –'

He stopped talking abruptly when he realised his hand had stopped to rest on her breast.

'I'm sorry.' He jerked it away so quickly that he fell back on the bed. 'I didn't mean anything.' He wanted to roll over and hide his face in the mattress. 'I'm always – I don't know – I'm so sorry.'

But Maggie didn't seem angry. 'Don't be,' she said gently. 'You're just tired and scared.' Her lips curled into the slightest of smiles. 'I've helped a lot of frightened men in my time. Of course, that was in a different world, a different lifetime.'

Nick looked up at her. 'I don't understand. Were you a nurse?'

Her smile grew at that. 'Not exactly. I helped the soldiers in other ways.' She sighed, looking away from Nick at the grimy space that passed for a window. 'I was – young. And I was desperate.' She turned back and looked straight at Nick. 'Well, I guess you could call me a camp follower.'

'Camp follower? For the soldiers?' Nick remembered reading about women like that in a book about the Civil War. 'You slept with them, you mean?'

She raised her eyebrows at his question. 'Well, a lady's got to make a living. I was a different person, then. My hair went down to my shoulders; it's curly when it's longer. And I had nice clothes, things with lace, that showed off my curves to good advantage.'

She sat down on the bed next to him. 'It's hard even to

135

imagine what I was like back then, what I thought and felt about the things around me. It really was a different world.'

Maggie smiled down at him. He was aware of her breathing and the smell of her sweat. Somehow, at this moment, she seemed more real to him than any woman he had ever known.

'But you gave that all up?' he whispered.

Her smile was somehow very sad. 'I did more than that. I fell in love. I ended up here with the Volunteers.' Her gaze wandered over to the brown smudge that passed for a window. 'There were a lot more of us, when we started. The Lieutenant – his name was Douglas. He was in charge, of all of us, I guess. He had spirit. He'd go after anything, even a wizard.' She glanced down at Nick. 'That's what killed him.'

She looked away again. Her cheek was wet. She was crying.

This was all wrong. The Volunteers were able to handle anything. But Maggie looked so lost, so vulnerable; not like a Volunteer at all.

'Hey,' he muttered, looking for some words that might comfort her. He propped himself back up, his elbows digging into the straw mattress. 'Maggie.'

She turned her head away from him. 'Oh, I'm being stupid. You can't afford to have feelings here.'

'Hey,' he said again, this time adding, 'I guess you have to cry sometimes.'

He brushed a tear off the bottom of her chin.

Her hand caught his. Her fingers felt very warm against his own. Maggie looked down at the hand as if she wasn't sure whether or not to give it back.

She turned to him then, the tears falling freely down her cheeks.

'Oh, Nick,' she whispered. 'If only – I wish I could –' Tears interrupted the rest of her sentence.

Before he even knew what he was doing, Nick leaned forward and kissed her.

Not that it was much of a kiss. Their lips brushed, really. Nick pulled back, feeling clumsy and stupid.

136

Maggie brushed a tear from the corner of her mouth. 'Oh, my.' She sat up straight on the edge of the bed. 'I don't think we're quite ready for that yet.'

Nick shook his head. He was so embarrassed. 'I'm sorry. I'm so sorry.' He raised his hands towards her, but then he didn't know what to do with them. What was he thinking of? He closed his eyes and started to shake again.

He felt her arms go round him.

'I think, tonight, you need someone to hold you,' she said softly. 'And maybe I need to hold on to someone too.'

She felt warm against him. The shaking wasn't quite so bad. Maybe, with Maggie close to him, he could stop it altogether.

She pushed him back gently as she lay down next to him. His breath escaped him slowly as he sank into the bed.

When he closed his eyes, he no longer saw the sword.

Pit looked hard at the lad before him. If his one eye scared the boy a little, all the better.

'Now,' he demanded, 'what be the message?'

'The travellers have arrived,' the boy repeated quickly. 'All should be in their rooms by nightfall. Their leader has already displayed a quantity of gold. We look forward to the arrival of your men at the usual time.'

'Fair enough!' he tossed the lad a tin coin. 'Mind you repeat me, word for word!'

The boy caught the coin mid-air. 'Yes, sir!' he cried, already running down the hill towards his destination.

Pit did hope that this messenger did a better job than the boy who had come to him earlier. That other boy had told him there were four, not three. And there was something about the woman being older too. What was the world coming to, when you couldn't trust messenger boys?

Oh, well, Pit thought as he climbed the stairs back to the inn. He had a few final preparations to make for his guests. But everything would be fine, so long as he got his cut.

Seventeen

Something warm and wet rasped across Jason's face. He jumped up, ready to fight some new threat to him and the Oomgosh.

Charlie barked up at him, tail wagging, ready to start some new game.

Jason was amazed how much the dog had changed since his fight with the light creature, back when they first visited Obar's castle. The dog had been wounded by the creature, then healed by Obar's magic. Jason wasn't sure whether it was the light thing's attack or Obar's cure that had made the dog into what he was now.

Oh, sure, he still sort of looked dog-like, if you still sort of looked at him the right way. Charlie had grown round, bone-like ridges over his eyes, and a great hump of muscle across his back. It occurred to Jason that Charlie looked a little bit like those statues of Japanese dogs his art class had seen on their field trip to the museum downtown.

'Hey, Charlie,' Jason called softly as he patted the new bumps between the dog's ears. Charlie leaned against him, almost knocking Jason off his feet. The dog was gaining weight too. 'You're not the only one around here who's changing.'

Jason thought about the fight they'd all had, earlier in the day, against those dark things. That was wild, what had happened with the wind.

If he listened to the Oomgosh, he could be a little bit like the tree-man and help him out. Jason liked that, in a way. The tree-man was strong and happy most of the time. Jason had never felt strong in his entire life. And happy? Well, sure, he had a good time when he fooled around with Bobby, and it felt pretty okay when that girl from his homeroom, Amanda, talked to him at school, and maybe he was proud when he got a good grade or something, but happy? He spent more time being quiet, or out of the way. His mother didn't want anybody making too much noise around the house.

Besides, nobody could be as happy as the Oomgosh.

'Pretty weird, huh?'

Jason looked up from the dog. Bobby had wandered over from where he had been watching his mother.

Not that Bobby's mother did anything like watch back. She seemed to be lost in her own private place, talking to her husband and son even when they weren't there, asking them about school and work and what they wanted for dinner. It was like she couldn't handle this world and had let her mind go back to that place they all came from, where she could be comfortable again. But she wasn't on Chestnut Circle, none of them was, and the longer they stayed here, the more Jason realised they might never get back to the Circle again.

Somehow, Bobby managed to smile. That was one of the things Jason liked most about his friend; Bobby could barrel through anything. And he didn't make fun of Jason's thick glasses or the fact that Jason was the clumsiest person on the face of the earth.

'Whaddya think's gonna happen?' Bobby asked, as if Jason was some kind of expert.

'I don't know,' Jason said. But if he thought about it, he did know. 'I think we're going to have to fight again, just to stay alive.' He looked down at his sneakers. 'And I think stuff is going to change that we can't even guess.'

The Oomgosh stirred and opened his eyes. 'I knew Jason was a fast learner,' the tree-man rumbled.

This time, Jason realised he would have liked it better if the Oomgosh had told him he was wrong.

'Yeah.' Bobby stared down at the dirt, his smile gone. 'I guess so.' He looked back up at Jason. For the first time ever that Jason could remember, Bobby seemed scared.

'My dad's gone,' Bobby said slowly. 'Maybe he's dead.

My mother can't handle it. I don't know what I'm gonna do.' With that, he tried to smile again. 'I guess none of us does, huh?'

'First, you survive,' the Oomgosh said. He groaned as he shifted on the ground. 'Then, with any luck, you will grow.'

Jason was glad, at least, that the tree-man was awake and talking again. He smiled at his old best friend. 'We can do anything when the Oomgosh can show us the way.'

The tree-man sighed at that, a low, gentle moan, like the sound of the wind that brings the rain. 'I will need a great deal of luck to do that. I think this is a time when luck is in short supply.'

Jason had never heard the tree-man sound so negative. Maybe he needed Raven to cheer him up. Jason looked up at the trees that surrounded them. The black bird was usually perched on one of the limbs at the edge of the clearing.

'Where is he?' Jason asked, more to himself than the others.

'Who?' Bobby asked back.

'Raven.' Jason took a few steps towards the centre of the clearing to get a better view. 'I thought I saw him a minute ago.'

'No doubt you did,' the Oomgosh rumbled.

'I can't see him anyplace!' Bobby called. 'Raven! You around, Raven?'

'Raven will only answer if he feels like it,' the Oomgosh said. 'Not that he is close enough to answer just now.'

Jason turned away from the trees to look down at the tree-man. 'You mean the bird's gone somewhere?'

'Raven has business everywhere.' At that, the Oomgosh smiled at last. 'After all, he is the creator of all things.'

Jason frowned. He had trouble thinking of that boastful bird creating anything. Jason always thought that whole 'creating' business was some little joke the tree-man and bird played with each other.

'Do you really believe that?'

The Oomgosh managed a dry chuckle. 'Do I believe? Who am I to question the likes of Raven?'

'So where's he gone?' Bobby asked.

The tree-man shrugged. 'Raven can fly anywhere.'

Anywhere? Maybe, Jason thought, the black bird had gone off to help some of the others find the dragon's eyes. But, according to Raven's stories, he could just as likely be off capturing the sun.

Bobby looked up at the sky. 'I wish I could fly anywhere.'

'Do not be so quick to wish,' the Oomgosh chided. 'Sometimes, and Raven will tell you this himself, to be able to fly anywhere is a great responsibility.'

Jason somehow found himself very annoyed at the way the bird could come and go without apology. 'So what do we do, wait for him? Raven will come back, won't he?'

The Oomgosh's smile still showed his pain. 'Oh, most certainly, Raven will come back if he can. But we will not have much time for waiting. Other things will occupy us shortly.'

'And what is that supposed to mean?'

Jason turned around and saw that Mrs Blake had walked over to listen to their conversation. From the tone of her voice, it sounded like she was getting angry at the roundabout way the tree-man often talked.

'As long as I touch the ground,' the Oomgosh replied patiently, 'I can hear every tree in the forest. Nothing goes on in these woods that I am not aware of. Now, I hear many people – perhaps close to a hundred – moving our way.'

'People?' The only large group Jason could think of were Nunn's troops. 'Do you mean soldiers?'

'Soldiers.' The Oomgosh nodded.

Mrs Dafoe stepped up next to Mrs Blake. 'Soldiers?' she asked shrilly. 'Coming for us? How can you be sure?'

The tree-man looked calmly back at her. 'The roots of the trees go everywhere. They are what holds this island together. Through them, I can hear the troops marching through the forest.'

In a faint sort of way, Jason realised, he could hear them too, a distant rumble that somehow came to him through the earth beneath his feet. He could make no sense of the noise, or vibration, or whatever it was before now, and had ignored it. But it was definitely there, like so many other things the Oomgosh had told him about.

Thomas stepped up next to the women. 'Trust the Oomgosh. He knows what he's talkin' about. Nunn's not gonna leave us alone.'

The Volunteer paused, looking at everyone in the clearing in turn.

'Time,' he said at last. 'Time for everyone to get ready to fight.'

Eighteen

So where was she?

Todd's feelings kept shifting, from guilt to joy to fear to giddy triumph. One minute he felt he was getting away with something; the next that this was what he should have been doing all along; a second later that he should never have separated from the others in this strange place, both for his sake and theirs.

The sun had already sunk behind the hill above Todd, plunging the whole town into one great, late-afternoon shadow. The sky was pink around the hilltop, and fading to deep blue above the ocean.

As far as Todd could figure out, this was dusk, and Sala should be here.

It hadn't been easy for him to get here either. It had taken a little fast footwork to get away from the others at that inn.

'The finest accommodations in town,' the overweight woman who met them at the door announced. 'When I heard there were new traders dealing in fine cloth, I knew this was the place you would want to stay.'

She had proceeded to hover about the four of them, showing them her fine dining area, her spacious rooms, the roof deck with a splendid view of the port, even her newly remodelled outhouses, with separate entrances for men and women! She seemed especially proud of that, although they just looked like a pair of outhouses to Todd.

But the outhouses had given Todd the chance to leave. After he had safely deposited Mrs Smith in her room, he had made his excuses to the two Volunteers, saying he had to take care of certain natural business. Wilbert and Stanley waved him away; they were both clearly exhausted by their sea voyage and the quick trading that followed.

By leaving that way, Todd figured he had maybe a quarter of an hour before the others even got curious, and possibly far longer if the Volunteers made good their promises and fell asleep. He might be able to get to the tavern and back before the others even knew he was gone.

Todd had felt exhausted too, until he had met Sala. Now he couldn't stand still. It had taken him perhaps two minutes to retrace his steps to where they'd met, and only a minute more to find the way to the back door of the tavern. There was an alley to one side of the building. Todd looked around to see if anyone noticed him, but the way people were hurrying up and down the main street, no one seemed to care. Probably wanted to make it home in time for supper, Todd thought. Whatever the reason, he hoped that no one observed him as he ducked down the alley.

The passageway was narrow, maybe five feet across, and reeked of garbage. It went on for some distance, though. The tavern was longer than he had thought, certainly longer than that crowded room he and his shipmates had visited. It must have some additional rooms in the back or something. Todd moved quickly, careful to step over the refuse strewn here and there on the muddy ground. Something shrieked in protest as he kicked a pile of greasy rags out of his way. Rats, Todd thought, or something like them.

Evening was rapidly taking over this narrow space and it was getting hard to make out details in the gloom. He could already see the first stars in the thin ribbon of sky at the alley's top.

The alley ended in a wall ahead and he still saw no sign of a door. There was nothing back here except for him and the rats.

He would never have noticed the opening if it hadn't been for the smell. He kept walking towards the back wall, seeing nothing, and the stench hit him between one step and the next. It was like going into an open sewer.

There, on his left, was a narrow passage between the extreme rear of the tavern building and the beginning of the next. As he approached the space between the walls, three feet wide at most, he could see a single dim light burning just beyond the gap. There was a lamp back there, hanging over a door.

And, if anything, the stench here was even worse.

He squeezed through the space, which opened up into a small yard. The area, which was maybe thirty feet across, seemed far smaller, since much of it was taken up by two great piles of refuse. The one on the right was mostly pieces of wood and cloth and paper; things no doubt to put in the fire.

The pile on the right was the one giving off the smell. In the dim lamplight he could see a few fish heads and bits of rotten fruit towards the top of the heap. Most of the stuff underneath had disintegrated into something unrecognisable, becoming softer and moister as it got closer to the ground. He almost stepped in a puddle of brown ooze that leaked from beneath the bottom of this mess. The foul water ran downhill into a ditch that seemed to drain beneath the next building over.

He wondered how anyone could live around this sort of thing. The reek was so strong Todd could hardly breathe.

But he had found the back door of the tavern. And there was still no sign of Sala.

He stood there for a moment, wondering what to do, when he heard the voices. One male, one female, they appeared to come from the other side of the door. Maybe the woman was Sala. And the man was her father? Todd moved closer to the door, careful not to step on anything that might make a noise.

He stopped only a few inches from the door, ready to bolt if the thing started to open. Even here, the wood muffled the sounds on the other side so that it was hard to make out every word.

'Should have –' the man's voice bellowed. 'Why haven't we got a message?'

'I showed them –' the woman's voice called back. Todd thought it sounded like Sala. 'That's all I could – fault if they didn't –'

'If you didn't –' the man roared, '– break those pretty legs!'

That sounded like a threat to Todd. Part of him wanted to break the door down and rescue the girl. But he didn't even know her!

And he didn't know what was on the other side of that door either.

Down, boy, Todd thought. Maybe this was all a mistake and he should get his butt out of here.

There was a heavy sound, followed by the girl's voice crying in pain. Todd found himself wanting to go in there all over again. It sounded too much like his own family, his father beating his mother, and Todd, too, before he got too big.

Todd heard footsteps. Someone was running down the alley towards him, splashing through the puddles and the mud.

He froze. Could he be wrong about the people arguing on the other side of the door? This might be Sala running to meet him after all. Who else would come back to this disgusting pit on purpose? Still, that female voice had sounded an awful lot like the girl he was supposed to meet.

Todd had to find someplace to hide, just in case. He looked at the two piles in the yard. There really was no choice.

He ducked behind the far corner of the woodpile, hoping it was far enough from the single light so that he would be covered by shadows. Something chittered at him as he hunkered down, another of the rodents, angry that Todd was invading its home. Todd hoped it wouldn't get angry enough to bite.

The steps splashed to a stop as a short figure pushed himself through the narrow opening and into the yard.

It was a boy, maybe ten or eleven. He strode up to the back door and knocked loudly.

'What is it?' a muffled voice demanded.

'I have a message for Snake, sir,' the boy replied.

The door opened with the whine of unoiled hinges. The tavern keeper stuck his face out under the light.

'I'm Snake,' he informed the boy. He looked back into the room, shouting at someone inside. 'Get away from the door!'

Snake, the owner, took a step out from the back of the tavern, half closing the door behind him. 'Now,' he demanded of the boy, 'what is the message?'

146

'The travellers have arrived,' the boy said in a rapid singsong. 'All should be in their rooms by nightfall. Their leader has already displayed a quantity of gold. We look forward to the arrival of your men at the usual time.'

'Good enough.' Snake fished something from his pocket and tossed it to the kid. 'Get out of here now!'

The boy nodded to the tavern keeper and took off the way he had come.

Todd held his breath where he knelt down behind the wood pile. So the Volunteers had been right. This Snake did plan to rob them! He had to get back to the others as quickly as he could.

But what about Sala? He'd hate to leave without seeing her, especially after hearing how badly her father treated her. The message the boy had delivered said something about 'the usual time'. That would take planning. It wouldn't happen right away. 'The usual time' was probably in the middle of the night, when the streets were empty.

So he could stay a little longer. He'd only talk to Sala for a minute.

Besides, maybe Sala could tell Todd something about her father's plans, something that would make sure Todd and his friends could avoid the thieves altogether.

Snake turned round and stomped back inside. He swung the door closed behind him, but it didn't latch, instead swinging back open an inch or so. The two voices from within were much clearer than before.

'I've spent too long back here already,' Snake said. 'I should be out front, tending to my customers.'

Sala, and Todd could tell for sure that it was her, said she needed to get a little air.

Snake groaned at that. 'I shouldn't give you any time for dinner at all. You've been mooning away all afternoon!'

Sala didn't answer.

'Are all daughters as worthless as you?' Snake's voice, while still demanding, seemed fainter than before, as if the tavern keeper was leaving the room.

There was no noise at all for a moment. Then the door creaked open again.

'Are you there?' Sala called. Her face looked even prettier in the lamplight.

Todd stepped out from behind the woodpile.

'Here I am,' he whispered. 'But not for long. What's your father want to do to us?'

'Whatever it is, he'll be doing it to somebody else,' Sala replied with a smile. 'Your companions were too smart for my father's stupid plan. Somebody else has fallen into the trap; and my father's men will steal somebody else's gold.'

Todd couldn't believe it. 'So you were going to show us that inn, knowing your father planned to rob us?'

Sala shrugged, her eyes wide in the dim light. 'What else could I do? I didn't want to, but my father would beat me if I didn't. I gave you every chance to get away. I do that with everybody, unless they're rich and stupid and deserve to be robbed!'

Todd glared at her. He still didn't like this.

She walked towards him, her slim figure silhouetted by the light from the open door. 'We didn't get to spend any time alone before. I never had a chance to know your name.'

He guessed he could at least give her that.

'Todd.'

'Todd.' She nodded her approval. 'It sounds strong.'

She stopped only a foot in front of him and smiled up into his face. Before all this business with her father Todd had wanted to kiss her. Hell, he still wanted to kiss her.

He glanced back at the open door. There was a table in the room beyond, piled high with pots and pans. It must be the kitchen and it looked empty.

'I heard some of what went on inside,' he said to Sala. 'Your father hits you, doesn't he?'

She looked away then, as if embarrassed that Todd had found this out. 'He only hits me where it doesn't show.'

Todd nodded. That was the way his own father used to push his mother around.

Sala stepped even closer, so that her breasts touched the front of his T-shirt. 'I just wish I could get away from here.'

She looked up at him again, all innocence. Did she want him

to take her with them? She probably thought the four of them were some kind of rich traders, living in luxury on some other island. He couldn't tell her the truth. He didn't really dare tell her anything.

He took a step back. 'You wouldn't want to get involved in what's going on with me.'

Her long red hair bounced as she shook her head. 'I don't know about that. Anything would be better than this. And, Todd?' She stepped close to him again. 'I would like to get to know you.'

'So would a lot of people,' a man's voice called from the kitchen door.

Todd looked up from Sala. Her father stood in the doorway. He held a crossbow, loaded with an arrow pointed straight at Todd's chest.

'You see how I have to protect my little girl.'

Sala made a whimpering noise, deep in her throat.

'My dearest daughter.' Snake shook his head. 'Neglecting her chores, staring off into the rafters. I thought there was a reason.'

'But, Daddy –' Sala protested in the smallest of voices.

'Move out of the way, now,' Snake commanded, anger growing in his voice. 'You know what happens when you disobey.'

'Oh, Daddy,' Sala said, her voice already defeated, 'do you have to kill this one too?'

Nineteen

She wasn't with the Anno any more. Things had changed once her mind led her through the fire.

She was no longer in the forest either.

Mary Lou floated, but not on water. She coasted on a wave of sound. There were voices here, all talking, too many voices to count. But the voices were only the start of it. Beneath them were other sounds, too; waves crashing on the shore, the chirp of crickets, the whisper of wind through the trees. She heard a bell ringing, the singing of birds, the sharp noise of someone chopping wood. It was as though she were in a place that collected every sound that ever was, and she were here to listen to them all.

Or, perhaps, to listen for something more. The sounds were all around her, layer upon layer, but as she heard each noise and identified it, that sound fell into the background. It was not that the sounds disappeared, exactly. It was more as if she knew they weren't important. They could be filtered out, so that she could explore the next layer of noise, fainter than the one before, and then the next layer after that. It was like one of those antique toys where you opened a hollow doll and found another smaller doll inside, also hollow, which held another, smaller doll; half a dozen hollow toys with secret treasures, until you found the tiny solid doll at the centre of them all, the heart of the toy.

The layers of sound were like that, bright noise that grabbed her attention for an instant before she went on to the next, subtler sound. But what would she find at the heart of noise?

The sounds were more delicate now; a baby's laughter, an

old woman's sigh, a drop of rain. But she had to go on.

More sounds; the blink of an eye, the flutter of a butterfly wing, a flower opening its petals to the sun.

And beneath that, the final sound, the one she had been brought to hear. A sound fainter still, a rumble so deep it was almost beyond hearing. But it was a vibration without a single source. Instead, it was everywhere.

Mary Lou knew she heard the dragon.

With that realisation, the other sounds fell into place, butterfly wings to drops of rain to chopping wood to bells tolling to the voices, talking all around her, as if, now that she had been shown the dragon, the lesson was done.

The voices pulled her away from her thoughts. She thought she recognised a couple of them. One of them sounded like Mrs Smith. Could the old woman be looking for her? Mary Lou tried to concentrate, to hear what Mrs Smith was saying, but the voice was gone.

This was maddening. She felt as if she was trapped in a place where sound had no boundaries, where every noise that ever was flew by to assault her ears.

But who said she was trapped? She had already travelled to the very heart of the sound. Maybe she could go elsewhere and ride the waves of noise wherever she wanted to go.

But where should she travel? She thought about following Mrs Smith, but the neighbour lady had her own dragon's eye and all the power that came with it. Finding her would not be a true test of what Mary Lou could do.

She'd look for Mrs Smith in a moment. First, she'd find someone else.

Mary Lou thought about her parents.

She saw a light ahead, the first indication that her eyes even worked in this place.

'Wait a moment,' a voice said by her side.

'What?' she turned, but everything else here was darkness.

'I thought you might want to know a thing or two before you started using this place,' the young man's voice replied.

She knew that voice, too. 'Garo?' she whispered.

'At your service,' he replied jovially.

How could it be? 'I thought you were dead.'

There was a moment's silence before he replied. 'Well. That is a distinct possibility.'

'I thought you were eaten by the dragon!'

'Well,' Garo added after another moment. 'Yes. That happened too.'

Mary Lou found herself getting angry. 'So how can you be talking to me?'

'Well.' If anything, Garo's tone seemed even more hesitant than before. 'You have to consider where you are, now don't you?'

What did he mean by that?

Her anger threatened to give way to fear.

'Has the dragon eaten me too?'

'Not exactly.' Garo chuckled, as if that was the silliest thing he had ever heard. His words started to tumble out, quick and glib, like the Garo of old. 'Not that the dragon wouldn't like to, mind you. But it's more like you're visiting, on one edge of that thing you call the dragon.'

'One edge?' Mary Lou asked.

'I'm afraid I'm not describing it all that well. It really is quite amazing. The creature exists on so many levels, in so many places. The dragon is everywhere.'

Mary Lou still wasn't ready to share Garo's cheerfulness. 'So am I trapped here?'

'Oh, no. The dragon has other plans for you, at least for the moment.'

'Plans? What plans?'

'How should I know?' Garo asked. 'Do you think the dragon tells me everything?'

Mary Lou shook her head, even though it was too dark for anyone to see. This was all too ridiculous.

'Why should I even believe you?' she demanded.

'You mean because I tried to sacrifice you to the dragon a little while ago?' Garo sighed. 'I suppose there really isn't any particular reason. Well, I did sacrifice myself in your stead, that should count for something. But, no. I think the only thing you'll believe is a demonstration.'

'Demonstration?' Despite herself, Mary Lou was curious.

'Surely. Concentrate on your father.'

Her father? 'What will happen?'

'At least you'll be able to talk.'

Wasn't that what she was trying to do before Garo whispered in her ear? If it truly was Garo. She didn't know if she should be angry, or scared, or just ignore this thing altogether.

Maybe it would be better if she could contact her parents and just leave this place.

She thought of her father. The light was back before her, even stronger than before.

'Daddy?' she called.

She heard her father's voice, talking to someone below her. 'Get ready to find some cover!'

It was working!

Garo's voice was fading away. 'You can see him now.'

'Where?' she asked. For her answer, the light before her blossomed out into a scene of the forest and soldiers. And there, standing behind the others, was her father.

What was he doing with soldiers? Was he in danger? But he seemed to be working with the soldiers, not fighting them.

She hoped she could ask what was going on.

Could her father hear her? 'How do I do this?' Maybe if she looked at him and concentrated. 'I don't know how –' Light pulsed around her father as he looked up at her. Something was happening.

The other soldiers were looking up at her now, and calling out one word over and over again. 'Kennake! Kennake!'

She had to ignore them and concentrate on her father. The halo of light still shimmered around his body, but she thought maybe that was only for her to see. He also looked a little frightened. And just because his daughter was talking to him from someplace up in the sky?

She hoped she could find some way to reassure him.

'Can you hear me?' she called out.

'Mary Lou?' he called back. So not only could he hear her, but he recognised her too!

'Daddy! I'm so glad I found you!'

Another one of the soldiers was shouting at her father. He

glanced at the other man for an instant, then turned his face back to the sky.

'Where are you?' he called.

'I'm not too sure.' How could she explain any of this, especially when the only information she had was all that nonsense from Garo? She actually laughed. 'I'm certainly learning my way around!'

Her father turned away again, as if he needed to talk to somebody else.

She was suddenly very afraid of losing him. She needed to say something else.

'They said I'd be able to talk to people!' she shouted. 'You're my first try.'

Come on, Dad, she thought. Turn round and talk to me.

Instead, the man next to her father looked up as the halo of light formed around him as well.

With a start she realised it was Todd's father, Mr Jackson. He didn't look happy.

'What the hell is that?' he demanded.

Should she talk to him too?

Jackson lifted something towards Mary Lou that glowed a sickly, bluish green.

Garo's voice whispered urgently in her ear. 'You have to leave. He has a piece of the dragon!'

A piece of the dragon? What was that supposed to mean?

'It could hurt your father!' Garo insisted. 'Trust me!'

'Oh!' Mary Lou called. 'This wasn't supposed to happen! Daddy, I've got to go!'

The forest scene faded to a point of light, then that, too, disappeared. Mary Lou was back in darkness.

She felt she wanted to cry. But she wouldn't let herself. Not in front of Garo.

She wished she could have stayed longer. She had so many questions. Why wasn't her father with the neighbours? Were her mother and brother safe? And how about Nick, and Todd, and all the others?

But she had a question for Garo too. 'Why did we have to leave? Were we in danger?'

The other voice hesitated again before it spoke. 'Danger? Some backlash might have hit your father. With us, I'm not too sure. But it would have been very inconvenient.'

Mary Lou had had enough. 'Inconvenient? I had to stop talking to my father because it was inconvenient?'

'Perhaps I've used the wrong words. That man would have attacked us with power from the dragon. But we're with the dragon now. That sort of thing leads to – complications.' Garo sighed. 'I'm afraid I'm not very good at this.'

Mary Lou could agree with that. ' What exactly are you good for?' she demanded.

'I am here to deliver messages. It seems the only role I am allowed to take.'

That's all he ever was, Mary Lou realised, an interpreter of sorts, first with the Anno, and now with the dragon. Not that he had been satisfied with that. 'I think you wanted to be more than a messenger.'

'Oh, that.' She could imagine Garo's charming smile. 'Well, I am never quite what I seem.'

But Mary Lou had had quite enough of Garo's charm too. 'And what am I doing here?' she insisted. 'Can I leave now?'

'No,' Garo replied, his voice much more sober. 'I don't think so.'

'Why?' Mary Lou was getting more exasperated with every word that came out of his mouth. 'Because of the dragon?'

'Everything is because of the dragon. It could take you in an instant. It could take anyone. I don't know why it doesn't.'

Mary Lou didn't know what to say to that.

A moment later, Garo spoke again. 'No, I think I have an idea. I think you have to discover why the dragon is waiting. It's your part. Everyone has a part to play.' He paused a second before adding, 'I think mine is almost done.'

Mary Lou waited for a long moment, listening to all those other voices around her. Garo was silent. She began to wonder if he had left her.

But then he spoke again. 'The dragon won't wait for ever.' His voice was softer than before, the barest of whispers.

'The dragon will consume us all.'

155

Twenty

This was a different kind of pain. The knife-point pricked at his throat. Evan Mills felt a trickle of blood run down his Adam's apple.

The man on the other end of the knife smiled, revealing half a dozen rotting teeth.

'I heard there'd be rich pickin's abroad tonight,' the man allowed. 'Didn't think it would be as easy as this – you bein' a cripple and all.'

If not for the very real knife at his throat, Mills would never have believed this. He held great power inside him and had a dragon's eye hidden in his pocket as well. And he could still barely walk. Oddly enough, physical movement seemed to tax him more than anything Rox or Zachs could come up with.

But the two things that shared his body were oddly silent now. He had managed to run for a moment in the desert. Zachs had used his fireballs and Rox had whisked them away from there with his sorcery. Perhaps all three of them had used up all their strength.

It would be ironic to come so far, only to be killed by a common thief.

Mills wanted to laugh. He had looked like a victim. He could barely drag himself from one doorstep to the next. And there he would collapse, winded, until enough time passed for him to struggle to his next resting place.

He had been glad it was so close to nightfall. He thought he might be less conspicuous after dark. He didn't think about attracting an entirely different kind of attention, until he was grabbed from behind and roughly tossed into an alley.

'What do you want from me?' he managed in a whisper. 'I don't have anything.'

Nothing, he thought, but a priceless jewel that might be his only hope of survival.

'If you give it over now,' his assailant growled, 'I might let you live.'

Give it over now? Did the thief already know about the eye? Wait.

Rox's voice was very faint. But the wizard was awake inside him. Maybe Evan still had a chance.

But somehow he had to stall until the wizard was ready.

'Give what –' he began.

'I've had enough of this!' The thief grabbed a hank of Evan's hair with his free hand. 'Time to cut you!'

The knife nicked quickly into Evan's cheek. He grunted, more at the suddenness of it than the pain.

The thief stuck his face right up into Evan's, so close that their noses almost touched. The man with the knife smiled again. 'Now, I can cut you some more, or you can give me all you're worth. 'Course, if you don't have nothin', like you say, I'll just have to get my fun slicin' you up.'

Evan felt his right hand growing warm. He knew that feeling. It was the beginning of Zachs's fire.

'All right, all right!' Evan groaned. 'Give me a little room, so I can get to my money.'

The thief let go of his hair. 'Even a cripple can learn, can't he?' He took a single step away. 'Man can't walk, he don't deserve any money anyway.'

His eyes narrowed as Evan stood up straight. 'Careful now!' He wiggled his knife. 'I can stab you faster than you can blink!'

And, Evan thought, I can set you on fire before you know what's happened. He looked down at his right hand, waiting for the ball of fire to form in his palm.

But there was no fire. All he saw in his palm was a dull glow.

Where is it? he thought. If we don't do something, we're going to die!

We are doing as much as we can, came the reply. We are doing this together.

157

So this was all they had. Well, if they couldn't beat a simple thief, they didn't deserve to hold the jewel anyway.

His hand was growing hotter. The lines on his palm shone like distant highways seen from a plane at night.

The thief got a glimpse of it as well. 'What's that? Are you hiding gold?'

This was it. He had to work with what he had.

'Nothing I won't give you!' Evan called, throwing his open hand against the thief's face. The thief screamed as his flesh sizzled beneath Zachs's heat. He pulled himself away, bits of cooked flesh still sticking to Evan's palm like scorched fat on a griddle. The burned man wailed as he staggered away, his knife clattering, forgotten, on the paving stones.

Mills leaned against a wall, exhausted again. The thief's wails went on for quite some time, fading at last like some agonised siren in the distance. No one came to see what made the noise. Apparently, in this place, it did not pay to be too curious.

'What's happened to us?' Evan said to the empty street.

'I believe it is a test,' the wizard's voice replied.

'Tests?' Zachs's voice cut in, but with little of his usual energy. 'Fie on all tests!'

'No,' the wizard said, 'I think we have to learn from this one, if we're going to live.'

Evan had had enough of standing up. He let his back slide down the wall until his seat met the pavement. 'What do you mean?' he asked.

'It seems to me that it was very easy for us to gain the dragon's eye.'

Mills wouldn't exactly categorise being tossed about by magical explosions 'easy'. Still, he could see something of Rox's point. He was still amazed at the way they'd tumbled at last against the desert obelisk, with the jewel in front of them, within arm's reach. And there had been another small miracle involved as well.

'We did steal the stone right in front of two very capable wizards –' he said aloud, '– wizards with far more power than the three of us combined.'

'Exactly!' the wizard Rox exclaimed as if Evan had proved his point. 'And why would that be?'

'Zachs is quick!' the light creature whispered. 'Zachs is clever.'

'But you are not so quick or clever as Nunn, the wizard who made you,' Rox chided. 'I don't think Nunn and Obar ever expected the three of us to be together. We had surprise on our side, at least at first. But what made us win?'

Evan didn't have an answer for that, and neither of the other beings spoke with his voice. He sat there for a long moment on the all too quiet city street and looked up at strange stars.

'Maybe', he said at last, 'we were just lucky.'

The wizard's voice chuckled at that. 'If we were, the luck came from the dragon.'

'What are you saying?' Evan asked. 'Why would the dragon give us anything? Is it because you've seen it before?'

The wizard sighed with Evan's lungs. 'I don't think anyone who has truly seen the dragon has lived. I have survived the creature's last coming, along with Obar and Nunn, mostly by hiding from it while it laid waste to the rest of the world.'

Mills was amazed. 'The three great wizards – all hid from the dragon?'

'The dragon is a fearsome thing. It was the only way to survive. Somehow, the dragon's eyes protected us, at least that time. Not, of course, that I really survived the experience. That was the time when the dragon destroyed all around us, and the three of us cowered in fear; the same time that Obar and Nunn chose to kill me and steal my stone.'

Mills still didn't understand. 'But, if the dragon is so horrible, how can you talk about anything like luck?'

'Well,' Rox replied after a moment's pause, 'perhaps "luck" is not the best word. But I do think we were meant to have the jewel, at least for now.'

If he had had any more energy, Mills would have thrown his hands in the air. 'Meant? By whom? By the dragon?'

The wizard sighed. 'Do you want to know the questions I ask myself? How I wonder if the dragon plans everything that happens here? How I sometimes think we are only pawns in

159

some larger game we cannot comprehend? That it doesn't matter what we do, our fate will be the same?'

'Zachs does whatever he wants!' came the whining response. Never had the light creature sounded more like a petulant child who wasn't getting his way. And never had Zachs sounded more powerless.

'Actually,' the wizard answered, 'in my more cheerful moments, I believe it does matter. All we really know is that the dragon has brought us all here, for some purpose we can't fathom. But I hope that we come here not as pawns but as potential, with the possibility that our own actions will cause us to succeed or fail.'

The wizard paused and hummed a snatch of melody, as if his positive thoughts would turn night into day. 'It sounds good, doesn't it? I have no idea if it is true. For all I know, the dragon will destroy us, like it has destroyed everybody since the beginning of time. Perhaps three people had this very conversation a thousand years ago. Perhaps three more will join in this fine discussion a thousand years from today.'

Mills opened his eyes suddenly. He had been drifting as the magician had been using Evan's mouth. 'This is all a great theory, but the stone, rather than giving us strength, seems to be draining us.'

'As I said, this is the test.'

'If it is, I think we're close to failing.' And there's another irony, thought teacher-turned-vice-principal Mills.

'But there must be a key!' the wizard insisted. 'If we can only find it, we will be worthy of the dragon.'

Mills tried to suppress a yawn. 'How can we find a key if all we want to do is sleep?'

'Perhaps we should sleep first. We at least need the energy to think. But we must find someplace protected, lest someone slit our throat before we have a chance to wake again.'

That, Mills agreed, was the most practical idea he had heard. Somehow, he managed to stagger back to his feet and, using the right-hand wall for support, made his slow way back into the cul-de-sac the thief had brought him to, looking for a dark corner where he might be safe for the night.

Twenty-one

It was certainly a puzzle.

With his own dragon's eye, Obar could track the jewel. Or so the theory went. And, in practice, he was led to the neighbourhood of the tavern. But the eye itself seemed elusive. One moment Obar's eye would tell him that the new jewel was straight ahead, a moment later that he had passed it by, or that it was to left or right, in the air or under the ground. The dragon's eye seemed to move about as quickly, and with as much reason, as a raindrop in a hurricane.

And he had to be careful with his dragon's eye, keeping it out of view of others, especially in a place such as this. As night fell, people left the streets, except for the occasional group of four or more, banded together for safety, Obar would guess. There were others out here, too, single individuals who lurked in shadows and gangs of rowdies looking to pick a fight. Some of these others would stop as Obar passed, deciding, no doubt, if he was worth their effort.

After all, he looked like an old man. He *was* an old man, really; with all that he had been through with the dragon, not even Obar could guess his own age. But he was sustained by the power of the jewel.

A couple of times, these low-lifes approached Obar, saying something like 'Father! I'd like a word with you!' or 'Help a poor beggar buy a meal!' He'd resorted to some small parlour trick to discourage them, had green light shine from his eyes, perhaps, or suddenly walked a foot off the ground. Usually he left these little dramatics to his brother Nunn, but now and again they had their place. Still, he had to be careful. Showing off his magic caused people to fear him. He couldn't stay too long here, then, or become too well known. If too many thought of him as a monster, he could be facing an angry mob.

So why couldn't he find the eye? Obar, frankly, had no idea. When the dragon had disappeared, so long ago, it had taken four of the eyes with it, and no amount of Obar's searching showed the slightest trace of their whereabouts.

Now, in short order, that Constance Smith had simply picked up an eye somewhere, and the young Mary Lou had announced that the remaining eyes were there for the taking. But Obar had one snatched away in front of him, and now the second one seemed to be always floating just beyond his grasp.

This was the dragon's doing. There could be no doubt about it. Even now, the dragon wanted to manipulate all of them, to lead them towards who knew what. Not that they couldn't escape the dragon; he was proof of that.

But, if he wanted the other eye, he feared he couldn't escape the dragon any more.

He stepped into an alley, out of sight of the few late-night passers-by, and pulled the green stone from the hiding place within his clothes. It glowed as he held it, an object both of serenity and power.

He looked at his eye, his little piece of the dragon. What did he really know about this thing?

The jewel gave him power. The jewel gave him strength. He had learned to use the jewel for a thousand different things. If he lost it, he would die.

But he still didn't understand it.

What did the eye really have to do with the dragon? Maybe the creature was aware of every time the magician used a tiny bit of its power. Maybe the last time the dragon scoured the world, Obar did not escape, but was spared for some other purpose.

He looked at the jewel, and thought, tell me what to do.

To his surprise, something answered.

Tomorrow, it said. Or something like that. But with that one word, Obar knew that he would find the proper time and place, and he would be shown the jewel at last. He suspected that he would not be the only one. But once the dragon had revealed its secret, it was up to Obar to seize the opportunity.

The jewels were more important now than ever. Obar had never known the dragon to pay so much attention to the details of humanity. The dragon must be coming soon.

But Obar had to wait. It was part of the dragon's plan. And only by accepting some part of that plan could he succeed.

The wizard sighed. At least now he could return to the inn and rest, perhaps restore a bit of his energy without using the gem in his hand.

He turned and headed back down the hill. He had been gone far longer than he had planned. He hoped nothing had happened to Maggie or Nick in his absence.

Nick woke up with a start. It was totally dark, and for a moment he couldn't remember where he was.

'Hush, now,' Maggie whispered beside him.

The world came back to him; the new world, with the inn, and the lumpy bed, and Maggie the Volunteer by his side.

'Wha –' Nick began.

He found a hand placed over his mouth.

'Whisper,' Maggie instructed. 'There are people about.'

She took her hand away.

'Other guests?' Nick whispered back.

'I think not,' Maggie replied as she shifted on the bed. 'Other guests would make more noise.'

Nick listened a moment to the silence. A board creaked in the hallway outside their room, but nothing more.

'I suggest we both get away from the bed,' Maggie continued, 'and the door. I think we're about to have visitors.'

Nick rolled over to the edge of the bed farthest from the door. He swung his feet silently to the floor, groping for where he'd left his sword and scabbard. Maggie had got out on the other side. Nick had no idea where she was headed. The room was too small to give them many good hiding places.

The door flew open with a bang, as if someone had kicked it. Three men rushed into the room, forming a line on the side of the bed nearest to the door.

One man held up a lantern as two others pointed swords towards the bedclothes. But there was no longer anyone there.

'They're not here!' One of the swordsmen looked back to the man with the lantern. 'Is this the right room?'

'Pit says at least two of them came up here and never left,' the lantern man replied. 'Search the –'

Maggie swung out from behind the door, feet first, kicking one of the swordsmen on to the bed. As he fell forward, she used his back as a springboard, diving and rolling by the leader with the lantern. Before the man could even turn, she hit the floor and kicked the lamp from his hand. It shattered against the wall above the headboard, sending oil and crimson embers down on to the bed as Maggie scooted out the door.

'Kill them!' their leader shouted in the half darkness, the only real light coming from the outside hallway. 'We'll find the money later.'

Nick stood up on the bed's far side. 'You're welcome to try.' He pulled his sword free from its scabbard.

The man who once held the lamp ran to the hallway, pursuing Maggie. The swordsman who had fallen on the bed pushed himself back so that the mattress was between Nick and him. The second swordsman had reached the foot of the bed and was inching around it towards the far corner where Nick now stood.

'We have him trapped!' the second man shouted as he rounded the bed behind his fellow, his sword held before him. 'This should be short work!'

Nick's own sword tugged in his grip, urging him forward towards battle. He took a single step, balancing on the balls of his feet, waiting for the fight to begin. He had done this often enough now so that his muscles knew how to move with the sword, adding force to the skill of the enchanted blade.

There was a sudden whoosh of air to Nick's left as new light flickered into the room.

The nearer swordsman risked a look away from his opponent. 'The bed's on fire!'

'Well, kill him quick then,' called the man on the far side of the bed, 'and let's get out of here! The bed's Pit's worry!'

Nick's sword was already slicing towards the swordsman as he looked back. The man had to raise his own weapon quickly, awkwardly, barely to parry the blow. But his sudden movement threw him off-balance, sending him stumbling towards the burning bed. He pulled himself up short, trying both to find his feet and face his opponent. He was too late. Nick's sword pierced his heart.

Nick knew enough not to draw the sword out at once. The space here was so narrow that the dying swordsman acted as a shield against his still-living companion beyond.

The sword quivered in Nick's hand as it accepted the blood, and he could feel again the blood energy flooding up his sword arm and through his body.

Nick glanced to his left. The fire had already consumed half the bed and filled the room with leaping shadows. The heat from the flames was making him sweat. Smoke rose to the rafters. In a moment he wouldn't be able to breathe. He would have to leave this corner, or he would be trapped. He stepped forward, manoeuvring around the end of the bed. The shrinking swordsman was still on the point of his weapon, Nick's sword-spawned energy enough so that he could carry the shrivelling husk forward with one arm while the sword drank its fill. The whole room around him seemed tinged with red, although whether that was the result of the flames or a gift from the sword, Nick didn't know.

'What are you?' the remaining swordsman called as Nick approached. 'What have you done?'

Nick angled his sword at the floor, allowing the blood-drained body to slip off the blade.

The man backed towards the doorway, but he was trapped by another fight in the hall with Maggie's and the third man's swords flashing back and forth.

'Keep away!' the second swordsman called as he waved his blade before him. 'I'm far better with this sword than my brother!'

'So I'm killing brothers today?' Nick replied casually. He could hear the blood pounding in his ears and the heavy breathing of his opponent. The whole world was crimson before him.

His sword needed more blood. Who was Nick to deny it?

His opponent held his own sword close to his chest. 'Listen,' he said quickly. 'This was all a mistake. Maybe we can work it out. I can go back to my employers, tell them there was nothing here. Bad information, you see –'

Nick stepped around the foot of the bed, his sword pointing forward like a hunting dog sensing prey.

'Too late for mistakes,' Nick said. The sword needed blood. And Nick needed the power it gave him.

It was only now, using the sword, fighting, drinking the blood of his enemy, that Nick felt alive.

He moved around the final corner of the bed, his steps as sure as a dancer's. The sword swayed in his hand, overjoyed there was more nourishment to come. The last blood-stains on the blade shrank and vanished as it drank them in, cleaning itself for its next meal.

His opponent's eyes looked very large in the firelight.

'No!' He dropped his sword and turned to run. 'You won't –' He pulled up short, barely avoiding the clashing weapons in the hall.

Nick's sword took the man in the back. Their latest victim screamed as the blade sucked his life away.

'What?' The final swordsman stumbled back, undone for a second by his companion's agony. Maggie stepped into his fallen guard, slicing him in the shoulder.

The wounded man looked startled for an instant, then enraged. He shrieked as he ran towards Maggie, flailing his blade in circles.

The power flowed into Nick, more than he had ever felt before, as if sword and handler were becoming one and the same. Nick had felt a little of this in their last battle, in the desert. It had been very difficult to give up that feeling. Only Obar's magic had pulled him away.

But Obar wasn't here any more. And Nick never wanted this feeling to end. He moaned with the sheer joy of it, the feeling of power and well-being that filled every inch of him. This is the way he would feel for ever.

Done with its newest feast, the sword angled downwards, throwing the dried corpse into the hall.

The last swordsman leapt back, jumping away from his fallen comrade.

Nick's sword took this one in the side, between the ribs. Nick shook as the sword drank even faster than before.

Out in the hall, Maggie said, 'That was more difficult than I'd hoped. I'm glad it's over. Nick?' She stepped into the doorway. 'Are you all right?'

All right? Nick had never felt better. The feeling was wonderful, power flowing through him in waves. He had trouble keeping his eyes open. Soon, he would be nothing but energy and would float above the world.

Finished again, the sword allowed Nick to free its blade.

Even with his eyes open, the world was a crimson sea. And the sea would go on for ever.

Nick felt his sword-hand rise again, ready to attack.

'Nick!' someone shouted. 'What are you doing?'

Nick blinked. He knew that voice.

It was Maggie. The sword wanted her blood too. This time, Obar wasn't here to stop it.

Somewhere deep inside himself Nick found the power to speak. 'Maggie!' he managed. 'Run!'

Maggie leapt aside. The sword slashed through the air where she had been a second before.

'No!' Nick shouted. He grabbed the sword with both hands, trying to pull it away. 'Maggie! Out of here!'

'What be this?' a voice called behind him.

Nick and his sword turned round. There, at the top of the stairs, stood Pit.

'An altercation?' Pit called in feigned surprise. 'They must have got by me while I slept. 'Tis fortunate you –' He stopped and stared past Nick into the room beyond. 'Fire! 'Tis a fire! Everybody out! Oh, woe is Pit!'

Nick was already running down the hall, his sword before him. He skewered Pit with one smooth motion, the innkeeper's single eye staring down at the blade as he died.

The energy poured into Nick again, sweet power, but never enough to fill him up. He would have more. He would have it for ever.

But not Maggie! No, he would deny the sword some things for as long as he could. He hoped she had got away. He wouldn't – couldn't – look back.

He breathed in time with the gulping sword, short quick breaths for the work ahead, work that would never end. Don't look back, he told himself. Never look back.

The sword was done and he threw the useless corpse to the floor. It tumbled down the stairs, so dry that the remains broke apart when they hit the landing, leaving little more than dust.

The sword before him, Nick hurried down past their most recent meal.

He would find what he needed on the streets.

Twenty-two

'Now,' Snake said with a smile, 'why don't the two of you join me in the warmth of the kitchen?'

So, Todd thought, Snake wasn't going to kill him right away. Maybe, if Todd talked fast enough, he could keep the tavern keeper from killing him altogether. After all, he'd got himself out of bad scrapes before. Not, of course, that any of them had involved crossbows.

Sala asked the question for him. 'So you'll let him live?'

'Where's your thinking, daughter?' Snake laughed. He seemed to be in a much better mood than before. 'This boy comes with a group of rich traders. We should be able to collect a fine ransom for him before we kill him.'

Todd was getting really annoyed at the cheerfulness of the tavern keeper. He guessed if it was only a matter of time until he was murdered, he might as well say something. 'You'll get money and kill me anyway? I've got a few friends who wouldn't like that.'

Snake roared with laughter. 'You've got friends? Well, then, I guess Snake will have to kill them too!' The innkeeper drew a thumb across his throat. 'Snake does what he wants around here. That's the great thing about Hopeless. It's who you know and what you'll pay.'

'Hopeless?' Todd asked.

'The name of the town! Oh, those fancy fellows down at the docks may call it Port Town or some such, but all us up on the hill know the real name of this place!'

He waved the crossbow at Todd. 'Now I think we've had quite enough conversation. It's time you went in and wrote a little note to your shipmates.'

169

Todd was becoming more amazed with the tavern keeper by the minute. 'You've already said you're going to kill me. Now you expect me to write a note?'

'Well,' Snake said with a jolly wink, 'you do have to decide if the rest of your life will be pleasant or painful. But, by my calculation, we've got fifteen fingers and toes to cut off before we even get to your writing hand!'

Todd had to force himself not to look down at his hands and feet. He wouldn't give this creep the satisfaction of showing fear. If and when he got out of this fix, it wouldn't be by talking.

Snake waved his crossbow towards the doorway. 'Now get moving, or I'll give you a demonstration of my cutting skills.'

Todd glanced at Sala as he turned toward the kitchen. At least the girl had the decency to look upset as he walked on by. This set-up seemed to have nothing to do with her. Hell, you could never trust fathers anyway.

'Now,' Snake mentioned as he waved Todd in front of him, 'Todd, was it?'

Todd almost stumbled with that revelation. That bastard must never really have left the kitchen. He must have heard every word Todd said to Sala.

'If you want to hide,' Snake said behind him, 'next time try the garbage.'

Todd felt the point of the arrow as Snake nudged the crossbow into his back. Todd led the way into the kitchen. It was a long room, with a great central table running its entire length, and a series of brick ovens and stoves on either side. At the far end of the room, beside a second door, hung three large cleavers and two large knives. The place smelled better than the yard out back, but not by much. Cooking smells were overlaid with the odour of something sour. Todd thought maybe it was rancid fat.

Snake continued to talk behind him. 'It is a shame that your three travelling companions met with ill luck and were tragically killed, oh –'

No! Todd couldn't believe it! Wilbert and Stanley and Mrs Smith, dead? How could Snake know something like that?

Todd wished again that he had stayed back at the inn, to fight and maybe die with his friends.

'Exactly when?' Snake mused.

Todd no longer felt the arrow in his back. He risked a glance behind him and saw that Snake had paused to consult a large clock on a shelf next to the doorway they had just passed through. The clock was a square contraption with a glass door that let you see the heavy weights beneath the clock face.

'– I'd say in another two hours or so,' Snake concluded. He looked back to Todd, his smile not quite so full. 'Let us hope they had plenty of money on their persons when they died – it will dispose me to like you better.'

So they weren't dead after all. At least not yet. Todd hoped that none of them would have to die. Snake had no idea of Mrs Smith's special powers after all.

They'd have an even better chance if Todd could get away from this place and warn them. If only he hadn't blown everything, just to meet a girl!

'We'll have to comment on their tragic passing in the note. Maybe, if you do just as I say, we'll even manage to feed you a meal or two.' Snake pointed the crossbow at the long table that filled the room's centre. 'Sit.'

Todd plopped down on a stool at the table's side.

The tavern keeper turned to his daughter. 'Sala. Pen and paper, if you please.' She nodded her head, and ran from the room as if her father was chasing her.

Snake turned back to the seated Todd. The smile had vanished from the tavern keeper's face.

'You want to run, don't you, boy?' He waved towards the knives on the farthest wall. 'Or maybe you'd like to stab me in the back? And surely you'd like to be alone with my daughter for a few minutes, for a little fun in the alley?' He chuckled, as if that last suggestion was particularly amusing. Even with the laugh, though, the smile didn't come back to his face.

'I'd love to have you try. Any or all.' Snake laid the crossbow down on the far side of the table, just out of Todd's reach. 'One move from you and I'd cut you down so fast your head wouldn't even know the rest of you was dead. It would cost me a lot of

171

money, but I'd love to do it.' Snake took a step closer, as if he'd fight with Todd right now. 'It would be worth it, just to see your blood pumping out on the floor.'

Todd stared up at the tavern keeper. For a moment, he thought it would be worth it too.

The door at the far end of the kitchen slammed open and Sala hurried in, a jar in one hand, a quill pen in the other.

The gracious smile returned to Snake's face. 'Now,' he continued to Todd, 'I want this note to be in your own words. It's just that your own words had better repeat mine.'

Sala placed the pen and the jar full of ink down on the table in front of Todd. Snake plopped a book down next to pen and ink. The book fell open as it hit the wood; it was full of columns of figures, a ledger of some sort.

'Use one of the blank pages towards the back,' Snake instructed. 'And make it sincere, or we'll enclose something personal of yours to let them know we're serious.'

Todd could have sworn he felt something then, like a tiny earthquake, the table shifting beneath his arms. But the tavern keeper didn't seem to notice. Instead, he stared off into space for an instant before dictating:

'I am in terrible straits. The others with me have met a bloody death. The only reason I am still alive is that I have convinced my captors that you will pay them a handsome sum for my return. Please obey all the instructions and pay the amount specified on the other note attached. It is the only way you shall ever see me alive.'

Todd started to write down what the other man had said. He needed a little time to find a way out of here.

'Then, of course, you sign your name.' Snake looked back at Todd and nodded smartly. 'That should do it nicely.'

He slapped Todd heartily on the back. 'I hope you have some good friends on board that boat. A high ransom equals a pleasant death.'

Todd didn't dare tell him there was no one left on board the boat they had come in. It was just one more thing that could go wrong, one more way he could die sooner. He watched the crossbow out of the corner of his eye. He knew Snake had put it on the table so that Todd would make a try for it. It was probably a good way for Todd to start losing fingers.

No, he'd have to find a way to surprise his gracious host. After that, maybe he could push Snake's head into the garbage out back. It didn't much matter to Todd if Snake's body was still attached.

The room lurched again, more suddenly and violently than before. In that instant, Todd thought he saw a flash of green. That dragon's eye was very close, then. Was it trying to show Todd its hiding place?

This time, even Snake seemed to notice the change. His smile faltered for an instant. But then both quake and light were gone.

With a final nod towards Todd, Snake picked the crossbow off the far end of the table.

'I've been neglecting my duties far too long,' he said in a much gruffer tone. He walked over to the other door. 'Sam! Get your ugly butt in here!'

Snake stepped back into the room as a new figure more than filled the doorway. The newcomer was so large that he had to duck beneath the door frame to enter the room. He was big the other way too, his massive girth just fitting down the aisle formed between the table and a great brick stove.

Snake talked to the big man for a moment in a low tone. From what Todd could catch of it, the tavern keeper was repeating the stuff about the ransom note, followed by the words 'and if he doesn't –'. The final instructions were beyond Todd's hearing.

Snake turned back to his captive one more time. 'Sam doesn't talk, but he has other strong points. He's quite good at crushing things, and pulling things apart.'

Sam grinned in agreement.

'Finish the note quickly and Sam won't need to help.' Snake paused by the far door, hanging the crossbow on a hook above the knives and cleavers. He glanced back at Sam.

'Tie him up as soon as the note is ready!'

The room shifted again before the large man could gesture in reply. The candles on the table blew out as a hot wind passed through, but it grew no darker, for bright green light shone suddenly through cracks in the ceiling and the walls.

The green light vanished. The room was still.

Sam lit a taper from a lantern that had survived the wind and went round relighting the candles.

'I was told this wouldn't happen.' Snake's voice was not much more than a whisper.

Even the huge fellow looked frightened as he darted about, as if only by lighting every candle and lamp in the room might they begin to be safe.

The power was very close. Todd had managed to use one of the dragon's eyes before. Could he make this eye do something as well?

'Well,' Snake said, his voice stronger, ' 'tis done now.' He turned to his daughter, who stood by the far end of the table. 'And you!'

He raised his hand as if he would strike her. 'We'll have a little talk once business is concluded.' His hand reached out for her, but slowly, almost tenderly. He stroked a lock of her red hair with his knuckles. 'Better yet, we'll talk up in your room.'

He left the kitchen, pulling the door shut behind him.

His lighting work done, Sam leaned against one of the ovens that wasn't in use. Sala looked from the big man to Todd. 'You'd better write the note. I've got to get to work cooking and cleaning up the kitchen.'

Todd looked at the open book before him. He supposed he should try to write some sort of note, just to buy a little time while he figured out some way to get away from here, or get closer to the eye. He looked up at the big man. Sam stared back at him, his gaze fixed on Todd's face. The massive man didn't even seem to blink.

Todd wondered how fast the big guy was. Maybe, if he could distract this monster, he could make a break for the back door. Except, then, he'd have to run back down that long alley and past the front door of the tavern.

And he'd have to leave the eye behind.

It didn't sound like the best of plans.

Hopeless was a good name for this place.

Sam pointed at the book and made a rasping sound deep in his throat. The big guy wanted Todd to get to work.

For the moment, he would. He picked up the pen, dipped it in the ink and brought it over to the book.

A great drop of ink fell from the tip, spreading a black stain across his half-written note. How could you write with these things anyway?

He stared at the quill in his hand, wondering suddenly if he could use it as some sort of weapon. But even though it had a sharp point, it was much too fragile, especially if he was going to use it against something like Sam.

The green pulsed again, the room filled with light as this time the table erupted before Todd, as if the centre of the wood before him had become a volcano from which green lava flowed.

Sam pushed his back against the oven, as if he might crawl inside to get away from the light.

The eye! Todd thought. Give me the eye!

But then the light was gone again.

Sam stepped forward, glowering, as if he hadn't been frightened out of his mind a second before. Maybe, Todd thought, those green lights showed all the time back in this room. This time, Sam grunted at Sala to get back to work. Apparently ordering others around calmed the large man down.

Pans clattered as Sala sorted through one of the many piles that littered the other end of the table. Sam stared down at the point where the green light had erupted a moment before, as if the old wood held some secret.

Sala retrieved an enormous frying pan and made her way down the aisle. She held the pan with both hands as she approached the large guard.

'Excuse me, Sam.'

As he turned towards her, she swung the pan so that it hit him full in the face. Sam was thrown back, his head cracking against the brick oven behind him.

Todd was on his feet immediately.

'We have to get out of here!' Sala called.

'We?' Todd asked.

Sala looked down at the frying pan. 'I have to go too. Father will do worse than kill me!'

The large man's eyes snapped open from where he rested, still standing, against the oven.

Todd shouted a warning.

Sam looked down at Sala. She looked very small next to him. He shook his head sadly, as if hurt that she would try such a thing.

'Sam!' Sala said between clenched teeth, 'if you don't get out of my way, I'll have to kill you!'

In answer, Sam reached forward to grab her. Sala danced back, barely avoiding his grasp. The large man pushed away from the oven, swaying for a moment as if he was having trouble gaining his balance.

Sala ran to the row of knives and cleavers. She grabbed the longer knife and turned back towards Sam as he began to walk slowly towards her.

'I'll use it!' she threatened, her voice more a hoarse whisper than a shout. 'I warned you when you did those things!'

Sam grinned at that and walked faster.

Todd turned away from the two of them. The back door was free and clear. Sala was trying to keep things quiet, to avoid attracting any more attention. And Sam couldn't talk. If Todd ran now, he had a good chance of getting out of here before anyone could raise an alarm.

Sala made a small, frightened sound as the large man bore down on her, a sound that froze Todd. He couldn't leave.

He looked back at Sala as she stabbed Sam in the chest. He stopped, staring down at the knife sticking from his breastbone as if he couldn't imagine how it got there. He pulled the blade from his flesh and tossed the knife aside. A trickle of blood ran down his shirt. He swung one great hand forward, catching one of Sala's arms as she tried to run away.

He lifted her up. She swung beneath his giant fist like a rag doll. He stared at her for a moment, the only sound his heavy breathing.

'No, Sam,' Sala whispered. Her eyes were wide and desperate. 'I can be nice to you. Remember?'

There was a loud snap as Sam lifted her higher. Sala screamed.

The giant was hurting her. Todd had to do something.

Where was the eye now?

To hell with the eye! He needed a real weapon and the large man blocked the aisle between Todd and the wall of knives. But Todd had learned a lot in a hundred playground fights. If somebody refused to get out of your way, you simply went around him.

Todd jumped on top of the table and ran, dodging past piles of pots and plates. The large man gaped as Todd ran by and leapt from the far end of the table to grab the crossbow.

The giant reacted at last as Todd hit the floor. Sam lumbered towards Todd, still holding the now limp Sala at arm's length.

The big man was moving fast. Todd swung the crossbow round to face his opponent and pulled the trigger. The arrow leapt forward, pushing Todd back against the wall.

The large man gasped as the arrow sank into his throat. As he clawed at it with both hands Sala fell to the floor.

The giant sank to his knees, his face turning a sickly shade of bluish grey. He couldn't breathe. The arrow must have crushed his windpipe. It broke off in his hand. He held the shaft up in triumph as he fell forward.

Todd approached him cautiously. He was no longer breathing. Still, Todd hopped back up on the table rather than climb over the huge form.

Sala groaned where she lay on the floor beyond Sam.

'Sala!' Todd called. 'Wake up!'

'God.' She grimaced as she opened her eyes. 'I think I broke something.'

It sounded to Todd like Sam had snapped a bone in her arm when he held her aloft. 'I'll get you out of here,' Todd whispered. 'I know people who can fix that sort of thing in no time.' It seemed to him that broken bones would be no problem at all for wizards.

'What is this mess here?' a voice remarked loudly behind them. Todd looked round. Snake had returned.

'I leave you alone for five minutes,' Snake continued, 'and

you kill one of my best workers.' The smile spread across his face one more time. 'I guess it's time to kill you too.' He reached back and pulled the largest of the cleavers from the wall.

But Todd was no longer defenceless. He had held on to the crossbow. He looked around quickly. There must be a supply of arrows someplace in this room.

Green light pulsed through the kitchen as the eye announced itself again.

Not now! It was so bright this time, Todd had to throw his arm in front of his eyes.

And then the light was gone again. Todd lowered his arm and blinked as he looked over to the tavern keeper.

'Looking for these?' Snake asked, as he held up a quiver that had been hidden under the table. He tossed the arrows back on the floor and started to laugh.

Twenty-three

Nick ran down the street, looking for blood.

Three men rounded a corner in front of him. They stared at the runner in surprise.

'Whoa, lad!' one called.

'Looks like he's seen his dead father's ghost!' the second one added.

'No, he's just been doing a little bit of theft, haven't you, boy?' the third one suggested with a laugh. 'Why don't you toss the money over here? We'll take much better care of it.'

'Careful!' the first one called. 'He's got a sword!'

'Oh, now,' the last one answered easily. 'We've all got swords.'

With that remark, all three men unsheathed their weapons from their scabbards.

'Now, why don't you just put that sword away,' the third man continued, 'and we can have a discussion like civilised thieves?'

'I – can't,' Nick managed. Whatever they were, thieves or tradesmen, he didn't want to have to kill them as well. It took all his energy to keep the sword from lunging at the three.

'And why, pray tell, is that?' the third man asked.

'I need blood,' Nick gasped as the sword took over again and Nick was beyond speech. The world turned a hazy red as it weaved a fantastic pattern, keeping the three others at bay.

'He's damned good!' one of them called.

'We may be able to get this boy a job,' a second one agreed. 'If our young friend would kindly put down that sword.'

Nick's arm darted between the two. His sword pierced the shoulder of the third.

The man screamed as the sword entered his flesh.

Power filled Nick in waves, so much power that it would take him beyond strength and make him weak again.

'What has he done to Axos?' one of the other swordsmen called in fright.

'The sword is cursed!' his companion agreed.

The two others returned the attack. Nick pulled at his own blade, but it seemed stuck in the dying man's flesh, greedily taking his life fluid.

Nick jumped back, hand still clutching the sword-hilt. He ducked one blade as the other struck him in the side. There was a moment of pain when the point lanced his flesh, but it was distant, as if the wound belonged to somebody else. Nick pulled his own sword free at last, staggering backwards, the gash in his side strangely warm.

One man watched Nick warily as the other tended to their fallen comrade.

'Is he still alive?' the one watching Nick asked.

'We'll have to get him help,' the other said as he kneeled down to lift the dying man from the ground.

'Ah, demon!' the first said as he supported the wounded man's other side. 'We'll have to find you and kill you another day.'

The two healthy swordsmen carried their dying comrade swiftly away. Nick stared after them, his sword tugging at his arm as if it wanted him to follow.

Nick tried to take a step after them, but the cobblestones refused to support his feet. His sneakers slipped from under him and somehow he found himself sitting in the street.

They had called him a demon. Is that what he had become?

The sword tugged again in his hand, left, and left again. He looked down at the blade.

The wound was on his left side. Now that the others were gone, the sword wanted his blood.

Nick shuddered. What was happening to him? He had less control over this weapon every time he used it. He had tried to kill Maggie twice. The sword gave him wild, euphoric strength, but only so he could kill some more. There seemed to be no end to it.

But there was an end. He could let the sword have its way, slicing into Nick as it took his own blood. It would fill him with energy as it drained his life away, until – what? Maybe he would explode with euphoria at the instant of his death.

This was no way to live. There could be worse ways to die.

'Okay, sword,' he whispered, letting the blade swing towards his wound. 'Our last meal.'

'Wait!' someone called from the shadows.

Nick pulled his sword back in front of him. It sounded like another victim. They seemed to be lining up tonight.

A figure stepped out of the shadows. Staggered would be a better word. This man could barely walk. But then, neither could Nick. Maybe they could have a swordfight in slow motion, one person waiting patiently for the other to parry his blow.

But maybe, Nick thought, he didn't have to kill himself. Maybe he could let go of the sword as it took this new victim, could leave the damned thing alone as it drank its fill of blood again. Maybe Nick could leave this place and never think of swords again. That is, if he could get anywhere with his own blood pouring out of him.

But if he was going to survive the night, he supposed he had better stand up. He somehow managed to get his feet under him and slowly lifted himself into a crouch. The hand without the sword touched the ground to keep him from falling.

He took a deep breath. The sword would give him strength to stand. It needed him.

'Nick?'

He looked at the man's face in the pale light of the stars. It was Mr Mills.

The sword sensed fresh nourishment. The strength was pouring back into him. He could stand easily. And the sword wanted more.

But not this. Not someone from the neighbourhood. Nick had to warn him away while he could still talk.

'Mr Mills,' he rasped, his voice a hoarse monotone, as if the exhaustion had stripped away all his feelings too. 'Get away from here. I can't control this thing.'

To Nick's surprise, Mr Mills laughed.

'I can't run anywhere,' his old vice principal replied. 'I'm not who you think I am.'

Nick had no idea what Mr Mills meant. Maybe it had something to do with the desert and Mills running from both Obar and Nunn. But Mills didn't look very healthy. He was walking bent over forward, like an old man in pain.

'Or should I say', Mills added, '*we* aren't.'

Nick could feel the vibration first in his sword-hand. It travelled down his arm and across his chest, spreading up and down, until his whole body craved the joy of blood.

'I can't stop this!' Nick cried as the sword lunged for Mr Mills.

The point stopped an inch from the neighbour's chest. The fingers on Nick's sword-hand went numb. The sword dropped from his fingers and clattered on the street.

Nick found himself sitting down again. The strength the sword had suddenly given him had just as quickly vanished.

'I didn't have to cut you,' Nick whispered. He looked up at Mr Mills. 'You did that somehow, didn't you?'

'Sometimes,' Mills said, his voice suddenly deeper, 'the magic will work.'

A moment later he added in a more normal voice, 'We did it. I'm not one person, I'm three.'

Mr Mills straightened up and stretched.

'Zachs can feel the fire!' he called, this time in the high, breathless voice of an eager child.

The voice turned deep and reflective. 'Some of the pain is gone.'

Nick sat there and watched, almost too exhausted to think. So Mr Mills had three voices. And Nick was slave to a blood-drinking sword. Both made an equal amount of sense.

'Remember when I said this was a test?' The deeper, elder voice sounded excited. 'I think we might have passed the first part of it.'

Mr Mills laughed in amazement. 'You mean, all we had to do was use our power?'

'It's quite possible,' the deeper voice using Mills's mouth replied. 'Maybe that was part of the problem. We were holding it all within, as if we were our own little universe. Maybe we have to let some of it go.'

He glanced at Nick and sighed. 'We are a complex creature.'

Nick nodded. They were all far more complex than he ever could have guessed back on Chestnut Circle.

Mr Mills shook his head. 'You mean that maybe the power isn't just for us?'

'It may mean,' the deeper voice intoned, 'that perhaps the power isn't for us at all.'

'Zachs doesn't need it!' the child interrupted. 'Zachs has power of his own!'

'Well,' the deep voice replied reassuringly. 'Perhaps you will again, once we have freed ourselves of our obligation.'

Mills looked down at Nick then, a hint of surprise on his face, as if he only now remembered there was somebody else there.

'Now, Nick,' he said with a grin, 'maybe we can do something about healing that wound.'

His wound? That was something Nick had almost forgotten about. He looked to his left and saw that his side was covered with blood. The damage must be worse than he thought. He still didn't feel any pain there. He couldn't feel anything at all.

'Now,' the deep voice rumbled, 'let's see if we can get close enough to it.'

Mr Mills groaned as he squatted by Nick's side. 'I'll know we're getting better when our knees begin to work. Now just sit still for a bit.'

Nick nodded. He didn't have the energy to do anything else.

Mills's fingers glowed green where he touched the side of Nick's shirt.

'There,' the deep voice murmured. 'It's closed.'

There was a moment of extreme cold where the sword had punctured his side. Then that feeling was gone too, replaced by a dull ache. Maybe that was better than no pain at all. Nick was too tired to check. He would have to take his – or maybe their – word for it.

For the first time, Mr Mills stood up straight. 'This really is amazing.' He smiled down at Nick. 'Come on now. I think we're going to be good for each other. But we have to find a place to get some sleep.'

Nick suddenly found this whole thing funny.

He started laughing. 'How can I?' he managed, gasping for air. 'I can't walk and you sure can't carry me.'

Mr Mills was silent for a moment before the deep voice answered, 'Well, we can't carry you in any regular sort of way.'

Mills spread his hands in the air above Nick's still seated form. 'Allow me,' the deep voice said.

Nick felt something like a mild breeze rushing all around his body. He looked down, and saw that he was floating, buoyed up by a gentle cushion of green.

Sure. Why not?

'Truly amazing,' Mills said.

'For now,' the deep voice agreed, 'it gets better every time. I'm sure it is more complicated than that.'

'Zachs will fly again!' the child cheered.

'With the dragon', the deep voice added, 'it is always more complicated.'

There was a dragon. Nick remembered that. And the green glow. That meant a dragon's eye. They were using a dragon's eye. Nick must be more out of it than he had thought.

'We will all fly again,' Mr Mills said in his own voice.

Nick's eyes closed as all the tension left his muscles.

He was flying now.

Twenty-four

There was more than one way to use a crossbow. Todd held on to the heavy wooden cross-piece with both hands, ready to swing it like a club.

Snake grinned at him where he stood at the entrance to the kitchen. 'You'd like that, wouldn't you, one on one? It's too bad I can't oblige you.'

He stepped aside and waved. Two other men strode forward into the kitchen. They both looked a lot like Snake, with muscles and beards and clothes that had never seen a washing.

Snake shook his head in mock sorrow. 'You could have got away, you know. You must like my daughter a great deal, don't you?' He glanced at the two men who had just entered the room. 'Maybe I'll let you live long enough to watch.'

Todd asked the question, even though he knew Snake wanted him to.

'Watch?'

Snake rewarded Todd with the return of his smile. 'I like to give my men a little treat.' He waved first to his prostrate daughter, then to the newcomers. 'I think these two deserve to be given a treat right now.'

A treat? From the smiles on the other men's faces, Todd knew just what that meant. Snake was giving his daughter's body to his men, and now two of them were going to rape her right in front of him.

'Hey,' Snake called to the two others, 'I can't always have her just for myself.'

All three of them found that hilarious.

Todd had finally found someone who could outdo his father.

This was as sick as anything he had ever heard. 'But your daughter's arm is broken!'

'I see.' Snake sighed. 'A special treat, lads. I'll have to charge extra.'

Todd knew that the tavern keeper was trying to enrage him, to make him do something foolish, maybe even attack them outright, his one to their three.

Well, this time, Todd thought, I might as well oblige.

After all, if he was going to die anyway, why not take one or two of these bastards with him?

He leapt back on to the table and ran, screaming, heedless this time of the pots and plates that scattered from his mad dash, for Snake.

Snake and the two others stared. They had probably expected fear. They might have expected a fight. They never expected crazy.

The two newcomers were slow in getting their weapons. Todd was on top of them in a second. He kicked the one on the left in the teeth, then jumped on the one to the right, pushing him into Snake. The cleaver in Snake's hand bit into the second man's shoulder. The wounded man howled as Snake freed his weapon with a growl.

'So you want it, do you?' Snake called to him. 'One on one, to the death!' He tossed his cleaver from one hand to the other and back again. 'Well, too bad you're not gonna get it!'

Something smashed against the back of Todd's head.

Snake's laughter filled the room as Todd fell to the floor.

Todd gasped for breath.

He opened his eyes. He had been drenched with water.

Snake proudly displayed the bucket. Behind him stood two of his men. One of them was the same as before, the one Todd had kicked in the teeth, and probably the one who'd hit him on the back of the head. But the man who got the cleaver in the shoulder had been replaced by a new face, this one with a scar from mid-eyebrow to mid-nose.

'Ah.' Snake smiled as usual. 'Good to have you back with us

now. You know that we can't do anything to you unless you're awake. It's no fun if you can't feel the pain.'

Todd found he couldn't move. He looked down to see his arms pinned to his sides by large strands of rope that circled him, front to back. He saw a wooden seat between his legs. While he was unconscious, they had tied him to a chair.

'Sorry we had to do that,' Snake said in a voice that wasn't sorry at all. 'But it will make you a much better listener.'

The tavern keeper pointed down at Todd's feet. 'Interesting shoes you have. We'll be taking them off in a second. We have a method to this, smallest to largest. You'll hardly miss your little toe at all.'

Snake shook his head. 'It is a shame, in a way. You show a certain talent. I could have used you, under different circumstances.'

Todd did his best to grin back at the tavern keeper. 'You mean before I started killing your men?'

Snake looked up towards the rafters, as if he couldn't be bothered by such trivialities. 'Oh, no, nothing as minor as that. No, killing a man or two is perfectly excusable under the right circumstances. It keeps the troops on their toes. Oh, I'm sorry.' He kicked at Todd's sneaker. 'Perhaps I shouldn't have mentioned toes.'

Snake took a step closer to Todd and raised the cleaver to give his prisoner a good look. 'No, my lovely Todd, looking at my daughter is the killing offence.'

The tavern keeper waved over to Todd's left. Todd turned his head and saw Sala seated in another chair not very far away. She wasn't tied to it, but from the way she sat – arms and legs pulled in, eyes staring at nothing – she might as well have been.

Snake smiled tenderly at his offspring. 'I may have to kill her too. But I'm the one to do that. She knows it and I know it.' He glanced back at Todd. 'After all, who's going to look out for a little girl if not her father?'

There was a knock on the door behind Todd; the door that led into the tavern.

'I knew we should have waited until everyone was gone. Still, it is a slow night, and it is almost closing time.' Snake sighed, resting the cleaver on the table just behind Todd's right side. 'Scar, see who it is. I am expecting a message.' He nudged Todd's shoulder. 'Maybe it is a few of my fellows with news of your shipmates' deaths.'

So that would have happened already? That was the one thing that made Todd feel more trapped and useless than anything else Snake could say. Mrs Smith, Wilbert and Stanley, they were like his old gang back at the high school. More than his old gang, they had all faced death together. If they had got killed because he hadn't been there to warn them, well – maybe he should just get killed along with them.

But he really didn't want that. What he wanted was to run a knife across Snake's throat while sticking another one in his belly.

Not that he could do anything, tied up like this. If only he could find some way to change the odds.

Scar came back into the kitchen. He walked over to Snake, as if he was waiting as long as possible to give his boss the message.

He jerked a thumb back towards the door to the tavern. 'There's a man who wants to speak to you.'

Snake sighed again, his whole life too great a trial. 'Doesn't he know we're closing for the night?'

'He says you'll want to see him.' Scar hesitated, as if uncertain of just what to say next. 'He's not one of our regular customers.'

'He's not? Maybe this will prove interesting.'

Snake turned back to Todd. 'You can see my difficulty. Torturing and tavern keeping rarely seem to mix.' He made a tsking sound with his tongue. 'Even in a place as noisy as this, screaming seems to distract customers.'

He tossed the cleaver down on the table and turned towards the door.

'I'll be back as soon as I can. You can use the time to say goodbye to your extra digits.'

He took a couple of steps away before adding, 'And I do hope nothing's happened to the lads who went to visit your fellows. If anything went wrong, I could get very upset.'

He saved his last glance for his two local lads. 'And don't get too friendly with my daughter – until I tell you to.'

Snake stepped out of Todd's field of vision, leaving his threats behind. But Todd had his mind on other things.

The eye! He needed it now, and he knew it was close. That other eye on board ship had worked with his anger to make that sea creature catch fire. He still didn't know what happened – maybe he used the eye, maybe the eye used him. But he smiled as he remembered the flames. He wished he had that eye here now; he'd show this bastard what his anger could do.

But where was that green light now? Why wouldn't it come and show him the way?

Sala spoke up for the first time since Todd woke up.

'I'm sorry about this, Todd.' She still sat, straight and drawn together, on the chair, but she had turned her head towards Todd. 'I wanted to get away from here, not get you killed.'

'Shut up,' Scar murmured, 'or we'll tell your father.'

She looked straight ahead then, away from the eyes of her father's men. 'He can't do much more to me.'

She was silent for a moment then, before turning back to Todd. 'If we both die,' she said softly, 'maybe we'll go to the same place, then.' She smiled the slightest bit, as if afraid to be happy.

Todd tried to smile back. Compared to what had happened in her life, it must have been a beautiful thought.

'I think now', Sala added, more to herself than anyone else, 'I'd rather die.'

If she really meant it, maybe Todd could at least help with that.

Todd didn't look forward to being tortured to death. If all else failed, maybe there was some way he could get Snake to kill him – or maybe both Sala and him – outright.

The door to the tavern room banged open behind Todd. When Snake came into view, he wasn't smiling. He looked shaken, his mouth quivering at the edges. Todd wished he could know what could upset Snake like that.

'It wasn't news of the others,' he said before anyone could ask a question. 'Something else. Oh, don't worry, Todd. We'll keep you alive until you can hear every detail of your friends' murders.'

He took a deep breath as he once again wrapped his fingers around the cleaver, as if he wanted to forget whatever had happened out in the other room.

'I took a minute out there to clear out anyone who doesn't belong here. So we're all alone at last.' He waved the cleaver at the man without the scar. 'Now, take off his shoe and we'll get on with the show.'

Snake's man tugged at the shoe, then pulled at the laces. He didn't seem to know much about sneakers.

Snake pointed the cleaver graciously in Todd's direction. His face was working back towards a smile again. 'Is there any last thing you want to say before you start screaming? To me? To my daughter?'

Todd realised this was his last chance.

'I'm not sorry at all about what Sala and I did together.'

He saw Snake staring at him. Maybe he was on the right path.

'At least she had the chance to find someone who could really make her happy,' Todd added quickly. 'Physically happy. Not like her pitiful old man.'

Snake looked from Todd to his daughter and back again. His faltering smile had faded altogether. 'What? When did you have time?'

'When you're young and strong,' Todd added with a grin of his own, 'it doesn't take time. Not like you.'

Her father shook his head abruptly. 'No. She knows better than to say anything like that. You didn't have the time, she wouldn't have the will.' The smile was back on his face. 'Still, I appreciate the sport. 'Tis nice when your victim's ready to play.'

But Todd wasn't going to give this asshole any more satisfaction. His own smile grew as broad as the tavern keeper's. He knew other ways to fight besides his fists.

'She's told me all about you. Not that there's much to tell. She tells me she laughs at you behind your back. Ask your men. She says that sometimes, when you leave them alone together, they all laugh at you.'

Snake's face showed doubt for a heartbeat or two. But the smile never really went away.

'You're a clever little shit, aren't you?' he said to Todd. 'You make me mad, I slit your throat. No screams and prayers for mercy as I slice one toe here, one finger there. We wouldn't have any time for our amusement.'

He turned to his daughter. 'Daddy's little girl would never do anything like that.'

Sala looked him right in the eye. 'I laugh at you all the time.'

For once, Snake had no reply. His fingers were white where he held the cleaver.

'Why don't you ask the fellows, father?' Sala was smiling now. 'They'll tell you how we laugh about how pitiful you are in bed.'

Todd was impressed. She could really play along. He liked her when she looked like this, smiling her defiance. It was too bad this little game was going to kill them both.

'Snake –' Scar began.

The tavern keeper stared at the cleaver in his hand.

And the world shifted again, and exploded into green light.

This time the green light reached out from the ceiling, or from a point just below, a dozen feelers blooming out to reach every corner of the room. No, not feelers, Todd realised, but branches, as if a glowing tree was growing upside down in this room as he watched.

The others cried out and shrank away from the sprouting light. But Todd waited for it to touch him. Touch him and give him the dragon's eye.

Maybe, he thought, this was the secret of the eye, or at least Todd's secret. He only had to wait until he was angry enough and the eye was at his service.

Green glowing leaves almost brushed against Todd's cheek. Another second, now, and Snake would be sorry that he ever smiled.

And then the light was gone.

Todd couldn't believe it. Why had it vanished now, when it had been so close, when he could already feel the power just beyond his reach?

'This has gone far enough,' Snake said in a voice without emotion. 'I kill him now.'

'I don't think so,' a woman's voice answered.

Mrs Smith stood in the doorway that led to the backyard. Could she have brought the green light?

Or maybe she was the one who made it go away.

'Lovely place you've got here,' she said. 'Wonderful smell.'

Snake's mouth dropped open. His murderous plans had, for the moment, given way to astonishment. 'Who in the seven islands are you?'

Mrs Smith smiled pleasantly. 'A friend of Todd's. And somebody you don't want to see.'

She reached into her pocket and pulled out her dragon's eye.

'You're a witch!' Scar exclaimed.

Mrs Smith smiled. 'I'm afraid so.' She held the eye before her. 'And you're in trouble.'

She frowned. The gem in her hand was a dull green in the light from the kitchen lantern. The eye seemed not to glow from within at all.

Snake's grin returned. 'It won't work, my lady. Those things never work around here. That's the real reason we call this place the Dragon Tavern.'

Snake waved to one of his men. 'Scar, go over and make sure our new guest is seated comfortably.'

Mrs Smith took a step back into the darkness. Without her magic, she could hardly move at all.

'Maybe after my men have taken turns with my daughter,' Snake called out after her, 'they will want a spin with you.'

'I think she's trying to get away, Snake!' Scar called back cheerfully.

'Now why don't you just stay still and make it easy for us?' Snake went on, his grin fully back at last. 'You know, I've always wanted to kill a witch.'

Twenty-five

'Follow me, Pator!' the Captain called to his new lieutenant as he marched out into the woods.

The former soldier from Nunn's army, no doubt still a bit startled by the sudden death of his travelling companion, hesitated an instant before he ran to follow. Still, the Captain had faith in Pator. Once the soldier realised that he would be treated fairly – but, more than that really, once Pator realised he was an important, perhaps even vital, component of the new world order – he would immediately fall into line. Pator was always very good at seeing reason.

The wolves, having made a quick meal of that very travelling companion, needed no such instruction. They fell in on either side of the two men, licking the remaining blood from their chops. They looked eager and alert, ready to do the Captain's bidding. As long as he kept feeding them, the wolves would be loyal for ever.

Oh, this was wonderful. This was the way the Captain had always wanted it to be. He was his own man with his own purpose, free of the senseless dictates of crazed superiors. Surely, he would have to kill another soldier or two, men that used to be under his command, in order to reach his goal. But what was a murder or two when compared with the ultimate freedom?

And something was happening in the woods, something that had to do with the dragon. He could still hear cries of 'Kennake! Kennake!' from fleeing men to either side of his little party.

Not, of course, that he had ever seen the dragon do anything beyond frighten and confuse people. That was something the

Captain had never really thought of before. It was always the threat of what the dragon might do, rather than any real action on the part of the legendary creature, that seemed to drive this world. It seemed to the Captain now that no one had ever really challenged the dragon. Even he was guilty of trying to protect himself from a creature he had never seen.

Now he wished he had been stronger and kept that gun he had found among the neighbours.

But he had new weapons now, weapons with claws and teeth who would be far more deadly with his mind to guide them, and far more productive with his sense of vengeance spurring them on.

It was only when his new lieutenant jogged up to his side that the Captain realised the rapid pace he had been keeping. He slowed a bit, nodding pleasantly to his second-in-command.

His lieutenant still seemed reticent to speak. 'Excuse me,' he said at last. 'Captain?'

'Yes, Pator.' The Captain smiled graciously. 'Speak freely. We are no longer under Nunn.' He wanted to make sure that distinction was clear.

'I was wondering.' Pator couldn't help but glance at the wolves around him. He turned back to the Captain. 'Where are we going?'

'A fair question.' The Captain nodded his head. 'We are going to seize a great opportunity.' He waved his right hand at the forest around them. 'Listen and you'll hear it. Chaos everywhere. I've never heard the men so afraid.'

Actually, the Captain realised, he knew none of the details of what frightened the soldiers so. He turned to his eyewitness.

'Did they see the dragon?'

'Actually,' Pator replied with a wry smile, 'what they saw was a teenaged girl.'

'Really?' The Captain had to keep himself from laughing. That was even better than the dragon. A teenaged girl, Pator said?

'I may have met her at Nunn's castle.' Yes. The more the Captain thought of it, the more convinced he was it would be the same girl. By way of explanation, he added, 'If you can survive visiting Nunn, it leads to interesting things.'

'But the men fear the dragon,' Pator continued. 'Anything unusual is blamed on the creature. And they hate the man who replaced you. I think a few ran from fear, and a few more ran to get away.'

The Captain considered this for a moment. 'So most stayed behind?'

'Most certainly. For most of the soldiers, the fear of Nunn is greater than the fear of the dragon.'

The Captain had expected more chaos in the ranks. This might be even more interesting than he had anticipated. But he had one more important question.

'And what about you, Pator?'

'Why did I run?' The smile returned to the lieutenant's face. 'Perhaps I didn't want to serve under a fool. Perhaps I was tired of working in fear. Perhaps I no longer care if I live or die.'

The Captain smiled back at that. 'Ah, Pator.' He clapped the other soldier on his shoulder. 'It sounds like you and I will do beautiful work together.'

They marched in silence for a minute. The frightened cries seemed to be lessening around them. Perhaps the Captain's replacement was finally getting his troops under control.

'Speaking of business,' Pator said after a moment, 'what do you intend to do once we reach Nunn's army?'

'I like a lieutenant who thinks on his feet.' The Captain nodded. 'I will do what I should have tried for since the day I got here. I will bring Nunn down.'

'Today?' The lieutenant looked both surprised and impressed, as if he half believed the Captain could march right in and do it this instant.

'Not entirely,' the Captain confessed. 'But we all must begin somewhere. It's time to make a raid.'

'Five wolves and two men against an army?' Pator laughed, but it was a good laugh, full of joy for what was to come. 'Then a raid it will be.'

The Captain laughed, too, at his lieutenant's matter-of-fact summation of their strengths. 'Oh, Pator, you know as well as I that we'll succeed.'

'With this bold raid of yours? I suppose I will once you tell me your goal.'

'Simplicity itself.' The Captain smiled up at the trees around them, wanting to take the whole forest into his confidence. 'I think it's time to take one of Nunn's beloved neighbours for my very own.'

At first, the sky had been everything he had hoped for.

The entity that had once been Hyram Sayre felt at last that he was free. He was no longer tied to a little scrap of ground, worrying how his grass would grow or whether some neighbourhood punk would run over his lawn. Now he could soar through the great blue-green expanses that circled this world, alone, aloof, his only company the occasional curious bird.

It had been thrilling, at first, to see the world like that; to watch all of the seven islands pass below and float far above the green, green sea.

Green was what he had longed for. And now green was everywhere.

But after a while it was no longer enough.

The ocean seemed to go on for ever. Oh, there were things living beneath the waves, creatures he could glimpse as he flew overhead, creatures he could no doubt visit if he chose to. But a life underwater didn't appeal to him.

There was a whole side to this world he had never been to, a place far beyond the seven islands and the great expanse of sea around them. Was the rest of the world nothing but ocean? Were there more islands on the other side, perhaps even a continent? Or would he fly until he found a great shape on the far horizon, and he would see the dragon smiling back at him?

Sayre could go exploring for ever. As far as he knew, he was eternal. But the idea did not appeal to him just yet.

He found himself flying back over the islands, each one different from the others. Some of them held people and some other things altogether. One was mostly desert, another nothing but rock. And none of them was as green as the island he had come from.

196

He found himself flying past this island more and more. It was his home, more than any place that ever existed when he was simply alive, for the green here filled his spirit.

But, he realised at last, even a god can get lonely.

Life was more than just the colours below him, or things observed at a distance. Life was also change.

Some of the changes were good, like the coming of the seasons. Others, like earthquakes and tidal waves, would destroy the green as surely as teenagers running over your lawn in the middle of the night.

The Sayre Deity had no doubt that he could cause an earthquake or a tidal wave, if he wanted. But why would he do that? That would put an end to green.

Instead, he had to be a part of the seasons. He had to be a part of change. It was time to walk again, surrounded by living things.

Once, when he was merely alive, he had been obsessed with a tiny patch of green. During the time he was dead, he had still embraced the colour, even though he had hardly any mind at all. But now his mind was growing constantly, filling with so many thoughts and experiences that one day he might think the whole world.

If he did that, he would make everything green.

It was time to return to the earth.

'This cannot be happening!'

Carl Jackson would not allow this. His perfect world was breaking up before him. And, as far as he could figure out, it was all because of some teenaged brat from his old neighbourhood.

'Keep to your ranks!' the new Captain called. 'Deserters will be shot!'

The troops milled about, some of them trying to re-form their units. He seemed to have kept most of them from running away.

A couple of the men on the edges of the crowd bolted for the forest.

'Shoot the deserters!' Jackson demanded.

Not a single man grabbed a bow and arrow. No one even looked up at Carl. No one appeared to be listening.

This was treason! Mutiny! He'd kill them all with the globe he held in his hand.

Jackson looked from the globe to the frightened men before him. If he killed them all, he would have no troops. He would never be able to fulfil Nunn's orders. If Nunn could give him a powerful globe like this on a whim, what sorcery was Nunn capable of when he was truly angry?

Jackson told himself to calm down, to think this through.

This was a small setback, nothing more. He hadn't lost many more than a dozen men. And it was no wonder that the soldiers didn't seem to hear him; he didn't even think they understood him. He needed his lieutenants to make his orders clear.

And this thing – this sudden apparition in the sky – had taken him by surprise. He'd plan for the dragon from now on, and warn his soldiers that they could expect a quick death if they didn't fear their commanding officer more than some imaginary creature.

So this could all be salvaged. He needed Harold. Where was Harold?

'Harry!' he called.

'Yes, Captain?' Harry and George were standing a bit behind him to his left, at one edge of the trail. Why hadn't he seen them there? The new Captain had to get a grip on himself.

He waved at the troops milling about. 'Tell these men to get back in formation! And ready to march!'

Harry barked out an order and the men quickly returned to their ranks, professional soldiers once again.

It was a good beginning, but the new Captain had to plan for the future too.

'Tell them,' he shouted to Harry, 'if we run across any deserters, they will be tried and punished! And, from this moment forward, should any soldier attempt to desert he will be summarily executed!'

Harry looked back at Jackson for a moment without speaking.

Jackson held up his globe. 'Harry! Say it!'

'Yes, Captain!' Harry turned away from him and spoke for a while in the guttural tongue.

How, Carl thought, could he be sure that his lieutenant was repeating his orders in the way Jackson wanted them presented? Especially after he had clearly questioned them a moment ago. It was not a situation to his liking.

This was something else that had to change. Once the new Captain had brought the neighbours in, he would humbly ask Nunn for the gift of language as well. For his triumphant return, that should only be the beginning of Jackson's reward.

Harold finished his speech at last. The soldiers still seemed restless and upset. It wasn't neat enough for Jackson. The whole world was too much of a mess.

'Harold! Have them stand at attention!'

Harry barked a short command and got the desired results. At least some of Jackson's orders were being relayed properly.

The forest fell into a sudden silence as the men snapped to attention.

Carl was aware of the sound of the wind in the trees.

A new sound came from the forest. It sounded like a wolf howl.

Another wolf answered from the other side of the trail. There were wolves all around them.

He heard a low murmur from the troops before him.

'Harry!' he commanded. 'They are to be silent!'

Harry's guttural order was interrupted by another voice in the forest, speaking in the same ugly tongue.

'Can you understand that?' Jackson asked.

'He says he is the true Captain of these men,' Harry replied, 'and some day he will ask them to join him!'

So the old Captain was out in the woods? Somehow, Jackson had got the impression from Nunn that his predecessor was dead. Not that it mattered. This first Captain no longer had the power of Nunn behind him.

'Nonsense!' Jackson called. 'He is a traitor to Nunn! As soon as the magician returns, I'm sure he will be destroyed! Repeat it, Harry!'

Harry spoke for a moment in the troops' tongue. If possible, the soldiers looked even less sure of themselves than they had before.

The first Captain's voice called out again from somewhere beyond the trees.

'He says', Harry translated, 'he controls all the wolves in the forest.'

All the wolves? Jackson would think that would be impossible.

But nothing was impossible here.

The voice from the woods said something else.

'But he will hold off the attack,' Harry continued, 'if he can talk privately with one of our number.'

The nerve of this man. Did he want a private audience with Carl Jackson now?

'What?' Carl called. 'Does he want to get me alone so his wolves can kill me?'

The voice in the woods said something new.

Harry turned back to Jackson, his face showing an even deeper frown than usual. 'Um, Captain? He wants to talk with me.'

To Harold? Why to a nonentity like Harold? Did this first Captain want to persuade Harold to leave Jackson and join his cause? Or maybe they had talked before and were already working together with their secret, guttural tongue?

No, Jackson told himself, that was going too far. Harry would never have had the chance to speak with this mysterious Captain. Besides, he was far too scared of Jackson and his globe to try.

Jackson would have to take a minute and decide what to do. It would be his first real command decision. He wondered if there was some way he could harness the globe's power to reach someone hidden in the woods. But he didn't know enough about Nunn's gift even to guess if that was possible.

At the back of the ranks, someone screamed. Had a wolf got him? It would be much too easy for the creatures. The forest loomed above either side of their new-made trail.

Others shouted, looking around for the screamer.

His predecessor was telling the new Captain he was taking

too long to make a decision. He couldn't allow this to get any further out of hand. He turned to his lieutenant.

'Harry,' he instructed. 'I will allow you to talk with him, if you remain in my sight. The soldiers will stand twenty paces behind you.'

That should allow them to pick off any wolves that would attack his lieutenant and keep Harry from having any thoughts about a change of allegiance. Pretty clever, for a guy who had just taken charge.

'Tell him, Harry!' Jackson called.

Harry and the man in the woods had a brief guttural exchange.

'That is acceptable!' Harry called back to his Captain.

Jackson nodded. Now all he had to worry about was what the old Captain had to say. 'Harry. Stay where you are. And tell the soldiers to move back to either side of you. We'll cover you if there's any trouble.

'And Harry?' he added after a moment's pause.

'Yes, Captain?'

'I expect a full report on your conversation when you're done.'

'Yes, Captain!' Harry called out something to the troops, who moved up and down the trail to give him a wide space to himself. Jackson moved to place himself behind one line of his own men, a vantage point where he could watch but still be protected.

A man stepped out from behind the trees immediately in front of Harry. It was the old Captain, although he appeared far thinner and more fragile than before. Some of the soldiers started to talk among themselves.

Jackson wanted to do something here. 'George!' he called.

His second-in-command trotted over. 'Yes, Captain?'

'Is there any way we can quiet these men?'

George frowned at the soldiers around him. 'I'm afraid I don't know how. Maybe we should have arranged some sort of signal. Harold could have taught me an order or two, if I'd thought of it.'

'Yes,' Jackson replied with an impatient frown of his own.

'*If* you had thought of it.'

'Sorry, Captain,' George said quickly. 'I'll talk to Harold about it as soon as this is over.'

That was all they could do, besides wait. Jackson turned back to the meeting before him. He didn't like the way these things kept slipping from his control.

There was a loud growl behind them.

'Sir!' George tugged at his sleeve. 'The wolves are attacking!'

What? So this supposed meeting with Harry was just some sort of diversion to get them off their guard? Well, Carl Jackson could not be defeated that easily.

'Kill the wolves!' he called to his men. 'Shoot to kill!' Maybe they wouldn't understand his exact words, but he hoped his meaning was clear.

And, indeed, a number of his soldiers had unshipped their bows and fitted them with arrows.

But the wolves wouldn't show themselves. A couple of the arrows flew as dark shapes darted between the trees, as if the wolves were running to attack them from someplace new. Jackson wished he knew how to give an order for his men to close their ranks, facing back to back in a circle, so they could be ready for an attack from any direction.

The wolves made no further noise and had disappeared from between the trees. Why were they waiting to attack again?

Jackson turned back towards the meeting on the trail.

Both Harry and the Captain were gone.

Twenty-six

Todd watched helplessly as Mrs Smith backed away from the door. There was a flurry of motion out in the shadows, too dim to see clearly. Was she trying to run before Scar could get to her?

A face reappeared at the door. But it wasn't Mrs Smith. It was Wilbert.

'No magic?' Wilbert grinned. 'Guess it's time for some good old-fashioned American know-how.'

He lifted a bow and arrow.

Scar had almost made it to the door. Even the bow and arrow didn't deter him. He kept on moving as Wilbert let the arrow fly. It hit Scar in the shoulder, spinning him round.

'That was a warning shot,' Wilbert informed the others. 'The next one will kill. Of course, why we're being nice to you after the terrible things you've said to Mrs Smith, I have no idea.'

Stanley appeared in the door next to him. 'Why are you jabbering while Todd's still tied up?'

But Snake wasn't quite ready to give up his prize.

'Craps!' he called to his other man. 'You down that side of the table, me down the other. We can take them easy!'

He held his own quiver of arrows again. The crossbow was where Todd had dropped it, on the floor almost midway down the kitchen's length.

'Are you looking for a fight, eh?' Stanley rewarded Snake with a rare smile of his own. 'I haven't had one in minutes at least.'

'Well,' Snake replied as he stopped just before the fallen weapon, 'I guess we'll have to oblige you.'

'The crossbow!' Todd warned.

Snake leapt back as an arrow hit the table by his groping hand.

'I think you're right,' Stanley said as he fitted a new arrow. 'Bows and arrows are best when dealing with the likes of these.'

'We wouldn't want to get our hands dirty up close,' Wilbert said with a grin. 'It might never come off.'

Both the Volunteers stepped fully into the room.

'Now,' Wilbert nodded at both Snake and Craps. 'If you would drop those weapons you're carrying?'

A cleaver and a knife both clattered on to the table.

Wilbert nodded to Sala. 'Now, young lady, what say you go on over there and cut our friend free. No sudden moves now. Both Stanley and I are awfully quick with our bows.'

Todd frowned. How could they even suspect Sala would hurt him? 'She won't do anything!'

Stanley nodded this time. 'So says the lad who got himself into this mess in the first place, eh?'

'Always a good judge of character, young Todd,' Wilbert agreed, poking his elbow into the other's ribs. 'Probably why he gets along with you.'

Sala rose from her seat and grabbed the knife that had been tossed on the table. She stepped behind Todd's chair. He could feel the ropes loosen on his back almost at once.

'You're handy with that too,' Wilbert remarked.

'I've cleaned a lot of fish and cut up a lot of chickens,' Sala answered.

'Yep,' Wilbert agreed. 'I can see you're Todd's kind of woman.'

'Shut up!' Todd called as he stood up and pushed off the remains of the ropes. 'She's been through a lot.'

'And you haven't?' Stanley shook his head. 'We were outside for a moment, listening in, while we got organised.'

Todd looked at the Volunteers in amazement. 'You were waiting out there the entire time?' He didn't know whether to laugh or be furious.

'Well, no,' Wilbert said. 'Only a minute, really. We had to

check out the territory first, see how many there were up against us. Once we knew that, we barged on in.'

'Mrs Smith was for coming in right away, eh?' Stanley added. 'But we discouraged her. She was already having some problems with her jewel.'

Wilbert began to walk slowly into the room, his bow aimed at Snake's chest. 'You weren't easy to find. We've been out looking for you half the night. Dear Mrs Smith, who usually finds things right away, couldn't see you at all. It was only when we thought about this cursed place, which may or may not hold the final dragon's eye, that it all fell together.'

Stanley followed the other Volunteer in, his bow pointed towards Snake's lackey. 'In other words, we finally came to the one place that Mrs Smith couldn't see.'

'So, Todd,' Wilbert asked, 'is your circulation good enough to give us a hand tying these characters up?'

Todd nodded as he rubbed at the rope burns on his wrists.

'There's another coil of rope beneath the table,' Sala offered.

'We only need to tie the men,' Todd volunteered. 'I'll vouch for Sala here.'

Wilbert laughed. 'Ah, Todd, lad. We knew you would.'

Sala smiled at that and placed the knife back on the table.

'Wasn't there an old woman with you?' she asked.

'Mrs Smith?' Wilbert frowned. 'She's trapped in that horrible smelling place outside until we can get our work done in here.'

'She has trouble walking on her own,' Todd explained.

'There's something I can do!' Sala called, already running for the back door. 'I'll go help her in!'

'Fetch the rope, Todd,' Stanley said.

Wilbert shook his head as Sala disappeared from the kitchen. 'It's the last we'll see of that lass. Too bad. Todd, you do have an eye for beauty.'

Todd looked up from where he'd pulled the heavy rope from under the table. 'You think she's not coming back?'

'Oh, I'll grant you that there's no love lost between her and her father.' He waved his bow and arrow at Snake. 'Let's start with this one, shall we? But there's no love lost with her for us, either, if you catch my meaning. I don't blame her a bit if she goes to find a healthier climate.'

Todd had never thought she would leave. But maybe Wilbert was right after all. Todd and Sala had been attracted to each other, but it had never had any time to go beyond that.

'Loop the rope around, lad,' Wilbert said patiently. Todd realised he was just standing there. 'I remember you're not the best with knots. Once you've got him enclosed, I'll do the honours.'

Snake glared at him, but didn't speak. That was just fine with Todd. He'd already heard enough out of Snake to last him for ever.

Todd heard voices just outside the door.

'Be careful now. There's a slight rise here.'

'Thank you, dear. I see it. Sorry to be such a bother.'

Mrs Smith stepped carefully into the room, with Sala guiding her elbow.

'That was no trouble at all,' Sala said.

Stanley glanced sceptically at Todd. 'Wilbert's opinions are not always true.'

'Most of the time!' Wilbert replied forcefully.

Stanley shook his head. 'Most of the time they are, eh? Except when they're not.'

'Here,' Sala said to Mrs Smith, 'why don't you take this chair here.'

Mrs Smith sighed as she sat. 'It's only at a time like this when I realise how dependent I've become on that dragon's eye. It is far more of a problem than I would like.'

'We all have doubts about our future, eh?' Stanley agreed. 'That's one of the first things I learned after being dumped in this place – you never have the faintest idea what'll happen next.'

'So our future could be wonderful,' Sala said quietly.

Todd turned away from Sala's smile. The way she was looking at him was a little embarrassing.

'And pigs can fly,' Wilbert added. 'Except, maybe pigs do fly around here somewhere.'

Todd looked down at his handiwork with a frown. 'I've

managed a knot or two,' he said to Wilbert. 'I'm sure you can do better.'

'That's the lad, Todd,' Wilbert replied as he moved forward to lend a hand. 'Always learning.'

Snake looked up at the approaching Volunteer. 'You might want to think twice before you do this.'

'The great man speaks!' Wilbert grinned as he looked around at Snake's bonds. 'And why might I think that way?'

'The dragon's eye.'

'He may have something there,' Mrs Smith called from her seat at the end of the table. 'I know it's somewhere near here.' She patted the pocket where she kept her stone. 'My jewel was confused in the tavern out there and here it won't work at all. The other eye must be very close.' She looked up at the ceiling, then down at the floor. 'For all I know, I might be sitting on it.'

'It's here somewhere,' Snake agreed before anyone could ask, 'but I don't know its exact location. It's none too healthy to know too much about some things.'

Stanley looked up from where he guarded Snake's lackey. 'Our host speaks the truth, eh?'

'But that's not what I wanted to say.' Snake jerked his head towards the tavern. 'There's someone out there –'

'Out in the public room?' Wilbert asked.

'Right,' Snake agreed. 'Someone who could guide you right to the eye.'

'Now let me get this straight. There's someone in the other room who knows all about the dragon's eye?' Wilbert's smile came back full force. 'And how many would you have waiting for us in the other room? What do you take us for? That one's even more transparent than your suggestion about an inn!'

Wilbert checked his knots a final time. 'Your handiwork wasn't bad, Todd. Let's get to work on this other fellow, shall we?'

'Excuse me,' someone said at the tavern door.

Todd looked up at the newcomer. Not that there was much to see. His hands and face were hidden by the voluminous folds of a large grey robe of the kind monks wore.

'You know,' the newcomer continued in a conversational tone, 'Snake here was telling the truth for once. Oh, I admit that's not a common occurrence. But there was only one waiting in the room beyond, and he does know as much as anyone about this remaining eye.'

'And that would be you, sir?' Mrs Smith asked.

'Oh,' the newcomer replied, 'I think that you'll find my credentials to be genuine.'

He reached a pale hand out of his robes and pushed back his hood.

The newcomer was Nunn.

Twenty-seven

Nick woke up at the first light of dawn. The sky above had gone from black to grey.

His shirt was stiff with blood, but there was no soreness from the wound beneath. He remembered Mills touching it last night, before he had lifted Nick up and floated him back down this cul-de-sac. They had found a small, open shed back here full of hay. It was the softest bed that Nick had ever felt.

He lay there for a long moment, watching the sky lighten through the open side of the shed, and thought about what had happened. Not before he met Mills; that was all a blur, but after.

Mills had made him keep his sword. At first Nick refused. He never wanted to see it again. But Mills had listed the reasons they couldn't let it go. If there was danger from the sword, it was better to know where that danger was. There might be some way to harness its power, so that Nick could use the sword rather than being used by it. Obar should have done that, apparently. But Mills said that Obar was never very good with fine details.

In the end, Mills had put the sword back in the scabbard for him so Nick wouldn't have to touch it. But Nick still wore the scabbard round his waist. It waited there for his next fight. He wondered if he would choose to die rather than draw it again.

Mills had also told Nick about what had happened to him. Or perhaps Nick should say them, for he had heard something of the story of Rox the wizard and Zachs, the child creature made by Nunn. And Mills talked about stealing the dragon's eye in the desert, and how the power of the eye had almost crippled him until he used some of it to help Nick.

Nick remembered staring up at the stars as Mills talked, this time with his own voice.

'Using that power, letting it leave us, that was the key. Somehow, maybe because of the strange thing that I've become, the eye was too much for us until we let part of it go. Only by giving away the magic could we hope to control it.' He took a deep breath, then let it out slowly. 'I can see our future, Nick. You get into trouble, we'll use our magic to pull you out. It works for everybody.'

Mills had laughed softly. And Nick had fallen asleep.

'Nick?' Mills's voice called out in the morning light. 'Are you awake?'

Nick nodded.

'How do you feel?'

'A lot better,' Nick admitted. 'Let's see what happens if I get up.'

He sat up. He wasn't dizzy in the least. He took a deep breath and stood. He felt great.

He looked down at Mr Mills. 'I could use a little bit of this magic every morning.'

Mills smiled up at him. 'You might have to watch out. It could be habit-forming.'

Just like the sword, Nick thought. He was sure that was what Mr Mills meant.

'Yeah,' he answered. The scabbard brushed against his leg. The sword dragged at his belt; it felt heavier than it ever had before. 'What do we do now?'

Mr Mills stood up in turn. He took a minute to brush the hay off his pants. 'We look for another dragon's eye. The sixth out of seven, I believe.'

This was one more thing Nick couldn't understand. 'Why do you want another eye when you can barely control the one you have?'

'The boy asks excellent questions,' a deeper voice said. Nick knew now it was Rox, the wizard. 'Every time a new eye appears, the world shifts. Things change. The world is different than before. There is no way of telling whether another eye would hurt us, or help us.' Mills looked over at Nick for a moment before continuing. 'And, there is another consideration. If we do not get the eye, one of the others does. The balance of power shifts, perhaps in a deadly direction. Nunn already holds two of the eyes. He would be very dangerous if he had three.'

'But what about the seventh eye?'

'It is somewhere near at hand. I think it will make itself evident soon.'

That still wasn't what Nick wanted to know. 'But it's the last eye, right? What happens when someone finds the seventh eye?'

'Then, I believe, we will see the dragon.'

Nick nodded. Obar had said something like that, although not so directly. It looked as if it was almost time for the big pay-off here. Whatever that was.

'Where are we going?' he asked as Mills led him on down the hill.

'I know where it is now,' the wizard in Mills replied. 'The one place that we can't see it.'

'You show yourself here?' Constance Smith was quite amazed.

'I have to,' Nunn replied. 'Otherwise I have no chance to find the latest stone.'

Nunn smiled. It was not a pleasant sight. Without the glow of his jewels, he looked even more like death, with sunken eyes and pale, parchment skin stretched over a fleshless face.

'Should we kill him?' Wilbert asked.

This would be the time, Constance realised, while Nunn's gems were as useless as her own. She never thought she could want to see anyone die in cold blood. But maybe that was before she got the jewel. Or maybe that only applied to people who were still human beings.

'Yes,' she agreed quietly. 'I think killing him would be for the best.'

'Wait!' Nunn raised a hand. The dead jewel looked like a malignant growth in his palm. 'Hear me out first. Then you can kill me later. What do you have to lose?'

No doubt this was more of Nunn's trickery. Or maybe his ego was so great that he couldn't conceive of dying.

Still, Mrs Smith was curious.

'All right,' she allowed. 'I'll give you a minute. Speak quickly.'

Wilbert looked over at the man he'd just begun to hogtie. 'You'll excuse us if we finish our business here.'

Nunn waved the Volunteer on. 'Oh, tie them up, by all means. They work for me, and even I often find them unmanageable. It is so hard to get good help around here.'

His sunken eyes looked quickly back to Mrs Smith. 'But I have to plead for my life. You shouldn't kill me for one simple reason: I don't think the dragon would want you to. Just as I shouldn't kill any of you. Ah, I thought that would get your attention.

'The dragon brings people to this place. Why? It looks for people to control the eyes. Otherwise, why would these seven gems exist? I think, if you can control one of the eyes, you are among the chosen.'

Nunn waved a skeletal hand at those in the room. 'The dragon has found a particularly talented group this time. In addition,' he added with a nod, 'he's allowed a talented few to survive from before.'

He paused to look from face to face around the room. 'What does it all mean? Maybe the dragon is looking for three, or six, or even seven people to control the eyes.' He held up both his jewels for all to see. 'After all, I may have overstepped my authority.'

What Nunn said made a certain sense. Mrs Smith had really just *happened* upon the jewel she now possessed, as if it had been meant for her all along.

She wondered if Nunn was right and they were all somehow performing for the dragon. Was the dragon leading them towards a fight, giving one dragon's eye here, another there, until their owners were bound to clash? It certainly seemed that way.

But even if she discovered how much the dragon controlled them, would that make any difference in what she had to do?

Nunn stared at her and smiled, quite satisfied with his argument.

Todd stepped close to her. He looked uncomfortable. He bent down near her.

'Mrs Smith?' he whispered. 'I need to go out back for a minute.'

She nodded. Magic or no, there were still certain needs that had to be taken care of.

'I think that would be fine, Todd, for a minute,' she answered. 'But don't go very far. Stay within shouting distance.'

Todd moved quickly towards the back of the room, only taking a moment to glance at the tavern keeper's daughter.

'I'm not spending another minute in here!' Sala announced the instant Todd was gone. She pointed at her father. 'Not while he's still here!'

She turned and ran out back before anyone could stop her.

Wilbert looked at the others in the room. 'Young love, huh?'

No one laughed. Mrs Smith wondered if both Todd and Sala had planned this, or if the tavern keeper's daughter had thought of it herself. Either way, she couldn't see any harm in it, not if they stayed close. Heaven knew, none of them had had time to relax or do anything personal since they got here.

'So what do we do with him?' Stanley asked, nodding over at Nunn. Both he and Wilbert did their best to look the other way as Todd escorted Sala from the room.

'What he talks about almost makes sense.' As much, Mrs Smith thought, as anything around here. 'We should let him live for a while. But we should also tie him up.'

'Tie him up?' Wilbert actually giggled. 'Ah, sometimes I do enjoy my work.'

'You do know', Nunn continued as the Volunteers advanced on him with the rope, 'that this is just the beginning. The prologue, if you will. The real drama won't begin until we have all the stones.'

Wilbert glanced back at Constance. 'What about if we gag him, too?'

Mrs Smith actually laughed at that. 'No. Let him talk.' She wiped the smile from her face as she turned back to the wizard. 'And what, Nunn, will happen then?'

'I think the world will change again, in a way that none of us can anticipate. I lived through the last coming of the dragon, but I hid from the beast. Oh, I'm not proud of that, but I wasn't ready to face it then. Or maybe I give myself too much credit and the dragon wasn't ready for me.'

Nunn glanced down at the ropes that Wilbert wound around him, then fixed his gaze again on Constance.

'This time, though, this time is different.' His voice rose with excitement as he spoke. 'This time the dragon chose all of us and this time there will be no escaping his wrath.' He leaned forward as far as the tightening ropes would allow. 'You know, of course, that no one has ever seen the dragon and lived.'

Mrs Smith nodded, more perplexed by the minute. 'So you tell us. But if we are all doomed, why are you so gleeful about it?'

Nunn grinned at that. 'Well, it's partly the adventure of it. And I also have a plan. You know, you really should have gagged me after all.'

He stomped his trussed feet upon the floor, calling 'Time, boys!'

The brick front of a stove rolled away as a trapdoor opened in the floor. Wilbert and Stanley scrambled for their weapons.

'Pick them up', a man in the tavern entrance called, 'and you're both dead.'

Six men emerged from the hole in the wall, and another four climbed up from the hole in the floor.

'Todd!' Wilbert called. 'Run, boy!'

'What?' It sounded from Todd's voice that he was coming back inside.

An arrow embedded itself in a beam an inch away from Wilbert's nose. The archer put a finger to his lips. It was time for Wilbert to be silent.

But not time for everyone. 'Get away, Todd!' Mrs Smith called. 'Get help! We're being attacked!'

She was rewarded by two sets of feet scrambling away.

'Very clever,' Nunn said calmly. 'You are one individual I cannot kill, by my own admission.' He sighed. 'Oh well. We'll catch them.' He pointed at a couple of men towards the back of the room. 'You two! Down the alley!' The two did as they were told.

'I have a lot of people here,' Nunn continued. 'Sometimes I think I employ half the island. Not that two children would be all that important –' Nunn caught himself with a sad smile, '– well, only the dragon knows that.'

He waved at the newcomers as they relieved Wilbert and Stanley of their weapons.

'My people were here all along,' the wizard explained. 'They could have overwhelmed you at any time. But I thought it would be better if you could see my reasoning first. Less chance for violence. I don't want to kill you, and you don't want to kill me.'

Nunn stood as soon as his bonds were cut. 'Nothing in this place is ever quite what it seems. I think this room will prove my point,' the wizard continued. 'The jewel is already here, but it is also completely unobtainable, until the dragon is ready. And the dragon is waiting, I think, for all the available candidates before it reveals its treasure.'

'Now let's all get comfortable.' The men started to move toward Snake and his sidekick. 'Oh, leave them tied up, they deserve it. We have to wait for the rest of our little party to arrive.'

Nunn took his own advice and sat back down. 'After that, of course, I'll take all the jewels and keep you as my prisoners. As long as all the players are present, I don't think the dragon much cares who's in control.'

One of Nunn's men sat down on the table at the side of Mrs Smith's chair. He grinned as he pointed a knife at her throat.

Twenty-eight

Why had the globe allowed this to happen?

Harry was gone. And Harry was the only one who could talk to the troops. Without Harry, he and his soldiers could do nothing more than stare at each other.

Oh, that Captain was so clever, causing the diversion with the wolves. Jackson bet the Captain was laughing now.

But no one laughed at Carl Jackson.

'Carl.' Someone was talking to him. 'Carl, you have to listen to me. One way or another, you've got to get a grip on yourself.'

Jackson took a deep breath and tried to blink the red rage from his eyes. He glanced over at George Blake.

'Don't tell me what to do.'

George hesitated for a moment before he spoke again. 'I'm sorry. I'm just trying to get us out of a bad situation. You know, Carl, maybe we should leave all this behind too.'

Jackson looked Blake straight in the eye. 'What are you talking about?'

'Think about it,' George insisted. 'The way Nunn talks, he's got everything under control. But Nunn doesn't talk about those people fighting him. Those people are our neighbours, Carl. And he doesn't even mention this other Captain, who seems intent on sabotaging our every move. If Nunn was so all-powerful, Carl, why isn't that Captain dead?'

Why was Blake telling him these things? Jackson didn't want to hear about any of that.

'There is no other Captain,' he announced. 'I am the Captain and that is what you will call me.'

He stared hard at George Blake. 'You will give the troops their orders now.'

'But Carl!' Blake protested. 'They won't understand me.'

'They didn't understand Harry, either, until Nunn did some of his mumbo-jumbo.' Jackson looked over at the globe. He always had it with him now. He almost felt it was an extension of his hand.

He waved the globe at Blake. 'And here's some of the mumbo-jumbo right here. You've seen how it works. All I have to do is think at it and it does just what I want.' He smiled. If the globe hadn't kept Harry, it could replace him with George. Carl knew he'd figure this out. 'George, we'll make them understand you.'

George still wouldn't listen. 'But Carl, we don't know –'

'Captain.' Jackson had had quite enough of this. If he had any options at all he'd get rid of Blake this instant. 'I will punish you if you do not call me Captain.'

'All right, then, Captain,' Blake tried again. 'What if this doesn't –'

Jackson had been very patient with his new recruit, giving him every benefit of the doubt. And he still wouldn't stop?

'I will kill you, George, if you say another word.' He held the globe up in front of George's face. 'Now stand there, and we'll make this work.'

Blake finally stood there and shut up. He was sweating a little bit, too. At last he must have realised Jackson meant business.

Carl stared at the globe. Now all he had to do was make the frigging thing work. He had to concentrate and think with the same directness he used with his other tasks.

He said it out loud, like an order. 'Make him talk like the soldiers.'

A dark-blue tendril floated out of the globe, somehow passing through the glass. It reached over to caress George's temple.

'Carl. Uh – Captain, this is strange.'

'Quiet, George!' Jackson shouted. 'Let it work!' He had half a mind to – but he had to make sure the globe knew what he wanted.

'Make him good with language!' he demanded. 'Make him speak both ways.'

217

'Cap – Carl.' George's voice sounded more like a moan. He batted at the tendril against his skull as if it was a living thing come to suck out his insides.

'Can't –' George's face was turning as blue as the smoke. He fell to his knees.

The globe was killing him.

Stop! Carl thought.

The tendril obeyed, snapping back inside the sphere like a rubber band.

George moaned again and rested his head in his hands. 'What was that thing doing? I felt like my head was going to explode. Another minute, I think it would have, too.'

Jackson stared at the thing. So it wouldn't do whatever he thought after all. What good was this wonderful magic globe if it wouldn't do what he wanted? He had half a mind to smash it.

But the globe had its uses. It would clear a path and it would kill people. The globe was good for destruction, and nothing more.

'What the hell am I going to do?'

Even Carl was surprised by the strength of the shout. It came from somewhere deep inside him, someplace that was always pissed off, but was doubly pissed by what had happened here.

He stared at his troops. Some of them looked uncomfortably back at him. But they were all still here. Even though they couldn't understand him, they were too scared to leave.

Understand him?

Carl suddenly remembered the first day he had come to this godforsaken place, when they had been taken to Nunn, and the Captain had disappeared. One of the other soldiers, maybe two, had spoken to them in English; not perfect English, something about being finished with the stew or sitting down or some such, but clear enough to be understood.

With any luck, one of those English-speaking soldiers was still with him. Hiding out here, not wanting to take responsibility.

Well, Carl Jackson was about to force responsibility on that man.

'Come on, George!' he called. Blake was still on his knees. 'We've got work to do.'

He turned to the soldiers and held the globe before him. 'Now!' he called. 'I know that some of you speak English. If you do, if you can speak any English at all, come forward and you'll be rewarded!'

None of the soldiers moved.

'Ah, my boys are being shy!' Jackson called. 'Very well, I will have to ask each of you in turn.'

He walked over to the nearest soldier.

'Do you speak English?'

The soldier looked at him as if he didn't understand at all. Either he didn't know the language, or he was a real good actor.

Carl held the ball before him. 'I repeat. Do you speak English? You have until the count of five to answer. If you do not answer me, I will kill you. Then I will go to the soldier next to you and ask the same question. If you try to run away, I will kill you. If you attack me, I will kill you.'

Jackson paused. The man before him shook his head. Was he saying that he didn't understand? Jackson would soon find out.

'Now,' he said, 'a final time: do you speak English? One, two, three –'

'Wait!' somebody called from the crowd.

Jackson stopped. 'I think we've got a volunteer.' He waved with his free hand. 'Please come forward.'

The man who had spoken pushed his way through the crowd. Jackson thought it might have been the same one who had talked about the stew.

'English,' he said tentatively. 'I have some – not so good, but some.' He stepped out in front of the crowd. 'Thought before you look for someone who speak – good English.' He frowned. 'What? Yes, better than me.'

Carl smiled. 'You'll be great. This is the best decision you've ever made. What is your name?'

'Name?' the soldier asked. 'Umar.'

'Well, Umar, you are my new officer! Do you understand?'

Umar hesitated for a moment, then nodded his head. 'Umar. Yes.'

'Umar.' Jackson spoke slowly and distinctly. 'For your first job, I need you to tell the troops to prepare to march.'

'March.' Umar nodded his head again. 'Yes. Umar tells.' He turned to the men and barked out a guttural sentence every bit as good as anything Harry had ever done, maybe better.

The soldiers quickly fell back into formation.

'Excellent!' Jackson cheered. He was on his way again, and even better than before. Someone like Umar would never question his orders like Harry or George.

He glanced over and saw that Blake still knelt on the ground. With any luck, Umar would work out nicely, and he wouldn't need anyone like George Blake anyway.

It would be pleasant, next time, to let the globe go all the way with Georgie.

But now he had his army back. Still, Jackson knew it wasn't enough.

He needed a triumph to cement his leadership.

They were on their first campaign. Captain Jackson's army. He was only supposed to capture the neighbours. Nunn's orders, after all. But he had to show his troops that he meant business.

Maybe he'd let some of the better soldiers, the ones who displayed special valour or some such shit, spend a little private time with some of the women. He wouldn't mind taking Joan Blake off her high horse himself.

But that still wasn't enough. Nunn or no Nunn, Jackson would have to kill a few of them, just to show how serious he was. Mills, to start. Maybe even Joanie, once he was done with her.

That would show his army he meant business!

Twenty-nine

By this time, Joan Blake thought she was ready for anything.

Anything, that is, but that sickly green glow in the sky.

'Is this it?' Rebecca Jackson whispered in her ear. 'Is this the dragon?'

Somehow, Joan had always thought the dragon would be somewhat larger than that, imposing even, and certainly a better colour than that dayglo thing descending towards them now.

Thomas came up beside her. 'Maybe I can shoot it down.'

Joan shook her head. 'No, we'd better see who – or what – it is first.'

'Exactly,' Rose Dafoe agreed sharply. 'This is the sort of thing Mary Lou would do.'

There was something in the tone of Rose's voice that implied it would be Mary Lou's fault, too. Maybe she also thought her daughter got captured by those little bald creatures on purpose.

For a second, Joan wished that light in the sky could be all their children, Nick and Todd and Mary Lou, coming back, safe and sound.

The green thing was floating down towards them, drifting like a falling leaf.

'It looks like a man,' Thomas announced.

'Sort of,' Rebecca agreed. 'Isn't part of him missing?'

Joan stared up with the others. Yes, the thing up there was definitely human shaped. Except that it did have a hole in the middle that showed the sky on the other side. Its sickly green colour was fading, too, as it drifted to earth, so that its features were slowly becoming more apparent.

'Oh my god,' Joan whispered. 'I think it's Hyram Sayre.'

'But Hyram's dead!' Rebecca exclaimed.

'Maybe', Rose suggested, 'you'd better shoot him down after all.'

'No, no, wait a minute,' Joan insisted. 'We know what this appears to be. But we don't really know what this is, and, until it threatens us, I, for one, will let it be. We have seen stranger things since we got here – I think.'

The green light flickered off like an old fluorescent bulb as Hyram settled to the ground. It certainly did look like Hyram, or what was left of Hyram. There was a part of him, where his stomach should have been, that was just a mess.

'Well,' Rebecca whispered in Joan's ear, 'what happens now?'

The thing that might be Hyram Sayre stood there, in the middle of the clearing, and stared.

Well, Joan thought, somebody had to say something. 'Hyram,' she asked, 'is that you?'

'Greetings.' The newcomer raised a hand in the way they used to do in old movies when the Indians talked to the Cavalry.

Nobody said anything back. What was there to say?

The newcomer cleared his throat. 'Um, that is – hello. I've never done this sort of thing before.' He smiled a bit sheepishly. 'Actually, I haven't spoken with anyone in quite a while.'

Well, it certainly sounded like Hyram Sayre.

'Hyram,' Rebecca said, 'we thought you were dead.'

Hyram nodded. 'Well, I was for a while, I think.'

'You still look it,' Rose agreed. She pointed towards his mid-section.

Hyram blinked and looked down at his middle. 'Oh, that's right. It's where the worms got to me. Part of the growing cycle, after all. It is a little distracting, isn't it?'

He frowned and placed a hand at the very bottom of the hole.

'Wait a moment,' he offered. He slowly drew his hand up the length of the hole, somehow drawing the two sides of his form in to meet in the middle on either side of a large, silver zipper.

Hyram frowned down at his handiwork. 'I hope that's all

222

right. With a little more work, I could probably imagine buttons.' He sighed. 'This omnipotence business is hard work.'

'I'm sure it is,' Joan agreed, more to keep the conversation moving than because she understood what he was talking about. 'Hyram, why have you come back here?'

This, at last, made Hyram really smile. 'I've decided to cease flying above it all and return to the living.'

Well, that was all very nice, Joan guessed with an hysterical sort of calm. First you get killed. Then you become omnipotent. What else would you want after that but to settle down?

'And do what?' she asked.

Hyram's smile faltered. 'I hadn't thought of that, exactly. Help things grow, I guess.'

'Help things grow?' Bobby Furlong had run up to join them. 'Hey, have you met the Oomgosh?'

Hyram's face went back to full frown. 'Didn't you used to run over my lawn?' He shook his head. 'Well, that's in our past.' His smile came creeping back. 'It's a whole new world, isn't it?'

He looked around in wonder, as if seeing his surroundings for the first time.

'I want to be one with the things of the earth,' he said, opening his arms to the great trees that surrounded the clearing, 'communing with them and helping them to flourish.'

'The Oomgosh already does that,' Bobby pointed out.

'He does?' Hyram's look of wonder sank into one of confusion. 'Oh, I see. Well, it still seems like important work. Maybe we'll have different approaches to the same job.'

Jason Dafoe walked up to the group. 'You said you can make things grow. Can you heal the Oomgosh?'

Hyram shook his head. 'Pardon?'

Joan saw what Jason was getting at. 'Our friend here was wounded in a fight,' she explained. 'We're worried about him. We were wondering if you could help.'

'Really?' Hyram's face lit up. 'Well, I'll certainly take a look.'

Jason turned and waved for Hyram to follow. The rest of the group tagged along, eager, Joan thought, to do something besides wait. And, as – well – *strange* as Hyram Sayre was acting, he did seem to have certain powers. It was amazing, Joan thought, how easy it was to accept that anything could happen here.

Besides, she thought, Hyram Sayre had always been a little strange.

'Jason,' the Oomgosh called from where he lay against a tree. 'I see you bring company.'

Jason shifted from one foot to the other, as if he didn't know where to start. 'This man here,' Jason began hesitantly. 'Mr Sayre –'

'I used to be Hyram Sayre,' Hyram agreed. 'Now I have a different purpose.'

'I can feel it,' the Oomgosh agreed.

'You can?' Jason asked, getting excited. 'This Mr – uh, this fellow here says he works with growing things. I thought maybe he could help you.'

'I can feel the potential in you.' The Oomgosh smiled up at Hyram. 'We both hold the power of living things and appreciate their beauty. In that way, we are brothers.'

Hyram smiled back. 'You look like a fine, tall tree. I've always wanted to make things grow.'

'Ah, this tree is sick,' the Oomgosh replied. 'He is filled with a poison that slowly seeps towards his heart.'

'Can you help him?' Jason asked Hyram.

The newcomer looked up at the boy. 'I don't know. I've never tried to heal anyone.' He turned back to the Oomgosh. 'I *have* caused grass and trees to sprout where there were none before. Maybe I can use that same energy on you.'

The Oomgosh sighed and closed his eyes. 'You are welcome to try, friend.'

Hyram Sayre knelt down by the tree-man's side. He extended his arms so that his hands were inches from the Oomgosh's rough skin. His hands began to glow the same putrid green.

Joan mentally chided herself. Hyram was trying to help the tree-man. She shouldn't be criticising his colour choices.

Hyram touched the tree-man's side. The Oomgosh's body lurched. He grunted as if he had felt a physical blow.

'Oh, dear,' Hyram said. 'What have I done?'

The Oomgosh opened his eyes. 'Actually, I feel much better.'

'Really?' Hyram asked, a little startled.

'Yes.' The Oomgosh sat up. 'Like spring is coming and the sap is beginning to run. You know what I mean.' He braced his good arm against a tree as he stood. 'Much better.'

'So he did heal you?' Jason called out behind the world's biggest smile.

The Oomgosh shook his head. His knee buckled a bit, and he had to lean slightly more against the tree to right himself. 'Not yet. But it is a beginning. The poison is still inside me, but now so is some of my strength. Perhaps the Oomgosh will last another season.'

The tree-man threw back his head to the sky. His laughter boomed out through the forest.

But, for all the tree-man's joy, Jason looked even happier.

The Oomgosh turned and rested his back against the great tree. 'I am afraid I have to sit again. Both standing and laughing were too much for my current state of recovery.'

'But it is better?' Jason insisted.

'It could not have been much worse,' the Oomgosh admitted.

'Perhaps', Hyram suggested, 'I should stay around for a while.'

'Maybe you can help in other ways,' Joan suggested. 'We can use everyone we can get.'

'Help?' Hyram smiled. 'Does it have to do with life?'

'Death, too,' the Oomgosh said.

'I've been there as well,' Hyram agreed. 'I'm your man. That is, if I'm still a man. I don't think I'm human, exactly.'

Human?

That was one of those things Joan didn't think was all that important any more.

Harold Dafoe didn't feel all that good about this.

For one thing, the wolves made him nervous. Especially when the other two humans left camp with only a wolf to guard him.

'Sit,' the wolf said, grinning at Harold with razor-sharp teeth. 'Rrrelax. Ourrr Captain will be back shorrtly.'

It didn't help one bit, either, that the wolves talked.

But he had nothing else to do but sit and reflect on how he'd got himself into this situation.

It was another case of someone else making the decisions for him. Of course, the way things had been going on the trail, the wisest thing in the world had been to get away from Carl Jackson. He wasn't sure if it was quite as wise to end up here.

Actually, Harold had made one decision on his own that had led to all the others.

That's how it all began, back there on the trail. One moment he was Carl Jackson's lieutenant, whether he wanted to be or not. The wolves were howling, the soldiers were frightened and Carl was fuming.

And then he had agreed to talk to the original Captain.

'Greetings!' the Captain had called to him in the soldier's tongue. 'How does it feel to be on one of Nunn's death marches?'

'Pardon?' Harold had been confused. 'What do you mean?'

'Oh,' the other man continued matter-of-factly, 'Nunn considers soldiers' lives to be cheaper than penny candy. He thinks nothing of losing half his troops in some fight or other. He knows the dragon will always bring him some more.'

Harold frowned. 'I don't think that will happen this time. We vastly outnumber the others. And they know us. We can probably talk them into surrendering.'

'Really?' the Captain asked. 'And who's going to do the talking? Your beloved leader?'

Harold stared at the other man. He realised what he had just said had more to do with his own hopes than anything approaching reality. As soon as you stuck Carl Jackson in the middle of those hopes, all you could do was lose.

'There is another way,' the Captain suggested.

That's when the wolves started up and somebody screamed. Jackson and his soldiers all rushed towards the other side of the trail.

'Time for us to be going.' Suddenly, as if they had appeared out of the air, the Captain was on one side of him, and another large and burly soldier was on the other.

'But –' Harold began as they lifted him off his feet and hustled him into the woods.

The second soldier took over the task of carrying him once they had lost sight of the trail. The Captain himself looked a little pale, as if he was recovering from a long illness.

'What are you doing to me?' Harold demanded.

The Captain waved for his soldier to stop. 'Do you want us to release you? Do you want to go back there? You know that your leader will consider you a deserter.'

Harold looked away from the Captain's face. That's exactly the sort of thing that Carl Jackson would do.

'I don't imagine your leader smiles upon deserters.'

Harold shook his head. Carl had already promised to shoot anyone who even thought about running away.

'Pator,' the Captain said to the second soldier, 'put our guest down. I think he will be walking with us the rest of the way.'

Pator did what he was told. And Harold walked back to the Captain's camp.

Where they had left him, a moment after they arrived, with a lone wolf for company and the promise that they would be back soon with food.

It seemed as if they had been gone for hours.

'Would you like waterrr?' the wolf inquired.

Actually, Harold thought, he was rather thirsty.

'There is a crreek, ten paces beyond that tree.' The wolf nodded to its left. 'Come. We will walk togetherrr.'

The wolf walked to his side, waiting for Harold to stand up and accompany him.

'If you strray from the path, I will have to give you a little nip,' the wolf remarked cheerfully. 'And blood makess me hungrry.'

Harold was careful to stay in the middle of the path. The stream was directly ahead, as advertised. He knelt down on the bank and dipped his hands in the water. It was surprisingly cold.

He cupped his hands and brought the water up to his mouth,

losing about two-thirds of the liquid on the way. Still, what made it down his throat tasted wonderful. He brought his cupped hands up a second time, being a bit more careful to keep them level with the ground, and got a bit more water in turn.

'My turrn,' the wolf announced as it stepped forward. It lowered its snout to lap up the water from the stream.

Even while it was drinking, it kept an eye on him.

Where would Harold go? As frightening as being surrounded by wolves might be, he was sure that being lost in the woods would be far worse.

The wolf lifted its head and pricked up its ears. 'We musst go back. They returrn.'

Harold preceded it back down the short path to the clearing and resumed his sitting position.

A moment later, a pair of wolves ran barking into the clearing, followed by the Captain and Pator, with the other two wolves at their heels.

'We have a feast!' the Captain called to Harold, holding up half a dozen carcasses tied together with rope. 'Fat birds felled with Pator's arrows. A wild hog that I caught with a stone from my sling. And, of course, the usual fine bush-rodents brought down by my troops!' He waved to the wolves. 'Now we start a fire, and then we eat!'

Harold realised he was quite hungry, too. He had no idea how long it had been since his last meal, when Nunn had fed the soldiers. But, he reminded himself, it was time to do more here than just eat and drink. He waited until after the Captain had started the fire to ask questions. 'What do you want with me?'

The Captain smiled at him. The scars on his cheeks kept this from being the most pleasant of sights. 'It's more what we don't want you to do.' He waved at the wolves, already eating, and Pator, who was plucking the birds.

'We fight against Nunn. He has overstepped himself. He is vulnerable.' The Captain made a fist. 'We want to scour him and those he controls off this island for ever. Of course, we will give those under him a choice. Join us, or die.'

He paused to study Harold for a moment before continuing. 'We shadowed Nunn's troops for a time before we made our decision. But it was obvious, from the first, that you were the only one capable of getting the wizard's plans to succeed.'

Harold was flabbergasted. 'Me?'

'Do not sell yourself short,' the Captain chided. 'With yor gone, see who is left: a leader who is crazier than I am, an assistant who doesn't seem to know where he is, and perhaps eighty soldiers who want nothing to do with either of them. Not exactly the recipe for a successful campaign.' The Captain laughed. 'You are the only one who could possibly have thought things through. But now you are with us.'

The Captain frowned, as if he had forgotten something. 'You are with us, aren't you?'

Harold nodded his head. Was he with them? It would be suicide to go back to Carl. Not that his chances might be all that much better here.

'Oh,' he answered as easily as he could. 'Of course.'

The Captain grinned and slapped him on the back. 'Congratulations, Harold Dafoe! You are the latest addition to the small but growing band of Free Islanders!'

The Free Islanders? Harold thought.

'Pator came up with the title,' the Captain admitted. 'I think it has a nice sound.'

He turned back to the fire. 'But come. We have a meal to cook. I'm looking forward to eating the fowl.' He glanced back at Harold. 'Have you eaten bush-rodent recently?'

Harold said that, to the best of his knowledge, he hadn't.

'Good!' the Captain cheered. 'The bush-rodent is yours. It's good once or twice, but after that it gets a little tired.' He grabbed two handfuls of plucked and skinned carcasses.

Pator strolled over as the Captain placed their meals on spits.

'You know,' he said softly to Harold, 'I believe he is crazy too. But he is the kind of crazy that can win.'

Thirty

'I should never have left.'

Sala pulled Todd's hand to slow him down. He stopped, mid-street.

'Why do you say that?' she demanded with a frown.

He wasn't sure. It was more a feeling than any particular reason. The two of them had planned to meet out back when they could find a moment. But they hadn't planned to run away until they heard what had happened inside.

'Nunn's got everybody,' he said after a moment. 'Maybe I could have helped.'

'And maybe you could have got yourself captured with the rest of them.' She took a step further down the street. 'At least now we might be able to get away from all of this.'

Todd laughed sourly at that. 'Not that I know where to go. All my friends are stuck back there in the Dragon Tavern.'

He gazed at Sala. She looked beautiful in this early morning light, her freckles golden on her skin.

'Do you have any place to go to?' he asked. 'Anybody who would help?'

Sala shook her head. 'They're all too scared of my father. If it comes to it, I know a couple of good places to hide.'

'Well, it may come to that too.' Todd looked up the empty street. 'It's awfully quiet out this morning. And awfully pretty.'

Now that they had stopped running for a second, Todd could really appreciate the view. The sun had risen out over the harbour; its lower edge had just cleared the water and the reflected light formed a golden path that reached to the docks.

With the sea breeze coming off the harbour, it smelled as if the ocean had washed the whole world clean.

'The rowdies are in bed,' Sala said softly, 'and the fishermen have gone to sea. It's the only quiet time around here.'

Todd looked back the way they had come. They had heard footsteps before, but they were gone now. 'This time of morning, you can hear people coming a long way off. That's good too. I expect Nunn is sending someone after us.'

Sala's voice sounded even smaller as she replied, 'Nunn – or my father.'

Todd turned back to Sala. She looked so small and frightened, he wanted to spend his whole life protecting her.

He longed to kiss her now, despite their danger and the friends they'd left behind, to take her in his arms for one bright moment, the two of them the only people in the world, the sea birds calling, the whole town bathed in golden light.

She looked up at him, wide-eyed, as if she, too, desired that kiss. He knew she would taste of the sea wind and a warm fire at night. Their lips were so close. He wanted this kiss to last for ever.

She pulled away. 'Someone's coming!'

He shook his head, the moment gone. There was no time to kiss while they were fighting to stay alive. He pulled her into the shadows of the buildings. 'Here, we'll find some place to hide!'

There, between two of the houses, was a narrow space, not even an alley, lost in the long morning shadows. Todd pulled Sala in after him. They were very close together. His hand brushed the linen of her blouse. He could feel her breathing on his cheek. She took his hand and clutched it tightly.

He could hear a pair of male voices in conversation, coming down the hill.

'It won't be far now.'

'And you think we'll see the others?'

'I'd be surprised if we didn't see some of them. We might be in for a bit of a fight.'

'As long as I don't have to use my sword, thank you.'

231

Todd knew those voices. He jumped from the alley, pulling Sala behind him.

The two others stopped as they saw them run out into the street.

'Nick! Mr Mills!' he called. 'How did you get here?' He never thought he'd be so glad to see a pair of neighbours.

'Magic,' Nick replied. He looked a little startled to see Todd, as well.

'It's much too long a story,' Mr Mills agreed.

Nick grinned at that. 'And how about you?' he called to Todd. 'Oh, that's right. You went on the ship with Mrs Smith! You were supposed to end up here!'

'This is Sala,' Todd continued, 'and I'm incredibly glad to see you, because we're in trouble.'

'The two of you?' Nick asked.

'No, I think we're all in trouble,' Todd replied. 'Nunn's here, and he's got Mrs Smith and Wilbert and Stanley.' Todd quickly explained the situation in the back room of the Dragon Tavern.

'That's where we're headed too, although, until now, I wasn't exactly sure it was the tavern.' Mr Mills paused to look back up the street. 'Someone else is coming.'

'Should we hide?' Sala asked. Her hand gripped Todd's tightly.

Mills held up a hand. 'No. We know these people. It's better if we wait.'

A moment later, Obar and Maggie strolled around a corner.

Obar stopped dead, Maggie stumbling to a halt beside him. Obar and Mr Mills looked at each other as if they were going to start a fist fight.

'This feels more like a small town than a city,' Todd murmured.

'Perhaps', Nick suggested, 'all roads lead to the Dragon Tavern.' He waved to the Volunteer. 'Maggie, I'm sorry. I've got –'

She waved him to silence as she stepped away from Obar. Todd had been wrong. The way the two men were staring at each other now looked more like a showdown in an old Western, where each waited for the other one to draw his gun.

'This one who looks like Mills,' Obar said to no one in particular, 'he's not who he seems.'

'And you are?' Mills shot back.

'Never trust a wizard,' Obar admitted.

'Unless another wizard wants the same thing,' Mills replied.

Maggie looked from one to the other. 'We're all here for the eye,' she said.

'Todd's found it,' Mills offered.

'It's in a tavern, the Dragon Tavern,' Todd added. 'But the dragon's eyes don't work there, in the back room. They don't work at all!'

'We've got other problems too,' Mills said. 'Nunn. Your partner in the desert.'

'I was stupid,' Obar admitted. 'Sometimes, I crave the power of the eyes so badly.'

The street was silent for a while after that.

Mills took a step forward.

'So we work together – for the moment?'

Obar's bushy moustache bounced as he nodded his head. 'For the moment.'

'And you won't join your brother?'

Obar seemed to want to turn away. He kept looking at Mills instead. 'It was the fear of seeing Rox again, the memory of what I've done.' He shook his head. 'I'm glad you're not dead, although I wonder if you're quite alive.'

Mills smiled at that at last. 'I wonder that myself. Hopefully, my definition will improve when we find the next dragon's eye.' He sighed then. 'There are other problems. Not only do the eyes not work there, but Nunn has reinforcements.' He looked to Todd. 'How many?'

'We saw around a dozen,' Todd answered.

'And my father,' Sala answered. 'He's the one who owns the tavern, he may have more.'

Maggie nodded at all of them, as if they had said enough. 'There's half a dozen of us. We'll put up a fight. Besides, maybe we can ambush their ambush.'

'There are more than six of us here,' Mills said in a deep voice. 'There are eight. Surely we can come up with something.'

233

'Well?' Maggie asked. 'What are we waiting for?'

She led the way. Obar and Mr Mills followed, with Nick, Todd and Sala taking up the rear.

'Eight?' Sala whispered in Todd's ear. 'Where are the eight?'

Todd shook his head. By now he knew there were things he just had to accept.

'Maybe', he whispered back, 'we can ask questions later.'

Thirty-one

'How?' Mary Lou demanded to the darkness. 'How do I do it?'

'If I knew that,' Garo's disembodied voice replied, 'do you think I'd still be here?'

She didn't like his attitude. 'You're laughing at me. You didn't used to do that.'

As soon as the words were out of her mouth, she was afraid she wasn't being fair to Garo. She was too upset to be fair to anybody.

Actually, she didn't even know exactly what she was asking. Did she want to know how to get out of here? Or did she want to find out how to fulfil the destiny the dragon had given her?

'No,' Garo replied, 'I did things that were worse. I tried to use you.'

His sudden seriousness startled her. But it made her thoughtful too. He had gone in her place to feed the dragon's hunger. She never thought she'd have the chance to ask him about it.

'You saved me in the end. Why did you change your mind?'

Garo laughed softly. 'I don't think my mind had much to do with it. Even then, with the Anno, it had been a long time since I had been alive. But, despite all that, you had made me feel human again.'

'Really?' What a nice reason. She thought about how much Garo had meant to her, for a little while, at least. It was only later, when she realised she didn't know Garo at all, that she recognised most of her feelings were just fantasies. And that she'd have to rely on herself, and not some phantom prince, if she was going to survive.

Still, it was nice in a way to hear him again.

'Well,' Garo returned to his bantering tone, 'as much as I could feel anything, considering the circumstances.'

He was quiet for a moment. The other voices surrounding them were still there, but somehow they had faded into the background. Had Garo done that? Had she?

Garo's sigh cut through the background murmur. 'I've always been very sorry about one thing.' He paused again, as if he had to drag each sentence from somewhere deep inside. 'I've never been able to touch you,' he said at last.

Mary Lou didn't know how to answer that.

The words poured out of Garo quickly now. 'I would like nothing so much as to leave this place and be with you, anywhere you want, even back in that old neighbourhood of yours. Maybe, if we were both real, flesh and blood, outside of this craziness, it would never work. But I'd love to try.'

Mary Lou had once thought of Garo as a prince. She wished she could feel that way again. But she couldn't.

Still, she thought he deserved a reply. 'After everything – that's nice to hear.'

'And I have got something new. I've heard your voice again. That's a gift I never expected.'

He laughed once more. 'It was impossible. But this whole world is impossible!

'You know', he added a second later, 'you're being used again.'

'What?' Mary Lou asked. Was Garo going to confess to some other horrible plan?

'The dragon is using you now,' he said instead.

'What do you mean?'

'No one should be in this place until they're dead. But the dragon has trapped you here. And he's going to keep you hidden – until when?'

Mary Lou had no answer to that question.

'I think the dragon is afraid of you,' Garo added.

It was Mary Lou's turn to laugh. 'Me?'

'No. You've got something, some power, some insight, that could throw off the way of things, or the way the dragon wants things to be. Otherwise, the creature never would have snatched you from the world of the living.'

'Garo! That's ridiculous.'

'Is it? Try to leave now.'

'But you were the one who showed me how to do it before. I saw my father.'

'Try it,' was all Garo said.

'Fine.' This time she thought about her mother.

The voices rose around her, as if they wanted to distract her from her task. They became deafening. She couldn't shut them out.

'No!' she shouted.

The voices retreated. But she had become distracted. Maybe if she thought about her father again.

The voices rose.

Dad, she thought. She would not be pulled away again.

The voices called.

Dad. She concentrated. If only she could see him for a minute, to tell him what was happening to her.

The voices shouted.

Dad. I need to see my father. She wished for the light to show her the way.

The voices screamed.

Dad. Dad. Dad. Dad.

The voices exploded inside her head.

'Nooooo!' she called, her voice as loud as all the others and maybe louder.

'You are overwhelmed by the voices of the dead,' Garo said matter-of-factly, as if he would expect nothing else. 'We surround you.'

But Mary Lou was not going to give up. Maybe she could find some way out of here if only she understood this place a little better.

'How did I find you, anyway?' she asked.

Garo thought for a moment before answering. 'I was suddenly here, knowing that I had to talk to you, to help you get around.'

'To keep me here,' she added. It did sound like the dragon was going to great lengths.

'You talked about a destiny,' she said slowly, 'and that the dragon might be afraid of that destiny. Maybe there's nothing the dragon can do to stop us.'

Maybe, she thought, she just had to think about bigger things.

She thought about the island, with the great trees, and the Anno, and her neighbours from Chestnut Circle, and the Volunteers, and the Oomgosh, and –

'What is that?' she called.

There was a great booming sound that filled the air around them, drowning out the voices.

'Have we made the dragon angry?' she called.

'Maybe you did,' Garo yelled back. 'I think I am largely beneath the dragon's notice. If I made it angry, I would cease to be.'

Garo's voice faded for a moment.

'Listen!' he said at last. 'I don't think it's the dragon after all.'

She could hear the difference too. The booming changed, grew higher, more distant, like a repeated call, or the cry of a bird. Mary Lou felt a sudden wind against her face, like the breeze from a pair of flapping wings.

'Caw!' went the cry. 'Caw!'

Mary Lou couldn't believe it.

'It sounds like Raven.'

'Well,' came the answering call, 'who else would it sound like?'

'Raven?' Mary Lou asked again.

'It took me long enough to get here,' the bird replied. 'It has been a long time since Raven has had to find his way around in the dark.'

'How could you be here? How could you be inside the dragon?'

'You mean because the dragon controls all things?' Raven laughed derisively. 'That is what the creature wants you to believe. The dragon is a pretender.' The bird cawed softly.

'The dragon, of course, thinks the same about Raven.'

'But why are you here?'

'What do you mean, why am I here? Raven is the creator of all things! He can go wherever he wants.'

'Oh,' Mary Lou replied, 'of course.'

'Now let's get out of here. Raven can't stand the stink of dragon fire.'

The stink of dragon fire? Mary Lou couldn't smell a thing.

But then she wasn't Raven.

She wished she could turn to Garo, to have a private word with him. But how could she do that in the absolute dark?

She thought about him instead. 'I have to go.'

'It's what we were both hoping for,' Garo called back. 'Think about me sometimes.'

She felt something hard nudge her shoulder, like the beak of a bird.

'And think of the dragon!' Garo's voice was fading back among the million others. 'What doesn't it want you to know?'

And then Mary Lou felt as if she was part of Raven herself and was soaring through space, flapping her wings.

Thirty-two

Nunn had finally decided to untie Snake and his men. They hadn't even bothered to tie up Mrs Smith. She didn't have the energy to run. But, even though she no longer had the power of the jewel, she had the power of her mind.

Maybe, she thought, there were other ways to get to Nunn. And maybe, if she was quick enough, there might be another way to get to the new dragon's eye.

'You speak well,' she said to him as they were waiting for the others, and the jewel. 'No doubt you were once a very cultured man.'

Nunn grinned at that. 'Before I became what I am today? No doubt. But that, my dear woman, was a long time ago.'

But Constance wasn't ready to leave it at that.

'What brought you here?'

'You mean besides the dragon?'

She shook her head. 'I think you know perfectly well what I mean. What changed you, and made you what you are?'

Nunn held up both his hands. 'The simple answer would be these, the dragon's eyes. They change everyone they come in contact with. You, too, no doubt, although you may still wish to deny it. Wait until the day you kill someone to keep your power. It will come.'

Perhaps it will, she thought. But I will never be like you.

A scream came from the public room next door.

Nunn looked sharply at Snake.

'It sounded like Stumpy,' the tavern owner explained.

'Who is?' Nunn prompted.

'He was one of the look-outs.'

'In plain view?' Nunn demanded.

'Well, no, he was supposed to be hidden.' Snake was beginning to sweat.

Nunn smiled back at Constance. 'Interesting. It appears that some of the others have arrived.'

'So what do we do?' Snake asked.

Nunn studied the dead jewel in his right palm. 'Do?'

'Your rivals are here!' Snake was beginning to sound the slightest bit exasperated. 'We should go out there and put them in their place!'

'Should we?' Nunn closed his open hand into a fist. 'I would think that's the very thing we shouldn't do.'

This was totally beyond the tavern keeper. 'What do you mean?'

Nunn smiled at Mrs Smith. 'That scream was an announcement. An enticement, if you would. About these rivals of mine; if they wanted to sneak up on us silently, they would. But no, they advertise.' He looked back at Snake, his smile gone. 'Why? To draw us into a little trap of their own and diminish our numbers.'

'Is that so?' Snake looked at the half dozen henchmen crowded around the room. 'Well, we'll simply attack them from the back!'

Nunn sighed. 'If you must.'

Snake slammed his fist on the table. 'And let's send a couple more of the boys through the passageways behind the walls!'

'Really?' Nunn nodded curtly, his eyes half closed, as if concluding some private conversation with himself. 'Now that idea may have merit. Even if they can't reach our adversaries, we may at least be able to spy on them and get some information.'

'Right!' Snake pointed to his men. 'Scar, you go out back and get Jack and the boys to circle around with you. Davy, you go through the hidden panel. One-Eye, you take the route down through the store-rooms. First one of you to reach the boys in the front room, tell them they've got work to do. Then let me know what you see. Be quick about it! And don't any of you take any chances!'

The three men rushed off their separate ways to perform their tasks.

'Now maybe we'll find out what's going on!' Snake announced.

'Or maybe we won't,' Nunn added. 'We'll certainly find out how well prepared our adversaries are.' He looked again at the two jewels embedded in his palms. 'Interesting. You become so dependent upon your jewels, it is difficult to do anything without them.'

He turned back to Mrs Smith. 'But all this business has interrupted a most pleasant conversation. Now, where were we? I believe you were trying to draw me out, perhaps discover some weakness of mine that you could use against me in the future?'

'Is that so?' Constance replied. 'Well, then, why don't you just tell me those weaknesses now and we can cut out all the small talk.'

'Oh, but I live for the small talk!' Nunn protested. 'You know, that might be a weakness after all. Beyond that, I have none.' He looked to his hands again. 'These eyes burn it out of you. Or rather, you burn it out of yourself, so that the eyes don't overwhelm you. I've seen more than one pretender to power destroyed by these things.'

'Really?' Constance replied. 'Well, then, we can only hope for the best.'

Nunn laughed at that. 'My dear lady! Sometimes you make me wish that I were human again, just so I might get closer to you.'

'While I, myself, only wish to get farther –'

Mrs Smith was interrupted by a crash from the other room.

'What was that?' Snake did not look at all happy.

'I imagine we will have to wait and find out,' Nunn said patiently. 'Do you have any idea how long it will take those men you sent out to spy?'

'For One-Eye and Dick?' Snake considered this for a second. 'Only a minute or two, unless they find something juicy.'

Nunn bobbed his head. 'Then we should hear from them shortly.'

Something else crashed next door, this time even louder than before.

Snake's head whipped towards the door that led to the tavern. 'They're tearing my place apart!'

'I would think that's an occupational hazard of your sort of profession.' Nunn sighed as he, too, glanced at the closed doorway that was keeping them away from all the action. 'Don't worry. Should this work out, you should have enough money to do the place over a dozen times.'

'And if it doesn't?' Snake demanded

Nunn's smile was gentle. 'Well, if it doesn't, you'll most likely be dead. Either way, though, you don't have to worry.'

A chorus of muffled shouts came through the door, followed by a third crash.

Snake stood up from his chair. 'I can't stand this. They're wrecking the inn.'

'They want you to go out there,' Nunn reminded him. 'We have to wait. We should be hearing soon from your spies.'

Snake looked to each of the entry ways that led behind the walls. 'You're right. Where are they? One-Eye's usually in and out!'

Nunn appeared lost in thought for an instant. He looked back to the tavern keeper. 'There isn't anybody else who knows about the secret passageways, is there?'

'The passageways?' Snake shook his head with a frown. 'Only a few of my most trusted men. Oh, and my daughter.'

Nunn's eyebrows rose. 'Really?'

'My daughter would never come back!' Snake's hand slashed through the air in front of him, rejecting the thought. 'She fears me too much.'

Nunn glanced over at Mrs Smith. 'Apparently, she has discovered another motive besides fear.'

'So what now?' Snake demanded. 'Do we wait for them to come in, or try to fight our way out?'

Somebody knocked on the door to the tavern.

Nunn waved for Snake to open it. 'I believe that will be your answer.'

Snake walked quickly over.

'Snake?' a voice called from the other side. 'Can I talk to you?'

'It's Scar,' Snake acknowledged. 'Should I open it?'

Nunn shrugged. 'I see no other choice.'

Snake jerked the door open, his free hand on the knife at his belt.

'Oh,' he said.

He stood there for a moment with the door open. If Scar was on the other side, Constance couldn't see him. And no one seemed to be talking to anybody else.

'Have him come in,' Nunn insisted. 'What's holding him back?'

Snake moved back. 'Scar,' he said.

The other man stepped into the room. He seemed to have lost his clothes and was wearing nothing but a rather soiled apron about his mid-section.

'They wanted to make sure I didn't have any weapons,' Scar muttered darkly.

'I'm surprised they didn't dress you in something with more frills,' Nunn replied. 'Well, at least someone has returned. And we know our opponents have a sense of humour.' He beckoned Scar forward. 'But come! I'm sure they gave you a message to deliver.'

'You want me –' Scar began. He looked across the room at Constance. 'But –'

'Oh, come now,' Nunn insisted, 'I do believe she's seen naked men before.'

'At my age', Mrs Smith agreed, 'you've seen almost everything.'

Scar took a couple more steps into the room, revealing more of his opponents' handiwork. While the apron covered a fair amount of his front, it had little effect on his backside. He was actually skinnier than Constance had guessed. And there were more scars than just the one on his face.

'They want to see the woman,' Scar announced. 'Mrs Smith. To make sure we haven't hurt her.'

Nunn nodded as if resigned to his fate. 'It makes sense. We'll probably have to untie everybody and get rid of all our weapons too.' He sighed. 'What I won't go through for a dragon's eye.'

He waved Snake and the others in Constance's direction. 'Carry her out there, so that we can get on with this.'

Snake nodded to two of his remaining henchmen. They moved forward and stood to either side of the chair. 'Now,' one of them said, and each of them grabbed one side and lifted her, chair and all. They carefully marched her down the length of the room.

'Oh,' Nunn called, 'and Mrs Smith? Please let us know what they want.'

Thirty-three

Nunn was furious, but he was doing his best not to show it.

Instead of trapping his opponents, they had trapped him. Instead of a fortress, he had a prison. And all because he didn't take one little girl seriously.

Still, as long as all of them gathered here, none of this mattered. All that was important was who gained possession of the sixth stone. And Nunn had many more plans for that, both inside and out of this tavern.

Nunn stared at Scar. The other man looked particularly vulnerable, standing there with only a scrap of white cloth around his middle. 'Do you have any idea what happened?' he asked most politely.

'Yeah,' Scar said. He scuffed at the floor with his bare feet. 'The jewels don't work in here, but they still do outside. And they got most of us out there.'

They lured them outside. It was pitifully simple, just like the tavern keeper and all his men. This was what happened when Nunn had to depend too much on others.

He did not want to get too upset. He had, of course, allowed himself to become momentarily distracted as well. Just as Mrs Smith had been looking for his weaknesses, he had been searching for hers. She was quite quick on the uptake, but he thought that maybe she was still just a little afraid of him. Nunn liked that in a woman.

Well, again, none of this would matter soon. He would have to hold his temper until his final plan took effect.

A woman appeared at the door, one of those forest people from back on his island with the brown-and-green clothes that blended in with everything. He'd never bothered much with them until now. That was another mistake, no doubt.

'We are ready to talk,' the woman said. 'After you untie my two friends over there.' She indicated the two men who had arrived earlier with Mrs Smith, both of whom were dressed in that same forest fashion. 'And', she added, 'all the weapons will be piled in the middle of the table, out of arm's reach, where everyone can see them. I am to stand here until those two conditions are carried out.'

'I would expect no less,' Nunn said most agreeably. He glanced up at Snake, who might be stupid enough to resist. 'Do it,' he said simply.

Snake pulled his knife from his belt and tossed it on the table. He told his one remaining man to do the same.

The woman turned, once the two males were untied. 'They've done it!' she called. 'You can come in.'

She stepped inside the room, moving beside the door. She carried no weapons either. Still, Nunn was quite sure she'd be formidable in a fight.

Snake's two men returned, carrying Mrs Smith in her chair. Immediately after them were Nunn's brother and the man inside whom Rox hid.

Nunn nodded to the newcomers. 'Is this all of you?'

'All that matter,' said the man with Rox inside him, Evan Mills. Or perhaps it was Rox himself who spoke. 'We had to post a few sentries ourselves.'

'Perfectly understandable,' Nunn agreed. And perfectly futile as well. If he had to, Nunn could trap everyone in this room in an instant. Not that they needed to know that just yet.

'So what happens now, dear brother?' Obar asked.

'You should know that as well as I,' Nunn replied. 'The dragon is ready to show us another eye, here in this room. But it had to wait until all the proper players were present.'

'Players?' Mrs Smith asked. 'I believe you mean the wizards?'

'Yes, those of us whom the dragon has already chosen. Once we are all together, I believe the dragon's intent will become clear.'

'Excuse me,' said the hairier of the two male forest folk, 'but you've got all the wizards here already. What's the dragon waiting for?'

'We have to be patient,' Nunn replied, his anger even closer to the surface. Still, he wondered a bit why the eye had not yet been shown to them. For a few moments before, while he had waited in the public room, he had seen a series of those sort of disruptions that the dragon seemed so fond of. But then, as soon as the others arrived, the disruptions ceased.

What could this mean? Perhaps, Nunn realised, he was really angry with the dragon.

'We can't wait here for ever,' Evan Mills said. 'Whatever is suppressing the magic here is hurting Zachs as well.'

An unexpected benefit, Nunn thought. 'Give it another minute,' he urged. The dragon had shown that the eye was coming, perhaps half a dozen times. It wouldn't stop now. 'Perhaps the eye comes from a long way off.'

'Or maybe the dragon has a sense of humour', the hairy fellow said, 'and has brought you all here for a joke.'

'Maybe', Mrs Smith said softly, 'Nunn is simply wrong.'

'*I am not wrong!*'

Oh, dear, Nunn hadn't meant to shout just yet. That put everything into motion a bit too fast. Well, he would just have to cope.

'I know more about the dragon that any of you,' he said, the model of serenity. 'This is the way the dragon dispenses its gifts. But perhaps we are overlooking something.'

He looked quickly about the room, hoping for some indication of the presence of the newest eye, a bit of green, perhaps, or a sudden light from around a corner. There was still nothing.

What had he missed?

'Maggie!' a young man's voice shouted from the tavern. 'We're under attack!'

'What's that?' the female forester asked. She took a step towards the door.

'They're not human!' the young man called. It was Todd. Nunn and he had had business before. 'Red-haired apes, like the ones we fought on the island!'

'What is this?' Mrs Smith demanded.

Once in a while, Nunn's plans were too efficient. He pulled a dagger from deep within his robes. 'I simply didn't want anyone to leave unexpectedly.'

'Or anyone else to get the stone,' Obar said in disgust. 'Brother, you're as predictable as you are corrupt.'

'Watch out!' Todd called. 'There're too many of them! They're trying to overwhelm us. We're gonna have to join you!'

The tavern keeper's daughter was the first to enter the room. Todd followed quickly, as if he didn't want the girl beyond arm's reach. 'Come on, Nick!' the boy cried.

And then the world shifted, as green light poured around them.

The dragon was ready at last.

Thirty-four

Nick had had to pull his sword, something he swore he would not do again. But it was a promise that he could never keep.

They had done their best to keep the creatures away. The ape-things had appeared almost out of nowhere, pouring through the front door and climbing in through the windows a moment after Nick had heard a shout in the back room.

Todd called out to watch for their spears, or poison sticks, as someone had called them back on the island. Luckily, only a few of the creatures carried them. The rest of the red-haired things sported short, curved knives, which they swung at the ends of their ape-like arms.

Todd had a knife of his own, but he also used his fists and feet to keep the creatures away. Sala had found a long club behind the bar and was swinging it at the things, knocking them back into their fellows.

And Nick had pulled his sword.

The ape creatures seemed so eager to rush at them that they almost impaled themselves on the point of Nick's blade.

But Nick would only allow the sword to drink for an instant before he freed the blade to accept one of the corpse's fellows. The power built more slowly in him during this battle, perhaps because of the lesser amounts of blood. He swore he wouldn't let that power overwhelm him this time.

The three of them held their attackers off for a long moment while Todd shouted a warning to the next room. But there were only three of them, against what seemed like a never-ending stream of the ape-things. They had to find a better place to defend themselves.

'We'll have to fall back into the next room!' Todd called. Nick nodded. There, they would only have to defend a narrow doorway, and they could get assistance from those already in there.

Todd scrambled on ahead to alert the others to what was happening. He stepped aside to let Sala through, then followed her into the room.

And a rush of green light poured from the room behind him. The ape-things screamed and surged away, trampling each other in their panic to escape.

Nick turned round, shielding his eyes against the glare.

Todd had told him that the back room was a kitchen. Just now, it looked like a kitchen under water.

It was as if the green light that filled the room was really water and four people swam through it. Mrs Smith, Obar, Mr Mills and Nunn; the four wizards floated in the middle of what should have been the air. And they all swam through this strange ocean, following a light which dodged and darted before them, shining like a guppy in a shallow, sun-filled lake.

There were others in the room as well. They sat or stood like statues, as if time had stopped for them.

But there was also another figure walking through the room, feet on the floor, as if the strange green light wasn't there at all.

Todd turned back to Nick and waved.

Nick almost laughed. It was just like Todd to be walking around in the middle of this madness. Heck, if Todd had his way, he'd beat the wizards just using his attitude! Nick hated to admit it, but he was starting to like that high-school bully. He'd been a little surprised they'd got along so well once they'd met here in the port town. But then, they'd probably been so busy fighting outsiders they'd had no time to fight each other.

So Todd walked through the green. But the wizards were much closer to the gem as it darted back and forth through the air – or water. Obar pushed Nunn out of the way, the frailer dark wizard tumbling away. But Mr Mills had cut in front of both of them and was angling his body to force the light down towards a corner of the floor, where he could trap it. But the light slipped between his legs and spun straight for Mrs Smith.

She seemed surprised by this opportunity, waving her hands and feet to halt her forward progress through the strange green sea and accept her gift. But all her waving only made her body spin round, the light bouncing off her knee. It angled straight down into Todd's palm.

Todd closed his fist. The light was gone.

Nick blinked, unable to see in the return to normal daylight.

'What the hell –' somebody yelled.

'The jewel!' somebody else responded. 'He's got the jewel!'

'Well,' Mrs Smith cut in, 'maybe he's supposed to have the jewel!'

Shapes were starting to come together in front of Nick's eyes. All four wizards stood on top of the table, their clothing plastered to their bodies as if they had all been caught in a torrential downpour. All the others, Todd included, looked perfectly dry.

Wilbert nudged Stanley with his elbow. 'I think the dragon has a sense of humour after all.'

'The stone!' Nunn screamed. 'I won't lose another stone!' The two gems in his own palms had begun to sparkle again.

'Zachs doesn't hurt!' Mr Mills called in that strange, high voice.

'The eyes!' Obar cried. 'They're working again!'

The wizards looked from one to the other. All held their gems.

'Get out of my way!' Nunn shrieked. He opened his hands and two beams of green spread across the room.

His beams were met by three others, mid-table.

The room seemed to explode. All four of the wizards yelled as they were thrown from the table.

Nunn scrambled to his feet. 'Not yet!' he called. 'I have a hundred ways to stop you!'

He slammed his fist into a panel on the kitchen wall. The panel moved aside. And then the kitchen ceiling opened, releasing a dark mass over everyone.

It was one huge net, Nick realised as it fell, a net made out of thick strands of rope, ensnaring each person they fell upon. Somehow, Nunn had managed to trap almost everyone.

Nick's arm began to shake.

He sheathed his blade before he could think of anything else. This time, at least, he had had some control.

Everybody was yelling at once in the kitchen. Nick waded into the mess. The nets had missed Sala and Maggie too. The mesh had mostly fallen in the middle of the room. Another trap, no doubt, although Nick figured this wasn't quite the way it was supposed to work.

'How can we get them free?' he asked the others.

'There are knives piled in the middle of the table,' Maggie replied, 'if we can get to them.'

'Wait a moment,' Sala said as she rushed past Nick. 'There's something in the other room.' She came back a second later with a six-inch blade. 'My father wants to be prepared for every emergency.'

Nick saw a couple of figures crawl from the far end of the net and bolt through the alleyway door. He was pretty sure one of them was Nunn. There was no way Nick could follow him. Even a cursed sword was no match for a pair of dragon's eyes.

Maggie got Todd free first. 'Hey, Nick!' he called, holding up the eye. 'Is this a trip, or what?'

'Put that away someplace!' Maggie chided him. 'I think there's more than one in this room who would like to take it from you.'

'Yes, ma'am,' Todd agreed, sliding it into one of his front jean pockets.

Sala ran over to him. The two of them hugged.

'I was so frightened,' she whispered up at him.

'Hey,' he replied, stroking her hair, 'I was only a little scared myself.'

It looked like Todd had made another conquest. Nick could never figure what women saw in that jerk.

'Here! Nick!' Maggie had made it to the other knives on the table. 'Grab one of these!'

He did just that, busying himself freeing the other prisoners of the net.

'Thank you, dear,' Mrs Smith said as he cut her free. 'This has not been the most dignified of mornings.'

253

She stood up. 'Nunn's gone, isn't he?' She looked down at the stone she still held in her hand. 'And my eye doesn't seem to work again.'

Maggie had freed Mr Mills and Wilbert, and was moving on to Stanley. Nick found Obar had began to cut through the ropes.

'Maybe there's some backlash', Obar muttered, 'with us using the eyes on each other.'

'The eyes are still working somehow,' Mills informed them. 'Zachs is not in pain.'

Todd fished his own gem out of his pocket. 'This eye isn't working either, or maybe I don't know how to start it going. Thanks, but I'll keep it,' he added before any of the others could make an offer.

'Maybe it has something to do with this place,' Mrs Smith suggested, 'some residual effect.'

Neither Obar nor Mr Mills looked very convinced.

It took only a moment for Maggie and Nick to free the last few prisoners of the net. Nunn, Snake and one of Snake's men had got away. They tied the remaining gang members together in the tavern room. As Wilbert mentioned, they'd get freed when the paying customers showed up for the night.

With that, the whole group, Obar, Mills, Mrs Smith, Maggie, Wilbert, Stanley, Todd, Sala and Nick, left the tavern together. It was still barely mid-morning and only the more respectable people were out on the streets.

Mr Mills looked at all the others. 'What happens now?'

Obar considered the question. 'I think that we have to find Nunn.'

'We?' Mr Mills said dubiously.

Obar glanced sharply at his fellow wizard. 'I think recent events have made it clear that the dragon is taking an ever more active part in this world. We can look on this as a warning. I think it's best if we work together to control as many of the eyes as we can before that happens.'

Obar seemed different than he did before. More direct. Nick guessed that he had no more time to be absent-minded.

'Granted,' Mills replied. 'Then I am with you. But where is Nunn?'

'He would return to his stronghold,' Obar replied, 'back to that island where we came from.'

'How,' Mills asked, 'without the powers granted by the gems, could we move all of us to another island?'

Obar shook his head. 'You know as well as I that, as magicians, we hold over certain residual powers from our time with the eyes. Although I feel even those might be dampened in this strange new climate.'

'We do have a ship!' Nick reminded them.

'So we do,' Obar said, shaking his head that he could forget something so big. 'And perhaps, with so many of us, we can somehow manage to sail it.' He waved for the others to follow him. 'Let's get ourselves to the harbour.'

Todd and Sala helped Mrs Smith down the hill.

'We are so dependent on our eyes,' she murmured apologetically. 'Me in particular.'

'I'm sure we'll get yours to work again,' Todd said. He seemed to swagger a bit when he talked about the eye. 'You have to give me some pointers on mine too!'

But the smile left his face as he looked past the old woman to the girl on the other side. 'I'm worried about you, Sala. Will you be all right?'

'What do you mean, will I be all right?' she repeated indignantly. 'I want to go with you!'

Todd looked back to Mrs Smith. In a way, she was the leader of all of them now. 'Can she come with us?'

'Oh, dear,' Mrs Smith began. 'And leave Sala's – well, there isn't much for her here, is there?' She smiled. 'I don't see why not. It will certainly be more pleasant for her with us than it would be for her to stay here and have to face her father. Maybe the two of you can get a little bit of happiness.' She stopped and sighed, as if she had second thoughts. 'Not, of course, that it will be at all pleasant when we reach the other island.'

'When the dragon arrives,' Obar replied, 'I doubt that anyone will survive, whether they are on this island or the other.'

Mrs Smith frowned at that. 'So you say. But what does any of us really know?'

Thirty-five

Jason started awake. Charlie was barking loud enough to wake the entire forest.

'What's the matter, boy?' Bobby asked, patting the dog's bony head. With Nick gone, Bobby had taken care of looking after the dog.

Jason looked up. The sky was growing the slightest bit lighter overhead. It must be just around dawn. Soon, it would be time to get up anyway.

'Charlie sees something over there, in the woods!'

Bobby and Charlie started over to check it out.

'Bobby!' Thomas called from where he stood watch. 'Wait a moment. We'll look together.'

Bobby paused for Thomas to catch up. Charlie galloped on ahead.

Jason looked down at the Oomgosh. He was sleeping, more peacefully, it seemed, than during the day before. So whatever Mr Sayre had done to him had seemed to help for the long run too. Jason just wished Sayre could give the Oomgosh more of it.

Charlie started barking all over again, running back and forth at the edge of the woods.

He was answered by a howl.

'Wolves!' Thomas called. 'Bobby, see if you can call Charlie back here!' He fitted an arrow into his bow.

'There's more than just wolves out here,' a voice said from the wood.

'Jason!' Bobby called back. 'It's your father!'

His father? Jason got up. He thought his father was gone for good, somehow captured by Nunn and locked away for life. That is, when Jason thought about it at all.

He watched as his dad, his actual dad, walked out of the woods. It was funny. It was like Jason had pushed his father so far out of his life, he didn't know what to feel. Not at all like the Oomgosh. Maybe somebody almost had to die before Jason could really feel something about them.

'Hey, Jason.' His father waved.

Jason took a couple of hesitant steps in his direction.

'Oh, yeah,' he managed to say. 'God, Dad, I'm glad you're OK.'

'Why don't you come over and –' His father stepped forward, arms wide, ready to give his boy a hug. Jason was surprised to think how much he'd like that.

His father stopped as his mother marched towards him.

'Harold Dafoe!' she demanded. 'Do you have any idea how worried –'

'Don't start with me now, Rose,' his father said, sounding about as firm as Jason had ever heard him. 'We'll talk once things have settled down.'

He looked back towards the forest. 'I didn't get here entirely on my own, though. I had some help. Help who wants to meet you.'

Another figure stepped out of the forest. Jason half expected it to be one of the talking wolves. He hadn't expected the Captain of Nunn's guard.

'You!' Rose Dafoe said accusingly.

'Yes, I'm afraid it is.' The Captain smiled and shrugged. 'I treated you very badly before. I'm here to make up for it.'

Thomas stared at him. 'I thought you were dead.'

'Hello, Thomas,' the Captain replied. 'I think in a way, I was.'

'You two know each other?' Bobby asked.

'Yes, we do,' the Captain answered. 'A long time ago I was a Volunteer.'

'And then you sided with Nunn?' Thomas was furious. 'I should kill you right here.'

'I wouldn't blame you for that, although there were circum-

257

stances that led me into this. I took care of my own, though, in my way. Didn't you ever wonder, after I disappeared, why Nunn never hunted down the last few Volunteers?'

'Thought we were beneath his notice,' Thomas admitted.

'Nothing is beneath Nunn's notice, especially where revenge is concerned –' the Captain allowed one eyebrow to rise, '– unless someone can talk him out of it.'

Thomas considered that for a moment. He nodded his head sharply. 'All right. Maybe we'll let you talk.'

'Thank you, Thomas. I appreciate it.'

The Captain seemed different to Jason than that last time he had seen him, when he was taking the neighbours to Nunn. Could that have only been a few days ago? For one thing, the Captain was thinner. But he also seemed quieter, as if he decided to talk instead of brag.

'Who?'

The cry was high and sharp and not quite human. Jason half expected some huge white owl to fly from one of the trees.

Instead, Hyram Sayre came rushing across the clearing, walking not on the ground but in the air.

'It's you!' Hyram stated.

This time, the Captain had no reply.

'You who killed me!'

'Yes it is,' the Captain admitted.

Hyram floated, seething silently, before his murderer.

'In a way', the Captain suggested softly, 'you might be better off.'

'What?' Hyram demanded. Then he added. 'Yes!'

He seemed to be losing definition around the edges, his hands and feet and head all glowing green. 'You know what I should –' he began. 'But I shouldn't!' he added.

The bright green overtook him as Hyram went flying out over the woods.

'I've done terrible things,' the Captain said, following Hyram until he was lost behind the trees.

'I think you have.' It was Mrs Blake who stepped forward now. 'We don't know what's happened to Hyram, or what he's capable of.'

258

The Captain was silent for a minute.

'So why'd you come here?' Thomas asked bluntly.

'To make amends,' the Captain replied, 'or at least whatever amends I can. To fight against Nunn, who nearly killed me, both spirit and body. If I can, to kill Nunn and make this world a better place.'

He looked at Thomas and the neighbours, all of those who had gathered around.

'Nunn is sending a small army against you, perhaps eighty men. There is no way you can fight that number by yourselves. I bring you three more men and five wolves who obey my every command. We are good at picking at the enemy, demoralising them, diminishing their numbers, then vanishing into the forest as if nothing had ever happened. Plus, that army was once loyal to me. I have a feeling that, given a chance, some of them can be turned to my way of thinking again.' He waved an arm around to include all of those before him. 'Together, we still might not be able to defeat that army, but at least we can put up a fight.'

He turned back to Thomas. 'I don't know if you quite believe me, but I also don't know if you have a choice.'

'We'll have to talk about it,' Thomas allowed.

'Talk quickly,' the Captain replied. 'You have very little time.'

Thirty-six

As they reached the dock, Mrs Smith saw another ship pulling out of the harbour.

The others saw it too.

'Look,' Nick called, 'could that be Nunn?'

'We'll know soon enough,' Wilbert answered. 'See if that vessel takes the same course as we do.'

Wilbert and Stanley took over, carrying Mrs Smith up the gangplank and on board the sailing vessel.

'That is', Wilbert remarked, 'if we can get this ship sailing. Stanley and I have always been strictly landlubbers.' They gently put her down on a pile of rope and canvas that made an acceptable seat.

'I was in the merchant marine,' Mr Mills volunteered. 'But after basic training, I held down a desk job. Mostly, I could tell you the names of things on this boat.'

Mrs Smith sighed. 'I wish this ship would just cast off for home.'

'Is there someone else on board?' Maggie said. 'I could have sworn I saw someone up in the bow. Funny. He looked a little like a cross between Stanley and Wilbert.'

A cross? That was from the spell Mrs Smith had left on board before she went ashore. As was the gangplank they had all used to get on board.

Did that mean that other spells might be working as well?

The ship jerked away from the dock, as if trying to free itself from its moorings in response to Mrs Smith's commands.

'I think the sailing spell still works,' she whispered. So whatever was dampening the eye's power at this moment appeared to have no effect on the earlier products of its magic. It made a certain sense. So much of this place had been built by this magic that chaos would result from its sudden removal.

And it seemed as if the dragon wanted to save the chaos for later.

'Hey!' Maggie called to the others. 'Free those ropes there! And Todd and Sala hop on board! We're under way!'

'Well,' Obar remarked, smiling at Mrs Smith. He waved towards the ocean as the boat sailed slowly out of the harbour. 'It seems that sometimes I can do something right.'

'Sometimes,' she agreed, 'when the dragon's eye doesn't get the best of you.'

Obar nodded as he looked at her quizzically. 'It's strange. You're the only one who's had the eye who hasn't succumbed to the greed for more.'

'I haven't had the eye for very long,' Mrs Smith admitted. 'Nunn is sure it will corrupt me with time.'

'No, I think that you handled it differently from the very first.'

'Maybe it's because I'm a woman. Perhaps I react to the eye in a different way.'

Obar shook his head. 'Or it could be because you're wiser than all the rest of us combined. Nunn and I are older than you, as is Rox, whose spirit is somehow hidden in Mr Mills. But we've spent almost all our lives in the pursuit of the eyes and what the eyes can give us. That leaves us with very little knowledge of the rest of the world.'

'Which I have, after forty years of being a suburban house-wife?' she asked incredulously. 'Not that I didn't do a lot of volunteer work, mind you.'

'No, it goes beyond that, to what you hold inside you. I think that, somehow, some of us have wiser souls.'

Mrs Smith smiled at that. 'Well, thank you, I think.' She'd never had her soul complimented before. Actually, she wasn't even sure how responsible she was for her soul's condition.

'It has to be Nunn!' Maggie called back from the position she'd taken up on the forecastle. They'd sailed free of the harbour and their craft was picking up speed. She pointed to the other ship, now only a dot on the horizon. 'We're following him directly!'

'So he'll get to the island before us, hey?' Stanley mused. 'Do you think he might come about and attack?'

'Ah,' said Obar with a grin, 'then there's a dilemma, isn't there? For I imagine Nunn is being propelled by a ship full of human sailors, while we're being sent in a ship powered by a left-over magic spell. Now, the question is, can a slightly tattered spell overcome and even pass real sailors with a knowledge of the sea?'

Mrs Smith realised he was proposing a race. 'Shall we try?'

'The helm is yours,' Obar replied. 'I designed this spell for your command.'

She felt a bit like a child again. 'How should I do it?'

The wizard glanced distractedly about the boat. 'Oh, I would make your commands as specific as possible.'

Specific? She supposed that left out something like 'Go ship, go!'. So perhaps, instead of simply telling the ship to go faster, she should address directly the method of propulsion.

She turned her head towards the sky. 'Sails!' she called, 'fill with wind!'

The sails billowed forward, even though the breeze was only moderate.

Wilbert whooped from where he leaned against the rail. 'We're really moving now!'

The wizard tugged at one side of his lengthy moustache. 'An excellent beginning.'

Sometimes she rather liked Obar. It was too bad he couldn't be trusted.

Mr Mills walked over to join them. 'You understand that all these factors – the loss of power of the gems, Nunn's flight across the sea, the convenient way that the spell still works for this craft – all of them point to us being led somewhere for the dragon's benefit.'

Mrs Smith realised from the tone of Mills's voice that Rox was talking.

'Well,' she replied, 'some of them do.'

Mills frowned at her response. 'Some, or all, I have never

seen the dragon interfere so much with the lives of the people on its world. I feel somehow that we are players in a drama where we are not allowed to see the script.'

'We have a saying for that where we come from,' Mrs Smith agreed. 'It's called "being set up".'

'Set up?' Obar asked. 'To be knocked down, perhaps.'

'Let us hope we have more of a chance than that,' Mills answered.

'Perhaps we will,' Mrs Smith said, 'if we can find some way to use our eyes together.'

Mills smiled at that. 'Now you're talking about the impossible!'

'We're catching up with the other ship!' Maggie called from up ahead.

The other boat, which had only been a spot on the horizon a few minutes before, was now quite close. Mrs Smith could see great black crosses on the sails.

'We'll be alongside her in another minute or two!' Maggie added.

'Try to give her a wide berth,' Obar told Constance. 'Gunpowder doesn't work with any regularity here, but they can shoot arrows and spears. If it's a pirate ship, they may even have a couple of giant crossbows that'll send flaming spears quite a distance.'

'Give a wide berth?' Mrs Smith asked a little doubtfully. She wasn't quite sure how to steer with the wind.

'Let me have a try at it,' Mills suggested. 'Merchant marine training, remember. I'll take the wheel.'

Oh. He could steer the ship manually. What a novel idea.

'Be careful it doesn't fight against your spell,' Obar cautioned.

'Release the rudder for a moment', Mills encouraged as he positioned himself behind the wheel, 'and let us steer.'

Mrs Smith was even less sure of what she was doing here. 'Free the rudder!' she suggested.

The boat pitched to one side as if the steering line had snapped, but the craft righted itself almost immediately.

'I've got it now!' Mills called. 'Had to get the hang of it!'

263

'Ship on the starboard bow!' Maggie called.

Mrs Smith looked ahead and saw the other vessel, maybe only a couple of hundred feet away. It was close enough, in fact, that they could see half a dozen angry faces peering at them over the rail. One of them was Nunn's. And there were others that they recognised.

'That's my father!' Sala cried.

'Snake is on board?' Wilbert asked. 'Maybe, once we get back to our island, we can return his hospitality.'

'He's going to catch us!' Sala despaired. 'Oh, I'll never get away from him.'

'Hush.' Todd pulled her close to him. 'I won't let him hurt you.'

Mrs Smith wished she could still feel the utter certainty of youth.

Her vessel gained on the other until the ships were side by side.

'I can only turn her aside so much!' Mills called as they approached the other ship. He looked overhead. 'Maybe it's the wind. More likely it's the spell!'

So, Mrs Smith thought, Obar's magic might end up destroying them all.

'That's a pirate ship for sure,' Maggie announced. 'I see a fire embrasure on board! They're going to try to burn us!'

Obar paced the deck. 'It's the one way they can stop us. The dragon's eyes don't work and these wooden ships will burn quickly down to the water line.'

A spear, maybe three feet in length, was launched towards them in a great arc. A rag had been tied behind the spear-point and set ablaze, so that it looked more like a fast-moving torch tossed in their direction.

The spear landed in the ocean a good ten feet shy of the boat. The flames hissed as they hit the water.

'Well,' said Mrs Smith, a bit relieved, 'that was well short.'

'Don't speak too soon,' Wilbert replied. 'They may just be determining the range.'

The other ship was angling towards them, decreasing the distance between the two.

'Is there some way you can steer away from them?' Mrs Smith asked Evan Mills.

'I don't know if that's advisable,' Mills answered. 'The spell, you know! We're going at such a good clip, I think we have a better chance of just outdistancing them. We only have to hold on a minute or two longer.'

A second spear was launched towards the forward end of the ship. It fell below Mrs Smith's line of sight as it headed for the bow. She closed her eyes, waiting to hear the flaming missile hit the wood.

'A miss!' Maggie called.

Mrs Smith opened her eyes and remembered to take a deep breath.

'But just barely,' Maggie added. 'If that one had been aimed a little better it would have hit us just above the water line.'

'You know,' Obar suggested, 'Nunn left in a hurry as well. They might not have the most experienced gunners manning those crossbows.'

'That may save us!' Mills called back.

Another spear flew from Nunn's ship, describing a much higher arc than either of the first two. The burning wood sliced through the corner of the smallest of the three sails overhead before falling into the sea on the boat's other side. They were finding the range!

The spear had passed through the sail too quickly for the fire to spread, but they had sustained their first damage. The next missile could burn the ship to the water line.

So much for inexperienced gunners. They needed to get away from here and Mrs Smith had only heard one suggestion that made any sense.

'Hang on!' she called to those around her. 'We're getting out of here.' She looked aloft again. 'Sails! Fill as though you were pushed by a gale!'

The sails above ballooned forward, bursting with the wind. The boat slammed ahead, the masts creaking so much Mrs Smith was sure they would break.

Mills looked up at the groaning sails. 'I'm not sure those masts will stand up to this!'

265

'They only need to do it for a minute!' Mrs Smith called back. She herself was worried that the smallest sail would rip from the torn corner, but so far it held.

Another spear missed their stern by a dozen yards.

And then they were beyond the other ship and still pulling away.

'Ease the wind in the sails', she called, 'just a bit!'

The sails above developed the slightest bit of slack as the groans of the masts went from full-throated cries to uneasy mutters. They pulled away from the pirate vessel more gradually, but pull away they did.

'Boat!' she called. 'Take us home!'

They would see Nunn again soon enough. But now they might have some time to prepare for him.

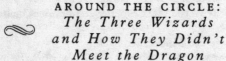

AROUND THE CIRCLE:
The Three Wizards and How They Didn't Meet the Dragon

There were three of them, then, the survivors of a battle for the three known stones; the first three dragon's eyes. Two of them were brothers, who now called themselves Obar and Nunn, the third a watchmaker who took the name Rox. They had had different names before; ordinary names from an ordinary world. They gave themselves new names for their new roles, the three great wizards. They had been so much younger then, inexperienced with the new-found power, and perhaps a little drunk with it as well.

When he first had a dragon's eye, Nunn thought he could do anything.

Rox had found his eye first and had learned the ways of magic from a wizard older still. And he in turn had trained the brothers. There had been a fiction, then, about how wizards had to work together, help each other, extend the great knowledge of magic. Although even that fiction contained chapters best unread, for Rox never talked about where he'd found his eye, or what had happened to his tutor.

So Nunn could fly and tear tall trees from the earth. And, with the help of Rox, he developed subtler skills, like being able to see to the beach on the other side of the island, or to transport yourself to that beach instantly. Every waking moment had been an adventure, better than the one before.

For a time, the eye had made Nunn feel invulnerable.

And then the dragon had stirred.

There was a reason, Rox explained, for their extensive study. The stones were a gift from the dragon and the dragon expected them to use them.

'To give something back?' Obar had asked.

'No,' Rox replied. 'To protect ourselves.'

There seemed to be no end of stories about the dragon. The stories were often sketchy and occasionally contradictory, but the stories were there, many from those who had held the eyes before.

Some said the dragon destroyed everything. Others that it only destroyed the wicked, or the mighty, or all but the specially blessed. But all said the dragon would come and destroy again.

This, Nunn realised, was the dragon's doing. It always allowed some whisper about it to survive. For, more than anything else, the dragon wanted fear.

The dragon stirred and the spells no longer worked the same. At first, the magic would fail for just a moment, as if one of them had forgotten a few of the words and only had to start the spell again. And then the whole world had begun to shift, both those things the three wizards had constructed from their magic, and those other things, like air and water and sky, that the magicians had once assumed were permanent.

At the end, they could see the changes in the dragon's eyes. The power in the eyes seemed to fade and flourish from moment to moment, like flickering candles.

And then, from somewhere far away, they heard it, whether because they were wizards or simply because it was meant for anyone with ears.

267

It was the first rumble of the dragon.

The sound had come in the night, a night without stars. At first, Nunn had just assumed the sky was blotted out with clouds. But after the deep rumble reached them through the earth, he began to wonder if the dragon had stolen away the stars.

The rumble was subtle at first, a slight vibration beneath their feet. But it was everywhere, and it was never ending. And it grew as the night lingered, lasting far longer than any darkness should, until it shook the tables and chairs and pots and pans, everything clattering at once, on and on, like an everlasting tremor.

But it did end, as suddenly as someone would snuff a flame. And in that instant the sky began to lighten at last.

To begin with, Nunn thought it might be the most magnificent sunrise he had ever seen. But that first pink at the edge of the world spread until the whole sky, a sky without a sun, was filled with a dull red glow, as if all the world beyond the horizon was on fire.

Nunn knew then that the dragon would destroy everything.

And the wizards, the three knowledge-filled, invulnerable wizards, looked out at the end of their world and asked themselves: how can we defend ourselves against *this*?

Still they hoped, and still they tried. Some of the sheds and outbuildings had collapsed during the night, torn about by the vibration. They had retreated to one of the few buildings still left intact, to consult whatever tomes remained, hoping somehow they might find some secret that would overcome the destruction they saw out in the world.

As the day that was like no other day progressed, the temperature continued to rise, until it became so hot that the three wizards removed most of their robes and still could barely move. A wind stirred outside in short, puffing gusts, like the hot breath of the dragon. It felt to all of them that the dragon was waiting for them, just beyond the door, and that it would not be done until it had taken them, along with the rest of the world.

But as the day lengthened, the dragon's eyes returned to life, flashing with power.

'There is nothing here to save us,' Rox said, slamming shut the last of their books. 'Perhaps we will have to give in to it at last.'

'No!' Nunn insisted.

'The eyes will protect us!' Obar agreed.

'Will they?' Rox asked. 'Or have they just been loaned to us until the dragon wants them back?' He balanced his own jewel on his palm, as if he might just throw it away.

Nunn was horrified at the elder wizard's capitulation. He would never give up.

'We can fight with the eyes!'

'I have no fight left.'

They had invested too much of their lives into these gems. Nunn would not see an eye go to waste. 'If you will not use it, I know someone who will.' He concentrated the power of the eye into a single narrow beam, but one with killing force.

'What are you doing?' Rox asked. His instincts worked even through his despair, as he met the force of Nunn's jewel with an equal one of his own. They were evenly matched.

'Why do you waste your powers? Why don't we surrender now to the dragon and be done with it? Rather a good death than a life that is ruled by fear.'

Nunn found that the jewel was shaking in his hands. 'Brother!' he called to Obar. 'You see what he wants to do. Act! Act now!'

Obar pulled out his own jewel and turned its destructive power towards their elder.

Rox managed to absorb the second attack as well, using his superior knowledge to defend himself. Somehow, Nunn realised, even with two jewels ranked against him, he might survive.

'Why do you bother?' Rox called out to his foes. 'The jewels, used this way, will exhaust themselves. The dragon will win in the end.'

But it had to end some other way. Obar had kept a knife and he pulled it now, plunging it past the magic into Rox's heart.

The dragon still waited. Nunn knew it only waited for the proper moment to take them.

Rox's jewel lay on the floor.

This went beyond brotherhood. This was survival.

They had to defend themselves. They would both die if they didn't have more power.

Obar had balked once the deed was done. He'd never before had blood on his hands. He stood there, wiping them on whatever cloth he could find, trying to get them clean.

But Nunn had a different purpose for his hands. He screamed as the gems sank deep into his flesh, safe from theft.

Rox looked up at him, somehow still alive, blood pouring from a hole in his chest. 'So the eyes are that important to you? You will leave me to die beneath the dragon?'

'Maybe I can save you that.' The energy of the eyes flowed from Nunn over the dying Rox. He let the jewels take over to do what they would.

Rox turned to dust as Nunn felt himself filled with energy, the first time he had ever absorbed another. The eyes had done it for him. He was startled. He would learn to enjoy it later.

'Nunn,' Obar whispered. He waved his brother to join him at the window.

The sky had become the sky again, full of bright sun and white clouds. The air was cool and slightly damp, as if rain was on the way.

The dragon was gone, here one minute, disappeared the next, without even time to fly away. It had simply gone somewhere else, as if the creature really existed in a separate time and place.

Why had it left? There were no answers. Perhaps it was simply time. Or perhaps, in watching Nunn and Obar, the dragon had learned all it needed to know.

Nunn found no relief in this sudden disappearance. Who knew when the creature would be back to take them all? He had to defend himself. He needed the third eye as well.

But the dragon was truly gone, and so was Obar. Perhaps his brother had guessed Nunn's mental state. Or maybe Obar had left to make plans to gain all three gems for himself.

And where there had been three wizards, now there was only one.

Thirty-seven

'No!' Nunn screamed as the other ship pulled out of range. 'I will not allow this!'

The crew members all busied themselves as far away from the magician as they could get. And with good reason. If the eyes were working, he would kill one of them just to calm himself.

But if the eyes were working, this never would have happened.

The dragon was closer. And when the dragon was closer, things changed.

Nunn remembered how powerless he had felt the first time the dragon had passed them by. How three wizards had hidden from the dragon and how two had survived. That was Nunn's story of the dragon, a story that bore no resemblance to any of the others he had heard or read.

Perhaps all the stories were different because every time the dragon rose was different as well. Or perhaps there were no answers to anything.

Still, Nunn found himself preparing for the next rising of the dragon. He used his jewels endlessly, pushing them against the edges of reality, so that he might adjust space and time, and go to some of those places that only the dragon had seen. He had contacted things both of this world and of the other places he stumbled upon, making promises, forging alliances, all to gain strength against the dragon.

He needed to know more. Sometimes it seemed as though he had been gaining knowledge for ever. But it always felt like much too short a time.

The dragon wanted something. There must be something he had learned that would protect him from the dragon. Already the creature was taking his magic away.

Soon it would take everything.

'Land ho!' the look-out called down from the crow's nest. He had seen their island goal. They were rushing, now, towards a battle with his brother and the others, and a far larger battle after that.

And Nunn had no way to prepare, with two dead jewels embedded in his flesh.

He glanced again at his hands, thinking at first that he had only seen the sun reflected across the facets of his stones.

But, no. There was something stirring deep inside, a first faint glimmer of life in the dragon's eyes.

Nunn laughed. There was more to be done. The eyes were his again. He would take these two and still gain an eye or two from his enemies.

No more hiding for Nunn. This time he would stare the dragon in the face.

The air was quiet. The air was safe. Here, the being who had once been Hyram Sayre felt he might find peace.

But peace was not with him yet.

His anger had come back to him there on the earth. First, in a little way, with a boy who might have mistreated his lawn. But that was another place, far away, a place that sometimes felt like a dream, and a person he no longer was. The seeds of what he had become had been planted in that distant place, but that life had been barren of the meaning he had found.

Below he could see the green, the peaceful green.

His thoughts flared back to the world below and the second man who brought his anger. His lawn was a thing of the past.

He found murder somewhat more difficult to forgive.

The sword had felt like fire as he was gutted, his bloody innards spilling out into his hands. When he had seen the Captain again he had wanted to give that fire back. He had wanted to burn and maim, to embrace destruction. The great being who was once Hyram Sayre could take his power and destroy the Captain in an instant. Worse, he wanted to do it!

But really only a part of him wanted that. The greater being would rise above it. Anger was the opposite of everything Sayre had been searching for.

But what should he do?

He could hide in the sky the same way he had once hidden behind his lawn. That was the secret of his life before: if his lawn was perfect, he would be perfect too. But it hadn't worked then. His perfect lawn had kept him from the rest of that other world.

The sky was free and quiet and empty.

And the sterile perfection of the sky would not work for him now.

To escape was not an answer. To escape was not to exist.

There was so much to do. He hadn't even chosen a name for his new self.

So much of this was new to him. He had to give himself the time to learn. He would have to return to the earth, travel again among both gentle creatures and murderers.

Only then could he begin to discover his true nature.

Thirty-eight

The globe in his hand told him he was close to his goal. The globe in his hand told him he and his troops could not be stopped.

Why didn't it warn Carl Jackson about the pitfalls he might run across along the way?

They knew he was coming. They had set up traps in the forest, traps his men could not see, sometimes, until it was too late. The worst of these were the deep pits, filled with sharpened stakes. 'Mantraps', his new lieutenant had called them. He had also told Jackson the traps were built by the wolves. It was damn funny, the superstitions these people had. They would have been a real laugh if Jackson didn't have a job to do.

Then there were the piles of dead trees blocking their way, and the dammed-up stream that created a pond they had to circle.

And every step of the way, each one more cautious because of what they found, they heard the real wolves in the forest. Actually, the constant howling was a bit of an advantage as far as Carl was concerned. The men stayed close, for they knew that what waited for them in the woods would be even worse than what they faced on the trail.

But even with the soldiers' vigilance, they would lose a man here and there at the back or sides of the formation; a lone scream followed by a series of growls. Occasionally, an arrow would come out of nowhere to pierce someone in the heart, another gift from their old Captain, who had turned from his men to run with the wolves.

274

At first, Jackson would dash to the scene of the latest murder and cause his globe to send a spray of fire into the trees. But all his efforts caught were a few burning leaves; the killers vanished back into the woods.

Somewhere, in the midst of their march from night to day to night, Jackson had begun to blame the magician for these troubles.

Nunn had promised him glory and had then disappeared. Nunn, who had limitless power at his command, and who could no doubt kill wolves and archers and trap-diggers with a single glance, had left Jackson and his men to get picked off, one by one, until half of Jackson's army was gone.

Umar, his lieutenant, did his best to keep the troops in line, cajoling, threatening, leading by example. George, on the other hand, slunk silently along at Jackson's side, not saying a word, no doubt blaming his leader for the accidental pain the globe had caused him.

Maybe, Jackson thought, if things grew even worse, he could use George as an example to the others. George's life meant nothing. Maybe his death could be of some value.

The globe in his hand suddenly sparkled. Something was going on inside the mysterious sphere. Jackson stopped dead, letting the other troops go on ahead.

There were figures inside the sphere, maybe half a dozen of them, standing in a clearing. Jackson realised he knew most of them. One of them was even his worthless wife! At last the globe must be telling him their goal was near.

'George!' Jackson called. His old neighbour looked round from where he had wandered ahead. 'Get Umar!'

George nodded and trotted off in search of the lieutenant.

Umar returned a moment later. 'Captain?' At least he was good about calling Jackson that.

Carl related what the globe had shown him.

Umar nodded smartly. 'We need to scout. Umar will do it.'

With that, he called for the troops to halt and pushed past them into the forest.

Only when his lieutenant was gone did Jackson start to worry. He needed Umar if he was going to win.

But what if Umar decided he didn't need Jackson?

The Captain let Umar get almost to the clearing before he stopped him. He had always liked Umar. It was tough to kill someone you liked.

'Umar!' he called, drawing his bowstring back.

Umar dropped his weapons and raised his hands before the Captain even finished saying his name. 'I am glad to see you!' he called, even though he was still looking the other way. 'Take me away from here. He is a madman!'

The Captain almost laughed. 'Umar. Turn round.'

Umar did as he was told.

'There's only one way to save your skin,' the Captain told him. 'We're going into battle too. You will be fighting for our side now.'

Umar shrugged. 'Fighting? It is what I know to do. Maybe we get others to join too.'

'Fine. We have work to do. Pick up your weapons, Umar.'

The Captain waved for the others to join them.

He had always liked Umar.

Joan Blake looked out over her little army.

The Captain had told them to be ready. The enemy was only a few minutes away.

Thomas had supervised the distribution of the weapons that Stanley had left for them. Not that many of them knew what to do with them. Still, Rebecca Jackson and Rose Dafoe had each taken a long knife, and they did know they would have to defend their lives. Bobby was actually pretty good with a bow and arrow. And Joan had surprised herself a bit when she found she preferred a hatchet. She liked the feel of the handle as she swung it back and forth.

Thomas had climbed up into the trees and was watching for the approach of the others. Harold had gone off with the Captain again. He seemed to think that it was his regular job. But all of them would be ready when it was time.

Even the Oomgosh had got on to his substantial feet, although he seemed to need a tree behind him for support. Jason refused to take a weapon, but Joan knew, from their last battle, that the Oomgosh somehow gave the boy a special kind of strength.

The only one who couldn't help was Mrs Furlong, lost in her memories. Joan had had to tie her to a tree and hope for the best, whatever that was. The best, Joan knew, might be for Margaret Furlong to die.

A light flared on the edge of the forest. Joan and the others turned, weapons before them, ready for the first attack.

Charlie started to bark as Hyram Sayre, or whatever he'd become, walked out of the woods.

'Well,' he said as he came towards the others, 'I decided to come back. It's not healthy, I told myself, to spend all my time alone.'

'Hello,' Joan answered, not knowing what else to say. She doubted this befuddled fellow would be much use in a fight. She hoped he wouldn't get in the way.

Hyram turned to the Oomgosh. 'And how are you doing? I would never forgive myself if anything happened to you while I was away.' He walked over to the tree-man, and his hands once again glowed green where they touched the Oomgosh's bark-like skin.

The Oomgosh stood up straight. 'Even better than before. Your hands have miracles inside, green man.'

'Green man,' Hyram repeated with a smile. 'Yes, I rather like that.'

The tree-man took a great, deep breath, as if he wanted to smell every tree in the forest.

'Were you here a week,' he said to Hyram, 'I think you would cure me completely. Not that we have a week.' He looked to the others. 'The Oomgosh is ready to help you in your battle. Now, should Raven return, you will have a true pair of fighters on your hands.'

Yes. Raven was gone too. So many of their number were not here. When Obar had sent Mrs Smith and himself on his little errands, he had sounded as though he would be gone for no

277

time at all. But then, Obar himself had said it: never trust a wizard.

Joan was happier, though, that Nick wasn't here. There was a very good chance that all of them in the clearing were going to die. She hoped her son had got himself to someplace safer.

'And how about you?' the Oomgosh asked Hyram. 'Will you join us?'

'You could call me Green Man again,' Hyram said. 'I rather like it.'

The Oomgosh smiled. 'Well said, Green Man. But we have a fight and could use your help.'

'A fight?' The Green Man frowned. 'I should – I don't know – I'm afraid of the violence in my nature.'

The Oomgosh nodded. 'It is something we all must deal with when it is time to meet our fate.'

BOOK 3

Dragon Waking

Thirty-nine

Todd never thought he'd be so happy to set foot on this stupid island. But this was as close to a home as he had on this world, and it was where he and his neighbours would make a stand.

There were a lot of them now on Todd's side, and they were strong. They had four of the dragon's eyes among them. If they could get the gems to work, the four of them could easily overcome Nunn. And after that there was only some indescribable battle with the dragon.

If they could survive all that, maybe things would quieten down. Maybe they would settle here, or maybe they could get back to Chestnut Circle. Maybe, somehow, he and Sala could have a life together.

'The gems,' Obar announced abruptly. 'They are glowing again.'

Mills nodded as he pulled forth his own eye. 'This is where the dragon wants us to have our battle.' He frowned as he examined the gem in his hand. 'The eyes are still exhibiting only a fraction of their power. They seem to be regaining their energy very slowly.'

'Much too slowly,' Obar added.

'Rather like a pot coming gradually to the boil,' Mrs Smith said. 'It is probably best not to plan on using the eyes over much in the immediate future.'

Mills slipped his gem back in his pants pocket. 'It appears that the dragon doesn't want us to have our battle too soon.'

Todd nodded as he watched the three wizards examine their stones. 'And the dragon is making the rules – for now.' A bit hesitantly, he pulled his own gem from the T-shirt pocket where he had it stored. Yes, there was a faint gleam to it now, as though there was the tiniest of lights deep inside.

Obar glanced sharply at him. 'I think the dragon may always make the rules.'

'And I think the dragon wants us to think that way.' After all, Todd had met the dragon, in his dreams or somewhere like that. And the dragon had smiled at Todd's anger. Todd felt that dream had been as real as anything that had happened to him since he'd come to this place; just as real and much more important.

Then the dragon, or at least the dragon's eye, had channelled Todd's anger to burn the sea monster.

These wizards talked about the dragon destroying the world. But they could also use these parts of the dragon, the dragon's eyes, for their own benefit, and maybe even against the dragon itself.

It didn't make sense to Todd.

He wondered if, somehow, there could be more than one dragon.

He looked back to the other three, the experts with the dragon's eyes. Why didn't they feel the same thing? Todd supposed he must be missing something.

The row-boat pulled up with Nick and the three Volunteers, the last members of their party to leave the sailing ship. Todd and Mr Mills waded into the shallows to help pull it ashore.

'Farewell to the sea!' Wilbert called as he jumped from the boat.

'And none too soon, eh?' Stanley agreed, as he followed Maggie. 'That was one sea monster too many, if you ask me.'

'Well, I missed the monster,' Maggie admitted. 'But there's a whole new world out there. Do you fellows want to be stuck on this island for the rest of your lives?'

'What?' Wilbert replied in mock outrage. 'But didn't you know we were going home? The dragon's going to have us all over to a big celebration and send us all right back to Newton. First, of course, it'll send us engraved invitations.'

Nick jumped from the other side of the boat. He frowned at Maggie when she spoke. He didn't seem to want to have the slightest contact with anyone.

It was strange, Todd thought. These days, Nick looked the way Todd used to feel.

'Yes,' Mrs Smith was saying behind him. 'I can feel the eye's energy again.' Todd turned to see her once more floating above the ground. 'I don't know if I can maintain this sort of thing and really fly about the way that I usually do.' Even as she spoke, she was already sinking towards the ground. 'I might have to hop from place to place for a while.'

'Let us see if we can find your neighbours,' Obar said, as he frowned at his own jewel. 'We were gone a bit longer than I might have liked.'

A green haze expanded out from the jewel to float a foot or so from Obar's head. Shapes moved about in the haze, but they were indistinct.

'Damn!' Obar muttered. He shook the jewel, as if trying to get a bit more power from the thing. Perhaps the shapes became a bit clearer, but it was hard to tell with the way they were moving. Most of them looked like people, and those people seemed to be going everywhere, running, jumping, smashing into one another.

'I believe your neighbours are about to be attacked,' Obar said quietly.

'Oh,' Mrs Smith replied with a frown. 'Will the jewels show us the way there?'

'I'm sure they will, eventually,' Obar agreed as the image vanished.

Todd looked at the two wizards. The neighbours were under attack and all they could do was frown? How could they be so cool about it?

Obar stared into his jewel as if he was looking for defects. 'Maybe I can conjure enough power to transport myself to the scene. My very presence there might quiet things down.' He squeezed the jewel in his palm. 'Oh, dear. I hope this works.'

Obar vanished.

'Isn't that just like him?' Mrs Smith asked. 'Wouldn't it have been better if we planned an attack together?'

'What about Nunn, eh?' Stanley interjected. 'He should be showing up on these shores in a few minutes himself. Shouldn't some of us set an ambush for him?'

Mrs Smith frowned. 'I think Nunn will have to wait. If his stones are in a similar condition to ours, he won't be able to do much damage for a while anyway. I think our first priority has to be the rest of our group.'

Wilbert stepped forward. 'The camp wasn't very far, as I recall. Maybe half an hour's quick march. We Volunteers should be able to see the trail clearly enough and maybe make it in half that time. That should let those of you with the stones go ahead and defend the others. We'll be your reinforcements.'

Mrs Smith nodded in agreement. 'Well, I may have to hop there, but I'll make it as quick as I can.'

'We'll be right behind you,' Mr Mills said in his deepest tones.

They would? This talk of people with the eyes included him, too. Todd wanted to get back to the others as fast as anybody. But how could he go anywhere when he had no idea how to use this dragon's eye?

'Good,' Wilbert agreed. 'Then that's what we'll do. Nick? Sala? You both look young and healthy. Try to keep up –'

He stopped abruptly as the scene shifted around Todd, the sky and trees blurring and moving, then re-forming. But it was a different set of trees now, trees that completely blotted out the sky overhead, and he could no longer hear the ocean.

Todd looked around and saw that Mr Mills was still with him, but the others had gone.

'What happened?' Todd asked.

Mills smiled. 'I just brought you somewhere else,' he rumbled. 'I've always been better at this transportation business than Obar.'

Todd didn't understand. 'Somewhere else? Are we close to the camp?'

Mr Mills's smile vanished. 'Oh no. We have something else that must be taken care of first.'

Todd took a step away from his old vice principal. He had got to know Mills fairly well over the years. After all, the vice

284

principal had been in charge of discipline, something Todd always seemed to need a lot of. At least in Mr Mills's book. But Todd had never seen the vice principal look as – well, intense – as he did today. As if Mills needed something and wouldn't be denied.

'This will only take a minute,' Mr Mills, or perhaps the wizard inside him, said. 'I want your dragon's eye, now.'

Forty

Jackson's worst fears had come true. Umar had not returned.

'What are we going to do, George?'

George just stared back at him, as sullen as Carl's kid, Todd. Well, maybe George could use a good spanking. The thought made Carl Jackson smile.

Not that he had time for it just now. Now was the moment to show everybody who was boss.

Who was boss. And it wasn't Umar or Harold, who weren't strong enough to stay with their new Captain. It certainly wasn't snivelling George. And it wasn't even Nunn, that preening pusbag of a magician who made all sorts of threats and promises and then went and disappeared like all the rest.

No, none of them could be the boss.

And it sure wasn't anybody from the old neighbourhood, either, like those judgemental bitches Joan Blake and Rose Dafoe, or that holier-than-thou Evan Mills. No babe ever was going to hold out on him, not even that cute piece Mary Lou. He saw the way she looked at him. She'd have a good time when he hiked up her skirts. But no, even she wasn't going to be the boss.

And it especially wasn't going to be his useless wife and his excuse for a son. They were probably having a fine old time now that he was gone, laughing at him behind his back the way they always did. He'd give them both a piece of his mind, slap that shit-faced boy out of the way and turn to the real source of all his problems.

His dear wife. What was she looking at all the time anyway? This was a new world and he was a new Carl Jackson, and he wasn't going to take anything any more. One look from her, one word, and he'd hit her and hit her and hit her again until she got some sense in her stupid fucking useless body.

He was the boss now, nobody else, and he'd show them all.

He had the power. That stupid useless Nunn had given it to him before he upped and vanished. And he would win. He would smash anybody who stood in his way. He'd show them all.

His army couldn't understand him? He didn't care how much those pansy boys would shake their heads when he talked, he'd show them just what he fucking wanted, and if they didn't do it pronto, he'd show them how to die.

This would work. He was surprised how easily it all fell into place. He'd let his doubts get in the way before, but no more. Carl Fucking Jackson was going to kick some ass.

'George!' he called to his main pansy boy. 'We're going to attack!'

Carl couldn't stop grinning.

George at least looked surprised.

'George, tell the troops to move out!'

George looked from Carl to the troops and back again, as if he had some trouble relaying his Captain's order.

Well of course. The Captain wasn't being specific enough.

'George! Tell them to charge!'

George blinked back at him.

Carl raised the globe before him. His smile got so big you could throw shit in there with a shovel.

'Oh, hell.' George turned to the troops. 'Charge!' he called.

The troops stared at their second-in-command. A few of them stopped and snapped to attention.

George turned back to his Captain. 'Look, Carl –'

But Carl wasn't taking back-talk any more. 'You're a pretty lousy officer, George. I should let this globe do a number on you right here. But I think it would be better if I demonstrated to the troops exactly what I wanted.'

He stared down at the globe and thought of fire.

Yes! The globe shot a line of flame, first to one side of the trail, then the other. Soon, this whole part of the forest would burn.

'Come on, now!' he called, waving them forward. 'There's only one way to go!'

Most of them started to follow, with only two hesitating in the rear. Two shit-faced pansy boys. He concentrated on the globe again and it lifted him aloft to give him a clear line of sight at those in the rear.

'Disobey a direct order, will you?'

Carl Jackson's new flame-thrower shot a great tongue of fire past the other soldiers, engulfing the malingerers in flame. It was quite impressive. They barely had time to scream.

Captain Carl Jackson waved his troops forward again.

'Charge!' he called.

He hit the ground running, as his army stampeded behind him.

'Now you're with me!' he cried. 'For glory!'

He knew just who the boss was.

The wolves heard it first.

But even Harold knew something was coming. He could see it in the way the wolves paced back and forth, sniffing the ground.

'It's the attack!' the Captain called. 'From the north! Headed straight towards the clearing!'

And Harold could hear the noise then too, a rumbling, crashing, roaring sound. It was a whole army, rushing as fast as they could, not even letting the forest get in their way.

'Well,' the Captain said. 'At least they won't be hard to find. Come on now, soldiers!' he called to all around him, both wolf and human. 'We'll attack their flank. We have to distract them. We have to put fear in their hearts. We have to make them forget they were attacking anyone!'

One of the wolves looked to the Captain. 'We take down ass many humanss ass we like?'

'As many as you can kill,' the Captain agreed. 'You will have full bellies tonight!'

The wolves howled with delight.

'Fressh meeat,' they growled in chorus.

The Captain slapped Pator's back and winked at Harold.

288

'For us, eating human meat is optional. Now, let's go!' The Captain broke into a trot as he waved the others forward.

Harold found himself running at his side. For once, he wanted to be there.

Nunn was certain there would be an attack.

He had instructed his men to land their boats most carefully, on a barren stretch of coast far from any hiding places. Still he expected the others to try and surprise him.

This was the time, while all the other wizards were working together, four eyes against his two, that they would finally do to him what he had always wanted to do to them. They would destroy him and rip his two dragon's eyes from the dust of his palms. He wondered if the four would fight over their new-found wealth. A pity he wouldn't be alive to see it.

But he had stood on land for a full minute and all was still quiet. He looked down to his stones. Yes, they warmed his skin slightly now; the power was truly returning. He sent that power searching for the ambush, from the sky, from the rocks or the trees beyond, or even from beneath the sea.

The dragon's eyes found birds and rodents and insects and fish, nothing more. What did this mean?

He could at least hope for a moment's reprieve. He turned to Snake. 'Send your men back to the boat to bring our guests.'

Snake grunted and did as he was told. None of the sailors was particularly happy about the rest of what Nunn had brought. But they didn't have to be happy. They just had to obey.

While he waited, Nunn set about weaving a portal with his two dragon's eyes; a window that would show him the other parts of the island, both his enemies and his friends. The weaving was weak, the images faint. There was barely enough power in the two eyes to sustain it. Nunn had to concentrate to keep the weave alive.

The jewels found Mrs Smith first. She seemed to be rushing not towards Nunn, but away. Then he got an image of that boy, Todd, along with the human vessel that now contained Rox, standing and talking in another part of the forest entirely.

The other wizards' actions made no sense. Did they have some different plan? Would they lure Nunn into a trap once he had travelled inland?

But then the jewels showed Nunn the fire, raging through the wood. And before the fire ran his soldiers, and before them their new Captain, all of them running into battle.

The battle! Of course! While he was gone, the soldiers moved as they had been instructed. And Nunn's magical opponents had been gone as well, fighting with Nunn on that pirate isle, and could not protect their own. They returned, and they found their friends under attack.

Nunn was forgotten.

Nunn chuckled. While his quest for the jewels had not worked out as planned, his island strategy was working to perfection.

The wizard closed his fingers over his palms, allowing the spell to dissipate. He turned back to the sea, where the longboats were bringing in his special passengers.

The humans did not care for the ape-creatures. But the short, red-haired creatures were fierce fighters with an appetite for blood. When properly instructed, they might turn a battle to Nunn's advantage.

Nunn would be certain that this battle would be far more than four jewels against two. He would bring everything and everyone to this fight, and show that his knowledge was more than a match for the raw power of the others.

He silently instructed his jewels to search for the shadows, and tell them he required their services again.

And he used his voice to tell the men to ship the boats, and both apes and men that it was time to follow him, for soon it would be time for battle.

Forty-one

Who did this guy think he was?

'Look,' Todd began, 'Mr Mills, or whatever your name is. I don't think this eye is mine to give away.'

Actually, in the short time he'd had the dragon's eye, Todd had had plenty of doubts about the power that literally fell into his hand. More than once he had been ready to chalk it up to some cosmic mistake.

But that was before this guy kidnapped him to who knew where and demanded that he give up his stone. Even if Todd's getting the dragon's eye was the biggest mistake ever, he still wouldn't give up the stone to a bozo like this.

Mills's eyes closed for a second. He took a deep breath. 'Todd,' he said in a strained voice, 'you should keep –'

Mills's head snapped back as if someone had hit him in the jaw. 'Who are you to tell him?' he screamed in a high singsong. 'Zachs needs the stone! Zachs needs the stone!'

Mills's head snapped back down so that he was staring straight at Todd again. 'There will be no squabbling,' the deeper voice said with great authority. 'We must do this if we are to survive.'

The vice principal shivered. 'So you say,' he continued with Mr Mills's normal voice, 'but you never tell us why. The first stone didn't exactly produce the results you had planned. Why would a second stone do any more?'

'Zachs needs the stone!' He threw his arms wide. 'Zachs needs to be free!'

Todd took a cautious step away from the twitching Mills. The other man was too caught up in his inner argument to notice.

'Will we be, Zachs?' Mills's real voice asked. 'Rox never tells us anything unless he has to. I'm sure it's as much a surprise to both of us as it was to Todd when we left the others and showed up –'

'I will not have arguments!' the wizard's voice took over abruptly. 'You do not understand the importance of the stones!'

'I know the importance to you,' Mills shot back. 'I can hear it in your voice, and maybe even in your thoughts. You're like a junkie who's finally found a fix. What will you do, Rox, collect the stones until you overdose on power?'

'Zachs can never have enough!'

All three voices were silent for an instant before the wizard responded. 'I am not alive without them. And the power enters you, too, Mr Mills. Soon, you will feel it; the need for the energy, know that to be without it is the same as death.'

Mills's gaze abruptly shifted, so that he looked Todd straight in the eye. 'But there is another reason for the stones. The dragon –'

Mills groaned, doubling over as if he had been kicked in the stomach. 'Oh god,' he whispered. 'It's happening again.'

All three voices tumbled out between his lips, as if talking might ease his pain.

'The jewel's power is growing beyond what I can handle.'

'Zachs – save Zachs!'

'We have to let – some of the power go.'

The three of them seemed completely lost in the pain. Todd glanced behind him. Another couple of feet and he could duck behind the trees.

'You're not going anywhere!' one of Mills's voices snapped.

Todd found himself jerked from his feet and pulled back before the other wizard, a green halo around his middle like a lasso.

He'd had enough of this. Todd would not be bullied.

Mills's face actually showed a weak smile. 'That is a little better. I have to use the power, or it will overwhelm me.'

So that was what was important to this three-headed guy in front of him? The guy needed to feel a little better. Yeah, Todd was used to that sort of attitude. It was like Todd didn't matter at all, once his father had his bottle, or Mills had his magic.

292

And now Todd had a great green lasso of his own. Or a great green whatever-he-wanted. The dragon's eye waited for him in his pocket. Before, he'd been a little scared to use it. But now he was mad.

Make me a knife, he told his own gem, and cut the line that connects me to Mills.

Green light flashed from his fingertips. Todd was suddenly spinning free.

Mills's head snapped up to stare at the retreating Todd. 'No!' He reached out a fist as if he might grab Todd back.

But then Mills jerked suddenly, his hands flailing spastically at his sides. 'Todd! Go now!'

'Zachs will win! Zachs will use the power!' With that, Mills's hands erupted into twin torches of green flame.

Mills screamed, as if this time the flame was burning him. He staggered back, the fire reduced to smoke. But the green light rose around him, shifting back and forth, the man inside changing, too, as if three sets of facial features were fighting for dominance of his skull. In a single instant, Todd swore, he could see all three of them at once.

But this gave Todd a moment's freedom and that moment might be all he had.

'Stone!' he called. 'Take me away!'

And the stone did just that.

Mary Lou didn't want to criticise her rescuer, but this particular rescue seemed to be taking a while.

'The dragon is tricky!' Raven called to her out of the darkness, as if he, too, was impatient with the delay. 'Raven wasn't supposed to show up. Not here, not now. The dragon is trying to hide the way out, cover everything with darkness. But who brought light to the world in the first place? Raven did!'

Mary Lou felt like they were flying endlessly. The exhilarating feeling of soaring through the air had long since calmed to monotony and even her newly discovered wings were getting tired.

'Raven sees light again! This way!'

Mary Lou felt herself bank to the left and turn about. That was another strange feature of her flight through the darkness.

293

Sometimes she felt she was riding on Raven's back, at others as though she was flying free, and once or twice, just like now, that she and Raven were one and the same.

But she saw the light now, too, a lone spot of green piercing the total absence of light, like a night sky with only a single star.

Raven and she swooped towards their discovery.

'It is a gem!' Raven called. 'A dragon's eye!'

'The last of the dragon's eyes?' Mary Lou asked, not really ready to believe it.

'It must be indeed. Raven doesn't think we were meant to find this. It's the dragon's hiding place!'

And they just chanced upon it? Sometimes Mary Lou wondered if anything happened in this place simply by chance.

But Raven flew closer and Mary Lou could see that, yes, it certainly looked like the final eye, simply floating here in space, or whatever it was that they travelled through.

'A very pretty prize,' Raven announced as they flapped their wings to slow down their forward progress, 'and one ready to be taken.'

There was a sudden burst of brilliant light behind them, as if someone had opened a door and let in the sun.

'Uh-oh,' Raven remarked. 'Mary Lou, would you see who that is?'

Mary Lou swivelled her head round, ready for her first direct look at the dragon.

'Hey, Mary Lou? What are you doing here?'

It wasn't the dragon after all. It was Todd Jackson. He stood on the edge of a forest, the scene surrounding him for twenty feet or so before it faded back into darkness. And Mary Lou didn't just see the forest; she smelled the trees and heard the calls of insects and birds. The forest was there, the doorway only a few feet away.

Todd smiled apologetically. 'Not, of course, that I know what I'm doing here,' he added quickly. 'Or, to be honest, exactly what "here" is.'

'You're here to give us a way out!' Raven announced as he perched on Mary Lou's shoulder. 'And you took your own sweet time about it!'

'Oh,' Todd replied. He glanced down at his hand, where he held a dragon's eye of his own. 'Sorry, I guess.'

'Raven is a font of forgiveness,' the bird replied, 'as soon as you get us out of here.'

'Well, I guess I can try,' Todd agreed with a shake of his head. 'Mary Lou. Why don't you take my hand?'

Mary Lou reached out towards him. Their fingers touched. His hand felt very warm.

'Hurry it up!' Raven made a clucking sound with his throat. 'Raven thinks this would be a fine moment for us all to be elsewhere!'

A deep, rumbling sound came from somewhere in the darkness behind them.

'Raven knew it was only a matter of time.'

Forty-two

There was a fire in the forest.

'This is something else Nunn will pay for,' the Oomgosh said darkly. Jason looked up to his friend. The Oomgosh's anger seemed to lend the tree-man as much strength again as the energy he had got from Old Man Sayre.

'Come, Jason,' the tree-man said. He glanced down at the boy with a smile. 'Dig your feet into the soil. Together, we will call the rain to wash away the flames.'

This time, Jason pulled his sneakers off. He placed his bare feet wide apart, as he saw the Oomgosh do beside him. The earth felt cool between Jason's toes, and far softer than he imagined the hard-packed dirt of the clearing could ever be. Still, his feet sank easily into the loam, until rich brown soil covered his toes.

'Now, Jason,' the Oomgosh urged. 'Hear the earth talking to you.'

Jason listened, but what came to him was not so much a sound as a feeling. He could feel the slow, almost imperceptible pace of the dirt and rock beneath him, settled in their way, only moved by the force of others; the gentle insistence of water as it pushed its way both above and beneath the dirt; the dizzying whirl of air, hot and cold, warm and cool, always moving, never still; and far away, the omnivorous rage of fire.

Somehow intertwined with all of this was the pure joy of growing things as they soaked the water from the soil and turned their leaves to the sky. And in the distance he could sense the first pangs of the plants' agony as all moisture was sucked from them by the heat of the fire.

296

'Now, Jason,' the tree-man called, 'we will bring the clouds.'

Instinctively, Jason understood this meant speaking with the water and persuading the air. Maybe, just as the dirt and trees talked to him through his contact with the roots and soil, so the Oomgosh spoke with him as well.

'I see them coming!' somebody called from up in the trees. Was Thomas acting as look-out? But the human voice was so faint, so much further away than the voices of the elements around him.

Jason had no time for people now.

Harold wasn't quite able to keep up with their Captain. Their leader ran like a man possessed, dodging trees and vines and whatever other obstacles stood in his way without breaking stride. Even the wolves were hard pressed to keep pace, their ears flat back as they dashed through the forest. Pator followed immediately thereafter, carefully tracing the footsteps of his leader. Harold took up the rear.

He held a sword in one hand and a bow was strapped to his back. Pator had given him some rudimentary lessons in both, but he couldn't say he was skilled in either. Still, running through the forest, weapons in hand, ready to mow down anything in his path gave him a sense of giddy freedom he hadn't felt since he was a teenager. If the boys in the office could only see him now. Then again, they'd probably laugh. He wondered if they'd keep on laughing after he'd shot the boss.

'Clossse!' the wolves howled. 'Clooossse! Meeat cloosse!'

The forest abruptly opened into a trail that looked as though it had been burnt from the wood. The Captain turned left, followed by his lupine troops. The soldiers were only slightly ahead of them, but Nunn's men were moving so quickly and purposefully that at first they did not realise they were being attacked from the rear.

'Wolves!' the Captain called to the five who ran to either side. 'Attack! Dinner time,' he added in a quieter voice as one of the wolves brought down his first soldier. 'A shame about this, really, but we have to make a statement.'

Some of the soldiers at the rear were stumbling to a halt as their fellows were being pulled to the ground. The wolves were efficient, going immediately for the humans' throats, then leaping to another assault as soon as their last victim's blood pumped on to the ground.

The Captain and Pator joined the attack, their swords drawn and hacking at the disorganised troops before them. Harold found himself only a few steps behind them, his sword above his head, screaming just like his fellows. It was like some great boyhood game, capturing the opponents' fort. Ready or not, here I come!

A hairy face suddenly stepped in front of him. It was one of the soldiers, the enemy. Harold was aware of the smell of sweat and blood. His arm shook where his sword-blow was parried by his enemy's blade, but his forward momentum almost made him plough into the other man. His bearded enemy grabbed Harold's shirt and pulled him from the ground.

This, Harold realised, was all too real.

Joan Blake wished, for one very intense and foolish second, that she could be back in civilisation, where women didn't have to fight to save their lives. Back on Chestnut Circle your biggest problems were paying the mortgage and conquering the crab grass. Joan didn't think she'd ever see crab grass again. Heck, after this, she'd just let it live.

It was strange how much she thought about her family and her house and her past, as Nunn's soldiers began to pour into the clearing. Most of the first wave of them fell into the traps Thomas had helped them devise; half a dozen soldiers maimed and broken in an instant. A couple more went down with arrows in their chests.

But four of the soldiers broke through. These were the ones they were going to have to kill, or the soldiers would kill them. It was as simple as that.

Bobby shot one of the four at close range. The soldier screamed as he pawed at the shaft that protruded from his eye.

The other three came straight for the women, who stood side

298

by side, their backs to a great tree. One of the men grinned at the women and said something in their strange language. Even though Joan didn't know the words, she understood him perfectly. Why don't you just put down your weapons and spread your legs? Certain sentiments were universal.

'Oh, god,' Rose Dafoe kept repeating softly, as if the litany might give her strength. 'Oh, god, oh, god, oh, god.'

The man who grinned trotted in front of the others. Joan remembered to breathe. If the men treated them so lightly as to come at them singly, they might stand a chance.

Now, Joan thought, they only had to follow through on the strategies they'd worked on with Thomas.

'Open arms,' she called to the two other women. Both she and Rebecca Jackson took a step away to either side, leaving Rose Dafoe directly in the soldier's path. Rose looked timidly at the man bearing down on her, the knife in her hand apparently forgotten.

The smile spread across the soldier's face again. He carried a knife, but his sword still sat inside its scabbard. He didn't think someone like Rose would take much persuading at all. He was almost close enough to touch her now.

'Not so fast, bastard!' Rebecca called. He grunted in surprise and turned towards the voice. That was Joan's cue to swing her hatchet. She aimed for the back of the soldier's neck. Somehow, the blade got turned round, but the flat of it hit the back of his head with a very satisfying thump.

Rose jumped away as the soldier fell on his face.

At that, the other two soldiers rushed forward. Joan took a couple of steps away and one soldier angled towards her while the other headed for Rose and Rebecca. Joan swung her hatchet back and forth before her, trying to make her opponent keep his distance. He grabbed his sword, pulling it most of the way free.

The other soldier grunted and stared down at the knife sticking out of his chest. His companion only looked his way for a second, but that was enough for Joan. She danced in as she swung her small axe. The hatchet buried itself into the flesh at the man's hip.

A great gout of blood spurted out as he fell to his knees. He looked up at Joan, finally pulling his sword free. He swung the blade back, ready to take her with him.

Rebecca ran forward, slamming the side of the soldier's face with a large rock. He fell forward, the blood still pouring freely from his wound.

The three women looked at each other.

'So far,' Joan said, 'still alive.'

They looked up as they heard a shout. Another group of men poured into the clearing.

'Oh, hell,' Rebecca muttered. 'Here comes my husband.'

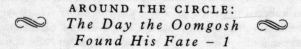

AROUND THE CIRCLE:
The Day the Oomgosh Found His Fate – 1

So it was that the Oomgosh roamed the world and took joy in all growing things. And, as has been related elsewhere, he came to know the ebb and flow of the seasons, and how much of life would wither away, only to return with spring.

Now the Oomgosh had wandered through the years and seen everything the whole globe over, except for one place; the house at the end of the world.

This house was as famous as it was mysterious, for the Oomgosh discovered that, while many had heard of it the whole world around, none had ever seen it for themselves. This made the Oomgosh curious, for he wished to embrace all the earth and everything within it. How had this single place eluded him?

Perhaps, he thought, it was because he had never looked for it.

Therefore he began his search in earnest, asking everyone he met, human and otherwise, if they could direct him to the house at the end of the world. And some told him that they had never heard of such a place, while others, at the very mention of it, became fearful and ran away. But a very few of them did know of it and could show the Oomgosh the way.

The first of these was an old woman, her back bent forward, her fingers twisted useless with age.

'It is very close,' she told the tree-man when he asked the way.

'And where is that?' the Oomgosh asked further.

But at that the old woman shook her head. 'My eyes are failing. I cannot see it yet, but I expect to shortly.'

The Oomgosh was excited to be near the house at last. He thanked the old woman and hurried on his way, climbing up one hill and down another. And there he chanced upon another man, who was pulling a wagon piled high with the bodies of the dead.

'There is a great battle taking place over the next rise,' the man explained. 'Someone must take charge of the results.'

The Oomgosh agreed that this was a sad but important task. He then asked the corpse-mover if he knew the way to that special house.

'The woman said it was nearby?' the man asked as he scratched at his head. 'Well, that house is not here. It must be on the other side of the battle.'

The Oomgosh thanked the man and hurried over the next rise. There, he could see the battlefield before him, with a dozen men loading carts exactly like the one the Oomgosh had just passed. But there were living soldiers upon the battlefield as well, for two lines of men were hunkered down in ditches and hid behind boulders. And all of them had weapons nearby and were waiting for the battle to resume.

The Oomgosh walked down into the battlefield and the first line of soldiers, seeing that he looked nothing like the enemy, let him pass. He then walked up to the second line of soldiers and asked them his question.

'Do you know the way to the house at the end of the world?'

The tired soldiers looked at each other and then back to the Oomgosh.

'It is that way!' one of the soldiers said at last, pointing behind them without looking. And then all the soldiers turned

301

away from the Oomgosh too, as if he might never have passed their way.

But the Oomgosh had no more time for battles or those who fought them, either. He was near his goal. So he climbed one final hill and stood on one final summit. And there, upon the other side, he saw a large house, standing all alone, built upon a cliff. The Oomgosh walked closer to that cliff, but the drop-off beyond seemed to go on for ever, for the ground below was obscured by clouds.

This, then, was the house at the edge of the world.

Forty-three

Harold Dafoe was pinned to the ground. He had failed in his first fight. Somehow, when he blundered into his opponent, he'd managed to get the man to drop his sword. But Harold's triumph was especially short-lived as he lost his weapon as well, and his foe grabbed him and threw him to the ground.

Now that they were both weaponless, Harold assumed he would be strangled. His career as an adventurer would be short, and not particularly glorious.

The face, and the body attached, were abruptly yanked away. Harold could breathe.

The Captain stood above him, a wolf on either side.

'Congratulations, Lieutenant Harold,' the Captain called. 'You engaged your man for a sufficient time to allow us to subdue the others.' He extended a hand. 'Now get up and join us, while we consider the fates of our prisoners.'

Harold let the Captain pull him to his feet. Pator and two of the wolves watched a cluster of seven soldiers. Three more lay on the ground. Not only were these three dead, but two of them were partially eaten, and the remaining wolf was working on the third.

The Captain turned to the seven living captives. 'Now, you all remember me, probably far better than you remember Nunn. I am taking Nunn's army away from him, one way or another. Therefore, you have two choices. You join me and I will once again be your Captain. Or you will be food for the wolves.'

The seven living soldiers all seemed to want to talk at once. 'We will join you.'

'Yes, we were hoping you would come back to lead us against that pig Nunn put over us.'

'There is no choice at all, really.'

'Exactly,' the Captain agreed. 'Consider yourselves members of the New Free Army.' He waved at the swords and what not scattered about them on the ground. 'Pator, see that they get some weapons.'

The wolf who was still eating raised its bloody snout to regard the Captain. 'Then we cannot eat any of theesse?'

'You do not want to over-indulge,' the Captain answered him with a smile. 'You will grow slow and tired, and your enemies will defeat you.'

The wolf looked at him sceptically. 'Will therre be no morre meat?'

'Oh, I wouldn't worry about that,' the Captain reassured the beast. 'We still have to talk with plenty of soldiers. I'm sure one or two of the others will want to disagree.'

The wolf regarded the Captain silently for a moment before turning away and howling at the others. 'Come! We musst eat quickly!'

All five wolves descended upon the three dead soldiers, tearing apart the remains with hearty growls.

'And we have other battles to fight,' the Captain called to everyone. 'Gather up what you want from the ground. We must leave to confront these soldiers' fellows.'

'And do what?' asked the bearded man who'd thrown Harold.

The Captain nodded to the soldier. 'They'll have the same choices you did. Either they will be killed, or freed.' With that, he sheathed his own sword, turned and hurried down the trail after the remains of Nunn's army.

Harold grabbed his sword and followed. He hoped that, in his next battle, he would do better.

Joan Blake looked at Carl and Rebecca Jackson, husband and wife on another world. Carl had somehow got past Thomas's arrows and brought a half dozen of his men with him. But he had stopped, the men clustered behind him, when he had seen his wife.

Rebecca was the one to break the silence. 'Carl. Why don't you listen to reason?'

At that, Jackson's face broke into a sneer. 'There she goes, Mrs High-and-Mighty. You always wanted to tell me off, didn't you? Well, now I'm holding all the cards. I've got a whole army behind me.'

And maybe he did have a whole army, somewhere. It was hard to tell how many men were with him. Thomas and Bobby had managed to keep some of them pinned down with their arrows. Of course, it didn't matter if Jackson had six hundred more soldiers hidden out there. The six with Carl would probably be enough to kill them all, if that's what they wanted to do.

Joan turned to the far side of the clearing where the great tree-man and Jason stood side by side, motionless. She had no idea what they were doing. Couldn't the two of them see that the women needed help?

It started to rain.

Bobby cried out. He fell against the tree he had been hiding behind. The soldiers were firing back. Bobby had an arrow in his shoulder.

Other soldiers moved cautiously from behind the trees at the edge of the clearing. The army was starting to show itself. What had happened to Thomas?

The rain got harder. It had turned to a downpour in a matter of seconds.

'Enough polite chit-chat.' Carl Jackson stepped forward, the cluster of men at his heels. Joan had the idea that whatever Carl did, the other men would quickly follow. He grinned at his wife. 'This one's mine.'

Joan heard thunder in the distance.

'Damn it, Carl,' Rebecca said softly. 'Don't make me.' Joan saw Rebecca still held her knife in her hand.

Carl reached out for her with a knife of his own. But he nodded to his other hand, which held a globe filled with some dark-blue fluid.

'In a minute', he whispered, 'you'll beg me for it.'

Something came streaking out of the woods and leapt towards Carl with a growl. Jackson screamed, throwing his hands in front of his face. Both globe and knife went flying.

It was only when Jackson had fallen to the ground, with Charlie on top of him, that Joan realised the identity of his attacker.

But Charlie was no longer the cute, neighbourhood dog that used to live in Joan's house. His jaws snapped shut on Jackson's arm as Carl shrieked.

One of the soldiers lunged forward and grabbed the globe. But he dropped it almost as quickly, adding his screams to Carl's, the flesh on his hands burned to black ash.

The rain was coming down in great surges, making it hard to see more than maybe twenty feet away. All but the closest soldiers had turned to grey shapes struggling through the mud. Joan remembered an earlier battle then, and what the tree-man and Jason had done with the wind. So maybe they were fighting alongside them after all.

She could still see them clearly enough when the five remaining members of Jackson's guard drew their swords and rushed at them with a yell.

She looked at Rose and Rebecca, both frozen before the attack. Joan wanted to shout something; come up with another one of Thomas's clever plans. But there were too many of them, coming too fast.

'Now,' the Oomgosh rumbled behind them.

A bolt of lightning streaked from the sky, hitting the upraised sword of the soldier in the lead.

He didn't have time to make a sound. The air smelled of ozone as he fell.

The four other soldiers dropped their swords and ran, losing themselves behind curtains of rain.

Joan stood for a moment, overwhelmed. She should do something else now, she knew, somehow press the attack back the other way.

But she was too surprised simply realising she was still alive.

They had brought the rain and they had brought the lightning. And Jason had helped.

306

Not that he was quite Jason any more. No, he was part of the roots and dirt beneath his feet, and they were a part of him. And he had other parts too; the air as familiar as if it had come from his own lungs, the lightning a spark at the end of his fingers, the rain just like his tears.

And he could hear the Oomgosh's thoughts, and feel his emotions, as if they were both portions of some great thing, something so big that Jason couldn't really define it. Maybe it was the whole island. Maybe it was the world.

There was both an anger and a joy in the Oomgosh as he led the rain and brought the lightning. Jason felt the anger too, rage at those who would destroy his forest, and the joy that came from joining with earth and sky to defeat nature's enemies.

He was vaguely aware of the clearing around him, and the drama that took place there between the folks from Chestnut Circle and Nunn's army. He had seen them all in brilliant relief when the lightning had struck down the man by his sword. But by far the greater part of his consciousness was joined to the elements around him, so that he felt every gust of wind and drop of rain.

He sensed the Oomgosh shift beside him.

'Jason,' the tree-man rumbled. 'You will have to control the rain by yourself for a time.'

Jason almost asked the Oomgosh why. But he could feel it too; the network of roots that held the island together felt the others coming – many others running towards them, others that weren't human.

The Oomgosh told Jason what he already knew. 'There are others approaching. We must find more ways to defend our friends. You know how to bring the rain and lightning. Keep the rain coming until all the fires are gone. You are the younger Oomgosh now.

Jason hoped he would be worthy of the honour.

The forest told him that someone new had arrived.

'What is this nonsense?' he heard with his ordinary ears.

The rain sputtered as Jason stared at the newcomer. The pale figure stood out, both with his common sight, and the feelings that came from the soil. It looked to Jason's human eyes like death, and felt to his forest senses like ice. It was Nunn.

Forty-four

Obar hoped he wasn't too late.

He willed the jewel in his hand to let him see through the curtains of rain. The dragon's eye dimmed, as if that simple request would use up the last of the gem's power. But the rain still faded, allowing the magician to see his surroundings.

The clearing around him had fallen into chaos. A couple of the soldiers were dead, a pair of the neighbours were wounded. Even with his diminished resources, Obar could tell that the rain wasn't entirely natural, and the placement of the lighting was all too convenient. He had never seen the Oomgosh do anything quite so impressive before. Obar wondered, with so little potency left in his jewel, if he could do anything nearly as powerful.

'Not the most auspicious of meetings, is it?'

Obar turned to find the source of the voice. There, on the other side of the clearing, stood his brother Nunn.

'Personally,' Nunn added, 'I was hoping for something far more glorious.'

He held up his hands to show his eyes; they sparkled dimly, with only a glimmer of their usual shine.

Nunn nodded at his lack-lustre gems. 'Yes, apparently the dragon does not want us to have our climactic battle just yet. So we'll have to have a smaller battle; just you and I.'

The dark wizard pointed to the jewel Obar held in his hand. 'Each eye holds but a fraction of its usual strength. And I would guess that all the gems are equal.' Nunn shrugged at the thought. 'So I am twice as equal as you. Dear brother, I will especially enjoy pulverising you with but a small part of the dragon's power.'

'You!' Bobby yelled from where he sat on the ground. 'What have you done to my father?'

Nunn waved pleasantly at the boy. The wizard seemed to be enjoying himself more with every passing moment. 'Why, you should know by now that I ate him, or at least his life energy. I intend to do the selfsame thing with my brother here, once I have taken his gem.' He turned his smile to Obar. 'Sounds a bit incestuous, doesn't it?'

Obar had had enough of his sarcastic brother. 'Why don't you do something besides talk?'

'No time for farewells?' Nunn showed Obar both of his gems. 'I'll make this quick then.'

But Obar had already concocted a spell that struck out towards Nunn, a spit of green fire that sliced through the rain before splitting into two, then four, then sixteen fireballs, so that the flaming globes swept down on Nunn from all directions.

'Clever,' Nunn admitted, as he spun about, sending bolts of power from his own eyes to make the fireballs explode, two here, then three more there, then a number of others one after another, until only four remained.

Obar wondered what Nunn was waiting for. His spell was obviously little more than an inconvenience to his brother. Unless Nunn's own jewels were so depleted that he couldn't immediately defeat the final four fireballs.

But the last four globes of flame were no longer sweeping towards Nunn. All four of them hung in the air, then began to describe a great lighted circle before Nunn. The dark wizard moved his hands up and down as if he were juggling. He started to laugh.

'What?' the laugh turned into a cry of surprise.

The four fireballs exploded as Nunn stared down at the arrow in his shoulder.

'That's for my father!' Bobby called from where he squatted, already fitting another arrow into his bow.

'How?' Nunn stared dumbly at the arrow piercing his flesh. 'Nothing gets through my defences.'

'When you have the full power of the dragon's eyes,' Obar

reminded his brother gently. Actually, there had been other arrows, and once a knife wielded by Obar himself, that had got past Nunn's sorcery over the years. But on those other occasions, he had always plucked them out with a laugh. He seemed to be having more trouble in these circumstances.

Nunn was as vulnerable as Obar had ever seen him since the day they had taken their dragon's eyes. This would be the time to end it all.

Not that his own eye would be much help. Well, if he had to, Obar would walk across this muddy clearing and strangle his brother with his bare hands.

He took one step forward, then another, careful to walk round the man and dog still rolling about in the clearing's centre.

'What are you doing?' Nunn called. Obar thought he might have heard fear in his brother's voice.

'Finishing this,' Obar answered. 'Just you and I.'

'Ah, would that we could. Unfortunately, I invited some others to our little party.'

The smile was back on Nunn's face as the red-furred ape-things rushed into the clearing.

When the apes arrived, Joan Blake knew this would never end.

'Oh, god,' Rose murmured as they poured from the forest. 'Oh, god, oh, god.' Her voice grew fainter, as if even that litany took too much energy.

Well, Joan expected all of them at least to fight back. 'Rose!' she called. 'Rebecca! Get over here! We can defend ourselves better if we stay together.'

Rose looked up from her reverie, blinking as though she was only now seeing her surroundings. Rebecca appeared out of the rain on Joan's other side.

'Let's back up,' Joan told the others. 'We can protect our backs with one of the big trees.'

Rebecca turned to her right. 'I'm bringing Bobby. He's hurt.'

Joan should have thought of that herself. But then, who elected her leader? She should be happy that the others were taking the initiative.

'Rose!' she called. The other woman seemed to be drifting off again. 'Back here with me!'

A tree loomed above them in the downpour. Rose and Joan huddled together as Rebecca half walked and half carried Bobby over to join them.

'Oh, Bobby,' Rose whispered as Rebecca and the boy joined them. 'You're really hurt.' Her hands reached out but didn't quite touch him, as if she wished to make him better but was afraid to try.

There was a dark spot of blood on his shirt, just below his collar. It was hard, with his rain-drenched clothing, to determine exactly how much he was bleeding.

Bobby tried to smile. 'I don't want to think about that.' He raised his bow. 'I've got a couple of arrows left.'

'Can you still use that?' Joan asked.

'I think so.' He pointed to the blood-stain on his shirt. 'I broke the arrow off. Part of it's still in my left shoulder. It's doing lousy things to my aim.'

'You should rest, honey. Maybe you won't have to –' But Rose's kind words caught in her throat as she saw four of the apes rushing their way.

Get it off me!

Suddenly, the dog was gone.

Carl Jackson pulled his protective arms away from his eyes. The dog was still there, maybe half a dozen feet away, but it was staring at something new that was running into the clearing, some other kind of beasts with long red fur.

Jackson had thought he was dead. His body was covered with bites and scratches. He could hardly move his left arm. His wrist was a mass of red, torn flesh and he thought he could see a bit of bone. He felt his face and found a piece of skin hanging off his cheek.

Carl Jackson managed to stand. Somehow he felt he should be in a lot more pain than this. He considered grabbing the dog from behind and twisting his neck round until it broke. But he had no guarantee that would work. He might do nothing more than get the dog to go for him all over again.

He needed his weapons. His knife and his globe.

As soon as he thought about the sphere, he saw it glowing dimly about fifteen feet away. He would have to move carefully. The dog was looking the other way, growling at the newcomers, and Carl would do anything not to remind the creature that he was still around to attack.

He took a single step towards the globe. The dog still looked away. Maybe the apes would kill the little bastard for him. Of course, it would feel a whole lot better if Carl got to blow the dog into bloody pieces. Then again, maybe the apes wanted to kill Carl too.

None of this was as clear as Nunn said it was going to be. But it would all be a lot clearer once he had got the globe.

Nunn couldn't stop himself from laughing.

When he pulled the arrow from his arm, he wanted to scream. The eyes had kept that kind of pain away for ever. But he laughed instead. The eyes would be back, two or three or maybe more. And what little power his own eyes held would keep him alive until then.

The apes shrieked as they tumbled into the clearing. The few remaining defenders fell back before their onslaught. The apes were messy killers, but they were quick. This should all be over shortly.

Nunn's soldiers were either dead or gone, except for his new Captain, who seemed to be getting eaten alive by a dog. Nunn would deal with his soldiers later. For now, he laughed at the lightning and the rain, and the way the storm turned the whole place to muck.

He had great reason to laugh. This moment was as chaotic as any that the wizard had ever seen.

There was a simple rule in this place: whenever chaos ruled, Nunn won.

There were things here that even Nunn couldn't believe. Like his brother actually rushing towards him across the clearing.

Seeing that old fool dressed in white and splashing through the mud made Nunn laugh even harder than before.

So it was that the tree-man found the house at the end of the world.

The Oomgosh, eager to discover the secret of this place, walked quickly to the front of the house. A great owl sat outside the door.

Now some believe that the owl is an ill omen and always comes before death. But others think of the owl as a harbinger of things to come and that good fortune might follow its great white wings.

So the Oomgosh nodded to the owl and walked up to the great door, which looked as though it was made of stone. And at the side of the door was a small, neatly lettered sign, which read:

'Only knock when you are ready.'

Well, the Oomgosh was as ready as he'd ever be, having seen all the world except for this one small corner. So he pounded his great fist against the door.

The door swung away quite promptly and there, on the other side, stood a young man who smiled up at him.

'Come in,' the young man said. 'I've been expecting you.'

The Oomgosh wondered how this could be. But as he had heard of this house, so perhaps had its owner heard of him as well. Therefore he gladly stepped inside.

The door swung shut behind him, apparently of its own accord, and the young man turned from the entry way and led the Oomgosh to a huge hall. This was easily the greatest room the tree-man had ever seen, large enough to hold a good-sized forest, if one would grow there. But it was difficult to determine the room's exact size for, while it was quite brightly lit at their point of entry, its recesses were lost in shadows.

Now the young man smiled again at his guest. 'You have seen everything, haven't you? Then it is time that you came here, to witness the one thing that you have missed.'

This was what the Oomgosh had come here for, although he had never put it into words. He would now see the final secret of the house at the end of the world. But what might that secret be, that it would be so different from the thousand things he had seen before?

Forty-five

Joan Blake concentrated on the hatchet in her hand.

Rose screamed as the apes rushed towards them. The apes screamed back.

Bobby's arrow caught one in the chest. That left three; one each for Joan, Rebecca and Rose. The apes all held knives as well. At least they wouldn't overwhelm the women with their weapons. But they had such long arms. If Joan and the others didn't distract them somehow, their three attackers would cut them dead before they could reach their own knives to retaliate.

The beasts raised their red-furred arms over their heads and shrieked again as they began their final rush.

'No you don't!' a shout came from their side.

Thomas jumped from behind a tree, driving his sword into the stomach of the ape on the right. Rose's ape, Joan thought absently.

But her thoughts snapped back to the battle. This was the distraction she had hoped for.

'Now!' she called to the other women, running forward, both hands holding the hatchet above her head.

The second ape had stumbled to a halt, half towards Joan, half towards Thomas and its fallen comrade. It bared its teeth at the Volunteer as its own knife swung down aimed at Thomas's chest.

'No!' Joan cried as she swung the hatchet down with all the force in her arms.

This time she struck blade first. The hatchet stuck in the ape's skull, just above the eyes.

Joan jumped back as it fell forward.

'The others!' Thomas called.

Joan turned and saw that the third ape had kept on running. It veered now, away from Rebecca and her knife towards Rose, who stared at the creature open-mouthed.

'Rose!' Joan called. 'Your knife!'

But Rose seemed to be beyond hearing.

'Oh, no,' Rebecca called as the ape passed her by. 'Nobody cuts up anybody ever again.'

At the last instant, Rose screamed and tried to run away. The ape's knife caught her on the leg. But Rebecca was right behind the beast. She used both her hands too, pushing her knife into the ape's back until the hilt stopped it from going further.

The ape screamed, reaching for the blade with its long arms. It fell to its knees, then to its side, its teeth snapping as the body spasmed.

'The thing's still alive!' Rebecca called.

Rose looked down at the knife in her hands as if this was the first time she had ever seen it.

The wounded ape's wildly groping hand grabbed on to her skirt.

'Oh, god,' Rose whispered. She fell to her knees, driving the knife into the creature's chest. The ape shrieked one more time before it went limp.

'Get your weapons back,' Thomas called. 'They'll be comin' again.'

Joan looked at the Volunteer and realised that one whole side of his tunic was brown with blood. He dropped to his knees and worked the sword free from the corpse. He looked up and saw Joan staring at him.

'They shoot enough arrows at you, one will get you sooner or later.' Thomas pushed against the sword, using it as a crutch to regain his feet. 'Don't have time to worry about it now.'

So three of them were already wounded. And the apes were coming again.

The apes were all around Obar, but none of them attacked. Whatever went on in their primitive minds, they knew they didn't want to clash with a wizard.

Obar skidded to a halt half a dozen feet in front of Nunn. 'This must end, brother.'

'Most certainly,' Nunn agreed, with his maddening smile. 'Except that our great and powerful dragon's eyes hardly work at all. How do you propose to stop me, brother?'

Perhaps it came from all the years of living in fear of what Nunn might do, or all the times Obar watched helplessly as Nunn destroyed all he had built. Or perhaps it was only because of that smile. But Obar did the only thing that came to mind. He rushed the other wizard with a yell.

Nunn yelped as Obar grabbed him by the shoulders. But Obar couldn't stop his forward momentum, his feet slipping and sliding across the wet ground.

The two wizards toppled together into the mud.

Another group of apes rushed across the clearing towards Joan and her fellows. This time, there must have been close to a dozen of them.

'Got any arrows, Bobby?' Thomas called.

'Just one,' was the reply.

'Well, make it count!' The Volunteer stood up straight. A groan escaped him as he lifted his sword.

Joan had retrieved her hatchet and taken one of the fallen creatures' knives. Rebecca had her knife back as well, but Rose stared down at her own weapon still impaling the dead ape.

They had been beyond lucky to survive the first two on-slaughts. Joan didn't think they had any hope of surviving the third. She turned again to her two silent allies at the very rear of the clearing.

'Oomgosh! Jason! If you can do anything, please do it now!'

Lightning flashed from the sky again, showing the whole rain-swept clearing for an instant, and perhaps another thirty apes beyond the dozen that rushed to attack. The lightning hit one of the apes in the lead, causing the red-haired thing to convulse and fall to the ground.

317

The others stopped. If not for the constant rain, it might have seemed as if time paused for a second.

And then, from somewhere within the ape pack rose a great, ululating cry. The apes bared their fangs and surged forward again, more quickly than before.

The lightning didn't stop them. If anything, it had made the creatures mad.

They were closing fast.

'Oh, hell,' Thomas muttered. He lifted his sword above his head. 'Come to me, you bastards!' he yelled as he rushed to meet them.

The clearing was getting closer, the forest further away.

'Mother!' Jason called. She was in danger. The roots told him about her fear, her helplessness. They were all in peril again.

'No, Jason,' the Oomgosh called. 'Keep your feet rooted firmly to the soil. You must keep the rain and lightning strong. Strike down our attackers and extinguish their killing fires.' He pulled one of his great feet from the earth.

'It is better if I go,' he called over one great shoulder. 'I know how to fight.'

Thomas was gone. Joan watched him wade into the pack of red-furred things, his sword swinging back and forth to catch as many of the apes as it could. But there were far more apes than that. They swarmed over Thomas, so that in only an instant all she could see was his sword swinging through the air. A second after that there was nothing but a great, screaming mound of red fur.

Thomas was surely dead. He had stopped the beasts' assault briefly, but for what? She stared at the hatchet, once again in her hand; one lone blade against so many beasts. Bobby was down to his last arrow, Rose seemed to be in shock. They had no other plans, nowhere to turn.

Joan Blake looked up. The Oomgosh was suddenly at her side.
'This will not happen,' he rumbled.

He walked past her, his steps firm even in the muddy ground. The red-furs freed themselves from their pile and turned to face their new opponent. But this time they did not rush to the attack. Instead, they formed a ragged line and moved forward slowly, knives held before them. Perhaps they remembered the Oomgosh from earlier battles. Whatever the reason, their attitude had changed.

The Oomgosh waved to the apes with his one good arm. 'Come, little creatures. If you want to handle death I will gladly show you its face.'

Four of the apes pushed their way past their fellows to join the first line. Each of them held a spear before him. Joan remembered those spears; the 'poison sticks'. The Oomgosh had lost an arm to these deadly sticks and, if not for the intervention of Hyram Sayre, the tree-man might have lost his life to the poison as well.

'One at a time?' the Oomgosh asked. 'Or all at once?'

As if in answer, one of the apes rushed forward and threw his spear. The Oomgosh did not even try to avoid it. The poison stick lodged in his shoulder as he hurried to meet his attacker. He picked up the ape and tossed it far back into the woods, the flying body soon lost behind the ever-present rain.

The Oomgosh kept moving ahead. He was in the midst of the apes, sending another flying before it had a chance even to bring up its spear.

Charlie darted into the mass of apes, growling and nipping at their legs and feet. He fled again a second later. Perhaps even the dog realised there were too many of them. One of the apes sent a spear after him, but it fell just short of the retreating tail.

'We should do something to help.' Rebecca stood at Joan's side. She was right. Joan had stood frozen here, too exhausted and shocked by the bloodshed around her even to think about what she should do next.

She pulled her gaze away from the battle to look at her old neighbour.

'Maybe the two of us can pick off stragglers at the side or something,' Rebecca suggested.

'It's worth a try,' Joan agreed. Anything, really, was better than standing here, waiting to die. The two women walked quickly towards one end of the cluster of apes fighting the

Oomgosh. At the moment, the tree-man had all of the enemy's attention.

He tossed another of the apes away and got another spear in his back for his trouble. The Oomgosh stumbled, but managed to regain his feet.

'Oomgosh!' Jason called out.

The rain sputtered overhead.

Why did Hyram Sayre even watch this? It was far too upsetting, far too bloody, far too much like what he used to be.

What was he thinking? He wasn't even Hyram Sayre any more. He was the Green Man. That's what the fellow who looked like a tree had dubbed him. And it was exactly the name for him.

But now the tree-man was in trouble. If Hyram didn't help – no, if the Green Man didn't help – that tree-fellow was going to die.

He wanted peace. He wanted to give life, to make things grow. The old Hyram Sayre was so angry, always wanting to destroy anything that interfered with his lawn. The Green Man shouldn't feel like that. Why did he even remember any of those thoughts?

Maybe it was because he had been only watching and not acting.

The Green Man could help the tree-man – the Oomgosh – to live.

But only if – the Green Man stopped himself. There were no more ifs. The old Hyram Sayre used to hide from the world behind his lawn. His new self couldn't hide behind his power. If the Green Man was going to be truly superhuman, he had to accept his responsibilities.

'I'm coming! I'm coming!' he called as he swept down from the sky.

The rain had turned the battlefield into a pond, with an inch of water above the saturated earth. When this was over, maybe the Green Man would come back here and make things grow. But first he had to help another life.

All fighting stopped below him as he paused in the sky overhead. He did have that effect on people; probably something to do with his spectral green glow. Actually, now that he looked closer, he could still see a couple of fellows rolling around in the mud, involved in their own two-person war. But they were beneath the Green Man's notice. He had no more time for the dirt of humanity.

He did, however, have a moment for this fellow who also tended the earth.

'Tree-man!' he called.

The large fellow – the Oomgosh, they called him – looked up at that. 'You,' was all he said.

'You need my help again,' the Green Man stated simply as he lowered himself to the tree-man's side.

The Green Man once again laid a hand against the other's bark-like skin and could feel immediately how much was going wrong within. He had sensed a weakness in the Oomgosh the last time he had shared his power, with the tree-man's body filled with unhealthy fluids.

Now the fluids were twice as strong as before, but still somehow the tree-man stood. This was surely someone worthy of the Green Man's gifts! The Green Man could not fight, himself. But he would give this warrior enough power to suppress all the poisons in his body, to fight with renewed strength to oppose the agents of destruction.

Yes. The Green Man liked the way that sounded.

His own power, the power of green, poured into the other. All of the tree-man's skin glowed green for the briefest of moments.

The Green Man withdrew his hand.

The Oomgosh laughed and plucked the spears out of his skin. 'Thank you. Would you like to join us?'

The being who had once been Hyram Sayre looked at the clearing around him. He saw the two creatures lashing out at each other in the mud, so covered with filth that they were both unrecognisable. He had once wanted to lash out like that. Those feelings could stir in him again. He saw the hate on the red apes' faces. He had felt hate like that before, hate at all the neighbours who laughed at him, at the teenaged cretins who destroyed his lawn – no, he would not go that way again.

'Sorry,' he managed. 'Can't.'

321

He had to fly away – now. Certainly the Green Man would be calmer in the safety of the sky.

Jason could barely hear the rain.

His friends were hurt and dying out there in the clearing. He wanted to run and join them. The lightning only seemed to enrage their bestial enemies. Hadn't there been enough rain to put out every fire on the island?

But the Oomgosh had told him to stay. Part of Jason still seeded the clouds to continue the storm. Part of him was ready to loose the lightning when it was needed. But most of him now watched the drama before him in the clearing.

Then Hyram Sayre had arrived out of the clouds and given the Oomgosh the benefit of his healing hands. The Oomgosh had stood up straight and stared at the enemy, as if he had forgotten all about the poison in his system. The thing that once was Hyram Sayre disappeared in a great flash of green.

But an Oomgosh at full strength was more than a match for any group of apes.

'What?' a caustic voice asked from somewhere in the sky. 'You've started already? You couldn't wait?'

The Oomgosh looked to the sky. 'Could it be?'

A black bird swooped down low over the battlefield. 'Take heart, my Oomgosh! Raven is here to the rescue!'

The Oomgosh's face brightened with his great familiar grin. 'My Raven! You have returned! My life is complete!'

Raven banked over the apes, who hissed and growled up at the newcomer. 'Ah, if only more would realise my true importance.'

The Oomgosh pushed aside the first ape who attempted to attack. 'But what has kept you?'

'I was not travelling alone.' Raven sailed over to one side of the clearing where Todd now stood. 'There is another as well. And even Raven had difficulty finding this place. There is far more going on in this world than Raven would like.'

'We saw a flash of green,' Todd explained. 'Raven took it for the dragon's eyes.'

'Either that, or the dragon,' the great black bird admitted.

322

'Either way, my wings grew tired. We flew to the light and here you are.'

'A flash of green?' the Oomgosh called, smashing two of the apes' heads together. 'Truly it was the ministrations of that strange being who has restored my strength. Fate has a way with you, Raven.'

'Fate is but another of my many names,' Raven agreed. He squawked as a spear barely missed his wing. 'Have these creatures no manners? Can't they see we're talking?'

'I'm afraid, dear Raven,' the Oomgosh agreed, 'that these creatures have no manners at all.'

Raven squawked at that. 'Then let us drive these things back to the other island where they came from!'

But the majority of the apes had not spent their entire time in awe of the Oomgosh and the bird. Another seven spear-wielders had stepped to the front of their ranks.

'Oomgosh!' Raven called as the seven beasts screamed and ran forward, all plunging their weapons into the tree-man.

The tree-man roared. Seven spears were stuck into his arms and chest. The Oomgosh ignored them as if they were the bites of insects.

'You will never be rid of the Oomgosh!' he cried to the apes before him. 'But the Oomgosh will be rid of you.'

He swept four of them out of the way with one great arm. But he stumbled with his next step forward.

'No!' he demanded. 'I am not finished. Let me stand until it is done!'

He grabbed an ape's head in his powerful hand and snapped its neck. He kicked another beast from its feet. But as he swung his leg, the Oomgosh seemed to lose his balance as well.

'No!' he called as he toppled forward. 'I am not quite –'

The earth shook where the Oomgosh fell.

'Oomgosh!' Raven called. 'My Oomgosh!'

The tree-man lay very still.

This couldn't be.

'Oomgosh!' Jason called as he pulled his feet from the soil.

The rain stopped abruptly, as if the sky had run out of tears.

323

And so the Oomgosh had come to the house at the end of the world, the place that held the one secret he had never seen before.

'Do not look so puzzled,' said the young man who was his guide. 'There is someone here I want you to meet.' He waved as if to lure someone from the shadows.

'Come here, boy.'

A smaller fellow stepped hesitantly forward. And although the Oomgosh had never seen this boy before, he was very familiar, from his toes that could dig into the earth, past strong legs covered with rough skin that held a hint of green, and a chest as broad as a tree trunk, up to a head covered with leaves and twigs where one might expect hair to be. The boy looked like a smaller version of himself; the Oomgosh as a child.

'We have been waiting for you for a very long time,' the man in charge remarked.

And the Oomgosh said something aloud then that he realised he had understood for a very long time. 'This is it, then, the very last place I will see?'

'Perhaps it is not the end,' his host answered gently. 'Perhaps it is the beginning of the last adventure.'

The Oomgosh knew from his travels that all things must make way for the young of their kind. And even the oldest tree must fall in its time.

The Oomgosh thought he knew the stranger's secret at last. 'Is your name Death?' he asked.

The young man smiled at that. 'Maybe my name is really Change.' He reached out towards both the tree-man and the boy. 'Come. Both of you, please take my hands.'

And both of them did as Change had asked.

'We have a great deal in common,' the young man told him with his touch. 'Only Change is eternal. But there will always be an Oomgosh.'

And the tree-man smiled a final smile as he fell, for as the world faded away, he knew that he had conquered death.

Forty-six

'No!'

This time, Joan Blake recognised the ever odder voice of Hyram Sayre before he even streaked down from the sky.

'He must be saved!' the former Hyram cried as he swooped above the clearing. 'Saved!'

The black bird looked up from where he had landed upon the shoulder of his fallen friend. 'Raven thinks this may be beyond even you.'

This only seemed to agitate the flying man further. 'I will help! I will! I cannot see such a noble life end like this!' He landed next to the prostrate tree-man. 'The Green Man does what he can!'

'Oomgosh?' Jason called as he rushed through the mud. 'Can you hear me?'

The Green Man placed both of his glowing hands on the Oomgosh's broad back. It flared for an instant, then faded and vanished.

'Green Man!' Jason called as he slid to a stop by the Oomgosh's side.

But the Green Man shook his head. 'I can do nothing if life is gone.'

He lifted his hands to the sky. 'It is too much for me!'

He turned to the apes, who seemed to have got over their surprise enough to think about resuming their attack.

'Why have you done this to someone who is a grower,' the Green Man demanded, 'not a destroyer?'

A pair of apes screamed at him then, and rushed towards him, their knives high above their heads.

The Green Man looked down from his attackers to the ends

of his fingers. 'This', he said as he looked up again, 'is for all of you who have defiled my lawn!'

Green fire erupted from his hands, engulfing the two apes in the lead and four more of their companions immediately behind them.

The Green Man was screaming now. 'There's more where that came from!' Another burst of fire spread before him.

'No one messes with Hyram Sayre!'

The last of the apes turned round and ran.

The Green Man screamed after them, a wordless sound, the equal of any of the apes' blood shrieks.

'Jason!' Rose Dafoe called as the apes rushed from the clearing.

But Jason Dafoe was running too.

Everyone had forgotten about Carl Jackson. What with this tree-man dying, and the guy with the green fire burning up all the apes, he guessed you could forget just about anybody.

It was a big mistake to forget about somebody with Carl's power.

It had surprised even Carl to see what had happened to his neighbour. Hyram Sayre had power too – that green fire stuff was nothing to laugh at – but he had gone completely off his nut. After burning up close to a dozen of those damned ape-things, all old Hyram could do was stare at his smouldering hands.

The apes were running. People were shouting. The wizards were still rolling around in the mud.

Carl would use this confusion to his advantage.

He would get them all.

But not quite now.

He grabbed his globe and ran.

Mrs Smith knew that she was too late the moment she arrived.

'Oh, dear,' she murmured. The clearing was littered with bodies. Most of them were either apes or Nunn's soldiers. But there were a couple of others whom she recognised.

Too late. With all she had learned and all her power, she was too late. She had brought the three Volunteers and Nick and

326

Sala as quickly as she could. It hadn't been good enough.

'Thomas?' Maggie called, running forward to what was left of the fourth Volunteer.

There was no doubt that Thomas was dead. His head stuck out at an odd angle from his shoulders and part of one arm had been torn away.

'He died fighting,' Wilbert called as Maggie stopped above their fallen comrade. 'That's all any of us could ask.'

Stanley spat at the muddy ground. 'And I think we're all going to get our wish, hey?'

But Mrs Smith wanted to know exactly what had happened. They could not bring back the dead, but if she knew the circumstances, perhaps she could save others from dying.

'Thomas is dead?' she demanded. 'And who else?'

'The Oomgosh,' Raven called from where he stood on the tree-man's still form. 'Raven's dearest friend. The Oomgosh is no more.'

Mrs Smith almost wanted the bird to repeat what he had just said. Somehow she had thought the tree-man would live for ever.

'Who is this?' Wilbert remarked, kicking at two interlocked figures rolling about in the mud.

'I'll kill you!' one of them managed. He was so out of breath that it wasn't much of a shout.

'Then I'll – take you with me,' the other one replied. 'Maybe it's better that way!'

'Obar and Nunn,' Mrs Smith said for everyone. Is this what they had fallen to without the full power of their dragon's eyes? 'Wilbert, do me a favour. Separate those two.'

Wilbert frowned. He was hesitant to deal with even mud-covered wizards.

'For some reason, none of the wizards seems to have much power just now,' Mrs Smith said reassuringly. 'Go ahead. If either of them gives you any trouble, my own eye will take care of it.' If, she thought but didn't say, her own eye had any energy left after bringing the Volunteers, Nick and Sala here.

'Maybe I can help with mine,' Todd added. 'I may need some assistance with how it works, though.'

Sala smiled up at him. She had managed to manoeuvre her

way through the mud to reach his side. Youth and enthusiasm, Constance thought. She wished that she herself didn't feel quite so exhausted.

Stanley strode forward. 'Let me help too, eh?' He grabbed one mud-caked form by the shoulders while Wilbert took the other one round the waist.

'On the count of three,' Wilbert instructed.

'I've always wanted to do this to a wizard,' Stanley agreed.

They pulled the two apart as Wilbert reached three.

'I will not be touched like this!' Nunn shouted.

'Right now,' Wilbert replied, 'I don't believe you have much of a choice.'

So these were the two most powerful wizards in the entire world? At the moment, the two looked like tired and foolish old men.

It was another sign, Mrs Smith realised, along with the deaths of her fellows and the strange shift in power of the eyes, that this whole world was changing.

She had the feeling that the change had only really just begun.

Leaves rustled in the trees at the edges of the clearing. She looked up and saw an owl perched on a branch above them.

'Who?' the owl inquired.

She had never seen an owl in this place before. The branches around it shook with the return of the wind. Mrs Smith noticed how quiet the world around them had been in the aftermath of the rain.

'Raven must go,' the bird announced as he flapped his wings.

'Where?' Mrs Smith asked.

'To fetch the Oomgosh!' Raven replied as he took flight.

Any questions Constance might have had died on her lips as Mary Lou stepped out of the tree. Right out of a tree at the clearing's edge, as if she'd been there all along.

Todd whistled. 'I was wondering where you were keeping yourself.'

Mary Lou acted as if she didn't hear Todd's voice. Instead, she stared straight at Mrs Smith, nodding once.

'Now it begins,' Mary Lou said.

Forty-seven

'Amazing', the Captain said to Harold, 'how quickly the ranks of our army grow. Isn't it?'

Very quickly, Harold thought, and almost too easily. Not that he was looking for another battle. By the time Nunn's fleeing army had reached them the troops had fallen into total disarray. There was no fight in them any more. Whatever had happened to them back in their own fight, the soldiers now gladly accepted any options open to them.

Only the wolves seemed less than pleased by this arrangement, since there were no dissenters to be eaten. Apparently, even with all they had consumed, the beasts were still hungry. They slunk about the edges of the human crowd, watching the soldiers with a mix of craving and fear. Harold wondered if their appetites could ever be satisfied.

The Captain, for one, appeared to be having a wonderful time. He hardly seemed to notice that it was raining as he strutted back and forth in front of his ever-growing army.

'Soon we will march to glory!' he called to all those before him. 'Soon we will march to our final battle, the destruction of Nunn.' The Captain didn't seem to notice how uneasy the mention of the sorcerer's name made his new-found troops. Instead, he called, 'No more fear, only glory!'

Harold wondered how the Captain could even begin to overcome a wizard. But then, this same Captain had stolen the wizard's army with remarkable ease.

But something else was bothering Harold. As the Captain's success had grown over these last hours, his interest in Harold lessened. Harold guessed he should be thankful for this. The

Captain, after all, only seemed slightly less crazy than Nunn. But it had felt so much better to have a purpose in this place. Maybe it had made the insanity of everything around here a little more bearable.

He walked a little way down the trail from the Captain. He was growing tired of his new leader's exhortations, on top of the wolves' grumbling, and the soldiers' confusion. He had to have a little quiet to reflect on what he needed to do. Not that he let the Captain's troops out of his sight. No, he felt as safe with this army here as he would anywhere in this place. Losing that safety was one thing he didn't want to risk.

As the Captain's voice faded with distance, Harold became aware of other voices ahead of him on the trail.

'I will not be a part of this!' one of them yelled angrily. 'This is not why I agreed to take the dragon's eye!'

'I don't know how you can help but be a part of this,' replied a second, calmer voice. 'We're all a part of this, until we find some way to disengage.'

'Let's fry him out!' screeched a third voice, high and grating. 'He doesn't want us, we burn him!'

'I don't think that's possible,' the patient voice replied. 'For one thing, my dear Zachs, you and I are inhabiting Mr Mills's body. We are his guests, welcome or not. However, I still believe, despite our initial problems, that the three of us together have a great deal of potential.'

Mr Mills? Could one of the people talking be Evan? Harold crept forward to get a better look. The trail twisted here, the huge trees obscuring the way ahead.

'Evan?' he called as he reached the turn.

He saw Evan Mills as soon as he passed the trees. The other man stood some twenty feet away, at the centre of the trail, all by himself.

'Evan?' Harold called again.

Evan Mills didn't seem to hear Harold at all. Instead, he appeared to be talking to himself, in three different and distinct voices.

'I don't want to be a part of that potential. Look what you tried to do to that boy –'

'And you interfered.' The calm voice was no longer sounding

330

quite so patient. 'What do you know about our needs? Only a wizard can save us from our current state.'

'Then free us all,' the third voice screeched out of Mills's mouth. 'Zachs needs to burn! Zachs needs to fly!'

Maybe, Harold thought, it was better that Mills didn't realise he was around. He stared at his old neighbour, who jerked his arms and legs every time his voice changed, as if his whole body wanted to alter along with his speech.

Mills raised a fist. 'I will not let you make decisions for me! If we do not work together, I will fight you.'

The fist relaxed as the hand waved away what was said before. 'Fight me? And how will you do that, you miserable human worm? You can't even guess how much power I will have, now that I have the eye.'

Mills suddenly fell into a crouch, arms forward, as if he was waiting to wrestle someone. 'We have the eye! And Zachs will take it away from both of you, and use it to burn this island to the ground, and fly far away!'

'Zachs, no!'

Mills jerked up, then hunkered down again, as though he had been snapped back by a rubber band. 'Zachs will burn up both of you, and take the jewel away!'

Mills's hands began to shake. 'Zachs, you're an idiot!'

'You must stop him.'

'Now you acknowledge my superiority?'

'No more talk!' The shaking hands were suddenly still. 'Zachs is taking you now!'

There followed a horrible noise, like a scream, that somehow contained all three voices.

Evan Mills fell to the ground. But he was far from still. Instead, he twitched violently, his back arching with one spasm, his legs and arms flailing wildly with another.

Harold approached him cautiously.

'Stop,' Mills groaned. 'Must stop.'

Harold wondered if there wasn't something he could do for his old neighbour. But he didn't even dare touch him. What if whatever had happened to Evan was contagious?

Maybe the Captain could help; he knew a lot about this

place. Mills had referred to a dragon's eye in his possession. Harold bet the Captain would get Evan back on his feet if they could get Mills to use his dragon's eye as a reward.

The rain had sputtered to a stop. Harold trotted back to his army, careful not to move too fast across the soggy ground. He only had to turn the corner of the trail to see that things were even livelier than before.

Four of the red-haired apes had somehow got themselves trapped in the midst of Nunn's men. The soldiers hurled curses at the beasts at first, and the words were followed by arrows. One of the apes tried to break through an opening in the soldiers' circle. Harold was surprised to see the soldiers let the creature pass until the wolf darted out of the circle after it, pulling the ape down before it could travel five paces up the trail.

The soldiers cheered as the other apes were dealt with in similar fashion.

Harold stepped carefully round two of the wolves tearing one of the apes apart. From the ape's screams, it was still alive until one of the wolves showed the kindness to tear out its throat.

'So shall the Captain always provide!' their leader called from the middle of his army. 'I think we should have enough to eat for quite some time. But come! The triumphant army should march forward and show themselves to our allies.'

But the Captain's smile waned as he looked past Harold. 'This damn place,' he muttered. 'Every time you get ahead of the game –'

What was he talking about? Harold turned round and saw the strange light in the sky.

'Everybody!' the Captain called. 'Down on the ground! Now!'

It was only when Mary Lou returned to the clearing that she remembered what the dragon had told her.

Not that the dragon had spoken to her, exactly. But the thoughts had somehow entered her head when she was in that place of voices, like a whisper that was clearer than the loudest shout.

She knew as soon as she stepped into the light that the dragon was stirring. And, because the dragon did offer certain choices, that soon she and all of the neighbours would be fulfilled. Or they would be dead.

Since she knew something of what was to come, she turned her eyes to the ground at the first sign of fire in the sky. For, even in its first glimmer, this fire was like no other she had ever seen. Rather, it was as if someone had taken away the clouds and replaced their sky with the surface of the sun.

Somebody? Mary Lou knew it was the dragon.

'I can't see!' somebody shouted.

'Look away!' someone else answered.

'What?' called a third voice, a mix of fear and frustration. 'Is he going to blind us before he eats us?'

But Mary Lou knew, from what she had been told, that the dragon was going neither to blind them nor eat them – just yet. The dragon was only stretching, flexing its fires as someone might flex her muscles after a long sleep.

She heard a sound in the sudden stillness, like the beating of a muffled drum.

'How can we save ourselves?'

'Maybe the eyes –'

'No!' Mary Lou replied, compelled to speak at last. 'Save the eyes! They may save us, but later –'

The dragon had also informed her of the times and places that things would occur. Or so she imagined. They came back to her slowly, like a memory from her childhood, or a dream she might have just before waking.

She knew now was not the time for confrontation. The seven eyes, both part of the dragon and separate from it, would only work again when the dragon was awake to accept them.

'What do we do?' another panicked voice asked. This time it sounded like Mary Lou's mother. 'What do we do?'

'We wait,' Mary Lou replied.

The muffled drumming was growing louder. Mary Lou realised that it wasn't drumming at all.

The blazing light vanished in an instant, as if the dragon had flipped a cosmic light switch. Mary Lou knew what she would see even before she looked up. The light was still there, but those on the ground were protected by a great shadow.

She raised her eyes at last. There, stretching across almost the entire sky, was the tip of the dragon's wing.

Forty-eight

Jason didn't know where he was going. He just had to run.

What had he been thinking about? This world was no different from the one he had left. No, it was worse, to give him someone like the Oomgosh, and then kill the tree-man right in front of him!

It was just like the way Jason couldn't trust what his parents said, or the way kids treated him at school. He had thought the tree-man would be different. The Oomgosh had shown him things, had seen things in Jason that everybody else had missed.

And he had said he'd always be around. Just like all the others, the Oomgosh had lied!

Jason couldn't trust anybody. He wanted to leave everybody behind for ever. The Oomgosh had taught him a lot about these woods. Maybe he could just disappear between the trees, become part of the ground and the leaves. Maybe he'd never have to hear anybody lie ever again.

Jason heard the scream before he saw the red shape hurtling towards him. It was one of those apes that they had fought back at the clearing; one of those apes that had killed the Oomgosh.

The scream was meant to frighten him, one boy against a beast with claws and teeth. But Jason was not in a mood to be frightened. He swung both his fists in front of him and screamed right back.

The ape collided with him, the creature's momentum almost knocking both of them to the ground. But Jason managed to grab it before it could use its hands or teeth. He lifted the creature above his head. It seemed to weigh nothing at all. The ape struggled in his grip, teeth snapping, as it tried to twist around and bite Jason's arm or shoulder.

Jason wouldn't give the thing a chance. 'This is for the Oomgosh,' he told the ape calmly as he tossed it away. The creature spun through the air, screaming again, until it crashed against one of the great trees head first, the screams silenced by the crunch of breaking bones.

Jason looked over at the thing he had just killed. It was almost as easy as crushing an ant on the sidewalk, back in that world he'd come from. He wasn't even breathing heavily. He knew, if he hadn't done something to the ape, the creature would have tried to kill him. But now that it was done, he didn't feel all that good about it. Killing an ape would not bring the Oomgosh back.

Jason flexed his arms. He could feel new muscles in his shoulders. The hair had changed on the top of his head. It crinkled and bent beneath his fingers, like tiny leaves and branches. He felt somehow he should be more surprised by these changes, but in some funny way he had expected them, maybe even looked forward to them.

'Ah.' A rasping voice broke into his thoughts. 'There you are.'

Jason looked up. Raven sat on the lowest branch of one of the great trees.

'What do you want?' he asked angrily. 'I don't feel like talking.' Actually, as soon as the words were out of his mouth, Jason wasn't sure that they were true. In an odd sort of way he was glad that the black bird was here.

'Ah,' Raven said again, 'but you and I always talk. After all, aren't we the best of friends?'

Jason felt the anger wanting to break out all over again. 'What are you talking about?'

'You are angry now at the way of things,' Raven agreed. 'But stop and think. Stop and feel. You have been given a gift.'

Why did the bird say that? But Jason knew, really.

'We have work to do,' Raven said. 'Come, my little Oomgosh.'

That word brought Jason's upset right back to the surface. 'Why do you call me that? He told me that the Oomgosh never dies!'

335

'And you know the truth of that,' Raven called back calmly. 'No one could have been closer to the Oomgosh than you.'

'If I'm so close, why isn't the Oomgosh alive?'

'Oh, but he is,' was Raven's reply. 'The Oomgosh never dies. But the Oomgosh does change from time to time. You're the Oomgosh now.'

So the words meant different things than he had thought, but they were true. Part of Jason still felt cheated, but part of him felt overwhelmed by the newness of all this. He brushed his hand again through the leaves and twigs that now covered his head, and looked at the Oomgosh's never-ending companion. Would there be new birds too?

'And what about Raven?' he asked.

The great black bird ruffled his feathers in indignation. 'Raven is eternal!'

Jason found himself amazed by the way that, even now, the black bird could be so full of himself. 'Sure, Raven. Whatever you say.'

'Ah yes, my young Oomgosh,' the bird replied with a raucous caw. 'Now you are truly speaking the truth!'

Raven flapped his broad wings, readying himself for flight. 'Come!' he called. 'We have work to do.'

Jason couldn't think of anything better to do than follow.

Half the forest seemed to be on fire.

For the first time since he had got the jewels, Nunn had thought about death. The dragon's eyes were barely working. His brother and he had resorted to physical force against each other, rolling about in the muck and the rain while a battle raged around them.

He looked down at his grime-encrusted clothes. Even the dragon's eyes were covered with a layer of mud.

But he had survived. He had got away from the others in the confusion. As a wizard in this place, Nunn was constantly tested. Survival was the only way to pass the test.

He waited there in the forest, still far too close to the clearing, for the fire in the sky to pass. After all, he had survived the dragon before.

But once the fire was gone from the air, he heard the whispers. He felt them, too, like a chill wind that cuts through the warmth of early spring.

At first he was annoyed. The shadow creatures were late. What good would they do him now that the battle was already lost?

Nunn, they called to him, as if he should give them some piece of his power in reply.

Nunn.

They were insistent. He could not ignore them. They did not keep their usual respectful distance, the distance he always demanded until he invited them forward. They must have sensed his weakness.

Nunn.

Did he hear triumph in that whisper?

He still had only the merest fraction of his power. The shadow things were gloating, knowing they had him at last. They would consume him with rasping teeth that fed on the mind before they took the body and there was no way to stop them.

The dark creatures drifted around him, ever closer, almost brushing now against his soiled robes.

'Get off me!' Nunn was startled by a scream that for a moment he thought might have come from his own lips. But the whimpering noises came from behind him.

He turned to see the shadow creatures settling towards Carl Jackson.

'No you don't!' Carl shouted at the silently floating pieces of dark. 'I've got this to protect myself!'

He still held the globe that Nunn had given him; the globe filled with the swirling essence of Nunn's power.

'Take that!' Jackson cried.

A line of green light shot from the globe to rip a hole through the nearest of the dark things. The thing crumbled into ash as its cold brethren whispered in fear.

Jackson laughed as he waved the globe towards Nunn. 'I thought that dog would rip my face off! It was like he was possessed.' He was bleeding from at least three major wounds and sported twice as many more scratches on his face and arms. 'But Jackson's stronger than anything. This globe you gave me guarantees that nothing gets the better of me!'

Nunn.

The shadow things had somehow floated further up into the air, disturbed by Jackson's destruction of their fellow. But it was only a temporary retreat. They had smelled Nunn's weakness and they wanted his life.

But Nunn was not ready to give it. Jackson had the globe and the globe would save them!

Nunn put on his very best smile. 'Most excellent, my Captain. Why don't you give me that globe again and we'll rid ourselves of these pesky demons.'

'Give it back?' Jackson frowned at the magician. 'But this only has a little bit of your power. You told me that yourself. Why can't you just blast them out of the sky?'

Nunn had had enough of this. He pointed a mud-caked finger at his underling. 'You will not question your master! Give that globe to me now!'

Jackson took a step towards the wizard, then seemed to think better of it. 'Those things are after you too, aren't they? And you can't defend yourself.'

This lackey's reticence only made Nunn angrier. 'That is nonsense! I have been a little weakened by my recent battles, and I want to save my remaining strength for the fights to come. Give me that globe and let's get this done with.'

He had lost all patience with Carl Jackson. He would do more than take the globe. He would consume Carl's energy as well. The strength of the two of them together would be more than enough to repel these soul leeches.

But instead of coming closer to Nunn, Jackson spun the globe about, shooting another arrow of light into a second of the dark things.

Jackson turned to Nunn and grinned. 'You can't do that, can you?'

'What are you talking about?' Nunn demanded. 'I'm the one who gave you that power in the first place!' If only he could get

338

that globe away from the fool, he could absorb both the power he'd put in the sphere and Jackson's life energy, just as he'd taken the energies of a hundred other souls. He held out his hand. 'Give it back to me.'

Jackson looked with suspicion at the wizard's outstretched arm. 'So you can do something to me like you did to Leo Furlong? I remember how smug you were when you had us all gathered around you in that first clearing. You were going to rule us all.' He grinned again when Nunn had no reply. 'Well, now I think it's time I ruled you.'

Nunn. Nunn. *Nunn.*

The shadow creatures were growing impatient. They drifted away from Carl Jackson, swooping in ever-tightening circles around the wizard. They would touch him soon and drain whatever strength he had with their bitter skills.

Nunn felt an all too human panic growing inside him. 'They know I am weak!'

'You want a hand?' Jackson asked cordially. 'All you have to do is ask.'

Light shot out of the globe in a broader band than before, catching four of the things in its glare. All four withered and vanished as the light swept by.

Nunn, the things cried, but the cries were fainter, the shadows further away.

Nunn.

The sky was suddenly free of shadows, their whispers faded to a lingering chill.

'You have driven them away,' Nunn whispered, surprised how well his power could work, even when used by other hands. But his gratefulness lasted only for an instant. After all, who was really responsible for the contents of that globe? 'My power has driven them away.'

But Jackson's grin only got larger, his voice more taunting. 'Is it your power? Or is it mine now?'

Nunn realised that this little drama had gone on for far too long. He grovelled before no one. And no one must know of his moment of weakness. He had to take this Jackson now, or he had to kill him.

Nunn wiped his hands against each other, trying to clean the mud from the surface of his gems. They glowed dull green once again, a sign that their strength would soon return.

He pushed his thoughts to the eyes embedded in his flesh, the eyes that were a part of him, and was rewarded with small flickers of fire, deep within the facets of the gems. Yes, the dragon's eyes would once again respond to his every command. He would force the power out of them and take Jackson now.

'Why don't you let me thank you personally?' he asked as he lunged forward to grab Jackson's wrist.

The smile fell from the other's face. 'What are you doing? The globe won't let you!'

It was Nunn's turn to smile as his grip tightened on the other. His gem rubbed against Jackson's skin. Nunn could already feel the warmth of the other and the warmth of the globe the other held – warmth Nunn badly needed.

'Ah,' he purred, 'but who made the globe in the first place?'

'And you gave it to me!' Jackson jerked his arm, trying to break free. 'It's mine to use! Stop him, globe! Stop him from taking me!'

Jackson's panicked exhortations only seemed to increase the flow of energy from the globe. The power felt wonderful as it surged into Nunn again, power both from the globe and from Jackson's life force.

'Now!' Jackson cried.

What pitiful ploy was he trying at the last minute? Whatever it was, it wouldn't work. The energies were flowing even faster now, so quickly that they threatened to overwhelm Nunn's senses. He felt as if he was drunk with the power that came to him.

The image of Jackson wavered before him, the first sign that his life energy was flowing into Nunn; the first sign of Nunn's triumph.

Nunn stumbled. Only his grip on Jackson's wrist kept him from falling. This much power, received this quickly, was somehow disorienting. The two dragon's eyes within his palms were not sufficiently recharged to filter it. He had to slow it down a bit, to keep from being overwhelmed.

Nunn had won. Why was Jackson laughing?

Surely, Jackson didn't understand –

Understand what? He had forgotten exactly what he was thinking about.

But he knew he hadn't felt this good in a long, long time. He might not have felt this good, ever.

So this was what Nunn felt like when he was full of the dragon's eyes?

Carl Jackson looked down at the twin jewels embedded in his new hands. Somewhere deep within him he heard Nunn's cries of anger. Well, the wizard within him would have to get used to the new order of things. He would think of far better things to do with the eyes than Nunn had ever dreamed of.

The dragon had vanished, the sky was once again half blue, half green, the glimpse of wing gone beyond the horizon. But the island was on fire. Mary Lou knew she had to do something about that. At the moment, she couldn't remember exactly what it was.

Mary Lou heard Raven before she saw him.

'There you are at last!' the bird called from somewhere in the sky. 'I have been searching for you!'

With that, she saw it appear in between the trees.

The black bird swooped low above her head. 'Raven's work is never done. Catch!'

A shining green gem dropped from Raven's claws, the final dragon's eye from that place of voices. It fell straight into Mary Lou's open hand. It was hot to the touch at first, but the warmth soon spread out into her hand, then up her arm and across her chest, flowing through her entire form.

With the warmth came the rest of the memories.

'The jewels!' Todd held up his brightly glowing dragon's eye. 'They're coming back!'

'The power is being restored to all of us,' Mrs Smith agreed.

'I assume', Wilbert asked for all the rest of them, 'that this has something to do with the dragon?'

'He has shown himself,' Obar agreed, pausing for an instant in the fruitless dusting of his ruined robes, 'and he has restored our power. Might this be some sort of a challenge?'

341

'Well, it's probably not a Sunday picnic, hey?' Stanley shot back. 'How can wizards who are supposed to know so much really know so little?'

But with her dragon's eye, Mary Lou was the newest of the wizards. And the dragon had given her a number of the answers.

'We can use the power.' She spoke flatly, as if reciting multiplication tables. 'We can defeat the dragon. But there is only one way to win.' She looked out over the assembled neighbours, the remaining Volunteers, the new girl whose name – Sala – seemed to pop right into Mary Lou's mind, Obar the wizard and Raven, who settled back on Nick Blake's shoulder. Charley looked up from where he had settled by Nick's feet, but the dog decided not to growl. All were silent, waiting for her to continue.

'But we can only beat the dragon by using all seven jewels together.'

Mrs Smith frowned at that. 'All seven? We already have four.' She shook her head. 'But the other three?'

Obar looked up from his constant brushing. 'Nunn will never agree.'

Todd looked down at his now glowing jewel. 'Mills tried to steal mine.'

'Mills?' Joan Blake asked pointedly.

'Rox,' Obar interjected. 'No doubt he has taken Mills over by now. He could be even more dangerous than Nunn.'

Mary Lou remembered how Garo had told her about Nunn and Obar killing Rox. And now Obar was calling his victim dangerous. She wondered exactly who was telling the truth.

Obar had said before that they should never trust a wizard. But now she was a wizard too. How could they possibly get all the wizards to work together?

'Maybe', Rose Dafoe said quietly, 'if we make them all understand that this is our only chance –'

But Mary Lou realised she had one more thing to say.

'We must do more than defeat the dragon. We must become more than the dragon.' She looked at the green gem sparkling in her hand. 'The jewels will show us the way.'

'Well I'm glad something's going to,' Wilbert snorted.

'Raven will show you the way too!' the black bird called. 'There are ways the dragon doesn't want you to know!'

'The time is almost here,' Mary Lou said, her dragon-taught speeches coming to an end. 'Come. We must put out the fires.'

'The Oomgosh will help!' Raven called as he launched himself back into the air.

The Oomgosh? Mary Lou frowned. Why didn't the dragon have anything to say about him? Or about Raven? Was the black bird right when he said there were other ways to win?

But her questions would wait, at least for an hour or two. The dragon had only brushed by their world in the midst of waking. They would all have to be ready when the great creature returned.

And when would that be? A minute, a day, a hundred years; that was one secret it had kept to itself.

But the dragon would return, no doubt before they were ready. Mary Lou let her jewel lift her in the air. She needed to put out the fires, make the world safe for them for this moment. They would plan for the moment of the dragon after that.

She waved for the others to follow. They all had work to do.

Epilogue

Where had everybody gone?

George Blake could have sworn this was the same clearing that all the neighbours had gathered in before. He had run away from Jackson at the first opportunity he could find. By the time they approached this place, Jackson was so full of himself he wouldn't have noticed whether George or anyone else was with him. George had hidden in the woods, hoping he could rejoin the other neighbours once things had quietened down.

They were certainly quieter now. There was no one here, no one alive, at least. The bodies of the dead, both human and some kind of ape, were spread over the muddy ground.

There was a new fire in the forest not too far away. Maybe, he thought, that was where the fireball that had filled the sky had landed at last. He wondered if he was in danger. Had the others run to escape the fire?

He scanned the trees that ringed the clearing, looking for other signs of life.

An owl watched him from up in the trees. 'Who?' the bird called, breaking the silence.

'What?' a woman's voice called back in confusion. 'What was that?'

George spun round. There, wandering down a trail that led away from the clearing, was another of the neighbours. Mrs Furlong. She did not appear to be very steady on her feet.

'Mrs Furlong?' George called. Maybe she could tell him where the others had gone. He rushed across the open space to meet her.

She smiled when she saw him. 'George? How are you,

George? We hardly ever see you any more.'

George didn't know how to reply to that. It sounded more like the sort of thing you'd say over the backyard fence, not in this strange new world.

As he approached, George saw she had a rope tied around her ankle. One end of it had been sliced clean.

Mrs Furlong waved her hands about with a frown. 'I'm sorry the place is such a mess. No matter how much I clean, I'm always behind.'

George stopped abruptly. She must be in a state of shock or something. She didn't seem to know where she was. He wondered what he could do. He certainly didn't want her to hurt herself.

'I expect Leo home any minute now,' she said brightly. 'Why don't you stay around for a while? I'm sure he'd really like to say hello, too.'

George nodded at that. He wondered if he could get her to sit down.

'We hardly ever see each other,' she went on blissfully. 'It's a shame we all get so busy. Life just sort of runs away from you sometimes.'

George nodded again, suddenly very sad. Margaret Furlong still thought she was back on Chestnut Circle, waiting for her husband to come home, maybe, so that she could start the cocktail hour. She didn't seem to see anything that didn't fit in with that particular reality.

It was a wonder she was still alive. Maybe, George thought, it was a wonder any of them was.

'Look at the grass around here,' she went on quickly, as if she was afraid of what might happen if she allowed too much silence. 'What a mess. Those neighbourhood kids have got completely out of hand.'

'Mum!' Bobby Furlong called from further up the trail. 'There you are!'

'Bobby! I'm so glad you're back. Your father should be here at any minute.'

'Mr Blake?' Bobby called as he came closer. 'I'm glad to see you too. But I was really worried about my mother. She – uh

345

– has trouble taking care of herself.'

His mother laughed at that. 'Oh, you men! You're always so over-protective.'

'Should we wait here?' George asked the approaching youngster. He saw that Bobby had one of his arms in a sling.

'The others should be back,' Bobby agreed, ' 'though I'm not sure when.'

'Your father will be here any minute,' Margaret Furlong insisted. 'He's always on time, your father. If there's something wrong, he always calls.'

'The others are putting out the fires,' Bobby said.

'The fire?' Mrs Furlong clapped her hands. 'What a good idea, Bobby. We'll go and sit by the fire and wait for Leo!'

'Who?' the owl called into the following silence.

Margaret Furlong sat down in the middle of the trail, her hands folded before her, her face turned towards the burning forest.

George sat down across from her to wait as well, wondering if the place Margaret Furlong found herself might be far safer than where they really were.

'I've never seen an owl around here before,' Bobby mentioned. 'I wonder if it means something?'

'Who?' the owl replied, spreading its great grey wings to rise from the tree and soar through the sky, above the heads of George and Bobby and Margaret, and out over the leaping flames and thick, black smoke of the wood beyond.

'Family and home, Bobby,' his mother replied. 'That's what really means something. Family and home.'

She closed her eyes, her face at peace in the firelight.